I heart Forever

Lindsey Kelk is an author, journalist and prolific tweeter. Born and brought up in Doncaster, South Yorkshire, she worked as a sales assistant, a PR, a silver service waitress and a children's editor before moving to New York and becoming a full-time writer. She now lives in LA.

Lindsey has written thirteen novels, including the *I Heart* books and the *Girl* series, as well as several standalones. A fan of lipstick, pro-wrestling and cats (although not all at the same time), she co-hosts the beauty podcast, *Full Coverage*, with make-up artist, Harriet Hadfield.

You can find out lots more about her here: http://lindseykelk.com and on Facebook, Twitter or Instagram @LindseyKelk.

I heart Forever

LINDSEY KELK

HarperCollins*Publishers*

This novel is entirely a work of fiction.
The names, characters and incidents portrayed in it are
the work of the author's imagination. Any resemblance to
actual persons, living or dead, events or localities is
entirely coincidental.

HarperCollins*Publishers*
1 London Bridge Street
London
SE1 9GF

www.harpercollins.co.uk

A Paperback Original 2017
1

A catalogue record for this book
is available from the British Library

ISBN:
B-format 978-0-00-823681-6
A-format 978-0-00-824018-9
Export TPB 978-0-00-823682-3

Set in Melior by Palimpsest Book Production Limited, Falkirk, Stirlingshire

Printed and bound by CPI Group (UK) Ltd, Croydon CR0 4YY

MIX
Paper from
responsible sources
FSC® C007454

This book is produced from independently certified FSC paper
to ensure responsible forest management.

For more information visit: www.harpercollins.co.uk/green

*For everyone who has been on this
journey since the beginning . . .*

I heart you.

PROLOGUE

'Angela?'

I looked up from a swamp of unfinished magazine pages to see my assistant loitering in the doorway.

'Cici?'

'You told me to let you know when it was seven,' she replied, tossing her icy long blonde hair over her shoulder. 'Because you can't use a clock like normal people.'

'It's seven already?' I said with a groan, sweeping all the pages up into a messy pile in front of my computer screen. I ran a hot hand over my forehead, into my own hair. My dirty blonde, very messy, and past-the-help-of-dry-shampoo hair.

'See how the big hand is on the twelve and the little hand is on the seven?' Cici replied slowly, pointing to the massive clock on my office wall. 'That means seven o'clock. Ninety minutes after you stopped paying me, for anyone who might be taking notice of that kind of thing. Not HR, obviously, since they went home hours ago.'

'Shit,' I muttered. 'I'm going to be late.'

Turning off my computer, I grabbed my Marc Jacobs satchel from the new coat stand I'd bought for my office. All that was missing now was a fold-out bed and a potted plant then I'd never need to go home. I paused for a second, wondering whether or not I could fit one in the corner. Maybe if I moved the coat stand . . .

Cici shrugged, her face perfectly even. I couldn't decide whether she looked so expressionless because she'd had really great Botox, or because she genuinely didn't give a shit. In my heart, I hoped for the former, but after years of working together, my head assured me it was the latter.

'You should go home,' I told her as I stuffed myself into my jacket, the sleeves of the cropped cashmere jumper I'd nicked from the fashion cupboard bunching up around my armpits. 'Thanks for staying late, I really appreciate it.'

'Yeah, whatever.' Cici didn't do 'grateful' unless it came with a hashtag. 'I'm leaving now, I have a date.'

'Me too,' I muttered. Casting a quick look in the mirror on top of my filing cabinet, I grimaced at my wayward eyeliner and sad, sallow skin. Had I been outside at all today? 'And we're totally going to miss our reservation.'

'But – you're married?' she replied, looking confused.

'You can still go on dates when you're married,' I explained, licking my ring finger and swiping at my undereyes while Cici gagged in the corner. 'It's not forbidden.'

She looked at me, completely scandalized. 'Does Alex know?'

'The date is *with* Alex,' I sighed as I gave up on my face. I'd fix it on the subway. 'He's leaving tomorrow.'

'Oh.' She frowned, clearly disappointed at the loss of potential drama. 'Whatever.'

'OK, great, see you in the morning,' I said, flying out the door as fast as my high heels would carry me. Which wasn't really all that fast, if I was being entirely honest.

'I'm sorry,' I shouted, the front door hitting the hallway wall with a bang. 'We had to pull a feature and I had to write a replacement and I lost track of time. Just let me get changed and we can leave and—'

'Or we could stay in?'

All the lights were out and my living room glowed with the light of a hundred tiny candles. He must have used an entire bag of the little Ikea tealights. I made a mental note to tell Jenny that yes, one human *could* need all those candles in one lifetime. The curtains were drawn, music played softly, and in the middle of the room was my husband, Alex, in all his worn jeans, faded Cramps T-shirt and barefoot glory. This was not a man who was dressed for the Chef's Table at Brooklyn Fare.

'But it's your last night,' I said, dropping my coat and bag to the floor and stepping cautiously across the room towards him. Do not set yourself on fire, do not set yourself on fire, do not set yourself on fire . . . 'We've waited months for this reservation.'

'That's true,' Alex took me in his arms and brushed my messy hair away from my face. 'So, I guess I could go put on a suit, get on the subway, pay four hundred bucks for some fancy dinner – and come home still hungry – or I could just stay here with you?'

He rested his forehead against mine and smiled. I

smiled back. Even now, he still gave me butterflies.

'Not a tough choice, babe.'

'But what are we going to eat?' I whispered, the rumbles in my stomach threatening to eat the butter-flies. 'We haven't got anything in.'

'It's all taken care of,' he said, nodding across the room. 'I am a man of many talents.'

Taking my hands in his, he led me over to our little dining table. It had been laid with more care than I thought possible, white linen tablecloth, proper napkins, single red rose in a miniature glass vase I was almost certain he'd borrowed from upstairs, and the classiest touch of all, two chilled bottles of Brooklyn Brewery's finest lager with the tops already popped. The doorbell rang and I imme-diately started for the door. It was an old habit I just couldn't seem to kill – what if it was post? Exciting post?!

'I got it,' Alex said, leaping nimbly through the candles and answering the front door.

I vaguely heard a muffled exchange while I stood by the table, unfastening the little buckles on my shoes and taking it all in. Ten weeks. He would be gone for ten weeks. No more kisses or romantic dinners à deux until November. Not that I was mad or sad or anything, other than extremely happy for my beloved husband. Honest. Only, I couldn't remember the last time things had been so easy. All my friends were happy, my parents were off on a cruise somewhere mobile phones didn't work, my job was going well, and things between Alex and I were perfect. Well, he was leaving me for months on end to go travelling around South East Asia but hey, what married couple didn't go through that on

4

your average Wednesday? No siree, no problems here.

'Dinner is served.' He opened the door with his foot and then kicked it closed behind him, two huge flat boxes in his arms, still steaming from the cool evening air. 'Get your ass sat down.'

'Pizza!' I clapped, delighted, all my worries about how much I was going to miss him devoured by the growling in my belly. If he wasn't the best bloody husband of all time.

'One porkypineapple for me,' he confirmed, moving the rose from the table to the kitchen top to protect it from the massive pizza boxes. 'And one disgusting tuna sweetcorn, specially made for m'lady.'

'You got them to make me a tuna pizza?' I gasped as I pulled back the lid and inhaled. 'Alex!'

Truly, this was a tremendous gesture of love. There were approximately fourteen thousand pizza restaurants in New York City and not one of them offered a tuna pizza on their menu. Even the places that sold tuna sandwiches as well, flat out refused to put canned fish on a plain cheese and tomato pizza. I'd been living in this country for six years and I still couldn't understand why it was the biggest possible transgression a human could make. Buy a rifle in the supermarket? Oh, OK. Empty a can of tuna onto a margarita pizza? No bloody way.

'I still don't understand why America refuses to embrace it,' I said. Who needed a seat at the chef's table when you had an entire tuna pizza in front of you?

'Because it's gross?' Alex suggested, settling down in front of his own enormous pie. 'And you should be ashamed of yourself?'

I shook my head, peeling one massive, slightly floppy slice off the bottom of the box, pinching the edges of the crust with my thumb and forefinger then folding it in half. Alex watched approvingly. He'd make a New Yorker out of me yet. As soon as he got me to give up the tuna.

'Firstly, they have it in Italy, where pizza comes from,' I said with a mouthful of cheesy goodness. 'And secondly, you're defending the eating habits of a country that puts cheese in tins *and* aerosol cans. You can't say squirty cheese is an acceptable food and then deny a woman her tuna pizza.'

'Easy Cheese is a basic American human right,' he replied, swiping a stray smear of tomato sauce from the side of my mouth with his thumb. 'I get it, you can't understand. You were brought up on toads in holes and spotted dicks, it's practically child abuse.'

'Ooh, I could go for a bit of spotted dick for pudding,' I said, still chewing my pizza. 'Have we got any custard?'

'You're disgusting – and I love you,' Alex replied. The grin on his face turned wistful as he watched me eat across the table. I felt my cheeks blush and wiped the corners of my mouth with the back of my hand.

'Do you think they have Easy Cheese in Cambodia?' I asked.

'I hope not,' he said. 'That's kind of the whole point of going. Get away from the Easy Cheese for a little while, try something new.'

'But I thought you loved Easy Cheese?' I said, pulling a piece of sweetcorn off my pizza and popping it into my mouth, avoiding his gaze. 'I thought Easy Cheese was the best thing ever.'

'I do love Easy Cheese,' Alex picked up his chair

and moved it around the table until we were side by side, 'more than anything, but my mind needs a break, though not from Easy Cheese. In a dream world, you know I'd take Easy Cheese with me.'

I paused to chew and swallow.

'Just to be clear, I was using Easy Cheese as a metaphor for our relationship,' I said, wiping my fingers on my napkin.

'Really?' Alex's denim-clad leg pressed against mine. 'I was definitely talking about Easy Cheese.'

I looked over at my husband's sweet, smiling face and bright green eyes and tried my best to look happy for him. He had been planning this trip for almost a year and I knew he was doing his best not to get too excited in front of me. We'd debated going travelling together but there was just no way. For one, I had what my mother would refer to as 'a proper job' and couldn't just nick off for months at a time and expect said proper job to be waiting for me when I got back. Alex had the time and the desire to spend weeks on end living out of a backpack. He was a musician, a proper one, in a band with a record contract that went on tour and sold records and everything. Well, he used to go on tour and sell records. Stills hadn't played any big shows in a couple of years and record sales were slowing down at an incredibly alarming rate. Bloody Spotify. He needed this trip and I knew it, I wasn't going to ruin our last night together by playing the 'poor me' card.

'There's still time for you to change your mind, you know,' Alex said, nursing his beer. 'This time tomorrow we could be on a river beach in Laos. This time next week, we could be checking out temples in Myanmar, next month dancing at a full moon party in Thailand.'

'You know that I would if I could,' I whispered, staring at his perfect features. His full lips, his sharp cheekbones, his shiny black hair that had obviously seen shampoo in the last forty-eight hours. 'You know I'd love it more than anything, but asking for two months off at work would basically be the same as handing in my notice.'

It was a complete and utter lie. Two months of nothing but Alex Reid, all to myself? Yes, please. Two months of living out of a backpack in dirty clothes, without telly or online food delivery? I just couldn't see it. The closest I'd ever come to roughing it was an abbreviated weekend at Reading Festival when I was seventeen and even that ended with my dad picking me up on the Saturday afternoon after I'd caved and tried to use the toilets. I hadn't seen the inside of a tent since.

'You could just quit,' Alex stage-whispered into my hair, one arm snaking around my waist. 'You could just leave.'

'I really wish I hated my job,' I replied, sliding my hand along his cheek. 'And having a home. And food. And things.'

'You do love things,' Alex agreed with a theatrical sigh. He squeezed my hand in his and my engagement and wedding rings pressed sharply against their neighbouring fingers. 'And I guess someone has to hold down a steady job. Looks like I'm stuck with Graham.'

Just because I would rather perform laser hair removal on myself than spend two months living out of a backpack did not mean I was fully OK with his going on this trip without me. Sure, I could play the supportive wife for a while but I'd seen *Eat Pray Love*, I knew what happened on these adventures.

'You'll barely notice I'm gone,' he said, picking up a piece of tuna pizza and sniffing it with great suspicion before taking the tiniest of bites. He looked to be struggling far too much for a man who was about to spend several weeks subsisting on flash-fried insects, but whatever, all the more for me.

'You're going to be so busy with work and I know Lopez isn't going to leave you alone for more than two minutes while I'm away. And I'm gonna call you all the time.'

'You don't need to convince me,' I promised and the butterflies fluttered back into life as he ran a finger along my jawline, brushing against my bottom lip. 'I'm glad you're doing this. You've wanted to go forever, I know.'

'It kind of feels like now or never,' he agreed. 'There's no tour, no record to promote. And I won't be able to do a trip like this once you're barefoot and pregnant.'

I almost bit his finger off.

'There's only one of us who's barefoot, right now, and I really hope neither of us are pregnant,' I replied, my voice just ever so slightly shrill. 'Unless there's something you want to tell me?'

'I didn't mean right this second.' He laughed at the look on my face with all the ease of someone who didn't have a uterus. 'I only meant, I won't be able to take off on a trip when we do decide to have kids. If we decide to have kids.'

'If,' I repeated softly. I wanted to commit to a 'when' but it still seemed like such a huge leap into adulthood. I still couldn't time my trips to the toilet properly when I was wearing a romper – how was I supposed to know how to raise a child?

'I'm glad you're going,' I said, forcing certainty into my words. 'It's just, you've never been away for so long before. I'm going to miss you, that's all.'

'I'm going to miss you too,' he said. Alex grabbed hold of both sides of my chair and turned it around to face him. 'I'm going to miss you every minute of every day.'

'That's clearly an exaggeration,' I replied as my heart began to beat just a little bit faster. His hands were still holding on to the seat of my chair and he leaned in towards me. He pushed my hair out of the way and pulled gently at the neck of my jumper, kissing my shoulder, my collarbone, my throat. 'You won't miss me while you're asleep.'

'I will,' he protested, whispering right into my ear. I shivered all the way down to my toes. 'I'll dream about you every night.'

'Well, that's just ridiculous,' I said, gasping as he pulled me out of my seat and into his lap. 'You can't control your dreams. You dream about whatever's in your subconscious.'

'Then let's give my subconscious something to remember,' he said, taking off my jumper and tossing it onto the settee. 'We've got twelve hours.'

'I've never been one to turn down a challenge,' I replied as I yanked his T-shirt over his head and ran my hands down his tight, taut back. 'You'd better set an alarm.'

Closing my eyes, I tried to concentrate on being right where I was. What good would it do to worry about what might happen? Alex would go, Alex would come back, and it would be fine. Everything was exactly how it should be, exactly at that moment. Now, all I had to do was keep every single thing in my life exactly the same, forever.

How hard could that be?

CHAPTER ONE

No one likes a Monday, especially a Monday that starts with an all-departments senior staff meeting that was scheduled last minute on the Friday before and takes place in the only windowless meeting room in the entire fifty-two-storey building. It looked as though the whole company had been herded in and they hadn't even provided pastries. Something drastic was definitely about to happen and they didn't want us to have our mouths full when it did. It was a huge mistake – everyone knew bad news went down better with a croissant.

'How come we're in the misery room?' Mason asked as he slipped into the seat next to me. 'Are they worried we're gonna jump?'

'It would be a nice day to be outside,' I said, gnawing on the end of my biro. Not nearly as tasty as a Danish. 'I just want to know what's going on.'

'You don't know anything?' He raised an eyebrow and crossed his massive legs.

'Nothing at all,' I replied, entirely innocent for once.

As well as being practically a giant and my best

friend Jenny's boyfriend, Mason Cawston was also a fellow Spencer Media employee. He was the deputy editor of *Ghost*, the men's monthly, and I knew why he was asking me if I had any idea what was going on. I'd founded *Gloss* five years earlier with Delia Spencer. As in Spencer Media, as in our employer. Our friendship meant I was usually pretty good with the goss, but not this time. There had been rumours flying around our twelfth-floor office for weeks and I'd been desperately fishing for details but the only solid thing I'd managed to unearth was a dastardly scheme to get rid of the free donuts in the canteen on a Tuesday. It was definitely upsetting, but I couldn't imagine losing out on one free Krispy Kreme a week was a good enough reason for Delia to be dodging me – and she definitely was dodging. Alex had been gone for almost two months and I hadn't managed to pin her down for so much as a happy hour cocktail, not even once. Something was officially up.

'None of the rumours I've heard have been reassuring,' Mason said, raising his eyebrows. 'And it's never a good sign when they drag people in first thing on a Monday. The last time this happened, people went back to their desks and they were gone. Literally gone. They literally removed their desks from the building.'

'They do tend to do all their best firing on a Monday,' I agreed, beginning to feel increasingly anxious. All right, so she hadn't been around for cocktails and gossip, but Delia would have clued me in if the company was planning to fire the entire editorial staff. Wouldn't she? An image of someone rifling through my office and loading my carefully curated stationery collection and imported packets of Quavers into a cardboard box flashed through my mind.

'I wish they'd just get on with it.' I slouched back in my chair and twisted my wedding ring on my finger, glancing nervously around the room. No one looked pleased to be there. 'McDonald's only serves breakfast until 10 a.m. and if I'm going to be out of a job, I want to be into an Egg McMuffin as soon as humanly possible.'

Mason let out a half laugh before noticing my entirely serious expression and covering it up with a cough.

'As long as this isn't a mass cull,' he said as the lift doors dinged open and the final lot of editors marched through the door. 'I was hoping you might be able to help me with something.'

'If I can,' I said, hesitant. It wasn't that I didn't want to be of service to my best friend's boyfriend but I was ever so lazy and now had a serious hankering for an Egg McMuffin. 'What's up?'

He opened his mouth to speak but before he could say a word the door to the meeting room closed with a bang and I looked up to see Delia and her grandfather, Bob Spencer, the president of Spencer Media, followed by a gaggle of harried-looking assistants clutching iPads who quickly lined the walls of the packed room, blocking all the exits.

'Good morning, everyone.'

I sat up straight and flashed Delia a small wave and a big smile, receiving nothing but a tight nod in return. Not a good sign. Slumping back down in my seat, I noticed she was wearing trousers. Delia never wore trousers to work. She was a woman who strongly believed in the power of a pencil skirt and once told me her very fancy, very old-fashioned grandmother only ever wore trousers during the war and had forbidden her and her sister from donning a pair of trews except if they were up against the same circumstances. Unless Delia and Bob were about to declare war on Anna Wintour and invade Condé Nast, I had a terrible feeling that this was not going to be a positive meeting.

'I'll get right to it; I'm sure some of you have heard rumours already so we figured it was best to make our announcements to the entire senior team at once.'

Bob didn't even wait to get to the lectern, instead delivering his speech as he strode up through the centre of the room. Delia followed before taking her place, standing shoulder to shoulder with her grandfather in her shit-kicking ensemble. They both looked sombre, Bob in his regular charcoal grey suit and white shirt, Delia sporting her smart black trousers and a scarlet silk top. It was perfect, you wouldn't be able to see the blood. I wracked my brains for the last time I'd seen Bob in the office and came up blank. Not that he hung out in the *Gloss* office or staff canteen opposite all that often, but there were usually stories of unfortunate encounters in the lifts or the general feel of a haunting whenever he was around. Everyone was terrified of Bob Spencer, except for his wife and his granddaughters. I'd seen salesmen in the fanciest shop on Madison Avenue run and hide when Delia walked through the door, afraid her grandfather might be close behind, but no one was more afraid of him than his employees. Most people said there were two ways to manage people, with a stick or with a carrot, but Bob had found a third: by scaring the living shit out of them. So far, it seemed to be working in his favour.

'We have some major changes to deal with today,'

he declared, slapping his hands on the lectern and loosening the bladders of everyone in the room. I looked over at Mason and he gave me a tight, supportive smile. I fidgeted in my seat, determined not to break into GCSE science class giggles. I hadn't been this on edge since the *Strictly* Christmas Special.

'So, I've been thinking,' Mason hissed into my ear. 'It's about Jenny.'

'Can we talk about it after?' I asked. I very much wanted to be paying attention if we were all about to be made redundant. It would be extremely embarrassing to have to ask HR to explain it over again while I was being removed from the building. He shuffled around for a second before shaking his head and leaning over to whisper in my ear, 'I'm going to ask Jenny to marry me.'

'Oh my god!' I shouted, spinning around in my seat to grab hold of his hand. 'That's amazing!'

Every single member of the Spencer Media family turned to look at me at the exact same second.

'I mean . . . '

Opening and closing my mouth like an awkward English goldfish, I couldn't quite manage to find my words. Instead, I thrust Mason's hand into the air, clasped in my own, and cheered.

'Yay, change!' I said happily. 'Change is good! I mean, choose change or stagnate and die!'

Mason yanked his hand out of mine and clamped it over his face.

'I choose the sweet release of death,' he whispered behind his hand, shuffling his seat away from mine.

'Of course . . . ' Bob cleared his throat at the front of the room while Delia tried not to smile. I sat back in my seat, doing my best to ignore the hundred or so pairs of eyes burning into the back of my head. 'Thank you for your support, Angela.'

We had a complicated relationship, me and Bob.

'The media landscape is not what it was ten years ago. Not even what it was just three years ago,' the big boss stated to a crowd of unsettled faces. 'We know this. It may be a little premature to declare print is dead, but it certainly isn't in rude health, and if we want to succeed, we need to be at the forefront of the media industry, not playing catch-up. I will not stand by and watch our publications flail and die like fish out of water. We should be setting the standard, not waiting to see what happens next.'

I bit my lip as I nodded in agreement, along with everyone else in the room. Mason was going to propose! Jenny was getting married! Flailing and dying! And something about fish?

'The new Spencer Media begins today. Right after this meeting, a press release will go out detailing our new corporate structure, starting with changes at the very top of our leadership team. With that in mind, I'd like to take this opportunity to announce my official retirement and the appointment of my successor, effective immediately. Please welcome the new president of Spencer Media, Delia Spencer.'

An en masse gasp was hastily drowned out by polite but enthusiastic applause as everyone in the room rose to their feet and clapped. I couldn't believe it. Jenny was getting engaged, Delia was taking over the entire company, fish were flailing and dying. Not even two minutes ago, I'd been planning to drown my feelings in reconstituted egg and now this was officially one of the best Mondays on record ever, narrowly beaten into second place only by the Monday

I'd seen Jake Gyllenhaal on the subway. He was eating a sandwich.

Bob gave Delia a brief, workplace-appropriate mini-hug and stepped off to the side, gesturing for her to take centre stage. My heart swelled and it was all I could do not to jump on my chair and whoop. As far as scary announcements went, this was one of the best. I was so proud of her, I could have wept. As Delia stepped up to speak, I watched ten years slide right off Bob's shoulders. And was he smiling? Truly this was a day for the ages.

'Thank you.' Delia inclined her head graciously and silenced the clapping without even trying. The woman was an enigma. How could someone be just as comfortable standing in front of a hundred people to casually announce she was taking over a multimedia empire as she was singing karaoke in front of four very drunk Chinese gentlemen on the Lower East Side on a Tuesday night? Although to be fair, there couldn't be that many people who regularly did both of those things. I flicked at my eyelashes to fight off a stray tear; she was my very own Wonder Woman.

'My grandfather started this company with one newspaper almost forty years ago and now we are home to over one hundred magazines, eighty websites and twenty-five podcasts that are part of twenty global brands, reaching consumers all over the world.' She broke off to smile and at least fifteen of the men in the room got a semi. 'To stay at the top of the global media market, we must not be afraid to make changes. It's not enough to maintain, we must always be developing, always looking forward. And that often means making difficult choices.'

Huh? I looked around at the fading smiles on my

colleagues' faces. That last bit didn't sound nearly as fun as the part about the podcasts.

'Beginning today, I will be restructuring our divisions to foster more progressive and creative brand development,' Delia said, still smiling.

I pulled my sleeves down over my fingers and chewed the inside of my cheek. No big deal, it was just a lot of management speak, nothing to be worried about. Delia wasn't Bob, Delia cared about people, not just money. Although she did like success. And it wasn't as though she hated money. Hmm.

'Instead of separating our brands by print, online and broadcast, we'll be working in streamlined brand groups. Our women's brands will all work together, our lifestyle brands, our men's brands. We will streamline our business models and foster a new sense of synergy through content creation to create new opportunities to reach our readers wherever they are.'

'Content creation?' Mason whispered. 'Synergy?'

'Isn't that the name of the computer in *Jem and the Holograms*?' I whispered back.

'After this meeting, we'll be separating you into your brand groups and your HR manager will go over the new structure.' Delia spoke with unquestionable authority. This was not a request, this was an order. 'And I'll be scheduling some time with all our editors individually over the next couple of days, to talk through any questions you might have and hopefully hear some great ideas about how we take Spencer Media forward.'

I looked down at the grinning T-Rex on my chest and for the first time since I'd bought it, regretted the decision to wear a bright red dinosaur jumper to work.

'Now, I'm going to hand over to Peter, our vice

president of HR and he'll detail the breakout groups.' She looked over at her grandfather, who gave her a nod and, against all laws of gods and men, flashed her the finger guns. Bob Spencer, doing the finger guns? Was it possible I'd fallen over and banged my head on the way into work? 'Thank you, everyone, I'm very excited about the future of our company and that future begins right now.'

Considerably less enthused applause clattered around the room, spurred on by the iPad-clutching assistants who quickly opened the exits for Delia and Bob and immediately locked us back in the second they were gone. As soon as the doors closed, the sound of applause was drowned out by panicked whispers and the clacking of acrylic fingernails against smartphone screens.

'Holy shit,' Mason exhaled. 'Restructuring and streamlining? This is not good.'

'But *Ghost* is doing fine,' I said, chomping down on the end of my pen until there was nothing left but a chewed mess. 'And *Gloss* too. We'll be OK.'

'Yeah, but what about *Belle*?' He nodded across the room to where the editor of Spencer Media's flagship monthly fashion magazine was sat staring at the wall, ashen-faced. 'Their circulation has been dropping for months. What if streamlining actually means folding?'

'Delia loves *Belle*,' I said, certain it was safe. 'There's no way she'd fold it. She started at *Belle*.'

'Not to make myself unpopular, but this is Delia Spencer, the new company president, not Delia Spencer, your friend,' he replied with an uncomfortable smile under his gingery beard. He had an excellent beard. 'So many magazines have gone in the last few years. And *Ghost* isn't doing *that* well.'

'So, you were saying something about proposing?' There was nothing like forcing a change in subject when you didn't want to deal with reality. 'Mason, this is so exciting.'

All the tension washed off his face and his eyes glazed over as he dug his phone out of his pocket.

'I've been thinking about it for a while but this is Jenny we're talking about, I want to get it exactly right,' he explained as I clapped along in delight. 'It's almost the anniversary of when we met so I was going to ask Erin if we could go back up to her house upstate, the place we met? I want to do it there. You know Jen better than anyone else. What do you think about this ring?'

Flicking around at the screen for a second, he pulled up a picture of a beautiful ring. Yellow-gold band with a cushion-cut diamond nestled between two baguette-cut sapphires. Very sophisticated, very elegant. Completely wrong.

'It's stunning,' I said, twisting my own emerald engagement ring around on my finger. 'But no.'

'No?' Mason looked down at the phone as the smile fell off his face. 'What do you mean no?'

Switching on my own phone, I opened my emails and tapped in Jenny's name.

'It's in here somewhere,' I muttered, poking my tongue out the corner of my mouth as I searched. 'Wait, yep, this is it.'

Clicking on a link, I held up the phone triumphantly.

'She sends me this about every three months,' I said as Mason blinked at the Tiffany Embrace engagement ring and took the phone out of my hands. 'And she's been sending it every three months for the last five years. This is the ring. This is Jenny's ring.'

Underneath his beard, I could see he'd gone awfully green. It was a diamond-studded platinum band with a huge brilliant cut diamond, surrounded by a halo of yet more diamonds. There were so many diamonds involved, it looked fake but according to the price tag, it most definitely was not. I figured I'd wait a while to email him the cost. From the look on Mason's face, he wasn't ready to learn how much Jenny's eternal love went for. Or the matching wedding ring she wanted to go with it.

'For real?' he asked.

'For really real,' I promised.

'If that's the one she wants, that's the one she'll get,' he said, recovering himself slightly. 'You don't happen to know her ring size?'

'Five and a half.' I slowly removed my phone from his vicelike grip. 'That is also included on her email. I'll forward you the details.'

He paused and took a deep breath. 'She is going to say yes, right?'

I bit my lip to stop my smile. He looked so nervous, I could hardly stand it.

'Of course she's going to say yes!' I leaned across my chair to wrap him up in a hug. 'But just to make sure, let's definitely get that ring.'

'So then, they got a ten for their samba but I really didn't think it was as good as the American smooth.' I screwed up my nose as I tossed two Sour Patch kids into my gob. 'Sometimes I don't even know how they work out the scoring, I really don't.'

'Yeah, that's a drag.'

'It's just not fair, you know? When everyone else is working so hard, he's so obviously the judges' favourite. I get annoyed.'

23

'I know you do, I know you do.' On a grainy Skype feed, Alex looked over his shoulder at the bustling marketplace behind him. 'So now I'm all caught up on *Dancing with the Stars*, you want to tell me what's really going on over there?'

'How's Myanmar?' I asked, cheerfully popping another handful of sweets. 'That's where you are, isn't it? Looks beautiful. When was the last time you had a shave?'

'It's amazing, and probably two weeks ago, and now seriously, tell me what's going on,' he ordered.

'Just some changes at work.' I tried to sound as casual as possible but I'd never been good at putting on a brave face. 'They're shifting some stuff around and I'm getting a new boss. Instead of a print division and a digital division, they're putting us all into brand streams. Which I'm sure I'll understand by the time I meet with Jo tomorrow.'

'Jo?' Alex scratched at his new scruff.

'Jo Herman. She's the new director of women's brands,' I recited through a mouthful of chewy sugary goodness. '*Gloss* is in good shape, I'm not worried.'

'I see,' he said calmly. 'Is that your first bag of Sour Patch Kids today?'

'No,' I replied. 'No, it is not.'

'I can come home.' Alex held his hand up to the screen of his phone until I could trace the concentric circles of his fingerprint on my laptop. 'There's only a couple of weeks left and I think it's very clear I could use a shower and a shave.'

A good wife would have immediately told him not to be so silly. A good wife would have thought about how excited he was the morning he left, how happy he was every time I spoke to him and the undeniable

24

joy in each and every one of his postcards. But I did want him home. I hated that he'd been away for so long, I hated waking up in a big empty bed every day then tripping over his slippers every single morning because he wasn't there to wear them. I hated cooking alone, eating alone, and then doing one person's dishes. But that was more to do with the fact Alex always did the dishes.

'Angela?'

'No, don't be silly. You'll be home soon anyway,' I made myself say. I might have been imagining it but I could have sworn he looked relieved. 'Where are you off to next?'

'Thailand,' he replied. 'Shawna's friend told us about this amazing beach called Koh Kradan. No ATMs, no roads even. They shut it down half the year but it just opened, so we should be some of the first people to visit this season. We're going to head out there tomorrow, kind of a last fling, you know? Before we're back to a New York winter. And then you know it'll be spring and we'll be off touring the festivals. Did I tell you? We got an email from the label and they want us to play like, thirty dates across Europe. Graham is so psyched.'

'Not even home and you're already planning to leave me again,' I smiled. It was good to hear him excited about getting back to reality, even if that reality was nicking off on tour all summer. 'Good riddance, that's what I say. Why even bother coming home in the first place?'

He laughed, knowing I was teasing. I would never tell him, but really, I was relieved. You'd think being married to a boy in a band would bring in the big bucks but over the last couple of years, the money had really started to fade away. Alex had always been good with his finances so things weren't exactly hard, but between streaming services and general piracy, the only way for Stills to make real cash was by touring and flogging T-shirts. Drunk people at festivals bought lots of T-shirts. Drunk people at festivals were my favourites.

'The place we're going is literally deserted, so don't freak out if I can't call for a week or so,' Alex added, immediately making me freak out. 'I'll email if I can, but if not I'll shout when I'm back in Bangkok and let you know my flight details.'

'That's fine,' I replied, overcompensating by adding about fourteen syllables to the word 'fine'. 'You'll be back before you know it, just go and enjoy yourself. Don't worry about me.'

I sounded more like my mother every single day.

'I like worrying about you,' Alex said. His lopsided smile shone through the screen. 'That's my job.'

'Your other job is to get me a present,' I informed him, returning his happy expression. 'A really nice one.'

He laughed and scraped his hair back from his face, showing off the tan line around his forehead. 'Consider it done.'

'And it's probably best you're not around anyway,' I said. 'Mason is going to propose to Jenny and I don't know if New York is ready for the attack of that bride-zilla.'

'Ahh, man, that's so great!' He looked truly pleased to hear the news. 'I'm so pleased for them. Tell them congratulations from me.'

I loved how much he loved my friend. Honestly, he was such an amazing human being, he made me want to throw up. That, or I'd finally found my limit on eating Sour Patch Kids, and that seemed unlikely.

A brisk knock on the door of my office made me look up. It was Cici, tapping at her Cartier Tank watch.

'I have to go,' I said with a sad sigh, reluctant to say goodbye. 'Meeting time.'

We tried to talk as often as we could but between the time difference and Alex insisting on travelling to countries where WiFi was not their strongest suit, it had already been five days since I'd last heard his voice and now I wasn't going to hear from him in over a week? I felt another pang of pukiness as he resigned himself to me signing off with a nod. I loved him so much, I wanted to vom.

'I'll try to call you again before we leave for the beach,' he promised. 'And I'll be home before you know it.'

'I love you,' I said, ignoring an impatient Cici who was busy sticking her fingers down her throat. 'Have you got plenty of snacks?'

'I ate crickets yesterday,' he said with a completely straight face. 'And Graham ate a boiled baby chicken still in the egg.'

'OK, I've changed my mind, you need to come home,' I ordered as he started laughing. 'I love you, Alex Reid.'

'I love you too, Angela Clark,' he said, his face relaxing into a smile. 'I'll talk to you later if you haven't overdosed on candy.'

I blew him a kiss, logging off my computer with one hand and emptying the sour sweets into my mouth with the other before beckoning Cici into the office.

'Sorry,' I said, holding a hand over my full mouth. 'Alex.'

27

'He's still on his gap-year adventure?' she sniffed and brushed non-existent crumbs off the chair on the opposite side of the desk before sitting down. 'I hope you got him vaccinated against Ebola and HPV before he left.'

'Didn't you go on a spiritual journey around India a few years ago?' I reminded her, trying to remember which vaccinations he'd had before he left. 'And HPV is an STD, I don't think you can catch that from travelling around South East Asia.'

'No, you catch that from boning skanks,' she replied, studying her glossy pink fingernails. 'But I'm sure he's definitely not doing that.'

'Did you want something?' I asked.

'I did, I do.' Cici combed her long blonde hair over her shoulder, the mirror image of her twin sister, Delia. It still unnerved me, how two genetically identical humans could be so different. On one hand, you had Delia, superhuman media mogul and now president of the company. As generous and gracious as she was ambitious, Delia always put the people she loved first. And on the other, you had Cici, a woman so concerned about the wellbeing of others, she once convinced an intern to take her new sleep medication for a whole week because she was worried it was making her gain weight. It turned out it wasn't but it did give the intern night terrors so that was something fun to report back to her doctor.

'I've been your assistant for, like, ever,' she began and I bit my lip before I could reply. As if I needed reminding of that.

'And I know I only got the job because my grandpa owns the company and my sister basically forced you into taking me on . . . ' She waved away the facts as though everyone found their jobs in the same way. 'But I'm good, and you know I am.'

'Yeah, I mean apart from the constant abuse and borderline bullying of the entire team,' I said with a nod, 'you're the best assistant I've ever had.'

I didn't bother mentioning the times she'd had my luggage blown up, sabotaged a press trip to Paris, fired our managing editor on press day (despite the fact she didn't have the authority to fire anyone), semi-kidnapped my goddaughter or even the fact she was the only assistant I'd ever had.

Didn't seem necessary.

'I know there are going to be changes with the new company structure and I want to be considered for something new,' she announced with the indisputable confidence of someone whose twin sister now ran the company her grandfather owned. 'I want a bigger role, Angela, I'm ready.'

Sometimes, her born-and-bred Manhattanite assertiveness still made my meek British skin itch.

'I'm not entirely sure what you've heard about the new structure,' I replied, scanning my inbox to see if a company-wide announcement had gone out since this morning's meeting but there was nothing. I was sure it wasn't due to be announced until the end of the day, Bob always liked to avoid distracting the worker bees while there was honey to be made. Cici was getting insider information and it didn't take a genius to work out where it was coming from (which was a relief, since the last IQ test I'd taken on Facebook had yielded less than impressive results). 'Nothing's been confirmed yet and I don't think there are going to be any staffing changes, to be honest, at least not at *Gloss*.'

'Yeah, I guess you should probably talk to Dee Dee. Or Jo,' she said as she pushed up out of her seat, flicking her eyes around my office. 'I've done my time here, Angela, it's only fair.'

'You work at a fashion magazine in Manhattan, Cici,' I pointed out, trying not to sweat over her little name drop. 'You're not doing twenty-five to life at Rikers.'

Even through my concern, I took a moment to congratulate myself on my knowledge of New York's prison system. And to think Alex said watching all those *Law & Order* marathons was a waste of time.

'Sometimes it's hard to tell the difference,' she replied. 'I really feel like my assisting days are behind me and I'd appreciate your support. I'd hate for us to be working against each other on this.'

'Well, I've enjoyed our talk.' I stood up behind my desk while Cici picked up the giant neon Troll doll on top of my filing cabinet and turned it over in her hands before setting it right back down and wiping her hands off on her wine-coloured midi skirt. It was Prada. I knew because she had told me. 'And I'll think about it. Like I said, I don't think there will be any roles opening up soon and we don't have the budget to create anything. Do you think you'd want to work at any of the other magazines?'

The audacity of hope.

She looked back at me as though I was mad.

'I feel like *Gloss* is my baby,' she said with a shrug as she walked towards the door. 'I wouldn't feel right anywhere else. I'm sure you, me and Jo will figure it out.'

I stared after her as she closed the door gently and tried my hardest to work out why everything she said always sounded like a threat.

'*Gloss* is *my* baby,' I muttered, opening a drawer and pulling out an emergency bag of Monster Munch. 'Why don't you go and tell Jo that?'

That was me, Angela Clark, super-mature, adult-extraordinaire, and absolutely, 100 per cent, winning at life.

CHAPTER TWO

'Never have I needed this more than I do today,' I said, chucking back half my cocktail-in-a-teacup in one go. 'Honestly, the day I've had.'

'Um, OK?' the waitress raised an eyebrow, clearly out of fucks to give and it was only ten past seven in the evening. 'Can I get you anything else?'

'Three more of these, please.' I pointed at my half-empty cup. 'For my friends. Who are on their way. Not for me.'

'Girl, no judgement,' she replied. 'You do you.'

'Still not entirely sure what that means,' I admitted quietly as she disappeared down the dark narrow bar. 'But I'll try.'

Even though I was twenty minutes late to The Dead Rabbit, I was still the first to arrive. It was a while since we'd been there and it was nice to sink into a comfy corner seat in the dimly lit upstairs bar. In days gone by, Jenny had been a big fan due to its proximity to Wall Street, Wall Street bankers and Wall Street bankers' wallets, but since she had settled down with Mason we hardly ever ventured this far south in

Manhattan. Even though they didn't live together officially, she spent almost every night at his Gramercy apartment, and her room in our old Murray Hill two-bedroom was little more than a glorified wardrobe.

Sipping the rest of my cocktail at a more dignified pace, I thought back to my Mason conversation that morning. Even though I was so excited for him to propose to my bestie, I knew keeping the secret was going to kill me. In general, people didn't tell me things they didn't want other people to know – case in point, Delia's taking over Spencer Media and reorganizing the entire business on the sly. I had a hard time keeping schtum: whether it was due to excitement, extreme tiredness or straight-up idiocy, I was not a safe space for secrets. But this time, I was 100 per cent going to hold my water. For two months. Two long months. Emptying the rest of my drink, I pushed the teacup away and stared off into the distance.

He probably shouldn't have told me.

'Hey, sorry we're late.'

Jenny and Erin blew into the bar in a cloud of perfect hair and expensive perfume. I surreptitiously stuck my nose into my own armpit to make sure my Dove was keeping up its twenty-four-hour freshness claim before Jenny hurled herself at me for a hug.

I pasted a bright smile on my face and clamped my lips together.

Don't tell Jenny about the proposal, don't tell Jenny about the proposal, don't tell Jenny about the proposal.

'Are you OK?' Jenny asked.

Don't tell Jenny about the proposal.

'Maso— *mais oui*,' I replied with a flourish to back up my sweet French save. 'Yes. Absolutely. Why wouldn't I be?'

She didn't look entirely convinced but she didn't ask any follow-up questions either. That went down as a win in my book.

'We had a meeting across town and I thought it would never end,' Erin said, explaining away their lateness and almost taking my eye out with her razor-sharp blonde bob. 'Traffic is a bitch tonight.'

'You could have taken the subway,' I suggested. 'No traffic down there.'

Erin and Jenny looked at each other and exploded into laughter.

'And that's why you're the funny one,' Erin smiled, shrugging off her oversized Burberry pea coat and dumping her Hermès Birkin on top of my MJ satchel on the spare chair. My bag slid to the floor sadly, ashamed to be in the presence of something so superior. Jenny grabbed it from the ground and passed the offending article back with a disapproving frown.

'You're still using this?' she asked, pulling a lip gloss out of her own studded leather Alexander Wang duffel. 'Angie, you must have like a thousand bags now, you have to let that thing go.'

'You're confusing my bag collection with yours,' I told her, stroking the soft, supple brown leather. 'Anyway, I love this bag. I think it gets better with age.'

'It doesn't, you should ditch it,' Erin assured me. 'Nothing does really. Red wine and George Clooney are literally the only exceptions to that rule.'

'We'll end up burying you with that thing,' Jenny sighed as I cradled my bag in my arms to shield it from Erin's cruel but worryingly accurate statements. 'Sometimes I think all my work with you was for nothing.'

'Give me a break,' I begged as the waitress reappeared with our cocktails, 'I've had a shitty day and my brain isn't up to it.'

'Same here,' Erin said, clinking her teacup against mine. 'I've been up since three – TJ has some kind of bug and I spent half the night stripping beds and cleaning up baby puke. And you know if he has it, Arianna'll have it by tomorrow.'

'To the glamour of motherhood,' I said, clinking her back. 'Cici announced she's been my assistant for long enough and wants a "bigger role" at *Gloss*. Also, they're completely restructuring the company and everyone is on the chopping block, which I probably should have mentioned first, so ha-ha, I win. Worst day in forever.'

Jenny peeled off her tight black sweater to reveal a low-cut black T-shirt and every man in the bar turned and looked.

'Mason emailed me about the restructure,' she said as she crossed her toned legs. If you got up and went running every morning like Jenny did, you could have legs like that, said the little voice in my head. I drowned it with another sip of my cocktail. 'You're overreacting. They haven't announced any closures yet.'

'The fact you added a "yet" on the end doesn't exactly fill me with confidence,' I told her. 'It's just unsettling.'

'Not as unsettling as that demon spawn twin, Cici,' Jenny corrected. 'Surely you've put up with her for long enough? It's time for her to disappear.'

'The worst part is, she's not actually wrong,' I admitted, washing away the words with a mouthful of gin. 'Most assistants move up after a couple of years and she's been with me for three. As much as it pains me to admit it, she's good at her job, even if her people skills are still, you know, a bit rough.'

Never had there been such an understatement.

'I only wish she wanted to move to another magazine, I know the rest of the team would like to see the back of her.'

Erin stretched her arms above her head until her shoulders clicked. 'I don't know how you sit in an office with that woman every day. I'd rather have an underfed hyena outside my office. Do you keep a loaded gun in your desk?'

'She *is* an underfed hyena,' Jenny replied for me. 'If not worse. Remember that time she threw out all the shoes under your desk?'

'She thought I wanted to donate them to the homeless,' I said weakly. 'She said she was trying to help.'

Jenny blinked in disbelief. 'Really, Angie? She thought you wanted to donate Chanel ballet pumps to the homeless?'

My stomach clenched tightly with the pain of loss and I took a sip to their memory. The worst part was, I was still paying off that credit card bill.

'I read about the restructure – we sent Delia congratulatory flowers, of course. You don't really think they're going to close any magazines, do you?' Erin asked, nervously clicking her fingernails. Erin owned a PR agency, the PR agency worked with the magazines, the more magazines closed, the more difficult her life became.

'*Gloss* is doing fairly well,' I said, repeating the same story I'd told a thousand times over already that day and hoped I'd start to believe it soon. 'I'm sure we'll be fine.'

Panicking would get me nowhere, I reminded myself. Listing all the magazines that had closed over the last three years would not help, I reminded myself. Imagining myself sat on the floor outside a Burger King with a sign that says 'will work for nuggets' was entirely unproductive.

'So, I had a shit day, Angie had a shit day . . . ' Erin looked at Jenny. 'Anything to add, Lopez?'

'I'm breaking up with Mason,' she replied casually, holding up her cup for a toast. 'So yeah, cheers.'

I stared at her across the table. Now my deodorant really had some work to do.

'What?' Confusion crumpled Erin's delicate features. 'You're kidding, right?'

'No,' Jenny replied simply. 'I've been thinking about it and he really isn't leaving me with much of a choice. So, I'm going to end it.'

'Is today National Everyone Make Dramatic Statements Day?' I asked, putting my cocktail down so I could fully and soberly concentrate on my best friend. 'Because if it is, I missed a memo. What do you mean you're breaking up with Mason?'

Jenny rolled her eyes as though we were the ones being irrational.

'We've been dating for almost three years,' she replied, all calm and rational and entirely unlike herself. 'He knows I want to get married, we've talked about getting married but nothing has happened. I told him back in the spring that I wanted to get engaged this summer, and if he didn't propose, I was going to have to end it. He hasn't proposed. How long am I supposed to wait?'

'You told him he had to propose or you'd dump him?'

I just wanted to be clear before I began screeching louder than an exceptionally miffed dolphin.

'Yes.'

Exceptionally miffed dolphin noises are go.

'That's not very romantic, is it?' I asked, my mind and my words racing. 'You can't break up with Mason because he hasn't met your deadline, what happened to an old-fashioned courtship? What happened to waiting?'

How could I tell her she couldn't finish with him because he hadn't proposed, because he had just told me he was planning to propose, without telling her he had just told me he was planning to propose? Just thinking about it gave me a headache.

'No, she has a point,' Erin said, resting her hand on top of Jenny's and giving it a reassuring squeeze. 'This is New York, you've got to put your cards on the table right away. Some guys are happy to date forever and never seal the deal. I told Thomas I wanted to be engaged within six months of things getting serious, that's how it is here, Angela. You were lucky to catch Alex when his light was on. Most of them need an ultimatum.'

I opened my mouth to argue but all that came out was a squeak.

'You have to play the game,' Jenny agreed. 'It's not easy out there.'

'Especially when you're over thirty,' Erin added.

Everyone looked down at the table and took a drink.

'I'm going to tell him tomorrow,' Jenny said, nodding to herself. 'I really don't think he'll be surprised. We've been seeing less and less of each other lately; maybe it's better to kill it before it goes sour. Maybe this is what he wants and he daren't admit it.'

'Just like a dude,' Erin agreed, clinking her cup to Jenny's. 'Ghost away and hope they break up with you.'

'But Mason isn't ghosting you,' I protested. 'You love him and I know he loves you.'

'And sometimes winning means knowing when to lose,' Jenny replied with a sad smile. 'I do love him, but I want to get married, Angie, I want kids. And I'm not getting any younger. If he's not going to give me those things, I'll find them somewhere else.'

I looked over at Erin for support but she looked away. Yes, she was happily married now but after two divorces, a failed engagement, and two difficult pregnancies that only came about after inordinately expensive help from the magical Dr Laura, Erin wasn't the first person to look to when you wanted someone to support your Happily Ever After rationale.

'But what if you gave him one more chance.' I was getting desperate. Jenny wasn't terribly good at sticking to her resolutions, she was forever making huge statements and hardly ever saw them through but there was a resignation in her voice that I did not like the sound of. 'I mean, when you tell him, he might propose. Maybe he's just waiting for the right time.'

'If he proposes after I tell him I'm breaking up with him, it's gonna feel like he's only doing it because I'm forcing him into a corner,' she argued. 'I gave him six months to decide whether or not he wanted to be in this for the long haul. I can't keep waiting around or I'll wake up one day and realize I'm forty. No offence, Erin.'

'None taken,' Erin replied. 'I'm in my forties, that's a thing. I might look amazing but it's still a thing.'

'Which self-help book are you reading right now?' I demanded, turning my back on Erin. She was not helping in the slightest. 'Is this Oprah? Did Oprah tell you to do this?'

'I'm not reading any self-help books,' Jenny mumbled into her drink as I waited for the inevitable follow-up. 'I got it from a podcast.'

'And podcasts are very wise but they're not right about everything,' I said firmly. 'I really think you need to give it more consideration, one more week.'

'Angie, it's November already,' Jenny stressed. 'I told him six months ago. What exactly am I waiting for? My ovaries to shrivel up and fall out my vahine?'

'They can do that,' Erin confirmed over the rim of her teacup. 'I've read about it.'

'No, they can't,' I said, pressing a hand against my stomach. There was that sick feeling again. 'You're both being ridiculous. This is why people complain about the American education system, you know.'

'I appreciate where you're coming from, Ange, but I'm not asking for opinions.' Jenny tossed her head, slapping the man at the next table in the face with her enormous hair. 'I'm just letting you know.'

Bugger. Bugger bugger bugger bugger. I tapped my fingertips against my thigh as she studiously ignored me. The conversation was officially over.

'So,' Erin blew out a deep breath as I stared across the table at my best friend. 'Did anyone else catch *Dancing with the Stars* last night?'

Three cocktails later, I rattled through my front door, dropping my satchel on the floor and peeling off my coat as I ran for the bathroom. I'd been desperate for a wee for the last three subway stops and sitting on the train outside the 9th Street station for fifteen minutes while the MTA got someone's phone off the tracks had not helped in the slightest.

Making it to the bathroom without breaking my neck

was almost as impressive as making it through my day without self-medicating. For the first two weeks of Alex's trip, I'd done such a good job of taking care of the apartment. I put dirty clothes in the wash bin and I put clean clothes back in the wardrobe. I put dirty dishes in the dishwasher and I put clean ones back in the cupboard. I ate proper meals at proper meal times, slept in my bed, and limited myself to two episodes of *This Is Us* per evening. But that was a long time ago. Now the place looked like a crime scene. Empty cups and takeaway cartons gathered in tiny huddles at either end of the settee and empty crisp packets had been carefully smoothed out and stacked up on the coffee table next to all of Alex's letters and postcards. And, if you looked very carefully, you could actually follow the trails of socks, shoes, jeans, several bras and the odd pair of pants all the way around the apartment and see where I'd been. David Attenborough would have had a field day.

I leaned back against the toilet cistern and stared wistfully at the beautiful roll-top bath that had won my heart when we first moved in. If only the day could be saved by a soak in the tub.

'Couldn't hurt to try,' I reasoned, waddling across the room with my jeans still around my ankles and turning on the taps. I missed Alex, but part of me loved living alone, even if I was reverting to some kind of wild, pantsless animal.

Leaving the rest of my clothes in a puddle by the side of the bath, I grabbed Alex's robe from the back of the door and toddled into the kitchen, looking for something to eat. Food was not love and it could not solve my problems, but it was delicious, and we hadn't really eaten a proper dinner so snacks felt justified.

I'd emailed Mason on the way home, asking if we could meet tomorrow after work to discuss DumpGate, or rather so I could convince him to bring Operation Proposal forward and head any dumpings off at the gate. There was no need to tell him exactly what Jenny had said; all I needed to do was encourage him to put a ring on her fourth finger before she flipped him off with the middle one. Naturally, I'd suggested we conduct this conversation at Tiffany.

And then I remembered.

When Louisa and Grace had come to visit for my birthday, they'd brought one of those massive slabs of Galaxy you can only get at the airport and, after eating half of it the second they left, then throwing it right back up two hours later, I'd made Alex break it up into little bars, wrap them in freezer bags, and hide them from me. I was almost certain there was still one left, wedged in between the ceiling and the top of the kitchen cabinets. For the first time in my life, my lack of restraint was about to pay off.

'I should take up parkour,' I muttered, hurling myself onto the kitchen top and wobbling upright. The belt of Alex's dressing gown swung around my knees as I felt along the top of the cabinets, hoping against hope that the chocolate would still be there. And only the chocolate. The last thing I needed was another nasty surprise, especially something cockroach-shaped.

Or washing-machine shaped.

Just as my fingertips hit Galaxy pay dirt, a deafening crash thundered through my ceiling, blowing up a world of dust and dirt. Coughing, blinking, and clinging to my kitchen cupboards – and the chocolate bar – for dear life, I waited for the literal dust to settle, my heart pounding in my chest. There, not six feet away from me, was a washing machine, sat right in the middle of my kitchen. And while we did need a new washing machine, I really would have preferred it if one hadn't just crashed through my ceiling from the apartment above.

'Angela?'

I looked up through the smoky hole to see Lorraine and Vi, the couple who lived upstairs, staring down at me with their hands covering their faces.

'Are you standing on the kitchen counter?' Vi asked, peeking through her fingers.

'Did your washing machine just come through my kitchen ceiling?' I replied, gripping the Galaxy more tightly than ever before.

'Um, sorry about that,' Lorraine pushed her clear acrylic glasses frames back up her nose as she spoke. 'Are you OK?'

I rubbed a layer of dirt and dust from my face and looked at the hand holding on to the chocolate bar. I was shaking.

'Absolutely fine,' I assured them. Stiff upper lip and all that. 'Are you both all right?'

'That was really intense,' Vi gripped Lorraine's arm tightly. 'I came in to see what the noise was and there it was in the middle of the kitchen and I'm thinking, what is the washing machine doing in the middle of the kitchen? And then boom! Jesus, what if it had exploded? What if *I'd* fallen through the ceiling too?'

'Yeah, I was quite surprised as well,' I replied. 'And, you know, right underneath it.'

'Should we call someone? Do you need to go to the hospital? Is it going to blow up?' Lorraine suggested, looking at Vi for confirmation. Vi looked at me and I looked back. Lawyers, both of them. Degrees from

Harvard. And as much good in a crisis as a pair of chocolate teapots.

'I think I'm all right and it's pretty late.' And I've had four cocktails, I added silently. 'No one died. Maybe we can sort it out in the morning?'

'Yeah,' she agreed with a sigh of relief. 'That sounds good. We're like, sorry?'

I was still stood there, frozen on the kitchen counter and not entirely sure if I was going to be able to get down. I wasn't quite sure what the proper etiquette was for when someone's washing machine fell through your kitchen ceiling but I was fairly certain it should include at least one cup of tea.

'Angela?' Vi said.

Ahh, here's the offer of tea. I smiled graciously at the redhead above.

'Your robe is kind of open.' She waved her hand awkwardly up and down her body. 'Just, so you know.'

'OK, thanks,' I said, yanking it shut and tying the belt in a tight knot under my boobs.

Both women slowly backed away from the gaping hole, leaving me perched on my dusty kitchen top, chocolate bar in one hand, cupboard handle in the other. I stared at the washing machine embedded in the floor, surrounded by broken tiles, rubble and shards of shiny wet floorboards with soapy water slowly leaking out around the somehow still intact glass door. Even though my kitchen had been destroyed, and even though I clearly could have been killed, all I could think about was what was in the washing machine and did the girls need it for the morning?

Very, very, very slowly, I clambered down from the kitchen top, careful not to stand on anything stabby, and tiptoed back into the bathroom, checking my heart rate on my Fitbit as I went.

'Would you look at that, it's up,' I noted as I turned off the taps. Instead of fighting with my hastily tied belt knot, I yanked Alex's robe over my head and tossed it on top of my day clothes before stepping into the hot water, opening the freezer bag and pulling out the bar of milk chocolate. I sank into the bath and let my hair soak around my shoulders before chomping down on the Galaxy. There was no time to break off individual squares, this was an emergency.

'Still,' I said to absolutely no one. 'At least tomorrow has to be better than today.'

CHAPTER THREE

The Tuesday morning team meeting was usually a pretty pleasant affair. After the madness of Monday when we sent the magazine to print, most people were either too exhausted or too hungover to kick up much of a fuss. And most importantly, I always brought donuts. Even as the editor, I was not above bribery.

Megan, my senior beauty editor, took the seat beside me and grabbed a delicious-looking, pink-frosted donut. I reached out to nab one before they were all gone, but before I could reach the box, my stomach turned. I hesitated. Too many cocktails and an entire bar of Galaxy was not a balanced meal but I was so hungry. Why hadn't I got bagels? Or pizza? Or pizza bagels?

'Have you heard the latest?' Megan asked.

'About Britney and the dancer and the box of cupcakes?' I asked. 'I refuse to believe it. Unless it's true in which case, it's amazing.'

'No, about *The Look*,' she peered around us and leaned forward with a furtive frown. 'Sophie says one of the girls at *Belle* heard the new brand manager tell the editor that it's closing.'

I felt a wash of something cold and icky run all the way from the top of my head to the tips of my toes.

'My first job in New York was on *The Look*,' I whispered urgently. 'They can't close it, *The Look* is an institution.'

Megan's eyebrows flickered upwards in agreement and she held a hand over her mouth as she chewed. 'I know,' she said. 'It's only a rumour but it's awful. Still, I know this is terrible to say but better *The Look* than *Gloss*, right?'

It was terrible to say but it was even more terrible that I was thinking the exact same thing.

'Spencer has got off so lightly with mags closing,' she said, swallowing a bite of donut. 'Condé Nast, Hearst, Bauer – they've all folded big titles. I guess we should have seen this coming.'

'I say we don't worry about it until we know what there is to worry about,' I said, turning my rings around my finger underneath the table. 'I'm almost certain the people at *Vegan Parent Quarterly* should be more worried than us or *The Look*.'

Personally, I still wasn't convinced that *VPQ* wasn't a front for some kind of underground meth operation, but Delia insisted it was a real publication. The world was a strange and confusing place sometimes.

'You're right,' Megan nodded in agreement. 'We shouldn't stress out so much, they're only rumours right now. Do anything fun last night?'

Drank too much. Ate too little. Listened to my best friend being a complete tool. Almost died.

'Nope,' I replied shortly. 'You?'

'I had a date,' she grinned. 'Tinder finally came up with something decent.'

'How was it?' I asked, sipping slowly from a tiny bottle of water.

'Not terrible,' she replied brightly. 'I know my bar is set kinda low but I liked him, he was nice. Not a serial killer.'

'Not a serial killer is about as low as you can go,' I said. 'But yay.'

'Probably shouldn't have gone home with him,' she replied, weighing up the decision on her face as I tried to hide my matronly shock. 'But that whole not sleeping with guys on a first date is a myth, right? It doesn't really make any difference, not if he likes you?'

'I feel like we have published that article more than once,' I assured her. 'All you can do is what's right at the time. And, you know, use several methods of protection.'

'Thanks, Mom,' Megan laughed before stopping short and biting her lip. 'Um, do you need me for this meeting because I kind of need to run out to the drugstore?'

'Go,' I ordered. 'Now. Leave the donut.'

Leaving her laptop and the rest of the sugary pastry on the table, Megan bolted for the door just as Cici appeared, long blonde hair pulled back in a ponytail and, for some reason, heavy-framed black glasses on her face. She turned her nose up as Megan ran by, slipped into the meeting room and closed the door behind her.

'Why are you wearing glasses?' I asked as she took Megan's seat, pushing her colleague's computer and breakfast into the middle of the table.

'I've worn them before,' she said, turning her phone to silent. 'I wear glasses.'

She definitely hadn't, and she definitely didn't, but I didn't have the time or the energy to investigate Cici's weirdness today.

'Hey guys, can we get started?' I waved to the team assembled round the table. 'Lots to get through.'

I was proud of my magazine. I'd come up with the idea for *Gloss* with the help of my friends – a cool, fun weekly magazine we gave away for free across New York City, and after five years of my literal blood, sweat and tears, it was now a real, live actual thing that was distributed all across America. Not bad for a British girl who had arrived in Manhattan with a weekend bag, a credit card, and no bloody idea what she was doing. Every time I saw someone reading it on the subway, I felt myself smiling – even if the celebrity on the cover had been an absolute nightmare, even if getting it to print on time had taken years off my life, it was still a kick. *Gloss* really was my baby, and like the parents of most five-year-olds, I'd lost more than one night's sleep over it. But like almost all the parents of most five-year-olds, I wouldn't have changed it for anything. I loved the team, they were all hardworking, dedicated, and while I wasn't about to offer any of them a kidney for shits and giggles, they made me love coming to work every day.

'First, I want to say how brilliant this week's issue is looking – loving your work, people.' I paused so they could all clap themselves and smiled while I silently wondered whether or not people applauded their own achievements in British magazine offices. 'Next, the Channing Tatum interview. Someone's going to have to go out to LA to do it.'

The entire table put up their hands.

'Really?' I eyed Jason, the managing editor. 'You

want to go to LA to interview Channing Tatum even though you've never conducted an interview in your life?'

'I'm not that interested in the interview part but I would like to hang with Chan,' he replied. 'And I am very happy to go to LA in order to make that happen.'

You and me both, I added, noting down names and silently lamenting the fact I couldn't just assign the job to myself. Being the boss was shit.

'Also, there's the Balmain feature to think about,' I said. 'We're going to be working with *Belle* on this one so it's going to be short notice but, short notice in Paris so not too much of a compromise. Sophie, you're good for that, yeah?'

The fashion editor nodded, jigging her shoulders up and down in a happy little chair dance.

'Do I get to fly first class?' she asked, giddy as the proverbial kipper. 'I love it when they give you the little pyjamas on the plane.'

'I'll buy you a pair of pyjamas and we'll save ten grand on the travel budget,' I replied. 'Or I can go to Paris instead? Save you the bother?'

She pouted and shook her head.

'Thought that might be the case. Right, super exciting, we've got a phoner confirmed with Irene Kim for the My Social Life column . . . ' I crossed off the points as I went. There was so much to keep track of and my brain felt like a Christmas pudding: only any good when covered in booze and just about ready to be set on fire. 'She's in Seoul, at the moment, and the call is set for four in the afternoon, her time.'

'What time is that here?' Sophie asked.

'I don't know,' I said, pulling out my phone to check the world clock. 'Oh. Three in the a.m.'

The entire table flinched at once.

'I know, but she's a really good get,' I pressed, as convincing as possible. From the looks on their faces, I was not very convincing. 'And she's got amazing social media; it'll make for a great column – she isn't doing a lot of press.'

'I would, but I've got the Bobbi Brown launch first thing,' Sophie said, piling regret into her voice even if she wasn't able to wipe the smirk off her face.

I looked to the entertainment editor. She shrugged, all apologies. 'I'm covering the Andrew Garfield premiere tonight and who knows how late that will go. I'm heartbroken, though, I love Ileen.'

'You mean Irene,' I corrected with a sigh. 'Fine, I'll do it.'

Classic. Everyone else gets to fly to LA and Paris and I get to wake up in the middle of the night to interview a model about her Snapchat. The joys of being in charge.

'OK, this is a fun one. You know Generation *Gloss* is coming up.'

For the past three years, we'd hosted an interactive reader event at the Market Design centre in Manhattan. A weekend of panels, makeovers, tutorials, meet and greets and general shenanigans that were made all the more stressful by the hangover everyone always had after the opening-night party.

'The event is all taken care of, but I need someone to manage the party,' I said, and offered the team a pleading smile. Every year previously we'd handed the whole thing over to an events production company but this year, unless there was an events production company that enjoyed working for literal peanuts, that was not an option. Yay, budget cuts.

'We're keeping the costumes so everyone needs to dress up as something,' I said, scanning my notes. 'Nothing says circulation increase like Kanye West in a toga.'

Jason shuddered at the end of the table.

'But who doesn't like organizing a party? It's all but done, to be honest, I just need someone to take over now it's a couple of weeks away, liaise with the sponsors, secure VIPs. All the fun stuff. Any volunteers?'

Silence. Either everyone had a mouth full of donut or the entire team had decided their job was done once they'd congratulated themselves on last week's work.

'Really, no one?' I tried again. 'Who could turn this down? Celebs, fashion, big massive piss-up, there's even a free frock in it for you. Seriously, no one?'

'I'll do it.'

Oh, sweet baby Jesus, no.

Cici looked at me, blinking behind her clearly non-prescription lenses. Her eyes were enormous, it was all very unnerving.

'I'll do it,' she repeated.

Well, bugger me backwards, Bob.

'You . . . it's . . . you want to?'

I tried to make eye contact with anyone else at the table and got nothing. What a bunch of absolute arseholes.

'I said I'll do it.' She tapped her fingernails against her phone, two tiny red spots blooming in her cheeks. 'So, can we move on?'

'Let's move on,' I nodded, flicking my pen against my notepad and trying to work out how to make it look as though every single member of my staff had suffered mysterious accidents in the same week. 'Thanks, Cici.'

'You're welcome,' she said, almost smiling.

Taking a deep breath, I looked back down at the agenda, attempting to focus. If this was karma's idea of making things up to me for the Monday I'd had, karma had a very dark sense of humour.

Later that afternoon I was drowning in admin, the least exciting part of my job. You never saw Miranda Priestly going through everyone's expenses and yet, here I was, trying to work out whether or not I'd get fired for allowing my news editor to expense three muffins. A knock at the door drew my attention away from the pile of Starbucks receipts and up to a tall, obscenely handsome man, glaring at me through the glass.

'So help me god, if you're a stripper . . . ' I stood up, pulled my skirt down and scuttled over to let him in. 'I warned you about this last time, Lopez.'

'Angela?' he asked in a crisp, clean voice.

'Yes?' I nodded, scanning him for a boom box, bottle of baby oil or Velcro strips on the seams of his trousers. They seemed sturdy enough.

'We have a four thirty,' he replied, stern features relaxing into an almost smile. 'I'm Joe Herman, the new director of women's brands.'

The smile on my face went blank and my lips pressed together until they were nothing more than a thin, pale line in the middle of my face. Joe? *This* was Joe? Joe was a man? A giant, handsome man? And definitely not a woman or a stripper?

'Shit,' I said sweetly. 'I mean, yes, of course we have. Come on in.'

Flinging the door open, the reinforced glass hit my filing cabinet with a sickeningly loud crack just as Joe stepped into my office.

'Don't worry about that,' I insisted, skipping past him in my high heels so I could clear some space on my desk. 'It won't break. We changed it to reinforced glass after the second time I smashed it. Now, can I get you a drink or anything?'

Joe shook his head, considered the two seats in front of him, and reluctantly sat down.

'That's a coffee stain,' I said, watching as his eyes lingered on the other empty seat. 'We're going to get it cleaned. Someone spilled coffee yesterday.'

Someone quite clearly meaning me.

'I'm not interrupting anything?' Joe asked, pulling an iPad out of a handsome leather briefcase and ignoring my explanation entirely. 'I'm still getting to grips with the scheduling system here. My assistant has had some trouble synching my calendar with everyone else's.'

'The calendar system is a bit rubbish,' I fibbed as I checked my schedule, which I had never, ever once had a problem with. 'Sometimes things don't copy over, but you're not interrupting at all.'

There it was, clear as day in the schedule: 4.30 p.m. – meeting with Director of Women's Brands, JHerman@ spencermedia.com. Nowhere did it mention that JHerman was a Joseph and not a Josephine. That would have been good information to have.

'Sorry, we're always a little bit hectic around here. Or I am at least, everyone else is great. I've been a bit scatty this week, actually. The other morning I couldn't remember if I'd left my straighteners on and had to go back home to check, and of course I hadn't, but you know how it is.'

I gestured towards his perfectly straight, swept back blond hair. There was no way it was behaving that well without help; the humidity gods of New York simply wouldn't allow it.

'I don't straighten my hair,' he said quietly.

'Of course not, sorry,' I replied. What a liar. 'Not that there would be anything wrong with it if you did.'

'But I don't,' he repeated.

'Noted,' I nodded. 'Sorry.'

'Please stop apologizing.'

'Sorry, I mean, of course. Yes.' I sucked in my bottom lip and took a deep breath in. 'Sorry.'

He dispensed with his starter smile and opted for a more professional semi-grimace.

'Angela.'

'Joe.' I clicked my fingers and pointed at him with the double guns. If it was good enough for Bob Spencer, it was good enough for Angela Clark. 'Shoot.'

'So, *Gloss*.' He crossed his legs, his perfectly tailored, charcoal grey trousers straining against some impressively chunky muscles. Not that I was looking. Well, yes, I *was* looking, but only in the sense that I had eyes and because he was sat in front of me, not because my husband had nicked off on a two-month, long-distance vacay and sometimes you're only human, goddamnit, and really, they were very big legs and—

'Angela?'

I looked up to see him staring at me across the table. My beloved, if poorly ageing Alexander Skarsgård poster rolled its eyes at me from its spot on the wall behind him.

'Sorry, I thought there was going to be more to the question,' I said, snapping to attention. '*Gloss*, that's us. We're really excited about the new strategy.'

If there was one thing I'd learned about corporate

life in the last few weeks, it was 'when in doubt, bullshit'. I'd originally been introduced to the concept as 'fake it 'til you make it' but I soon realized it wasn't so much faking it as talking whatever absolute shite the other person wanted to hear until they went away and left you alone.

'But you don't know what the new strategy is yet,' Joe replied.

Well, he had me there.

'We're still very excited.' I looked longingly at the door, wondering how upset Delia would be if I just kicked off my Choos and legged it. 'About the whole new strategy brand extravaganza.'

My new boss continued to stare at me across the desk while tumbleweeds blew through my empty brain. Of all the times for the voice in my head to decide she had nothing to say.

'You're English.' Joe uncrossed his legs and something that could have almost passed for a real smile appeared right above his chiselled jaw. I wasn't sure if it was a statement or a question, so I just smiled back and gave half a nod. I didn't want to scare him off if he'd decided to play nice.

'My girlfriend is English,' he continued. 'But she lives here now, obviously.'

'I wonder if we know each other,' I replied while giving myself a mental telling off for assuming this insanely well put together man with incredible hair and no wedding ring, who was in charge of the women's brands at Spencer Media, must be gay. There had to be at least one perfect-looking straight man, if only to make all the others feel terrible. 'It feels as though every British person in New York is connected in some way or another, even if it's just from devouring fish and chips with your bare hands at A Salt and Battery twice a year.'

We looked across the desk at each other for a long moment and I imagined what kind of a woman would snag a man like this.

'Probably not?' I said, shaking my head and sitting back in my chair.

'Probably not,' he agreed. 'But back to *Gloss*.'

This is all going to be fine, I reassured myself as he flicked around at the screen of his iPad. The magazine is in good shape, you're doing a good job. They actually said that, at your last appraisal: you're doing a good job. No one knows how much stationery you steal, or about that time you followed Chris Hemsworth for fifteen blocks after Mason tipped you off that he was coming into *Ghost* for an interview. *No one knows.*

'I hear you're doing a good job,' Joe said, still flicking through his notes.

SEE, my brain shouted, IT'S ALL OK.

'But *Gloss* is a small part of a big machine,' he went on. 'I'm sure you're already expecting to hear this, but there are going to be changes in the next couple of months.'

'Changes?' I replied. 'What kind of changes?'

'The kind of changes that take us from the third most profitable media company to the first,' he stated. Dear god, Joe Herman was a confident man. 'And those kind of changes aren't always popular.'

'No,' I agreed, my knee bobbing up and down underneath my desk, my black tights catching every time. 'I suppose they aren't.'

'But this isn't high school, we're all adults,' Joe said. 'No one is here to be popular.'

I was, I wanted to say. I was there to be popular. Being popular was great, as I was certain he already knew. There was a distinct air of Captain of the Football Team about this man.

'My job will be to look at how our brands can work more closely together to maximize our workforce.' He held his hands out in front of him and then clasped them together to reinforce his point. 'We have three separate women's brands with three entirely separate editorial, sales and marketing teams, talking broadly to the same audience, *Belle*, *Gloss* and *The Look*. That doesn't make sense.'

'It makes sense to me,' I replied. 'People don't only read one magazine.'

'People barely read magazines at all,' he argued. 'You're aware of how quickly *Gloss*'s online readership is growing versus your print numbers?'

I swallowed and shuffled myself upright in my seat. Why hadn't I prepared for this meeting? Apart from forgetting I had it altogether, why didn't I have all the latest numbers in front of me? One minute I was signing off receipts for manicure dates with Beyoncé, and the next I was fighting for the future of my magazine. This was not how I'd planned to spend my Tuesday afternoon.

'Next week we'll be announcing a consolidation of the marketing teams,' he announced. 'Instead of having one team per mag, we'll have one team per brand stream.'

'You're going to make people redundant,' I said slowly.

'Certain positions will be eliminated,' he replied. I felt as though I'd stepped into a bucket of ice water. People I knew were going to lose their jobs, six weeks before Christmas. It was like the first hour of a Lifetime movie without the happily-ever-after resolution tacked on the end. And I should know, I'd seen every single one of them.

'Once the new marketing team has been established,' Joe added. 'We'll be doing the same thing with the sales teams.'

'And then the editorial teams,' I guessed. He nodded and my knee crashed into the underside of my desk, knocking over my pencil pot. I righted it with trembling hands.

'Nothing is confirmed,' Joe said, resting his hands on his knees and graciously looking away as I calmed myself. 'And we don't want to worry anyone at this moment in time, so this conversation will be strictly confidential.'

'I wasn't about to call everyone in to announce the good news,' I replied, full of fire for my magazine, for my team. 'My people are good, Joe. They're creative, they work hard. You won't find better people doing what they do anywhere in this building or anywhere else in the city.'

It took me a moment to realize my voice had risen, I was half out of my chair and the entire team was watching through the glass walls of my office. Pushing my hair behind my ears, I cleared my throat and sat back down. Joe leaned forward and a full, wolfish grin appeared on his face. He had fantastic teeth. The utter bastard.

'I heard you were passionate about what you do,' he said. 'And I heard you have a great staff at *Gloss*, so there's no need to go to war just yet. I won't lie, Angela, I like passion and I like balls. That attitude is going to serve you well in the new Spencer Media.'

Joe's eyes lit up as he spoke and I was suddenly very, very worried. '*Gloss* doesn't have the heritage of *Belle* or the familiarity of *The Look* but it is a fresh and vibrant brand. With you, I see growth potential. My job here is to prune the dead wood and encourage new buds and I already know I don't need three mags in print with three full editorial teams and three editors to run three very similar outlets.'

Oh shit. Shit shit shit shit shit shit shit. Shit.

'Is *Gloss* a bud or are we dead wood?' I asked, my brain completely blank. I'd never been much of a gardener, as the dead succulent on my windowsill would attest.

'*Gloss* is a branch on the Spencer Media tree,' he corrected, 'that will either flower and bloom or wither and die.'

Such a reassuring man. Clearly Delia had employed him for his gentle way with words.

'I'm meeting with all the editors in my brand stream this week.' He flipped at his iPad and raised his eyebrows. 'And then I'm out of town for Thanksgiving. I'll schedule a follow-up meeting with you as soon as I'm back so we can discuss my strategy.'

'Fantastic,' I said with altogether too much enthusiasm for someone who felt as though they'd just been slapped across the face with a four-day-old kipper.

'I have to say, I was very curious to meet you.' Joe reached across the desk and took my hand in an absurdly firm handshake. 'You didn't take a traditional route into this job and you seem to be excelling. I know Delia has a tremendous amount of faith in you.'

It should have been a compliment but instead, it felt like a question. A massively unsettling, wanky, unanswerable question.

'Hopefully I'm not too much of a letdown,' I replied.

He cocked his head in agreement and I almost vaulted across the desk to knock him out. He was a monster. A horribly attractive and impressively tall monster.

'Let's get that follow-up in the diary,' he said, still squeezing the life out of my right hand. 'Great to meet you.'

'You too,' I managed to half stand and almost smile at the same time and it felt like too much of an achievement. 'Looking forward to our follow-up.'

Like a hole in the head.

Considering my words with a nod, he released his handshake, leaving white indentations across the back of my hand that turned red as I flexed my fingers. I watched him walk out the door and close it carefully behind him, counting to ten before I picked up the phone.

'Hey, what's up?'

Jenny answered on the first ring.

'Are you busy after work?' I asked. 'I need a drink.'

'Yeah, I can be done by six if I hustle,' she replied. 'You want to get dinner?'

'There can be food,' I said, my skin prickling from head to toe. 'As long as there is alcohol.'

Jenny made an unconvinced sound down the line. 'We got drinks last night.'

'Yes, we did,' I replied. 'What's your point?'

'Fair,' Jenny acknowledged. 'Meet at the St Regis? I'm sure it's nothing a martini can't fix.'

'Let's hope that's true,' I confirmed, suddenly aware of the seven staffers peering through my glass door. 'Gotta go, see you in a bit.'

I hung up the phone and waved everyone in.

'Was that the new boss?' Megan asked. 'The new brand director?'

'They put a man in charge of women's brands?' Sophie, the fashion editor, looked confused. 'I don't get it.'

'What did he say?' Jason gnawed on his thumbnail as he spoke. 'Are there going to be cuts?'

'Um,' I squeaked. 'Everything's fine?'

'Then why were you jumping out of your seat and shouting?'

Trust Megan to expect truthful answers. Why couldn't she accept my sugar-coated lies like everyone else?

'He said he could get me tickets to a secret Taylor Swift show,' I told her, not quite managing to meet her eyes as I spoke. 'Everything's fine. There's no news, which, I'm reliably informed, is good news.'

Jason pouted. 'My friend Stevens who works in sales says they're going to close five titles by the end of the year.'

'Your friend added an "s" to the end of a perfectly good name just to look more interesting on Grindr,' I replied, concerned that an assistant in the sales team had better insider knowledge than I did. 'So, let's not give him more credit than is due. I'll fill you all in properly at the team meeting in the morning,' I promised. Another lie, I'd clearly be dodging the facts for as long as humanly possible. 'But there's nothing for any of you to worry about. He actually said a lot of nice things about *Gloss*. So, the best thing we can do is keep everything as it is. We're doing such a good job, let's keep that up.'

I watched as they filed out of the office, all relieved giggles and sighs. At least it wasn't a complete lie;

there wasn't anything for them to worry about at that exact moment. There was at least a good week before they needed to start shitting themselves.

Until then, the only person who needed to worry was me.

CHAPTER FOUR

The St Regis was a great choice for an emergency after-work drink. It was a fancy hotel with a classy bar that made you feel like you were either a very important person or a very expensive call girl, depending on which boots you might be wearing at the time. Nothing terrible could happen at the St Regis, it was altogether too swanky for that, they simply wouldn't allow it. There was something about necking a twenty-five-dollar cocktail that made the rest of the world disappear, leaving just you, your booze, and an extortionate credit card bill to take your mind off whatever troubles you'd trotted in with.

'It's six ten,' Jenny greeted me, pushing a French martini down the bar and tapping her wrist where a watch was not. Jenny never wore a watch. She claimed to have an innate ability to tell the time, but I suspected it had far more to do with the fact that she never went more than fifteen seconds without looking at her phone.

I hopped onto the bar stool next to her, wondering for the first time how appropriate my outfit was for the venue. A corduroy dress with a stripy T-shirt underneath was great for a fashion mag, but not all that wonderful for the King Cole bar of the St Regis. The two older gentlemen in three-piece suits certainly didn't seem to share my appreciation for Free People's finest work.

'I had to finish proofreading an article about the psychology of nail shapes,' I said, smiling to myself before turning back to my friend. 'Did you know that almond-shaped nails mean you're more likely to be faithful?'

'What do these say about me?' she asked, flashing ten Chanel Rouge Noir stiletto-shaped nails in my face.

'That you're a sweet homebody who is good with animals and children,' I replied, ferreting around in my handbag for my phone. Alex hadn't been in touch all day and I didn't want to miss him if he called.

'Not that I'm complaining about a two-night back-to-back Angelathon,' Jenny said, admiring her nails before she wrapped them around the stem of her cocktail glass. 'But what was so bad about today that called for emergency drinks? Did you get busted photocopying your ass again?'

'That was one time,' I said defensively. 'I was just curious. And I still had my tights on, so it barely counts.'

She raised an eyebrow and supped.

'I met my new boss today,' I explained, gripping the base of my martini glass and twisting it around in shiny circles.

'And it was amazing and he loves you and he's already given you a promotion and a raise and every other Friday off?'

'Exactly that,' I agreed. 'Except the opposite.'

She gave me a quizzical look. 'So, you have to work every other Friday?'

'Keep your fingers crossed I keep working at all,' I said, pressing my fingers into my temples. 'We had a really fun, confidential meeting where he basically told me he's going to sack about half the staff, just before Christmas. Delia has hired the Grinch and given him complete authority over my magazine. A mean, tall, super-handsome, impeccably dressed Grinch.'

'He's hot?' Jenny asked.

'Not the point,' I replied. 'But yes. And it doesn't help.'

'Shit, doll, I'm sorry.' She reached over the bar and swiped a little glass bowl of snacks. Truly, she knew the way to my heart. 'That sucks. I just figured you wanted to lecture me about my decision without Erin here to back me up.'

'Well, since you mention it . . . ' I slipped my phone into the pocket of my skirt so I wouldn't be tempted to spend the entire night looking at it. Just like Jenny was at that exact second. Just like Jenny always was. 'You know I love you and I am Team Jenny all the way, but are you really, really sure this is the best idea you've ever had?'

'Best ever,' she nodded, taking the olive out of her drink and pulling it off the toothpick with her teeth. 'Like, even better than that time I invented that keychain with a phone charger attachment.'

'You didn't invent a keychain with a phone charger attachment,' I reminded her. 'You superglued your keyring to a phone charger and then you loaned it to someone in a bar, forgot about it and had to call a locksmith at 3 a.m. to get your locks changed.'

A flicker of remembrance crossed her face before

she went on chewing her olive. I turned green as a wave of nausea washed over me. I hated olives, all briny and green and evil. I liked my martinis the same way I liked my bread and my cheese, so French they should be wearing a beret.

'Did I?' she replied, knowing full well that she did. 'Whatever. I was worried about it but now I've made my mind up and I know it's the right thing to do. Lisa Vanderpump says if you've told a guy what you want and he won't give it to you, it's time to move on.'

Puffing out my cheeks, I counted to five before I opened my mouth to speak. I wanted to count to ten but there was just no way.

'If Lisa Vanderpump told you to jump off a bridge, would you do it?' I asked. Jenny paused for a moment while she considered the question.

Her phone sparked into life on the bar before she could answer me and she pounced on the illuminated screen.

'Expecting a call?' I asked.

'No one in particular,' she said, pushing it away with a sigh as the screen flickered back into darkness. I couldn't help but notice she still had the photo I had taken of the two of them kissing on New Year's Eve as her wallpaper. Maybe there was still hope. 'Like I said, things haven't been the same lately. He's hardly ever available and he's distant when he is there. I'm telling you, Angie, I have to end things before he does.'

And maybe there was literally absolutely no hope at all.

'Please don't rush into it,' I begged, sloshing my untouched drink all over the bar. For twenty-five bucks, you wanted a generous pour but my mum still gave me half a cup of tea at a time when I was at home, so there was little to no hope of my picking up a full martini glass without a fair amount failing to find my mouth.

'He's going through a lot of stuff at work, trust me. Things are crazy right now, with the new brand managers, all the rumours flying around. He's worried he'll be out of a job soon, that's not exactly ideal, is it?'

Jenny narrowed her dark brown eyes at me.

'Since when were the two of you BFFs?' She slid her neat and tidy glass away from the pool of vodka, pineapple and Chambord that was slowing spreading across the bar. 'I thought you hardly ever even saw each other?'

'We don't,' I said, mopping up my mess with a napkin under the watchful eye of a waiter. 'But I know how stressful things have been at Spencer lately. For everyone. And I know I sound like a broken record but he's such a good person, Jenny, and is it just me or are his arms getting even bigger?'

Try as she might, she couldn't help but smile at the mention of his giant biceps.

'They are,' she confirmed. 'I measure them every week.'

'You're a match made in heaven,' I replied, grabbing another handful of napkins. 'Really creepy heaven, but still . . . '

'Let me get that for you.' A not-at-all-impressed waiter came over with a clean cloth to clear up my spillage, just as my phone buzzed against my thigh.

'Ooh!' I leapt out of my seat and held it in the air. Jenny raised an eyebrow while the two older gentlemen further along the bar audibly tutted in my direction. 'It might be Alex,' I stage-whispered in apology. 'Give me a second. Don't dump Mason until I'm back.'

I ran-walked out of the bar and into the hotel lobby, pressing the green button as I went.

'Hello?'

'Angela?'

It wasn't Alex but it was a man, leaving me momentarily stumped. Literally no men ever called me on the phone unless they wanted me to donate to their charity or my dad needed to know how long to microwave a baked potato and my mum was out with the WI.

'Speaking,' I replied with great reluctance. Once they had your name, it was so much harder to tell them you didn't want to give twenty dollars a month to help rescue dogs or the New York Philharmonic or whichever political candidate was complaining the loudest this week.

'It's Mason, I'm outside the store, where are you?'

Bugger. I'd completely forgotten about my plan to meet Mason. Here I was listening to Jenny explain why she wanted to dump him and all the while I was supposed to be helping him buy her an engagement ring.

'I got stuck in the office,' I fibbed, looking back over my shoulder at Jenny, who was, predictably, flicking through her phone. 'But I'll be there as soon as I can.'

'I hope it's soon enough,' he answered. 'I'm pretty sure the security guard is about to make a pass at me.'

Hanging up, I walked purposefully back to the bar. Jenny could always tell when I was lying so this was going to be awful.

'Hey,' I picked up my bag from the floor without making eye contact, 'so, I need to run back to the office. I'm so sorry, I completely forgot.'

'But I just ordered another drink,' she said, pointing

at the stoic bartender. He shook his cocktail shaker in confirmation. 'Can't it wait?'

'It can't,' I said. She looked annoyed but not as though she was about to go nuclear. 'But I can come back if you want to wait?'

'What's going on?' she asked sharply. 'What could be such an emergency that you have to go deal with it right now?'

'Uh, Kris Jenner has announced she's running for president,' I rambled, putting my phone on the bar and dropping my bag on the floor while I fought my way back into my Topshop biker jacket. 'We've got to change the cover story. I'll be back in fifteen minutes. Twenty tops.'

Jenny propped her elbow up on the bar then rested her chin in her hand as I struggled with my outerwear.

'You OK, hun?' she asked calmly.

I leaned in to kiss her cheek then turned and ran.

'Twenty minutes, tops,' I shouted again as I left.

The doorman gave me a curt nod as he held open the main doors and I peeled out onto 55th and took a right on Fifth Avenue, dodging tourists as I ran the whole block up to Tiffany. Panting, I came to a sweaty halt in front of Mason, swiping strands of hair away from my forehead as I caught my breath.

It was the perfect crime.

'That was fast,' Mason said with suspicion as I held up a finger, waiting for my breathing to calm down. I really was out of shape. Sometimes, it wasn't enough for your jeans to fit, I told myself. First thing Saturday morning, I was going to rejoin the gym. Probably.

'I ran,' I explained, choosing not to worry as to whether or not Jenny had bought my story. By the time I got back, she'd be three martinis deep into her evening and wouldn't care in the slightest. 'Let's do this.'

'You're sure this is the right ring?' he asked as I sailed through the door with all the confidence of a woman whose friend was about to spend thousands of dollars on diamonds while she excused herself and used their lovely toilets.

'I could not be more sure,' I said, guiding him directly to the lifts at the back of the store. This was not the first time I had made this trip. I was fairly certain Jenny had played tapes of exactly what to ask for while I slept back when we had been roommates. The knowledge was just there, as certain as the sky was blue.

'Which floor for you both this evening?' The elevator attendant smiled warmly, clearly presuming Mason and I were a couple. I wasn't sure if it was the massive grin on my face or the light sweat that had broken out on his forehead, but we definitely looked like two people shopping for a massive rock.

'We'd like the engagement rings, please,' I said, my tone triumphant. Even though this ring wasn't for me, I was beyond excited. This was Jenny's dream and I got to play a part in making it come true.

'Wonderful,' he replied, hitting the button for the second floor. 'Do you know what you're looking for or is this an adventure?'

'Oh, we know,' I replied. I'd never felt so good about buying something that wasn't for me. 'We know exactly.'

I threw Mason my biggest grin and he returned it with a shaky smile of his own.

'Have fun,' the attendant said as we arrived at our

floor with a ping. He added a wink just for me as I stepped out onto the glorious showroom floor. 'And congratulations.'

For six thirty on a Tuesday night in November, Tiffany & Co. was surprisingly busy. Multiple couples hovered over display cases with wide eyes and feverish expressions. Credit cards hovered in mid-air, and everywhere I looked, bright, white ice sparkled under the specially designed lights.

'It's over here.' I led Mason over to the glass counter that held the Embrace rings. It had been a couple of months since Jenny and I had 'popped in on our way past' but the rings hadn't moved. I imagined the risk of fifty thousand dollars falling into a crack in the floor or half a mill getting hoovered up by the cleaners really wasn't worth that hassle. 'This one.'

And there it was.

Jenny's ring.

Bold, bright, and almost obscenely sparkly, it was La Lopez herself in jewellery form.

'Good evening.'

A shortish, baldish, pleasant-looking man appeared behind the counter.

'Is there anything I can show you this evening?' he asked with an encouraging expression.

'We'd like to see the half-carat Embrace,' I said, pointing at the glass but not quite touching. It wouldn't do to leave fingerprints in Tiffany. 'Right, Mason?'

'Yep,' he squeaked. 'We would.'

'A beautiful ring,' the assistant said as he opened the cabinet and reached inside to gently pull out the display tray. 'This really is one of my favourites. Such a glamorous option, a truly romantic offering for an elegant woman.'

He stopped to take a breath and consider my plum-coloured corduroy pinafore dress and stripy T-shirt ensemble.

'Oh, don't worry,' I said, looking down at my own toddler-inspired outfit. 'It's not for me.'

'Quite,' he replied before placing an almost identical, only slightly larger ring beside the first. 'Just for size comparison, this is the one-carat version of the same ring. It's still quite tasteful, perfectly suitable for daily wear. Slightly larger central stone.'

There was nothing slight about it. The new ring looked like something Barbie might have worn around her dream home. Even Elizabeth Taylor would have said it was a bit much.

'I think we're fine with the first one,' Mason gulped.

The assistant nodded. 'Is there anything else I can show you?'

'No,' Mason replied.

'Yes, please,' I countered. 'Have you got anything that's really massive?'

Mason elbowed me in the ribs as he stared at white diamonds on black velvet.

'Not for you,' I replied, eyes glazing over at the pretty things in front of me. 'While I'm here, I might as well.'

The shortish, baldish assistant amiably opened up neighbouring cabinets and laid several giant rocks out on a separate tray. Mason continued to eyeball Jenny's ring but made no attempt to touch it. Even though I'd seen it a million times, Jenny had never allowed herself to take the ring out of the cabinet. We only ever looked at it from behind the safety of the glass. Up close, it was even more stunning than I remembered. The central diamond sparkled under the store's lights while the halo of smaller stones shimmered with a subtlety that belied the fifteen-thousand-dollar price tag.

'It's gorgeous,' I whispered, as I slid a two-carat canary yellow solitaire onto the little finger of my right hand. 'She's going to be so happy, Mason.'

I held my breath as, very slowly, a huge smile broke out underneath his beard. He looked at me, and I realized there were tears in his big manly eyes. 'This is it, this is the ring. It's Jenny's ring.'

As soon as he said it, I began to well up.

'Oh,' I sniffed, scratching my cheek with an enormous sapphire as I wiped away my own tears. 'Mason, she's going to be so happy.'

'Thank you,' he said, draping his arm around my shoulders. Given his ridiculous lumberjack build, he had to reach down quite far to give me a half hug but I wrapped my arm around his waist as the assistant gave us one happy nod and silently disappeared to fetch a ring box. 'Part of me can't believe I'm actually going to do it, but as soon as I saw the ring, I knew it was right. I want to ask her right now, I don't even want to wait.'

'Don't wait!' I agreed, tears streaming down my cheeks at the thought of the proposal. 'Do it right now!'

'I'm going to call her.' Mason wiped his eyes with the back of his ringless hand and pulled his phone out of his pocket. 'Maybe she can meet me for dinner, she's probably still at work.'

'No, I know where she is!' I reached up to snatch the phone out of his hand. 'She's right next door, we were having a drink at the King Cole bar before I met you.'

Mason looked at me, confused. 'I thought you said you were at work?'

'I did but I lied,' I said happily. 'I forgot I was meeting you and I went to meet her but then I told her I had to go to work and – and none of this matters! Let's go and do it now, her hair looks nice and she's just had a manicure. She'll be ecstatic.'

'OK.' Mason ran both of his hands through his sandy hair then threw his arms out wide. 'I'm doing this! I'm going to propose to my girlfriend!'

Before I could object, he grabbed me around the waist and hoisted me off my feet, twirling me around in a circle.

'Oh, steady on,' I said, grabbing his shoulder with one hand and clapping the other over my mouth. 'I've been feeling a bit gippy all day.'

Slowly, everyone on the shop floor began to clap.

'Whoo!' yelped one overly enthusiastic man in a backwards baseball cap across the way. 'Congratulations!'

'Oh no,' I said, mortified. Whether it was sheer embarrassment or the fact a man was wearing a backwards baseball cap in Tiffany, I couldn't be sure. 'Oh, Mason, put me down.'

'Yeah, Mason, put her down.'

Still holding me hoisted three and a half feet up off the floor, Mason turned to reveal a decidedly unecstatic-looking Jenny Lopez.

'What the fuck is going on?'

'Jenny, I—' Mason, startled, seemed to have completely forgotten what he was doing in the most famous engagement ring shop in the entire history of the world. 'What are you doing here?'

'Duuuuude, busted.'

Backwards Baseball Cap Man gasped on the other side of the store and I realized everyone in Tiffany & Co. was watching us.

'What am I doing here? What are *you* doing here?' Jenny demanded. Her face was almost the same shade of red as her nails and her hair was wild. She was furious. 'Angie left her phone on the bar so I was going to take it to the office but when I followed her out, she didn't go to her office. She came here. To meet you.'

'You followed me from the bar?' I scrunched my eyebrows together, perplexed. 'How did it take you this long to find us?'

'Because I had to pee on my way up here, OK?' she yelled, hurling my phone at me. 'Someone left an entire martini on the bar and I paid seventy-five dollars for three drinks. I knew you were lying to me – tell me what the hell is going on!'

'Jenny . . . ' Mason dropped me like a bag of hot dog shit and I stumbled forward into the glass counter. Before she could say anything else, he dropped to one knee and everyone in the shop held their collective breath. 'I have something I want to ask you.'

Behind him I gestured wildly for her to come closer but she didn't move. The fury in her eyes began to shift into wide-eyed shock and her red cheeks faded to white.

'I've been thinking about this for the longest time,' Mason went on, inching closer to his girlfriend, still on one knee. Even kneeling he was almost as tall as I was. He really would be a handy person to have around if you needed something getting down off the top of the wardrobe. She had done well. 'Since I met you, my life has changed completely. You make the bad days better and you make the good days fantastic – and I need you to know how much I love you.'

'Oh.'

Jenny looked up at me as she realized what was happening. From my spot at the counter behind Mason, I gave a nod so big I thought my head might drop off.

'This isn't exactly how I'd envisioned it,' Mason said, 'but you are the most exceptional, intelligent, ridiculous, beautiful and incredible woman I have ever met and I want to spend the rest of my life beside you.'

He really was very good, I thought, tearing up again as I trained my phone's camera on Jenny's face. Impressive proposals were one of the upsides to dating a professional writer.

'Jenny?' he reached out and fumbled on the counter for the ring. 'Will you . . . '

'Yes?' she said, manically combing out her hair with one eye on my phone.

Mason opened his mouth to seal the deal but instead of saying 'Will you marry me?' he barked like a wounded sea lion and keeled over, huge, rolling sobs shaking his giant shoulders. Jenny looked at me with fear in her dry eyes. There was a chance this wasn't exactly how she'd imagined this going down.

'Mason?' I said, poking him with my toe. 'You all right there?'

'I'm just so happy,' he choked out each word in between a fresh wail. 'Jenny, I want to ask you, will you . . . will you?'

Just as I thought he was going to get through the sentence, he rolled over again, tears streaming down his face and getting lost in his beard before they pooled into a stain on the front of his plaid shirt. For the want of a comprehensible sentence, he held out the ring and squealed.

'I will,' I mouthed at Jenny over the top of his prone, checked form.

'I will!' she said, rushing towards him and skidding to the floor on her knees to plant a kiss on his lips and, most importantly, get the ring on her finger.

'Congratulations!' I shouted, circling around them with my phone, still recording the perfectish moment while all the staff and customers breathed a group sigh of relief and began a round of thunderous applause. It was like something out of a very expensive, slightly odd, fairy tale.

'Dude!' yelled Backwards Baseball Cap Man. 'Sweeeeet.'

'Yes, congratulations,' the assistant added, while Jenny and Mason continued their celebratory make-out session on the floor of Tiffany & Co. 'Will sir be paying with cash or credit?'

'Oh, it's credit,' I said, handing him the credit card Mason had left on the counter before slowly removing all my borrowed baubles. Who walked around New York with thousands of dollars in cash on them? And were they currently in the store and looking for a new British friend? 'Thank you so much for your help.'

'Not at all,' he replied, smiling at the newly engaged couple. 'It looks perfect on her. I'm so glad he decided to go with the one-carat ring, so much more impactful than the half carat.'

I bit down on my lip as my eyes opened up, saucer-wide at the sight of the half-carat ring still on the counter. Down on the floor, Jenny was laughing deliriously, staring at her own left hand. There wasn't a snowball's chance in hell he was getting it off her finger now.

'What's the price on the one-carat ring?' I asked as the assistant quickly and carefully put everything away. 'Just out of interest.'

'That one is actually 1.18 carats, and will be twenty-one thousand five hundred,' he replied without looking up from the task at hand. 'Plus tax.'

There was that nauseous feeling again.

'Worth every penny,' I said, snapping another photo. It would be nice to have as many as possible before Mason saw the price tag and had an aneurysm. 'It's a fairy tale come true.'

'Angie!' Jenny crawled over to me and hauled herself upright. 'I'm engaged!'

'I know!' I replied, watching Mason sign for the ring without reading the slip. Wow, that was going to be a rough day when his credit card bill came in.

'My wedding is going to be perfect,' Jenny whispered, glittering eyes locked on her dream ring. 'Just you wait and see.'

And for some reason, I couldn't help but think it sounded more like a threat than a promise.

CHAPTER FIVE

When a washing machine crashed through my ceiling a week earlier, it had been somewhat disconcerting. But now I had become oddly used to squeezing past the hunk of Hotpoint determined to get between me and my breakfast cuppa.

Right after they completely destroyed my kitchen, Lorraine and Vi had promised they would have it all sorted out before the weekend, but after a failed attempt at trying to pick it up and drag it out to the street on our own, I'd been living with what could have passed as modern art to some people, and a huge hole in my ceiling, for more than a week. On Sunday morning they'd lowered down a basket of pastries and, after that, it was fair to say I wasn't nearly as upset about the situation as I could have been.

'Good morning!' Vi called through the Hello Hole as we'd christened it. I waved back and grabbed a Tetley teabag out of the pot and tossed it into my travel mug. You could take the girl out of England, etc. 'Sweet outfit. Big day at the office?'

'Trying to make a good impression.' I flipped the

ends of the black ribbon I'd tied in a bow around my neck and prayed the white silk shirt wasn't a mistake. 'Do I look presentable?'

She squatted down to take a closer look and I gave her a quick twirl.

'Very nice, the shirt is smart, the skirt is sexy, everything's working for me,' she gave me a thumbs-up and I poofed up my little black mini. 'Great getaway sticks, lady.'

'And now it's black tights season again and I don't have to shave every day, you'll be seeing a lot more of them,' I replied, returning her thumbs-up as the kettle boiled.

'And if all else fails, you can just spill water on your blouse and call it a day,' Vi suggested. 'Your boss is a dude, after all.'

'Note to self, buy water,' I said. 'Thank you.'

'I'm sorry it's taking so long to get everything figured out.' She pulled at the hem of her Harvard T-shirt as she folded over to sit on the floor. 'Lorraine's brother's best friend is a builder and he specializes in restoring townhouses and period places. I'm really hoping he can come and take a look tonight.'

I poured boiling water from the kettle into my travel cup and swished the teabag around until the water was more or less brown before removing the bag and tipping in half a pint of milk. My mother would have died if she could see what passed for tea in this house these days.

'Any chance he'll be able to clear this out?' I asked, tapping the washing machine with my black Saint Laurent pointed pump. 'If I'm honest, a great big washing machine in the middle of a small kitchen is more of a problem than the Hello Hole.'

Naming the gaping chasm in the ceiling had probably been a bad idea. It now felt more like something from a Nineties sitcom than a potential structural disaster.

'You're telling me,' Vi sighed. 'I've got Lululemon leggings in there – no way I'm going to be able to save them now. I guess it's better not to try and force it open, though, right? In case it explodes or something?'

I chose not to tell her how I'd spent fifteen minutes trying to jimmy the door open with a butter knife three nights earlier. It was late, I couldn't sleep and curiosity had got the better of me. Bloody thing would not budge.

'Well, it *is* a washing machine, not a nuclear bomb, but I think we should probably leave it alone,' I said, sipping tea as weak and feeble as I was.

'I'll text as soon as I know when the builders can start.' She rolled upright and waved through the hole. 'Have a great day and show that boss man who's really boss.'

'It is actually him,' I replied with a wave of my own. 'He's been quite clear about that.'

'Eurgh, patriarchy,' she muttered as she vanished from sight. 'Catch you later.'

'I wish I was a lesbian,' I mumbled, staring up into Lorraine and Vi's beautiful kitchen. There was an actual herb garden in the window box. The only thing in our window box was pigeon shit. 'I wonder if there's a course you can take.'

'There is,' Vi shouted, apparently still in her kitchen. 'But they'd make you leave your hot husband and I know for a fact he does all the cooking in your house.'

'Noted,' I called back, my cheeks flaming red as I

barrelled out of the kitchen and towards my front door.
'Thanks, Vi.'

Park Slope was one of my favourite parts of New York
and not just because I lived there. It was post-
Halloween and pre-Thanksgiving, meaning the giant
cobweb decorations and animatronic skeletons were
gone but the pumpkins remained. Every single stoop
was covered in gourds, plastic, ceramic and even some
real ones. If you'd left real pumpkins on the doorstep
in my village when I was growing up, someone would
have lobbed them through the neighbour's greenhouse
by the next morning – we just wouldn't have known
what else to do with them. The streets all round mine
were wide and tree-lined and all the houses looked
like they'd come straight out of a Woody Allen movie,
usually complete with a neurotic man chasing a much-
too-good-looking-for-him younger woman to boot.
There was the odd modern concrete block dotted here
and there, but, for the most part, our neighbourhood
was all elegant brownstones and townhouses. It looked
like the New York I knew from the movies. That was
the strange thing about my city, even if you'd never
stepped foot in the place, you already knew it by heart.
The skyline, the streets, the parks and the subways,
New York belonged to everyone.

Sipping my tea as I walked down to the 9th Street
subway station, I let myself dream of buying a townhouse all to ourselves one day. Our apartment was
one of two in the building; we had the ground floor
and the basement while Lorraine and Vi had the top
two floors. Maybe if I didn't get fired, I'd become the
editor of *Belle* someday and that dream would become
a heavily mortgaged reality. Or perhaps Alex and the

guys would get back in the studio and write a block-buster album that made oodles of money. It had to be a possibility, didn't it? Coldplay didn't seem to be hurting for cash and Adele could definitely afford to spare a bob or two. I turned the corner past my favourite Mexican restaurant and the fancy underwear boutique next door, then nodded to the man inside the neighbouring juice bar, promising my liver I'd go in and get one tomorrow. There just wasn't time today, it had nothing to do with the fact I couldn't deal with even the thought of a green juice when my stomach was full of tea.

Just as I was about to put my foot on the steps down to the subway, my phone started ringing. Mother. I considered not answering but the passive-aggressive voicemail I'd have to listen to when I got to work didn't bear thinking about.

'Ahoy hoy,' I answered, holding the phone between my shoulder and cheek as I patted myself down for my MetroCard. 'How's life at sea?'

'Your father's had enough,' my mother announced from wherever they might be. There was no time for pleasantries when you were sailing around the world, it seemed. 'Once in a lifetime holiday, this. Round the world cruise and the silly old bugger has decided he doesn't like boats. Will you talk to him?'

'I'm actually on my way to work.' I leaned against the wall of the bodega and cursed myself for answering. I could have just deleted the voicemail. 'Can I call you back? I'm going to be late and I've got a meeting.'

'Why are you leaving for work so late?' she demanded. 'You can't be messing around, popping in when you feel like it. They'll sack you as soon as look at you, these days. Lesley, from the library, her son worked for Thomas Cook for twenty-two years and one day his car broke down so he couldn't clock in on time and when he got to work, they'd put all his things in a bin bag in the car park.'

'I'm almost certain that's not true,' I said wearily. It wasn't even eight thirty and I was already exhausted. 'But I do need to go.'

'Speak to your father and then get yourself to work,' Mum ordered before bellowing at the top of her lungs in my dad's general direction: 'David, it's Angela. She wants to talk to you and hurry up with it because she's late for work.'

'I don't want to . . . ' I closed my eyes and waited for Dad to come on the line. There was no point arguing.

'Angela?'

'Hello, Dad.'

'Why are you late for work? What's the matter? Is there an emergency? Do you need us to come to America?'

I'd have been offended by the hope in his voice if I didn't know he just really wanted to get off that bloody boat.

'I'm not late yet, everything's fine,' I told him, ignoring the disappointed sigh on the other end of the line. 'I just haven't heard from you in a while.'

'There's not that much to tell you, love,' he replied, his voice mopey. 'I must have walked every inch of this boat a thousand times and if I never see the sea again, it'll be too soon for me. Did your mother tell you it's fish at every meal? Every meal! And not proper fish like at home, weird fish. Big ugly things with their eyes still in. And who eats prawn cocktail at breakfast? It's not right, I'm telling you.'

'How long have you been on board?' I asked.

'Four days,' he replied.

'And how long have you got left?'

'One month, three weeks, two and a half days.'

Hmm.

'You know, if you really hate it, you could just get off and stay in a hotel,' I suggested. 'But I think you should try to give it a couple more days at least. See if you can't get your sea legs.'

'I've no interest in sea legs,' he replied with uncharacteristic grumpiness. 'If we were meant to be at sea for weeks on end, we'd have fins and gills. Have I got fins and gills? No, I haven't. It's nonsense. And there's no one on board who gives a monkey's about the cricket.'

'Well, that's just terrible,' I said, checking the time on my watch. Eight thirty-six. 'I've got to go, Dad, but I'm sure it'll be better soon. It's a once-in-a-lifetime cruise — you've been looking forward to this forever.'

It wasn't true. Mum had been looking forward to it forever and Dad had been looking forward to Mum shutting up about how she'd been looking forward to going on a cruise forever. Poor old bastard.

'Are you sure you're all right?' Dad asked. 'You sound tired, love. Are you getting enough rest?'

'We both know there's no such thing,' I answered with a yawn to prove my point. 'Just busy with work and home and everything. I promise I'm fine and Alex'll be home soon so he can take over the household duties.'

'Angela, you know I love you, but let's not pretend you've become any more familiar with the Hoover just because Alex has been away. I bet there's dust an inch thick on every surface.'

'Never thought I'd say this but can you put Mum back on, please?' I said. 'Go and enjoy your breakfast prawns.'

'Annette,' he shouted without moving the phone away from his mouth, deafening me in the process. 'She wants to say goodbye.'

'Tell her I said bye and to get to work,' Mum barked back. 'I'm having a wee.'

'She says—'

'Yep, I heard,' I said, pressing my index finger into my ear to stop it ringing. 'Talk to you both later, love you.'

I hung up and dropped my phone into my bag just as the downtown F train began to rumble down the tracks and into the station. If I could make that train, I'd be at my desk before nine. Sprinting down the steps and along the corridor, I swiped my MetroCard and hurled myself through the open doors of the train just before they closed. Coughing, I straightened my jacket and lowered my head to avoid sharing my victorious grin with my fellow passengers, assorted commuters, students and, for some reason, a man dressed as a clown. Face paint, curly wig, giant shoes, the whole shebang. I tried not to stare. New Yorkers don't stare and they don't smile in public.

The last thing I wanted was for the clown to think I was a weirdo.

I knew my journey had been altogether too smooth when I arrived at Spencer Media and the lift doors opened for me as soon as I pressed the button. Inside, I was greeted by my new brand director, sharp as Cici's nails, in a three-piece suit with a coffee cup the size of his head.

'Hi, Joe.' I raised my own travel mug up in his general direction and hoped none of the buttons of my blouse had come open en route. 'Happy Wednesday.'

He squinted at me like I was making a joke he didn't understand.

Oh god, I thought, trying to look down without making it obvious. My buttons *had* come undone.

'It's Tuesday,' Joe replied slowly.

'Sorry?' I blinked, trying to shrug my jacket closed over my shirt, just in case.

'Today,' Joe said. 'It's Tuesday. Not Wednesday.'

'Is it?' I pursed my lips as I checked the little screen on the inside of the lift. Sixty-three degrees, no chance of rain and well, bugger me, it was in fact Tuesday. 'So it is.'

'Yes,' he confirmed. 'All day.'

'Right, right,' I said, searching for a way to save the conversation. 'Doing anything nice for Thanksgiving?'

'I'm leaving for my family's house in Vermont this evening.' He edged slowly away to the other side of the lift as it chimed softly to announce our arrival at the twelfth floor. 'We're going hunting.'

'Of course you are,' I replied with a forced smile, not at all hoping he would get run through by a moose. 'That sounds . . .'

I couldn't even fake my enthusiasm to finish the sentence. It sounded appalling.

'I'm looking forward to our meeting next week,' Joe said as I held the door open on my floor. 'I have a lot to discuss with you.'

What kind of sadist said something like that right before he left the state?

'Can't you just tell me what's happening now?' I

asked. 'You can't leave me in suspense over Thanksgiving, surely?'

'No,' he replied. 'Enjoy your long weekend, I'll see you next week.'

'Not if I see you first,' I said with a wink, immediately regretting it as I stepped out and the lift doors slowly closed on Joe's horrified face.

Most of the team was already busy at their desks as I made my way over to my glassed-in corner, shaking my head at my own ridiculousness. Five days out of every seven for the last four years I'd managed to maintain a general sense of professionalism, more or less. And in just one week and only two interactions, I was fairly certain I'd convinced my new boss that I had all the professionalism of a blind skunk.

'I got you a coffee and a bagel.' Cici snuck up behind me, making me jump as I opened the door to my office. 'I need to talk to you before the morning meeting.'

'It's Tuesday today,' I said.

'Yeah, it comes after Monday, right before Wednesday,' she replied, making herself comfortable. I noticed she was wearing her fake glasses again. 'It's about the Generation *Gloss* party.'

'Bring me that bagel and we'll talk,' I bargained, dumping my bag on the filing cabinet and taking off my jacket to reveal my perfect, professional outfit. Hadn't done me any bloody good so far. Stupid Tuesday. 'And can you tell everyone we're pushing the morning meeting back an hour?'

'What's going on?' Cici asked, a flicker of genuine concern on her face as she took in my shirt and skirt combo. 'Why are you wearing adult clothes? Did you have an interview this morning?'

I looked down at myself and smiled. That was almost a compliment.

'Don't worry about it,' I said, covering up another yawn. 'Sorry, I'm not sleeping that well at the moment; it's only because Alex is away.'

'Right, probably, gross, whatever,' she nodded, tapping away at her iPhone. 'So, about the party.'

'About the bagel,' I countered. 'I'm starving.'

I turned on my computer and an alert popped up to let me know Cici had already rescheduled the meeting. I automatically reached for a handful of gummies. If I had any teeth left by the time Alex got home, it would be a miracle.

'Here,' Cici tossed an unappetizing paper parcel on my desk before settling down in the chair across from me, a notepad and pen in her hand and a small plastic container in her lap.

'You're eating?' I said, shocked. I couldn't recall ever seeing Cici eat before. Drink, yes. Juice, possibly, but consuming actual solids? Unheard of.

'I started working out with a new trainer,' she said, wrinkling her nose at the container in front of her. 'He says I have to eat more.'

'Oh, what a nightmare,' I commiserated, opening up the squished bagel and taking an enormous bite before I'd even swallowed my gummy sweets. I was a monster. 'What's going on with the event?'

Cici opened up her notebook while I ate, one eye scanning my inbox as my emails loaded. Nothing from Alex, three from Jenny and only one spending alert from my credit card. I had to tell them to stop messaging me every time I used my card – it was almost putting me off shopping.

'The venue is all confirmed and I'll have the quote

from the security firm by the end of the day. We have three different Snapchat geofilters and a dedicated Instagram sticker, Selena confirmed, and Justin declined so that all works out. The only issue right now is the drinks sponsor.'

Cici peeled the top off her breakfast and pulled out a small, sad-looking flatbread, covered in some kind of brown paste.

'The vodka company pulled out but I have a friend who does PR for Kiki, it's a new organic tequila? And she says they'll cover us. Does that work? I think they're a good brand fit.'

The smell of her food hit me like a slap in the face. Without time to run, I doubled over and retched into the bin under my desk.

'Works for me,' I replied grimly. 'What else?'

'Oh my god!' Cici squealed, pushing her chair backwards and cowering in fear, even though she was clearly several feet away and on the other side of a bloody massive desk. 'Are you wasted?'

'Stone-cold sober.' I grabbed hold of a tissue and dabbed my mouth. 'What are you eating? It smells revolting.'

'I *was* eating leftover tapenade crostini from Fig & Olive,' she said, putting the lid back on the container and dumping it in the larger bin by my door. 'But now I've lost my appetite, thanks. My trainer is going to be so mad when I don't gain weight this week.'

'You can tell him I gained enough for both of us,' I assured her, taking a small sip from the bottle of water on my desk. 'That explains it, I can't stand olives these days.'

Cici closed her notebook. 'Smelling olives makes you throw up?'

I gestured towards the puke station that had previously been my bin.

'I've never liked them, but yeah, just the smell completely turns my stomach at the moment.'

She sat back down and stared at me.

'You're pregnant.'

The second virtual slap of the day. I looked up at Cici and the room rushed towards me. Overtired, overworked, yes. Up the duff? Absolutely not.

'Don't be ridiculous,' I said, almost ready to puke again at the very thought. 'So you want to use Kiki Tequila? That should be fine, it's not like we're wedded to vodka. I like a margarita as much as a martini and why are you still staring at me like that?'

'You're pregnant,' Cici repeated.

'I am not,' I told her, slowly lowering one hand to my stomach and trying to remember when I'd had my last period but I had no idea. Just like I had no idea what day it was.

Oh.

'Come with me,' Cici instructed, beckoning for me to stand up then taking hold of my wrist and dragging me out to her desk.

The entire office was empty. As soon as Cici had sent out the email delaying the morning meeting, they'd all scarpered to Starbucks before I could change my mind. Only Jason was still at his desk and he kept his eyes on his screen. He barely tolerated Cici's existence at the best of times and expended a considerable amount of energy that could have gone into his job, simply trying to pretend she did not exist.

'Which one do you want?' she asked, dropping onto her knees and opening a huge draw full of colourful boxes. 'I've got First Response, Clear Blue, Equate . . .

I'd say it's a little late for Plan B but just in case I'm wrong, I always have a stash if you need it.'

She looked up at me, sooty black lashes framing her eyes perfectly behind her glasses.

'But I'm not wrong because you're definitely pregnant.'

'Shut up,' I whispered, glancing over at Jason. There was no need to worry, he had his headphones on and was furiously typing something to someone, determined not to acknowledge me or my assistant. 'Why have you got all this? It's like a bloody branch of Boots in there.'

'I might not have been a Girl Scout, but I do believe in always being prepared,' she replied as she fished through the morning-after pills and jumbo packs of condoms and pulled out three different pregnancy tests. 'Let's go.'

The ladies' bathroom on the twelfth floor was always busy. We were right next to the canteen, and even if they weren't planning to eat (and most women at Spencer weren't), our toilets saw a lot of traffic from people pretending to get food when, really, they just wanted to take a break or, worryingly often, enjoy a small cry. Instead of using the regular loos, Cici led me to the individual bathroom around the corner, meant for families, people with wheelchairs, and women who needed to pee on a stick in peace.

'You know how to do this, right?' she asked, tearing open the boxes and handing me three different white plastic wands. I shook my head, even though I did. My thoughts and actions weren't quite matching up.

'It's easy,' Cici said, miming the whole procedure. 'You literally hold them under you while you go, that's it. You ready?'

I was not ready. To pee on the stick in front of Cici Spencer or see Cici Spencer pretend to pee on a stick.

'Angela?' She stooped to look me squarely in the eye. No one should ever employ an assistant who was almost a foot taller than them in heels. 'What's wrong?'

I didn't answer. What if she was right? What if I *was* pregnant? This wasn't how it was supposed to happen, chucking up at the first whiff of a briny snack and then pissing on a paddle with my nemesis in the office bogs. I should be in my own home, surrounded by candles and white flowers, with Alex right next to me and a gospel choir in the next room, ready to sing the bit from *The Lion King* when Simba is born.

'It's like ripping off a Band-Aid,' Cici assured me. 'Better to get it over with. Putting it off isn't going to change the result, trust me.'

She placed her hands on my shoulders and gave me a none-too-gentle shove in the direction of the toilet. There wasn't a door to close, just a screen that separated the loo from the sink, and even though I needed to do the test and really quite badly needed a wee, there was part of me that was still far too British to go to the toilet with another woman in the room. At least, not when I was stone-cold sober.

'I'll be right over here,' she said, from behind the screen. 'Just pop the cap and pee on that sucker.'

If I really tried, I could almost convince myself it was Delia.

'Do you want me to set a timer?' she asked.

'Yes please,' I squeaked. I was a woman of many talents but I wasn't about to pee on a stick with one hand and start a stopwatch on my phone with the other. Spilling booze on a phone was shameful enough, weeing on it was something altogether more shameful.

'Thank you.'

It turns out there is no elegant way to pull down your tights and wee on a variety of plastic sticks in the work toilet. Thankfully, I'd downed a heroic quantity of tea since waking up and I'd been practising my Kegels since year ten when Louisa brought in her first ever copy of *Cosmo*, so I was pretty OK with stop-start peeing. But my brain was still struggling with the situation. One minute I was running late for a meeting, the next I was waiting to find out whether or not there was a tiny human being inside me.

Clicking the cap back on the last test, I rested all three on the top of the square, metal toilet-roll holder and silently congratulated myself on not getting any wee on my hands. My mum would have been proud. My mum. Any second now, she might graduate to grandmother. And my dad would be a granddad.

'The first time I took a pregnancy test,' Cici announced on the other side of the stall, breaking my chain of thought, 'Dee Dee ran out to Duane Reade and made me do it in the ladies' lounge at Barneys. It was negative, thank god, but she made me promise, if it wasn't, I would call it Barney. Even if it was a girl.'

I glimpsed her beautiful black patent shoes underneath the partition and made myself laugh, even if it sounded hollow in my own ears.

'And I remember this one time, Dee Dee thought she might be pregnant but the tests kept coming back with no clear result so she made me take a cab out to New Jersey so she could get a blood test in the emergency room because she thought if she went to a hospital in New York, someone would recognize her and tell our mom.' She paused to let out a happy sigh. 'And that was the only time I ever went to New Jersey.'

'That's funny,' I said, even though it wasn't. She was a fool to herself; there was no sales tax on clothing in New Jersey.

'Angela, I think it's time to check the tests,' Cici said. 'Do you want me to look or do you want to do it?'

'I'll do it,' I said, my voice strange and soft and unfamiliar.

With a deep, determined breath, I picked up the first test. And then the second. And then the third.

'So?'

She looked at me impatiently as I rounded the partition, three white plastic sticks wrapped in toilet paper in my hand.

'It's probably against the odds that all three of them could be wrong, isn't it?' I asked, looking at myself in the mirror behind her. My face was pale, my eyes were wide, and my tights were still around my ankles.

'Oh,' Cici replied. 'Wow.'

'Yep,' I replied, laying all three tests out on the sink. Each and every one was positive. 'You were right – I'm pregnant.'

CHAPTER SIX

'See, the thing is, I can't be,' I said as Cici closed the door to my office. 'There's no actual way, so there must be something wrong with the test.'

'All three tests?' Cici asked.

I began to pull out the wadded tissue I'd shoved up my shirt. Three pregnancy tests up my sleeve and one baby in my uterus.

'All three,' I agreed. 'I can't be pregnant.'

'Why not?'

I thought about it for a moment.

'Because?'

It wasn't a great argument but it was all I had. I was pregnant. Up the duff. With child. Knocked up. Expecting. In the family way. Preggers.

'If you're looking for a silver lining, at least no one will be able to tell for a while,' Cici said, rubbing her hand theatrically over her stomach. I looked up and then looked down at my belly. 'Because, if it was me, everyone would be able to see it right away but with you, it's not like you're—' She sucked in her cheeks and clapped her arms tightly to her side. 'You know?'

'Thanks,' I replied. 'That really makes me feel better.'

'You can't pretend this isn't happening,' she declared. 'I'll tell everyone you had an emergency and you should go home.'

'No need, I'm right as a bobbin,' I insisted as the room span around me. 'Fit as a fiddle.'

I was determined to remain calm. I flicked my mouse until my computer sprang into life and hoped for something that might prove I hadn't woken up in a parallel dimension.

'I don't know what a bobbin is,' Cici replied. 'But I do know a girl in high school who pretended she wasn't pregnant when she knew she was and she ended up having the baby in the middle of gym class.'

'No, you don't.'

I rolled my eyes at the thought of Blair Waldorf popping out a baby on the floor of the sports centre at Cici's *Gossip Girl*-alike Upper East Side prep, but Cici stood firm. Making sure the door was securely closed, she trotted over to my desk in her skyscraper heels.

'You should see a doctor,' she ordered. 'You eat too much sugar and you drink too much tea. Pregnant women aren't supposed to buy English candy in bulk and then binge-eat it when they think no one is watching. I'm going to call your OB and make an appointment.'

I pressed my hand against my stomach, feeling around for some sort of proof that there was anything to go away in the first place. How could I be pregnant? I didn't feel pregnant. Slightly nauseous, slightly tired, slightly gassy, but that wasn't too far removed from your average Tuesday morning for me. Especially when I'd fallen asleep with my hand in a bag of Cheetos.

'So, you're freaking me out.' Cici took off her ridiculous black spectacles and pushed them onto the top of her head. 'It would be awesome if you could start talking any time soon.'

'I'm pregnant,' I whispered.

'OK, that's it, I really think you should go home.' She stood glaring down at me with her hands planted on her hips. 'Do you want me to call Alex? Or that hateful friend of yours with all the hair? I'm sure she'll be desperate to know. Or I could call your mom. Wait, do you have a mom?'

That got my attention.

'If you call my mother, I'll have to kill you,' I said, refusing to even entertain that conversation. 'I'm really fine; all I want is to get on with the day. What time is it?'

She looked down at her watch.

'Almost nine thirty.'

'Let's get on with the morning meeting then,' I replied, scraping my damp hair away from my forehead. Was it hot in here or was it just me? Well, me and the baby. Oh god, the baby. It would never be just me, ever, ever again. 'Oh, and can you get me a coffee?'

I was fairly certain she wouldn't bring me a tequila shot, even though that was very much what I wanted.

'You can't have coffee. Caffeine is bad for the baby.'

Definite no on the tequila then.

'You should go home,' Cici insisted, more gently this time. Almost as though she was genuinely concerned. First with the eating, and now with the empathy. Who was this woman and what had she done with the real Cici? 'You puked in your trash can, you look like a hot mess, and literally no one wants you here right now. You're of zero use to anyone in this building.'

I wondered whether Cici and Joe had gone to the same charm school.

'Maybe I should go home,' I muttered, more to myself than to my assistant. The idea of sitting in my office for the next eight hours and acting as though everything was normal seemed impossible. 'I can call Alex, have a lie-down, come back tomorrow, all refreshed.'

'Still pregnant, though,' Cici pointed out.

'One would assume,' I replied, pulling my bag out from underneath my desk. 'Can you send a team email to let everyone know I've gone home sick? You can say it's food poisoning.'

She shook her head immediately.

'Food poisoning means pregnant,' she explained. 'Or hungover. Which they would probably buy. I'll say personal issue then everyone will think someone died or Alex left you. That way they won't ask questions.'

'Thanks,' I said slowly. 'Good to know. Thank you.'

She skittered backwards as I went give her a hug on my way out, wrapping her arms around herself.

'Don't.' She shook her head. 'People will know something's wrong.'

'Right, gotcha.' I nodded, a little sad at the idea of someone being so unhuggable it would raise an alarm. 'Seriously, though, thank you for the tests. And the bagel before the tests. And, you know, everything.'

She rubbed her hand up and down her tiny upper arm and cast her eyes across the room. Genuine moments between the two of us had been few and far between over the years and, clearly, she was not comfortable. Thinking about it, genuine moments between Cici and *anyone* seemed a bit thin on the ground. Other than her sister and a small assortment of Upper East Side clichés she was photographed with on Page Six, it didn't seem as though she spent that much time with that many people.

'I'll see you in the morning,' I said, grabbing my Marc Jacobs parka from the coat rack and juggling my satchel between my hands as I slipped my arms inside. 'Call me if anyone needs anything.'

'Don't worry, I doubt anyone will,' she replied. 'And I'll get someone to replace your disgusting trash can before the entire office voms.'

Nice moment, officially over.

It took exactly thirty-seven minutes to get from the office to the 7th Avenue F train station in Park Slope. As soon as I set foot on the platform, I began to sprint towards daylight, up the steps and out into the bright, winter sunshine, phone in hand. There had to be a chance Alex would answer, just a tiny, slim sliver of a chance. I imagined him zonked out on the perfect beach, lying on glorious white sand in front of azure blue seas, while I all but ran through the streets of Brooklyn, fighting with my front door while praying for his phone to get a signal.

'Please be there,' I repeated over and over, clamping the phone between my shoulder and my clammy cheek. 'Please, please be there.'

The first three times, the call went directly to voicemail, Alex's sleepy tones telling me not to leave a message because he never listened to them anyway. On the fourth try, the call connected.

'Come on!' I threw my bag down on the settee and punched the air. 'Now bloody well answer the phone, Reid.'

'Hello?' A scratchy voice clicked across thousands of miles. 'Angela?'

'Alex!' I had never been so happy to hear someone say my name in my entire life. 'Are you there?'

'We – we're driving,' he stuttered. 'Is something wrong?'

'No,' I replied, welling up. 'Nothing's wrong. I'm – wow, I don't know how to say it.'

'You're breaking up,' Alex said. 'I got the nothing's wrong part. You're OK?'

'I need to talk to you,' I said urgently. I walked up and down the room, trying to find a better signal but I was fairly certain the problem wasn't at my end. 'Can you hear me now?'

'Babe, are you there?' he asked. 'I can't hear you at all. I'm going to hang up.'

'No!' I wailed, hurriedly pressing the speakerphone button. 'Don't hang up, I need to talk to you.'

'Let me call you back,' he sighed. 'I'm not getting anything on my end at all.'

I jumped onto the sofa, balancing on the back, one hand gripping the wall, and holding my phone as high into the air as possible in the other.

'Are you still there?' The static on the line echoed through the empty house. 'I can hear you, can you hear me at all?'

'I'm hanging up now,' Alex said. 'If you can hear me, I'll call you right back but we're almost at the coast. If the call doesn't go through, I'll try again as soon as I can. I love you.'

'I'm pregnant!' I shouted. 'I'm pregnant, Alex. We're having a baby.'

My phone beeped three times and then his name disappeared from the screen.

'I'm pregnant,' I said to myself, climbing down and collapsing softly onto the sofa. 'We're going to have a baby.'

Silence. There wasn't a single sound in the entire apartment but for the first time I realized I wasn't alone. Eeep.

'You're not calling back, are you, you arsehole?' I said softly. 'What a bloody brilliant time for you to go off the grid.'

Resting my hands on my stomach, I stared at my not-quite-flat stomach. I was having a baby. I was having *our* baby. I was going to be a mum and Alex was going to be a dad. A huge, face-achingly wide smile found its way onto my face.

Bloody hell.

CHAPTER SEVEN

After a fitful afternoon spent napping, considering calling my mum then thinking better of it, worrying about what might be happening at the office in my absence, standing side on at the mirror in the bedroom to see if there was any evidence of a bump, and reading every available article on the internet, I was relieved when Jenny called to see what I was doing. There was only so long you could sit around being excited on your own and I'd given up on getting through to Alex after about four hours. He wouldn't mind my telling Jenny, I rationalized. I couldn't keep something this huge all to myself until he decided to return to civilization, I had to tell one other human or I'd go completely insane and, clearly, Cici Spencer didn't count as a human.

'I'm so glad you didn't have plans tonight,' Jenny said, greeting me on the corner of 8th Avenue and 14th Street. She waved the back of her left hand directly in my face with an enormous grin on her face. 'Mason had to go out of town for a work thing and I was like, um, I just got engaged, I can't sit in my apartment staring at the walls, can I?'

'Not really,' I said, bracing myself to deliver the news. 'Jenny, I—'

'I texted Erin last night and she was like, when can I see the ring? And I was like, how about tomorrow? And she was like, let's order in, open a bottle of champs, start wedding planning?' She was talking at a mile a minute, her hands flying around in front of her. 'I picked up some magazines from Barnes & Noble at lunch. Do you have any idea how much wedding magazines cost? Actually, yeah, I guess you do.'

'I got some news today,' I started again. 'I really want to talk to you about it.'

'About the job?' Jenny asked, not waiting for a reply. 'Cool. We were up all night talking about the wedding. And boning, obviously, but we already agreed on a bunch of stuff.'

'Such as?' My news could wait.

'We're thinking destination,' she said, the smile never leaving her face. 'We both love Maui, so that's the most likely option. We want to keep it small, just us, immediate family, close friends. I want it to be so special.'

'Sounds perfect,' I replied. 'Any idea when it'll be?'

Don't say next summer, I added silently. Don't say next summer.

'Probably next summer,' she replied.

Bollocks.

'It'll depend on the place, I guess.' Jenny pushed her masses of curls behind her ears where they stayed for a second before immediately springing back around her face. 'Mason is going to look at some resorts. He wants to pick the place.'

I couldn't quite believe my ears. I'd assumed total wedding-related breakdown was imminent, but here she was, rationally including her fiancé in the plans for her small, special wedding. I was naturally very concerned.

'Hey, before we get to Erin's place I wanted to ask you something,' she said. 'While it's just me and you.'

With a concerned smile, I bundled up my announcement and nodded.

'Angela Clark.' She stopped in the street and took hold of both of my hands. 'Will you be my maid of honour?'

'Yes!' I shouted as loud as my English-girl-in-public lungs would allow. 'Yes, I will! Wait, do I have to buy my own dress?'

'Traditionally, in America, yes,' Jenny began jumping up and down on the corner of 8th Avenue and Horatio, 'but we both know I'm way too much of a control freak to let that happen.'

Starting as she meant to go on.

'This is so amazing, thank you,' I said, tears prickled at the corners of my eyes, and they had nothing to do with the bitter wind that whipped around the Manhattan high-rises. 'You're not going to make me wear anything stupid, are you?'

'I'm going to buy two dresses,' she replied, dragging me into a tight, warm hug. 'A really cute one and a really heinous one. Which one you get depends on how good of a maid of honour you are between now and then.'

I thought back to Jenny's behaviour before *my* wedding. By her reckoning, I should have made her walk down the aisle in a bin bag.

'I'll do my best,' I said, throwing up my best three-fingered salute. 'Brownie Guide promise.'

'I'm going to ask Erin to be a bridesmaid, but I

wanted to ask you first,' she said as we looked left and then sprinted across the street. Who had time to walk to a crossing when it was freezing out? No New Yorkers I knew. 'That way I could always draft her in if you said no.'

'Why would I say no?' I asked, puzzled.

'Because it's me,' she replied, smiling sweetly. 'Planning my wedding. In New York.'

The reality of what I'd just agreed to hit me like a ton of pastel-pink sugared almonds. In the next nine months, I was having a baby and a bridezilla and all bets were off when it came to which one would be the most stressful. I'd spent all afternoon looking at photos of episiotomies, and in that moment I wasn't entirely certain I wouldn't choose one of those over an afternoon of wedding dress shopping with the world's most demanding woman.

What did an enormously pregnant woman wear to a wedding? Did they make maternity bridesmaids' dresses? Maybe one with those little flaps that let you pop your boobs out for a feed. If they didn't make them, they were missing a trick. I wondered if Jenny would be mad if I gave birth the week before the wedding. Or the week of the wedding. Or, please god no, at the wedding. I refused to let my baby come into the world surrounded by doves: everyone knows they're nothing but albino pigeons with good PR.

'Now,' Jenny said. 'What did you want to tell me?'

I looked at her shining face and sparkling ring and shook my head. I couldn't do it. I was going to be pregnant for nine months, Jenny could only be newly engaged for a matter of days. Even though I wanted to tell her more than anything, my news could wait at least twenty-four more hours.

'Um, there's a new Beyoncé song coming out,' I replied, crossing my fingers inside the pocket of my parka. 'Yeah, it's supposed to be amazing.'

'All hail Queen Bey,' Jenny said, touching her fingertips to her lips and then blowing a kiss to New York City. 'Maybe she heard about my engagement and wanted to celebrate.'

'Maybe she did,' I agreed, snuggling into my insufficiently padded jacket. If I died of pneumonia before she made it down the aisle, I wouldn't be maid of anything. 'Maybe you could have her play at the wedding?'

Her eyes lit up with worrying inspiration and I sent Mason a silent prayer as we made our way through the winding streets of Manhattan's West Village.

'That's weird.'

I pulled out my phone to check the time as we arrived at Erin's. She hated early guests, it was a pet peeve she claimed stemmed from all her years working in PR where no one likes Johnny Right On Time. Personally, I deeply appreciated the first person to arrive at the party – it meant I wasn't going to be sat there on my tod, re-enacting my surprise nineteenth birthday party when Louisa told everyone the wrong time and the surprise was that no one showed up.

'What's weird?' Jenny asked, fluffing out her curls on Erin's doorstep.

'I've got fourteen missed calls from Erin but no voicemails.' I looked up in panic. 'Is this an *SVU* thing? What if she's being burgled right now and she's trying to tell us?'

'Or what if she's butt-dialling you?' Jenny suggested,

dampening my enthusiasm for home invasion with wide, warning eyes. 'Or her kid has her phone?'

'Also possible,' I conceded. 'But still, why isn't she answering the door?'

'Because you haven't knocked?' She reached across me and belted the big, brass door-knocker against the stately wooden door. 'Seriously, Angie baby, I worry about you. Please stop watching so much *Law & Order*.'

'Yeah, whatever,' I muttered.

It was a promise I could not keep.

'Before you come in, you have to swear you're going to be calm.' Erin opened the door with a truly fearful look on her face. 'Swear it.'

'Is someone there?' I hissed, grabbing Jenny's arm. 'Blink if you want me to call the police.'

'Someone is here,' she replied, stepping to the side and letting us into the house. With great reservations, I followed Jenny inside. 'But I think we'll need an ambulance before the police get involved.'

'Congratulations, Jenny,' my friend muttered as she tossed her jacket on the foot of the stairs. 'That's a beautiful ring, Jenny. You're going to make a beautiful bride, Jenny.'

Sadie Nixon, Jenny's roommate, sort-of-supermodel and definite pain in the arse, stood in the middle of Erin's sitting room, holding an enormous bottle of Perrier-Jouët champagne in one hand and a samurai sword in the other.

'Oh god,' I whispered, trying to pull Jenny and Erin back into the hallway. 'She's finally lost the plot. She's going to kill us all!'

'Guess what?' Sadie screeched at the top of her high-pitched voice. She didn't wait for us to guess. 'I'm getting married!'

She sliced the top off the bottle of champagne, sending a shower of golden liquid shooting through the air to drench Jenny from head to toe.

Exactly seventeen minutes passed between La Lopez excusing herself to use Erin's guest bathroom and the sound of her high heels clicking down the staircase. I sat on the sofa, tuning in and out of Sadie's story and mentally listing all the potential murder weapons in Erin's apartment. Depending on how creative Jenny was feeling, this place could practically be the set of a *Saw* movie.

'Jennifer!' Sadie jumped up from her spot on the couch and hurled herself at her roommate. 'You were gone so long I thought you'd fallen in.'

Were Jenny not my best friend, I would have taken a photo. Her hair was tied up in a bun, soaking from her impromptu shampoo and her face was very much lacking the smile I'd seen when I met her earlier in the evening.

'Look at my ring!' Sadie thrust her left hand under Jenny's nose, waiting for a reaction. 'Look at it!'

'Can I see?' I asked, throwing Jenny a life raft. Sadie immediately dropped Jenny like a hot rock and bolted across the room, skidding across the polished floor in a perfect baseball slide to show off her canary yellow diamond.

'Look,' she said, waving it right under my nose. 'Isn't is gorgeous?'

She really didn't need to bring it that close. I could have seen this ring from my apartment back in Brooklyn; it was so big it was obscene.

'Now, forgive me for being dense,' I nodded to confirm its utter humungousness, 'but I didn't actually know you were seeing anyone.'

Try as I might, I couldn't seem to recall the last time I'd seen Sadie in person. Sure, I had to walk past her impossibly peachy bum every morning on my way to work (it was displayed on billboards all over the city and a fine backside it was too) but it was months since I'd actually been in the same room as her. And from the look on Jenny's face, it was just as long since she'd had any real one-on-one time with her glamorous roommate.

Jenny sat silently on the edge of an armchair across the room, her left hand jammed right up into her right armpit. Erin hovered anxiously, a fresh bottle of champagne in one hand and a massive roll of kitchen towel in the other. It had taken the two of us almost the same amount of time Jenny was upstairs to soak the spilled champs out of her carpet.

'OK, so, it has been kind of a whirlwind.' Sadie flushed. Her usually blonde hair was dyed a light, golden red and she was wearing a deep scarlet lipstick that set it off perfectly. 'I'm sure Jenny told you, I've been in Georgia, filming a TV show.'

Jenny had not told me.

'Being real for a moment, I'm getting older and modelling is a young girl's game,' she sighed. I tried to remember exactly how old she was, but Jenny assured me Sadie personally updated her Wikipedia page every year to make sure she would never officially be a day over twenty-five. 'And I wanted a more long-term plan, something realistic to fall back on. My mom was always worried when I was younger because modelling is so fleeting and she always wanted me to go back to school, so I sat myself down and I thought, what's a really solid, reliable career for me?'

'And you chose acting?' I asked. Across the room, with her eyes closed, Jenny nodded.

'Yeah!' Sadie laughed. She crossed her insanely long legs and sighed. 'It wasn't easy right away, it took me two whole weeks to find a job.'

'Wow,' I replied with one eye on my best friend. It was like watching the dial on a nuclear reactor in a James Bond movie. Any second now, she could blow. 'You were so dedicated.'

'It's just a CW show,' she said, pulling on the ends of her strawberry blonde hair. 'And they made me colour my hair which sucked because it's so hard to get blonde right, I mean, look at yours, you know?'

I ran my tongue over my teeth and looked away.

'But it was worth it. On the first day, I met Teddy.' She pressed her hands against her heart and swooned backwards onto the wet-through carpet. 'And now we're engaged!'

'And who's Teddy?' I asked politely.

'Teddy Myers?' she replied, shooting upright and looking at me as though I was demented. 'He's the lead in *Were*? My show?'

I looked back at her blankly.

'I can't believe you don't know him,' she tutted, pulling a brand-new, bedazzled iPhone out of the pocket of her skintight jeans. 'I thought you watched all the TV.'

'So did I,' I muttered before a photo of a tall, tanned, generically handsome man in next to no clothes was pushed into my face. 'Oh, *that* Teddy!'

'I knew you'd know him,' she purred, gazing longingly at the screen.

Who? Erin mouthed across the room.

I replied with a tiny shrug. I had no idea who this man was. In the past, Sadie had only ever dated athletes. She had three requirements for men who wanted to get into her Victoria's Secret Fantasy Bra: they had to be taller than she was, make more money than she did, and they had to make that money playing with balls bigger than the ones in their pants. She'd gone out with baseball players, football players, and basketball players. No snooker players that I knew of, but then I'd only been friends with her for a few years. To the best of my knowledge, this was her first actor. And her first engagement ring.

'We were filming last weekend and we were staying in his cabin outside of Atlanta . . . ' She looked over at Jenny and smiled beatifically. 'He has a cabin.'

'Sweet,' Jenny replied.

'And he gets down on one knee and pulls out this ridiculous ring and I know it's super soon, but what was I supposed to say?' She flashed her hand in my face again. 'Look at the damn thing!'

'I think Jenny has some news as well,' Erin said, putting down the kitchen towel but keeping the champagne, for toasting purposes or to use as a weapon, I wasn't sure. 'Jenny?'

Sadie looked across the room with bright eyes and a damp butt.

'Mason and I got engaged,' she said sulkily.

'What?' Sadie shrieked, running across the room on her knees. It was quite an impressive feat – she really was much more limber than I expected her to be. 'Jenny, this is so beyond!'

She wrenched Jenny's hand out from under her arm and immediately began oohing and ahhing at the ring.

'Let me get a selfie,' she insisted, her ever-present phone already in her hand. 'Bridal besties!'

'No, it's OK,' Jenny protested, pulling away.

Sadie considered Jenny's visage for a moment, then nodded in agreement.

'Yeah, maybe just our rings,' she agreed, waving her hand in front of her face. 'This isn't a good look for you.'

Jenny patiently held out her left hand, her gorgeous ring twinkling under the flash of Sadie's phone before disappearing next to Sadie's canary yellow monstrosity.

'This is going to be so amazingly, perfectly, incredible,' Sadie said as Erin handed out glasses of champagne. 'I'm so happy.'

I took my glass and suddenly panicked. What was I supposed to do? I couldn't drink this? And dear god, did I want to. While the others were preoccupied, I quickly dumped three-quarters of the glass into a potted plant at my side.

'We can plan our weddings together! Although, I was going to call you and let you know, I'm officially moving out. Teddy has a loft in Bushwick and I'm moving in with him. Actually, I've moved; I took all my stuff over this afternoon.'

'You've moved out?' Jenny asked, looking slightly shocked. Even though Sadie travelled constantly and routinely made noises about moving in with her boyfriends, she never actually took her stuff and left. 'Seriously?'

'Yes, seriously.' Sadie waggled her ring at her former roommate. 'I'm *engaged* now, Jenny. I live with my *fiancé*.'

Jenny breathed out slowly.

'You're not moving in with Mason?' Sadie asked, chugging her champagne as though it was pop.

'Eventually,' Jenny replied, flicking non-existent dust off her shoulder defensively. 'I'm practically moved in already, I'm there all the time.'

'Yeah, I guess. Wow, can you believe this is happening for us at the same time?' She sighed happily before nodding over at me. 'You know what this means, Ange? You're going to have to have a baby just to keep up!'

'Ha!' I barked wildly, really leaning into the laugh and waving my almost empty champagne glass around for all to see. 'A baby! Can you imagine?'

Sadie turned up her tiny nose.

'Nah, not really,' Sadie replied before turning her attention back to Jenny. 'Oh, Jenny! What if we had a double wedding?'

Jenny spluttered into her champagne flute in reply and chugged the rest of the glass.

'I can't imagine anything more exciting than sharing my big day with one of my best friends,' Sadie declared, holding her glass out for a top-up while Jenny's face went from grey to green to white. 'Or maybe that would be too weird. You're probably not planning anything as big as us. Teddy has pretty much invited all of Hollywood, our budget is a little out of control. That's probably not what you're going for, right?'

Jenny responded with silence, an angry vein throbbing in her temple.

'Whatever,' Sadie sighed happily. 'I just know we're going to have the weddings of the century.'

And just like that, a monster was born.

It was late by the time I arrived home. Once Sadie started talking, it was almost impossible to get her to stop. We went over everything, from wedding dress designers to Teddy's leaked sex tapes. It was a little disconcerting, meeting my friend's intended via videos of him getting a hand shandy from one of his former co-stars but Sadie didn't seem to mind. Par for the course in showbiz these days, Erin assured me. You were no one until your sex life had been splashed all over the internet. All the while, Jenny had remained suspiciously silent. Her bridal magazines stayed in her handbag and her dreams of getting married in Maui remained between us. Before I left, I suggested meeting after work the following night for a bridesmaid bonanza do-over, sans Sadie, and she hadn't taken much convincing. She hadn't mentioned actual murder but I still had a horrible feeling I had somehow volunteered to be her accomplice.

Too exhausted to walk all the way to the subway station, I hopped in a cab right outside Erin's townhouse, surreptitiously taking a photo of the driving licence details and sending it to myself, just in case. Jenny was right, I had to stop watching so much *SVU* when Alex was out of town.

Kicking off my heels the second I walked through the door, I knew immediately that someone had been in the house. I grabbed one of the shoes from the floor, brandishing it above my head as I proceeded slowly into the living room, quickly flipping on every light switch in the apartment as I went. By the time I reached the kitchen, my heart was thumping so loudly I was worried it might deafen the baby. Turning on the overhead kitchen light, I realized the washing machine was gone. The rubble, the hole and messed-up floor remained but the Hotpoint missile and Vi's Lululemon leggings had disappeared. On the kitchen top there was a piece of lilac notepaper, neatly folded in half and weighed down with a cellophane-wrapped cookie.

I opened the cookie and took a bite, belatedly hoping it wasn't poisoned.

Dear Angela, we managed to get our builder in early – YAS! He's coming back tomorrow am to start on the ceiling, we still have the spare key to your place in case he needs access while you're at work so don't worry! xoxo L & V

Looking around the one washing machine kitchen as I swallowed, the room seemed so oddly empty.

PS Enjoy the cookie, it's vegan, gluten and sugar free.

I took another nibble. They had to be lying – it was delicious.

Obviously, the builder had already been in the apartment. Had they given him the keys or had they let him in? It was pitch-black and completely silent inside the Hello Hole so my neighbours were either out or in bed.

'You're being paranoid,' I said, my voice breaking the stillness of the apartment. 'So what if the builder has keys? Jenny has keys, that's far more dangerous.'

The water in our tap always took too long to run cold. I turned on the faucet and grabbed a glass from the sink, rinsing off a new layer of dust and debris, presumably a super-fun result of the washing machine removal. Gulping down the first glass, I poured another and walked back into the living room, tossing my handbag onto the settee. Turning on the television was an automatic reaction, but as I flipped through my tenth channel, I realized nothing was going to take my mind off the matters of the day.

My skirt felt tight, although that probably had more to do with the food in my belly than anything else, and I rolled onto my side to unzip and wriggle free of it without standing. It was a skill I was altogether too proud of.

'You're so lucky to have me as your mum,' I said, patting my stomach and staring at the waistband of my black tights. It was still genuinely incomprehensible that there could be a living thing in there but that was the same thing I said when Alex told me a mouse had been living in the bathroom drawer for at least a month and I hadn't noticed and it had turned out he was right about that. There was a baby, in my belly, right that second. I just couldn't process it. Too big, too impossible.

Speaking of Alex, he still hadn't called back. This was what happened when you tried to be a cool wife who sent her husband off travelling without you: you ended up alone and pregnant, a million miles from your partner while a nameless, faceless builder ran around the city just waiting for you to fall asleep so he could break in, tie you up and re-enact the scariest bits from *Silence of the Lambs*.

'It puts the lotion on its skin,' I lisped to myself as I stared up at the patterns on our ceiling. A lot of New York apartments had old tin ceilings with patterns pressed in. It had been painted over so many times, the geometric designs had been almost entirely smoothed away. I always wondered about the other people who had stared up at the ceiling, what their stories might be, where they were now . . . whether or not they were waiting for a murderous contractor to sneak in.

'Do you want to watch *Moana*?' I asked my stomach, turning on the DVD player. 'It's really good, totally appropriate for someone your age.'

118

The bump did not respond but I decided to take its silence as tacit approval.

'I wish I could talk to your dad,' I told it as the DVD whirred into life. 'He doesn't actually know he's your dad yet, but he is, and he's great, you're going to love him.'

I bit into the witchcraft cookie and chewed thoughtfully. It was nice to have someone to talk to, even if no one else knew it was a someone just yet. Only me. This was all mine.

'He's very clever, your dad, so that's handy,' I said. 'And he's very practical. He always knows what to do when something breaks or stops working. I just order another one from Amazon, but nine times out of ten, he can fix it. And he went to school here, which means he'll be able to help you with your homework because I'm useless at maths and I don't know anything about American history. I am good at other things, though.'

But what? Bagging a bargain at Bloomingdale's wasn't going to help a baby for at least fourteen years, and that was only if it turned out to be gay or a girl. I'd heard there were straight men who liked shopping, but I'd never met one in the wild.

'I'm good at reading maps and I know the names of loads of YouTubers.'

There, that was something Alex didn't know and it was true – I didn't want to start our relationship off with a bunch of lies. Mostly because I wasn't absolutely certain the baby couldn't read my mind. I knew it didn't strictly have a mind of its own yet and was more of a teeny tiny frogspawn than a person but still, it was in there, we were connected. I wasn't going to go around telling my unborn frogspawn that I was a super genius only for it to pop out and discover I couldn't even beat my dad on *Candy Crush*.

'They probably won't have *Candy Crush* by the time you're old enough to play it.' I patted my stomach, not sure who I was trying to reassure. Me or my baby.

Oh.

My baby.

A loud noise outside the front window crashed through my sentimental moment. Leaping off the sofa, my skirt fell to the floor, pooling around my feet and for the want of a better weapon, I grabbed a Jimmy Choo. High heels had served me well in the past and I wasn't above using one to batter a burglar now. I peeked out the window to find a big ginger cat rootling around in a pizza box. He looked up and me and miaowed loudly.

'Apologies,' I said, waving a conciliatory shoe in his direction. Closing the blinds, I returned to my spot on the sofa, keeping the stiletto close by.

'Your dad might call,' I told my nano-bump. 'We should stay up in case he does, just for a bit. And to make sure whatever random builder has my spare key isn't a serial killer.'

It didn't reply but it didn't complain either.

'We're going to get on just fine,' I said. Patting my stomach, I pulled a blanket up over my chin and settled in for my first night alone with my baby, one hand on my stomach, the other on my shoe.

You really couldn't be too careful these days.

CHAPTER EIGHT

When people call New York 'the city that never sleeps', they're usually talking about the shenanigans people get up to after one too many cocktails, the karaoke bars that never close, or the dawn walks across the Brooklyn Bridge, Alex singing in my ear while I carried my high heels in my hand. How things had changed. I might have had my high heels in my hand all last night, but instead of pulling a walk of shame the morning after the night before, I was as clean and fresh as a daisy as I passed by all the dirty stop-outs on the subway as I headed into Manhattan at 7 a.m., on my way to a doctor's appointment.

'The good news is, everything looks great,' Dr Laura, friend of Jenny's and superstar OB-GYN, announced from somewhere between my ankles. 'You're between eight to ten weeks along. Closer to ten, I would say. Do you recall the date of the first day of your last period?'

'I'm not even certain what day today is,' I replied, dazed. 'Ten weeks?'

How could there have been a little person living inside me without my knowing for ten weeks? I thought I had nine months to prepare, all the websites I'd read had said forty weeks but I'd just had ten weeks pulled out from under me. I was already a quarter of the way along. Then again, I'd found a packet of Polos in my coat pocket three weeks earlier that had expired in 2009 so maybe this shouldn't feel like such a shock.

'Honestly, I'm not sure,' I admitted. 'I don't really keep track and things have been so busy since Alex has been out of town. I hadn't realized how late I was until, well, I realized how late I was.'

'Don't worry too much about it,' she said, flipping on a screen suspended from the ceiling to show a black and greenish-grey image I'd seen on what felt like a thousand Facebook walls.

Ladies and gentlemen, welcome to your uterus.

'This,' she pressed a cold plastic wand to my stomach with one hand and pointed to the screen with the other, 'is your baby. Congratulations, Angela Clark, you're going to be a mommy.'

'Oh fuck,' I whispered as I stared at the screen.

'Oh . . . ' Dr Laura turned the same shade of pink as the soft cotton smock I was currently sporting. 'I'm so sorry, is this a sensitive issue? Do you want to talk about it?'

'No, it's not that,' I replied, realization hitting me like a ton of bricks. 'You said Mommy, not Mummy. I'm going to have an American baby.'

Dr Laura laughed, slightly more relieved than amused, as she froze the picture on the screen. I, on the other hand, wasn't quite sure what she was laughing about. It was a legitimate concern. I couldn't be a mom! I didn't have the training. Moms wore straight-leg mid-rise jeans, they had neat, side-parted bobs and drove SUVs to soccer practice. I wanted to keep my jeans skinny and my hair long and sleep in while Alex took the kid to watch football down the pub. Could you even take kids to the pub in America? These were questions I hadn't even thought to ask.

'I know it's sometimes tricky for people this early into the pregnancy but,' she pointed at a grey blob that appeared to be pulsating in the bottom corner of the screen, 'can you see your baby?'

'That's it?' I gazed up at the screen, not entirely sure what I was expecting, but it didn't look like anything. Then again, the thing was still tiny and still in my belly; it wasn't going to be holding a giant lollipop and waving at me from inside its cot, was it?

'That's it,' she confirmed. 'There will be much more to see at your next appointment.'

That was it. That thing, bopping around in the corner of my uterus. That was my baby.

'Is that to size?' I squinted at the screen. It felt like something impossible, like winning the lottery, finding a pair of Louboutins on sale in my size or Michael Fassbender moving in next door.

'No,' Dr Laura made the image even bigger. 'The baby is around the size of a pea right now.'

A pea. All this for something the size of a pea.

'And when can you tell me what it is?' I asked, crooking my neck to try and get a better look. It looked relatively chilled out, which was good news, because it meant it was already taking after its father.

As she moved the wand off my stomach, the live streaming special, *Inside Angela Clark*, froze, and my baby became a static image. Immediately, I wanted her to restart the scan but instead, she began cleaning the gel from my belly. 'You mean the gender?' she asked.

'Well, I'm assuming it's human,' I replied. 'So, unless there's something important you want to tell me now . . . ?'

'Twenty weeks. Unless you want it to be a surprise.'

I shook my head. Absolutely not. No more surprises for Angela, not even of the Kinder variety.

'Surprised enough, to be honest,' I said. 'Book me in for that scan.'

'The only thing I'd like you to be careful with is your blood pressure.' Dr Laura turned to a small printer at her side, pressing buttons until it whirred into life. 'It's way too high. You need to avoid all unnecessary anxiety otherwise you're going to end up on bed rest and I know that sounds great but it really, really isn't. Is there anything going on right now that could be causing undue stress?'

Oh, I don't know, I thought to myself. Husband AWOL in South East Asia? Best friend's wedding? New boss? The prospect of my staff losing their jobs? The prospect of *me* losing *my* job? Potential murderous builder running around Brooklyn giving copies of my keys to every criminal in the five boroughs? *Completely unexpected and unplanned pregnancy*?

'Not that I can think of,' I replied calmly.

'Good,' she said. 'Keep it that way.'

She handed me a small, black-and-white image of the inside of my womb. It was weird, I avoided looking at photos of the outside of my stomach at all costs, but I couldn't stop staring at this one.

'That's it?' I asked, pulling my legs out of the stirrups. They seemed oddly comfortable. 'I'm done?'

'We have a lot of literature for you to take away and read,' Dr Laura said, nodding. 'And I'm going to prescribe some vitamins, but other than that, yes. Felicia at the front desk will schedule your follow-up visits.'

'But there's a baby in me?' I'd always been exceptionally talented at stating the obvious. 'You're going to send me back out into the streets with a photo and some vitamins? I've never had a baby in me before, I don't know what to do.'

'Angela, women have had babies in them for literally hundreds of thousands of years,' she said, resting a gentle hand on my shoulder. 'And everything will be great as long as you keep that blood pressure down. But there are some antenatal classes in your area I can recommend if that would make you feel better?'

'I don't know,' I replied, suddenly doubtful. 'Will it?'

Classes made me anxious. What if I wasn't as good as the other mums? What if they'd been preparing for months, drinking juice and doing yoga rather than drinking gin and doing sod all?

'The classes can be really helpful,' Dr Laura smiled. 'I'll have Felicia send you the details.'

'Any chance Felicia could have the baby for me as well?' I suggested. She raised her eyebrows and sighed and I realized I'd outstayed my welcome. 'Thank you for fitting me in this morning,' I said, giving her a small hug, holding up the sonogram behind her head. 'I appreciate it.'

'You're going to be just fine,' she said again. 'Both of you.'

Both? Oh god, I was pregnant. Just when I was starting to feel better, she had to go and start me off all over again.

Three years earlier, Jenny had dragged me to Dr Laura's office to get fertility tests. Back then, I'd been so impressed with the calming, spa-like décor, I'd taken photographs of the waiting room and sent them to Louisa back in England. She replied with a photo from the doctor's in our village at home. Grace, my goddaughter, was holding up an issue of *Take a Break* magazine from 2009. But even the soothing natural tones and comfy couches couldn't calm me as I stood at the desk, waiting for Felicia to finish on the phone.

Out of everything going on, I couldn't decide whether I was most worried about my unnecessarily high blood pressure or the fact I still hadn't told Alex I was even bloody pregnant. Work, Jenny, and my seafaring parents were going to have to wait for my anxiety levels to go down before I even considered dealing with them.

I couldn't believe I still hadn't heard from Alex and yet I remained absolutely certain that I wasn't going to have to raise this child alone because he definitely wasn't dead in a ditch – I would know if he was, wouldn't I? On the other hand, I was certain I could feel the beginnings of RSI in my thumb from refreshing every possible inbox, waiting for Felicia to hang up the bloody phone.

'Angela?'

Hearing someone say your name in a questioning tone of voice was hardly ever a good thing, and today it definitely wasn't. I turned to see Delia, my friend and now ultimate big boss, standing behind me in the waiting room. Without thinking, I rammed the sono-gram down the back of my jeans and went in for a hug.

'Hello, you,' I said into Delia's glossy, highlighted hair. 'What are you doing here?'

She laughed and pulled a strand of hair out of her nude lip gloss.

'It's an OB-GYN,' she replied, still smiling. 'What do you think I'm doing here?'

'No way,' I gasped. 'Are you pregnant?'

'Holy shit, no!' Delia pressed her hands against her chest, her eyes opened as wide as they would go without falling out onto the floor. 'Are you?'

Cue hysterical laughter.

'Not even,' I snorted as I choked on my words because, oh fuck, I was. 'I was passing and Dr Laura is a friend of Jenny's and I've met her once or twice so I thought I'd stop in and say hello and see if she could maybe fit in a quick pap smear or get a coffee or something. You know, standard. You?'

Delia pressed her lips together into a thin, restrained smile. 'Birth control.'

'Birth control, yeah,' I sighed. 'That makes a lot more sense. And it stops you getting pregnant! It's basically the opposite of pregnant! Good for you.'

I held my breath for a second, waiting for Delia to call me out on my spectacularly bad cover-up but she was already scanning emails on her phone.

'And this would not be a great time to tell my grandpa I've decided to screw my career and get knocked up,' she replied, actually shivering as she dropped the phone back in her bag. 'Besides, I'm pretty sure you've got to be sleeping with someone to get pregnant. I can't remember the last time I did anything other than work.'

'I don't need convincing of that,' I said, keen to get away from the subject of career-destroying pregnancies. Brilliant bloody timing, Clark. 'It feels like I haven't seen you in months.'

It didn't *feel* like months, it *was* months but I was trying to be nice and trying to change the subject.

'I know, it's been crazy with all the changes. I finally understand why grandpa was hardly ever around when we were kids,' she lamented, shrugging her Chanel Maxi Flap Bag onto her shoulder. It was lucky Delia was such a nice person, otherwise it might have been hard to empathize with a woman toting an eight-thousand-dollar handbag to a pill check-up appointment. 'We haven't even talked about Jenny and Mason. I'm so happy for them! Can we try to do cocktails soon? Me, you, Jenny? Erin if she's around?'

'Let's do it,' I nodded, already trying to come up with excuses as to why I wouldn't be able to drink. Stupid baby. 'Jenny is terrifyingly organized already. There's every chance she'll have actually had the wedding by next week.'

Delia leaned in and lowered her voice. 'She's not pregnant, is she?' she asked before straightening up to clarify herself. 'Not that it matters if she is.'

'Not as far as I know,' I replied, thinking back to all the champagne she put away at Erin's house. 'I think she wants to get it all locked down. Once she's made her mind up about something . . . '

'She usually changes it two weeks later?' Delia finished.

'I think Mason is going to hold her to this one,' I said with a smile. He had to, he was going to be paying off that ring for the rest of his life. 'Hopefully we're not looking at a repeat of The Great Pomeranian Puppy Debacle of 2013.'

'Sometimes I think about that dog,' she replied with a soft, wistful smile. 'Anyway, I need to go see the doctor and I'm pretty sure you have a magazine to run. Have you met with Joe yet? Isn't he amazing?'

'Amazing,' I replied, smiling with every single one of my teeth. 'Just the best.'

Definitely not an intimidating wanker who existed solely to test me and already thought I was a complete idiot who didn't know how to read a calendar. Although in fairness, I'd brought that last one on myself.

'I knew you'd love him; he's such a visionary,' she said with far more confidence than was warranted. 'Did he tell you his girlfriend is English?'

I nodded.

'Yes, he did.'

'And do you know her?'

I shook my head.

'I do not.'

'Eh,' Delia shrugged. 'We should all go get dinner sometime. I'm sure you'd get along.'

'Oh, I'm sure,' I agreed, wondering whether Delia actually believed all British people were best friends. I had a feeling anyone who was involved with Joe Herman and I wouldn't have too much to chat about, unless she also spent ten dollars a month on a VPN service just so she could hide her internet IP address and watch the latest episodes of *Come Dine With Me* on Channel Four's website.

'Let's get those drinks in the diary,' Delia reminded me as a nurse in soft-pink scrubs called her name.

'You bet,' I replied, sweating as I headed out to the lifts.

This was going to be a long nine months.

CHAPTER NINE

'Are you out?' Cici asked as I staggered past her desk at the end of the day.

Spending the night on my settee had seemed like such a good idea last night, but I'd barely slept a wink. Add that to my early morning doctor's appointment, an entire afternoon of budget meetings, and an email from my mother informing me that my father had almost got into a fistfight with the head of the onboard kids' club because he crept up on him while dressed as a lobster, causing Dad to have 'a little accident', and I was very much ready to leave. Everyone else was long gone, either having nicked off at lunchtime or disappeared dead on the dot of five. It was the day before Thanksgiving, a holiday I forgot about every single year until Alex reminded me – only this year he wasn't here to give me the nudge . . .

'I'm meeting Jenny,' I confirmed, wishing I was headed home to my bed. 'Is everything OK?'

'You should go home and rest,' she said, flipping down the screen of her laptop. 'You look terrible. Like, worse than usual.'

'Thanks,' I muttered.

'Drawn.' She wasn't finished. 'Like something is sucking the life out of you. Which it kind of is.'

'I don't really have time to chat about this right now, but I am touched.' I glanced up at the clock on the wall, the last thing I needed was for Jenny to storm in here. 'I'll see you tomorrow.'

'Angela!' She stood up and slapped her hands on the desk. I stopped and blinked. Cici had never actually shouted at me before. Sneakily tried to ruin my life, yes, but never actually shouted. 'I'm serious. You need to take better care of yourself, you look like balls.'

Ignoring the insult, I let myself smile a little at her genuine concern.

'And also, I want a job on the editorial team.'

The smile faded away.

'Cici, you can't be serious?' I said, looking at my assistant. Her pout suggested she was. 'We don't have any openings right now."

'You could find one,' she replied. There was a fine line between confidence and arrogance and Cici straddled it like an Olympic gymnast. I hated myself a little, but I couldn't help but be impressed. 'I've decided. I want to be an editor like you.'

It was the most terrifying thing she could have said.

'We can talk about it tomorrow,' I promised, desperate to get out the door. 'But if you're really serious about getting into an editorial role, this isn't the best timing. We've got all the restructuring going on and I don't know what we'd be able to offer you.'

'Yeah, but I read this thing that said you should aim high and then, even if you fail, you'll fail high,' she said as she reapplied her hot pink lipstick without looking in a mirror. That skill alone was probably enough talent to get her my job at some glossy mags. 'So, I'm aiming high.'

'And where did you read that?' I asked, dreading the answer.

She shrugged. 'Instagram?'

It checked out.

'We'll talk about it on Monday,' I said softly. 'Big plans for tomorrow?'

Splaying out her fingers to check her impeccable manicure she sniffed.

'Dinner, family, the usual,' she replied. 'I'm sure we'll all be kissing Dee Dee's ass as is de rigueur.'

Ooh. Tension.

'You've got loads to celebrate too,' I said, desperately trying to think of something. Anything. 'Your hair looks amazing right now.'

She looked up from underneath her eyebrows, her face grim.

'Yeah, well, I hope you have a really nice couple of days off,' I mumbled, turning on my sensible heel and making swiftly for the lift. 'I'll see you Monday!'

November was always an unpredictable time in New York. When I left for work that morning, it had been a little chilly. When I stuffed an entire calzone down my neck at lunchtime, it almost felt like spring, and now, as I jogged up the steps of Union Square station, looking for Jenny, the weather was full-on arctic blasts. She'd sworn she was leaving work just before I got on the subway, but I couldn't see her anywhere as the cold wind burned my cheeks. The red lights and turquoise green tiles of Coffee Shop were calling to me and I could already taste their guacamole. If she didn't appear soon, I was going to be two orders deep before she even arrived.

'Hey, Doll Face!' Jenny swooped in on me from out of nowhere, her curls tied back in an unruly bun and uncharacteristic trainers on her feet. So it was true: put a ring on a woman's finger and she truly gave up. 'Check us out, totally on time.'

'What are the odds?' I concurred, greeting her with a kiss.

I'd decided not to tell her about the baby until I'd told Alex, and I couldn't tell Alex until he called me. I'd already drafted seventeen emails with the good news but it just didn't feel right; you couldn't give someone news like this over email, at least not if you were expecting them to stick around. Besides, after Sadie's spectacular three-thunder-stealing carats of engagement ring, I didn't want her to feel shoved even further down the totem pole of good news. The baby would wait.

'I'm so hungry,' I said, setting off towards the restaurant. 'Is it me, or does it feel like a fries for the table night?'

'Wait, wait, wait! So, surprise.' She jumped in front of me and threw up her trademark Jenny Lopez jazz hands. 'Since we're going to be eating ourselves blind at Erin's Thanksgiving extravaganza tomorrow, I managed to get us the last two bikes at SpiritSpin.'

No. There was no way. Absolutely, one 100 per cent not possible.

I'd heard all about SpiritSpin and it just wasn't happening. Spinning in and of itself was bad enough, but spinning by candlelight with a deafening soundtrack, surrounded by model-types in tiny Lululemon sports bras when all I wanted to do was consume my own bodyweight in mashed avocados was pure torture.

'I haven't got my stuff,' I said, shaking my head. 'I can't go.'

'I brought you stuff from work.' She held up a baby pink backpack, stuffed to bursting. 'We're working with a new athleisure brand and I've got it all. Tights, tank, bra, thong, socks and shoes. Everything you could need.'

Thong? Thong? No.

'Let's go shopping,' I replied, going straight for the jugular. 'I haven't been to Sephora for ages, we should look at wedding make-up.'

'I know you think you don't want to go,' she grabbed my arm and began pulling me towards 18th street, 'but once you try it you'll love it. It's totally addictive.'

'I haven't eaten,' I yelped, looking longingly back at Coffee Shop. 'You can't work out on an empty stomach.'

'There's a protein bar in the backpack,' Jenny replied.

I stood fast, refusing to move.

'A murderous builder has keys to my apartment and I have to get home to make sure he hasn't filled my kitchen with traps inspired by the *Saw* movies.'

'Is that true?' she asked, squinting against the cold.

'The builder part is,' I admitted. 'I can't confirm or deny the rest of it.'

'Come on, Angie baby,' Jenny whined. 'I need this, I just got engaged.'

'Really?' I muttered as I gave up and followed her across the square. 'You'd never know.'

Technically, all the leaflets Dr Laura had given me recommended maintaining exercise during pregnancy but since I did next to nothing other than the odd yoga class and half-arsed run around Prospect Park when the weather was nice or I had new trainers I wanted to show off, throwing myself into a ridiculous pseudo-spiritual spin class at the end of a tiring day seemed beyond stupid.

'Come on, Ange,' Jenny whined, threading her arm through mine and pulling me close. 'Erin cancelled on us because she has to do something with her kids, and after that shit Sadie pulled last night? I need to keep my mind occupied.'

'Well, kids do need quite a lot of attention,' I argued, internally wincing at how quickly I would have agreed with her a week before. 'Don't be too mad at Erin.'

'I know,' she said regretfully. 'I just want her to be more excited about the wedding. I've been a bridesmaid for her three times now. Three! And she's too busy with some recital to even look at the one bridesmaid dress.'

'Arianna has a recital?' I was confused. 'She's only four, isn't she? How is she having a recital?'

'So much worse than you think,' Jenny clucked. 'It's TJ's Baby Mozart class. She's had him enrolled since he was three months old.'

Having a baby in New York was definitely not going to be the same as having a baby in England.

'Wait, how come I haven't seen the bridesmaids' dresses?' I asked. 'Did you send them? Have I missed them?'

Jenny shook her head and pulled the zip of her hoodie up to her chin.

'No, I wanted to whittle down the choices before they came your way,' she said. 'You're terrible at making decisions, babe. Typical Libra.'

'Spoken like a true Leo,' I muttered, following her through the door into SpiritSpin.

'Good evening, Spirit Seekers,' A gorgeous, willowy woman with Beyoncé hair and a twelve-year-old boy's body bowed as we walked inside. As she stood upright, I noticed her nametag. Serenity.

'Are you here to join us on tonight's journey?'

'We are,' Jenny said, handing over her credit card. I didn't even like to think what she had paid for these classes, at least thirty dollars each. Sixty dollars for forty-five minutes of torture. If I wasn't in my current condition, that was four very nice cocktails in a fancy bar. Or twelve cocktails in a not so nice one. Either would have been a better option.

I had been raised well enough to know it was rude to stare, but it was too hard not to. The reception was fairly dimly lit with the only real lighting over at the merchandise area where a group of the most perfectly formed women I'd ever laid eyes on oohed and ahhed over $100 T-shirts.

'You'll be following your dreams on bikes number four and number six,' the girl behind the counter breathed. 'They're both in the front row so you'll have the full benefit of Guru Brian this evening.'

Guru Brian?

'Can I swap to one in the back?' I asked.

'No,' she snapped. 'You have to stay on the bike you're assigned or else it confuses the system.'

Serenity by name, not so much by nature.

'This is just a normal spin class, isn't it?' I asked as Jenny clipped my reluctant feet into the pedals of my spirit cycle. 'Just with candles and stuff?'

'Pretty much,' Jenny said, fiddling with her own pedals to avoid meeting my eye. 'There's music and they show videos on the screen behind the guru. And they kinda move the bikes around sometimes.'

'They do what?'

I tried to pull my feet out of the pedals but I was stuck.

'What do you mean, they move the bikes around?' I yanked the handles backwards but nothing shifted, not even a little bit. This was not good. 'Move them how?'

'Babe, calm down,' she sighed as she shook out her shoulders. 'We'll do maybe a ten-minute warm-up, then some sprints, and then they just tilt your bike back a little so you can work your core while we're doing hill climbs. It's super fun.'

Mine and Jenny's idea of fun was sometimes really, really different.

'Good evening, Spirit Seekers.'

The lights dimmed in the room as Guru Brian approached the elevated bike in front of me. There was nowhere to run, nowhere to hide. This was happening whether I liked it or not.

'Tonight we take another step on our journey, not only to fitness and wellbeing, but to discovering who we really are,' Brian said, fiddling with his Madonna-esque microphone as he gracefully hopped onto his bike.

I looked across at Jenny and saw she was already pedalling, her eyes closed, hands pressed together in prayer. I tried to look behind me at the rest of the rows, but turning and pedalling at the same time was beyond me; instead I concentrated on listening to Guru Brian and not falling off the bike and breaking my neck.

'This isn't that bad,' I whispered, leaning forward in my saddle and concentrating on feeling good about the fact the saddle was killing my arse. If it could still cause bum-ache, my backside couldn't be as massive as I imagined it was.

Continuing to pedal, I imagined myself on the front of one of those fitspo magazines. Maybe being pregnant would help me turn over a new leaf, maybe I'd get totally into wellness and healthy eating and start working out every day. Perhaps I'd be one of those mums who has weird abs showing on the side of their baby bumps.

And then the bass started.

Glancing at the bikes on either side of me, I saw everyone lean forward and attempted to shift my weight.

'Oof, that is harder than it looks,' I grunted. Without touching anything, my pedals suddenly became very, very heavy.

'Who are you?' Brian asked as low, spacey music began to boom out of speakers in the ceiling. 'Who do you want to be? Where do you want to go today?'

'Bed,' I muttered, pressing all the buttons on my bike's console, trying to ease some of the tension out of the pedals, but nothing seemed to work. It still felt as though I was pedalling through quicksand and my hashtag FitMama dream was over. 'So, this is how I'm going to die.'

'Be it, believe it,' Brian shouted as the music got louder and faster. 'We can be whoever we want to be if we travel together on our SpiritSprint. You can soar! Let this ride take you there!'

'Shit!' I shrieked as my bike began to tip backwards and the screen behind Brian became a bold blue sky dotted with fluffy white clouds. 'What's happening?'

Whether Jenny, the Guru, and the other twelve people in the class were ignoring me or too busy trying not to die on their own buckaroo bikes, I wasn't sure. The only thing I was certain about was just how badly I wanted to get off the bike and onto the ground. The solid, non-moving ground.

'Bike number four!' Guru Brian yelled over the thumping dance music that was pumping so loudly out of the speakers I could feel it in my lungs. I looked up, swiping sweaty strands of hair away from my face, and realized he was shouting at me. 'Bike number four, you're lagging behind.'

'I'm trying,' I screamed as clouds of white smoke billowed in from god knows where. Within seconds, the floor had vanished and it really did look like we were riding on top of clouds. That, or I had actually died and gone to heaven, if heaven looked like a nightclub in Rotherham from 1999.

'Pick up the pace, number four,' Brian scolded from the front of the room as my bike tilted further back. 'We can only realize our dreams if we all move as one. Do you want to realize your dreams?'

'No, I want to get off!' I wailed. 'I don't like it!'

'Breathe,' Brian instructed. I looked over at Jenny for support but not only was she pedalling happily, the bitch wasn't even holding on to her handles. Somehow, everyone else in the room was lifting tiny hand weights above their heads and, dear god, was she *smiling*? 'Breathe through the experience. There is no such thing as pain, just sensation. Feel it, accept it, move through it, and join us on the other side.'

Even though I'd only been pedalling for a couple

of minutes, my legs were already burning, but I couldn't stop them moving. I wasn't sure if the bike was actually dragging my feet around with the pedals, or I'd genuinely just gone slightly mad.

'I can't do this.' I sat up, legs still whizzing around in circles and searched for someone to help me. 'I have to get off this thing. How do I stop it? Why won't it stop?'

'Angie, just relax,' Jenny shouted. 'Just breathe and feel the music.'

'I can't breathe and I feel sick!' I was starting to panic. 'Jenny, you've got to get me off this thing.'

It wasn't a heated spin class, but as far as I was concerned I could have been in a sauna. I was hot, I was out of breath, and I was scared – but for a shocking change, I wasn't just afraid of making a fool of myself. Was this bad for the baby? It certainly felt bad for the baby. Although I wasn't especially looking forward to everyone else's reaction when I threw up, which I was almost certain to do.

'Number four, I need you to inhale through your nose and exhale through your mouth,' Brian instructed. 'Take in the joy and let go of your fear. You're holding yourself back.'

'Yes, I am and you should be thankful,' I told him, sweat dripping off me. 'Get me off this bike now – I think I'm going to puke.'

'You'll regret it if you give up,' he insisted. 'Keep pushing yourself. You're an eternal being, don't let these earthly sensations prevent you from reaching your true potential.'

'I'm not an eternal being, I'm *pregnant*!' I yelled. 'Get me off this bike!'

'STOP THE MUSIC!' Brian screamed in a voice so

high-pitched, I assumed Alex's ears would be ringing all the way in Thailand. The second I dropped the P-bomb, the smoke machine cut out, and by the time Brian had released my feet from the spin bike slash instrument of torture, the floor was nearly clear.

'Don't sit down,' the guru ordered. 'Walk it off.'

With a face like thunder, I collapsed at the side of my bike, lying flat on my back in a pool of sweat while various people fanned me with little white towels and held out bottles of water. When I looked up, there was only one person left on her bike.

Jenny, with her mouth hanging open.

'Are you OK?' Serenity from the front desk asked. 'Do you need an ambulance?'

'Did she sign a release?' Brian hissed in her ear. 'Make sure we've got the paperwork.'

One bike over, my best friend was gripping the handles of her bike as though she was me two minutes earlier. Weak and pale-faced, I propped myself up on my elbows. Was she shaking?

'Jenny?' I said. 'Are you all right?'

'You're having a baby?' she asked in a tiny, little girl voice.

I nodded.

'You're genuinely pregnant?' She bit her quivering lip. 'Because you've said all kinds of shit to get out of exercise before.'

'Genuinely pregnant,' I replied. 'With a baby.'

'What else would she be pregnant with?' Serenity whispered to Brian above me.

'You're having a baby!' Jenny squealed, her entire being exploding with joy. 'Get me off this goddamn bike, my best friend is having a baby!'

Rather than unfastening the clips on her bike, she

kicked her way out of her shoes and threw herself onto the floor, covering me from head to toe with sweaty Lopez.

'Hi, baby!' She pressed her face against my belly, arms wrapped tightly around my waist. 'I'm your Aunt Jenny. Your cool Aunt Jenny. You're not even here yet and we just took our first spin class together, that's how cool I am.'

She looked up at me with huge, happy eyes.

'Angie, there's a goddamn baby in you,' she said, pointing at my stomach.

'I know,' I said. My face ached and I realized it was from smiling. 'It's mental.'

'Excuse me, but, like, do we get a refund for this?' one of the extremely toned women in the back of the class asked. 'I feel like we're not getting a full SpiritSprint experience this evening.'

Jenny gazed at me with the smile of a saint before turning to stare down the other woman.

'My best friend just told me she is pregnant and you will shut the fuck up!' she yelled. The girl shrank back into the darkness of the studio as Jenny turned back to me with a sweet smile.

'You wanna go get fries?' she asked, picking sweaty strands of hair off my face. I nodded and allowed her to heave me up to my feet. 'Let's go get fries.'

With Jenny's arm around my shoulders, I waved goodbye to Brian and Serenity and followed her through the door and back out to the real world.

Eight and a half minutes later, we were in a booth, in Coffee Shop, halfway through our first plate of chips.

'Can you see it?' I asked as Jenny played with the

143

sonogram, viewing it from every angle. 'It took me a minute, but it's this blob in the corner.'

'It's like a magic-eye picture,' she replied, squinting and holding it at arm's length. 'I feel like I should be looking for a sailboat.'

'Only this is a human being that is inside me.' I took the picture back and put it away safely in my satchel. 'A little bit more life-changing than a sailboat.'

'Oh honey,' she said, risking her life by taking one chip off my plate. 'You've obviously been going sailing with the wrong people.'

I pulled at the waistband of my SpiritSpin leggings. Jenny's guess at sizing had been optimistic or these were actually a child's medium, not an adult's.

'Do you think it's a boy or a girl?' Jenny asked.

'Don't know,' I replied.

'Have you thought about names?'

'No.'

'Can we call it Jenny?'

'What if it's a boy?

'Jenn, double "n".'

'No.'

'Do you feel pregnant?'

'Not really?'

'Do you have any weird cravings?'

'Chips?' I replied, pulling the plate closer to me. 'An entire plate of chips I don't have to share with anyone?'

'Have you had morning sickness?'

'Yes.'

I pushed the plate further away.

'You must be so excited,' she said, staring at my stomach. I pulled my white cloth napkin up a little

144

bit higher. Nothing to see here. 'Angie, you're going to have a baby.'

'Yep,' I replied. It was strange and wonderful and terrifying to hear someone else say it. Now it was real. 'It feels like waiting for Christmas when you're seven. I know it's coming and I really want my presents but first I've got to stare at said presents for nine whole months before I can open them.'

'And carry them around with you all the time,' she added.

'And then keep the presents alive forever,' I said slowly.

I couldn't get the plate any closer and so we both picked up a handful of chips and stuffed our faces.

'Whatever, Aunt Jenny is beyond happy about this,' she said, pinging the strap of her sports bra as her sweatshirt slipped off her shoulder. 'I'm gonna buy it candy and take it to movies you don't want it to see. Oh, Angie, we're going to be so happy.'

I felt an expression forming on my face that I'd only ever seen on my own mother. Slightly disapproving, slightly threatening, entirely maternal. Was this a thing that happened when you got pregnant? Did you open up an entirely new collection of mannerisms? Was I suddenly about to start telling people I wasn't angry, just disappointed and spitting on tissues to wipe their faces?

'What did Alex say?' Jenny asked as the waitress brought over her glass of wine and refilled my water. 'Is he coming home?'

'I haven't actually told him yet,' I admitted, dipping a chip in an enormous splodge of tomato sauce. 'He's on some beach in the middle of nowhere with no reception, no internet. I can't get hold of him and it's killing me.'

'I know before Alex?' She pumped her fist through the air, almost colliding with a passing pensioner. 'Yes! Screw you, Alex Reid, I found out first. It's my baby now.'

Smiling, I held a hand over my face to cover my extremely full mouth.

'And you're not mad?' I asked. 'What with the wedding coming up and everything? Obviously, I didn't plan it, but surprise, it's happening.'

'Angie, honey,' she saw her opportunity and nabbed two more chips, 'the only thing I'm mad about is that you didn't drop the B-bomb on Sadie last night and shut her yap.'

It was a fair point.

'Forget about Sadie,' I instructed. 'What are the chances of her actually marrying this dude? They've known each other for about ten minutes. It isn't real life, it's celebrity life, I write about it every day in *Gloss*. They're Kim and Kris; even if they make it down the aisle, it'll all be over in three months, tops.'

'I want her to be happy,' Jenny said, wiping her fingers to signal that she was done with her dinner. All the more for me. 'But it's a drag. I know my wedding will be perfect but it's still going to suck, seeing your super-mega-hot model friend try on hundreds of thousands of dollars of wedding dresses in a ten-page spread for *Brides* magazine when you're waiting in line in the snow at 6 a.m. for the Kleinman's sample sale to open.'

'Jennifer LaToya Lopez, we both know there's no way you're getting your wedding dress from the

Kleinman's sample sale,' I replied, putting my stern face on. I was not going to entertain this 'woe is me' fantasy for a moment longer than necessary. 'Do you want to marry Teddy Myers, teen heartthrob werewolf? Or any man you have known for approximately four minutes?'

'No.'

'And do you want your wedding plans plastered all over the tabloids?'

She looked as though she was considering it.

'You don't,' I informed her. 'I work in magazine publishing and trust me, you really don't.'

'She's going to get so much free stuff,' Jenny moaned. '*I* want free stuff.'

'Says the girl who works in PR,' I said. 'Shush, Lopez. You're being ridiculous.'

'Wow, you're already totally in mom mode.' Jenny leaned back against the booth and exhaled happily. 'You're having a baby and I'm getting married? This is all so insane. Is this *The Matrix* or are we, like, grown-ups now?'

'Let's not get carried away,' I warned. 'I stayed up all night watching Disney films because I really had convinced myself a psychopathic builder was going to let himself into my house in the middle of the night.'

I glanced around the restaurant. What if he was watching me right now?

'Oh! Brainwave!' She clapped loudly and the man at the next table, who had been subtly checking out her cleavage, jumped out of his skin. 'You can move in with me! Until Alex gets back, I mean. Sadie is gone, so your old room is empty, and I can look after you and we can plan the wedding together. You don't

147

even need to go back to Brooklyn tonight, you can borrow my stuff tomorrow and we'll get you a tooth-brush from Duane Reade. Come on, Angie, it'll be like old times.'

It was a tempting offer. Not only could I walk to work from our old apartment, meaning longer lie-ins, but she was in such a good mood I could probably borrow her Louboutins for my meeting with Joe and get grilled cheese sandwiches and everything bagels with tuna salad delivered from Scotty's Diner across the street. And also, all those nice friend-type things she had said. But mostly the shoes, the bagels and the grilled cheese sandwiches.

'Did Sadie take her bed with her?' I asked.

'We'll get a mattress protector from *Bed Bath and Beyond* on the way home,' Jenny replied, reading my mind. 'Besides, you already caught babies, you can't get that twice.'

'It's not babies I'm afraid of catching,' I said with a shiver. 'But really, are you sure? I have to get up to wee about seventeen times a night and I can't drink or eat sushi while I'm pregnant. I'm not even sure who I am any more.'

'Angela Clark,' Jenny reached across the table and laid her hand on top of mine, 'we may not have sushi but we'll always have pizza.'

My best friend was so clever.

'And you know what?' she said, throwing back her glass of wine. 'Maybe I'll give up alcohol with you, like, in solidarity. And also, to help lose the five pounds I've decided I need to lose.'

'You don't need to lose five pounds.' I clinked my glass of water against her glass of wine in a toast. 'But I would love to be your roomie again.'

'To old times,' she said with a smile. 'And new beginnings.'

'Old times and new beginnings,' I replied. 'And to definitely getting that mattress protector on the way home.'

CHAPTER TEN

'What do you mean, you're going to Thanksgiving?' Mum asked. I pulled a blue Sandro shift dress over my head, considered my reflection in the bedroom mirror then yanked it off and chucked it back on the bed. 'How do you go to Thanksgiving? You can't go to Christmas.'

'Thanksgiving dinner,' I clarified to my phone as I slid on a little black Nanette Lepore dress. It was sleeveless, so I wouldn't get too hot, but the white lace collar seemed too dressy. 'We're all going to Erin's house for Thanksgiving dinner.'

'I don't get it,' she replied. 'Why did they have to go and make up their own Christmas? And without the presents! It's bonkers, if you ask me.'

'No one asked you,' I said quietly, considering my limited wardrobe choices. I'd only been able to bring so much over to Jenny's and, inevitably, everything I now wanted was still back in Park Slope.

'And I don't know why you're going,' Mum sniffed. 'I know you're married to one, but you're not American.'

'It's not a religious thing, Mum,' I replied, plumping

150

for a pretty printed smock dress from Maje. Cute, smart, but with plenty of room for a Thanksgiving food baby. And, now I thought about it, a real baby as well. I'd been maternity shopping without knowing it for the last six months. 'You just eat a big turkey dinner with your friends and family and give thanks for all the good things in your life.'

'Sounds a bit happy-clappy to me,' she said. 'I don't want you joining a cult like Tom Cruise.'

Only my mother would confuse Thanksgiving with Scientology.

'Is Dad having fun yet?' I asked, searching for an appropriate pair of shoes. 'He's been very quiet online.'

'He's been very quiet in general,' she said with a sigh. 'He's taken to sitting at the side of the pool in his jogging bottoms and a jumper, reading books about serial killers. People are starting to talk, Angela. I'm certain that's the reason we haven't been asked back to the captain's table.'

'I've got to go,' I said as Jenny poked her head around the bedroom door. 'But I'm sure he'll cheer up soon.'

'I don't know,' she replied. 'They had Steak Diane on at dinner last night and he barely touched his. I'm starting to worry.'

'Is that you, Mrs C?' Jenny asked, giving my Acne ankle boots a thumbs-up. 'Happy Thanksgiving!'

'Happy Thanksgiving to you,' Mum shouted sweetly. 'I'm thankful that Angela has a friend like you, Jenny.'

My mother was such a suck-up sometimes, it was unbelievable.

'Aww, Mrs C, that's too cute.' Jenny smiled across the room while I faux gagged. 'We have to go now, but do you think you'll be coming to visit soon? We miss you here in NYC.'

I shook my head, slicing my arms through the air in front of me. Why would Jenny even joke about something like that?

'Oh, I don't know, Jenny,' Mum replied. 'We've still got a long while left on the cruise. Maybe next year.'

'Maybe next year,' Jenny said, back to her, dodging the pair of balled-up socks I lobbed at her head. 'Say hi to Mr C for me.'

'Will do,' Mum sang down the line. 'Bye, girls, have fun at Thanksgiving.'

'We will, Mum,' I said as I pressed the red button to end the call. 'You test me sometimes, Lopez.'

'That's my job,' she replied, running her hands over her skintight purple sheath dress. 'Does this look good?'

'It looks snug,' I said, ever the diplomat. 'Are you sure you wouldn't rather wear something a bit roomier for dinner?'

She held her arms up above her head and shimmied her hips.

'Nope,' she replied. 'I'm on my wedding diet, this will stop me pigging out.'

'So, it's a tactical frock.' I flipped out the hem of my smock. 'Mine too, just the other way around. You do realize you don't need to lose weight, though? You're practically miniature. If you get any littler in the waist, we're not going to be friends any more.'

'It's not my waist I'm worried about,' she frowned, patting her backside. 'It's the junk in the trunk that's the issue. Most wedding dresses don't leave a lot of extra ass room.'

'They do if you go for a ballgown,' I replied. 'Nothing but extra ass room.'

Jenny shot me the filthiest look I'd ever seen.

'OK, no ballgown,' I replied quickly. 'Well, don't think of it as junk in your trunk, think of it as fantastically practical things that you need in case of an emergency. Like a torch and a first-aid kit.'

She pouted and gazed at her gorgeous figure long enough for me to be certain we weren't seeing the same thing reflected back in the mirror.

'It's not a wedding dress body,' she said. 'Sadie has a wedding dress body, all tall and willowy. This is a Hervé Léger, drop it like it's hot bod. It has no business wearing Vera Wang.'

'Oh good, you've lost your mind.' I grabbed my parka from the bed and shooed her out of the room. 'You're going to be a beautiful bride, Sadie is going to be a different kind of beautiful bride, and more importantly, right this second, we are going to be late.'

'Next time your mom calls, I'm going to tell her you're pregnant,' she threatened, flouncing out of the front door. 'Think about that, Clark.'

'Sometimes you are stone-cold,' I said, locking the door behind us as she laughed.

Jenny Lopez, the dirtiest player in the game.

If Sadie's champagne shampoo had caused any permanent damage to Erin's carpet, I certainly couldn't tell. The sitting room of her West Village townhouse was impeccable, as it probably should be for someone who employed a full-time housekeeper. Even though it was dull and grey outside, the house was beautifully lit with low lamps and strategically placed candles, highlighting all of Erin and Thomas's beautiful collection of things. This was the kind of place I wanted to own one day. Maybe if Alex wrote two really successful albums and I became the editor of *Belle*? And we won the lottery?

'Ladies . . . ' Thomas strolled into the sitting room as we handed out coats to our hostess. 'So glad you could join us, Happy Thanksgiving.'

'Happy Thanksgiving,' I replied, grazing his cheek with mine in a downtown air kiss.

Thomas was a nice man, as far as I could tell, but other than his wife we had nothing in common. He didn't watch TV, he only listened to jazz, and he used the word 'summer' as a verb. I knew he did something on Wall Street and had somehow survived the financial crisis unscathed, but even if someone held a gun to my head, I couldn't tell you exactly what he did for a living. I'd always regarded money men with great suspicion, especially someone with as much money as Thomas, but if Erin said he was OK and he was prepared to feed me on a national holiday, who was I to judge?

'Dinner smells amazing,' I said, staring at a painting on the wall where the TV should be. Maybe it flipped over to reveal a dead fancy flatscreen? 'You must be happy to have the day off.'

'I worked this morning,' he replied as Erin disappeared to open the door again. 'Thanksgiving is a tricky one – the rest of the world doesn't stop so we can eat too much turkey.'

Mmm, too much turkey.

'I suppose not,' I agreed. 'Where are the kids?'

'Upstairs.' He nodded backwards and took a deep breath. 'Arianna is having one of her days. Four going on fourteen.'

'Imagine what she'll be like when she really is a teenager,' I replied, laughing.

Thomas looked at me, silent and stony-faced.

'Or, you know, don't,' I said, looking off over my shoulder. 'Mason!'

Jenny's fiancé appeared in the doorway with Erin behind him. I noticed she was wearing a beautiful white apron over her fancy silver dress even though there was no way on god's green earth that she'd even stepped foot in the kitchen. Jenny had already told me they'd had the entire meal delivered from Jean-Georges. It was half the reason I was there.

'Hey!' We exchanged cheek kisses with actual human contact before Jenny pounced on him, sliding her arm through his and resting her head on his arm. They really were a gorgeous couple, she was mad if she thought they would look anything other than stunning in their wedding photos.

'Dinner is served,' Erin announced, giving a gracious sweep of her arms to usher us through the sitting room and into the formal dining room.

Her house was like the TARDIS. Most New York homes were the opposite, they looked pretty big from the outside but when you went through the front door, it was just a rabbit warren of tiny studio apartments. Most of my friends didn't even have proper kitchens, and one of the girls at work had a shower squeezed in next to her stove. Erin and Thomas had managed to achieve the opposite. From the outside, it looked like any other bazillion-dollar West Village home, narrow, tall, and in close proximity to Sarah Jessica Parker. But once you were inside, the whole place blossomed, the sitting room led to the drawing room, the drawing room led to the family room, and the family room led to the kitchen. Upstairs was Erin and Thomas's bedroom, a home office, and a guest bedroom; and on the third floor, if you could be arsed to make it up that far, the two kids' rooms, a shared playroom, and the nanny's room. Because of course there was a nanny. I wasn't including all the bathrooms because if I did, it made me sad. I'd never quite got to grips with America's obsession with a toilet per person, possibly because the thought of cleaning that many lavs made me want a nap. Erin must go through so much Toilet Duck, I mused as we passed one of the downstairs powder rooms.

'You didn't tell me your new boss was Joe Herman,' Erin said, taking a seat at the head of the table, peeking at me over an enormous flower arrangement in the shape of a turkey. 'Wow.'

'You know him?' I asked, moving left and right, trying to make eye contact.

Erin growled, grabbed the floral turkey and dumped it on a side table behind her. Thomas raised an eyebrow.

'What?' she challenged.

'My mother sent that,' he replied.

'I would think it's quite clear to everyone here that *I* didn't choose it,' she said smoothly, retaking her seat and ignoring Thomas's tightly clenched jaw. 'And yes, I do know him. Of him, at least.'

Mason cleared his throat and began talking to Thomas, ignoring the tension at the table.

'Don't worry about him,' Erin instructed, picking up her fork with her right hand. The pumpkin-stuffed agnolotti I'd read about on Eater.com was already on the table. 'He's tired. TJ was up all night and I made him deal with it. Now he's sulking like the baby that he is.'

'Good to know,' I replied, sucking in my stomach.

'Joe Herman used to be head of digital at Hearst,' she said as she dug into her dinner happily. 'He revolutionized their online platforms. I was kind of surprised to hear he'd gone into print publishing at all, but it made more sense when I heard it was at Spencer.'

'Massive fan of *Belle*?' I theorized.

'Massive fan of your assistant,' she corrected. 'They used to date.'

Oh, fan-bloody-tastic.

'As I understand it, Delia, Cici and Joe all went to the same college and he dated Cici on and off for a while although from what I hear, she saw it as more off than on. He's been pining after her ever since she broke his heart and cheated on him.'

'I want to be surprised but I'm not,' Jenny said, pushing her pasta around her plate without actually eating a bite. 'But it's a worry, no one with a decent head on their shoulders could be in love with Cici Spencer.'

'Anyone with a penis in their underpants could be in love with Cici Spencer,' I replied. Mason and Thomas both looked up at the same time. I held up a hand in apology. 'It doesn't matter, he told me he has an English girlfriend so even if he was crushing on the evil Spencer twin, he must have got over it by now.'

'Sure,' Jenny nodded, raising a glass of white wine to her lips. 'That's why he gave up a huge job at Hearst to run the women's magazines at Spencer.'

'It's kind of a side step,' Erin said as I picked up my own wine, wet my lips and then put it right back down on the table without drinking a drop. Self-restraint was so hard sometimes. 'I'm sure he's there on a promise of moving up fairly quickly.'

'You're sure he's not there on another kind of promise?' I asked. 'But thanks for the heads-up. If he starts sending me notes asking me to ask her out for him, I'll let you know.'

'I know you're joking, but the media industry in New York is even more like high school than actual high school,' Jenny said. 'Only we have HR instead of guidance counsellors and the lunches are slightly better.'

'You're not wrong,' I said, accidentally on purpose letting the tiniest sip of wine pass my lips. Oh, so good. 'I have a meeting with him on Tuesday. He's really dragging this new strategy stuff out. Honestly, I think he's just trying to make me sweat and it's totally working.'

'It's all so macho,' she replied with a judgemental tut. 'Leave you hanging, make you wonder what's going to happen. He's just trying to keep all the power.'

'But he already has all the power, he could fire me tomorrow if he wanted to,' I reminded her, wilting at the very thought. Maybe I could have one more tiny sip of wine. 'Keep your fingers crossed that's not in his "strategy". How are things going on *Ghost*, Mason?'

He sucked the air in through his teeth and Jenny squeezed his huge bicep. It was a sweet gesture, but his arms were so massive I wondered whether or not he could even feel it.

'I don't know,' he said, leaning back in his chair. 'Lincoln, our new guy? He seems like he's going to be cool but there's something about him I don't trust. He's all "hey, we should all go see the Jets next game" to your face then goes to his office and sends you a brutally direct email insisting we pull any article that actually requires budget. I feel like staffing cuts are coming.'

'We've had the budget cuts talk as well,' I commiserated. 'I honestly don't see where we could cut anything and keep the magazine going.'

'Just keep a slot open for me,' Mason said, adding an awkward chuckle to the end of the sentence. 'You never know, I might need you to find me a job.'

'You're not really worried, are you?' I asked.

'No, he isn't,' Jenny answered on his behalf. 'How could they fire Mason? He won a Penny? He interviewed Kanye West and managed to make him seem almost entirely sane?'

'That kind of thing doesn't matter to the corporate folks,' he replied with a shrug. 'I've asked Gregory, my editor, but he's keeping this one close to his chest and that's not a good sign. He tells me everything – seriously, he told me about his affair and he won't tell me about this.'

'Gregory's having an affair?' I asked, stunned. Mason pulled an awkward face and I wondered if that was why Gregory hadn't told him who was getting fired. 'Sorry, not the point.'

'He told me not to stress, maybe we're not losing anyone. There's always growing pains with a new structure.'

Everyone around the table made agreeing noises.

'And I have better things to think about right now, right, Lopez?'

'Yeah, you do,' she replied, kissing the tip of his nose.

'How's the wedding planning going?' Erin asked. She and Thomas looked away from the PDA at the exact same moment.

Never missing an opportunity, Jenny flashed her ring around the table for everyone to enjoy. It really was bloody beautiful.

'It's only been a few days.' Jenny rested her hand on Mason's forearm and gazed at the ring, turning it this way and that so it could catch the light from different angles. 'We haven't really decided on anything yet.'

'We decided Maui, didn't we?' Mason asked, smiling down at her. 'But we're not totally sure where or when. We want to keep it real low-key.'

'I wish *we'd* done a destination wedding,' Thomas said approvingly. 'Or eloped. Or just gone to City Hall. The whole thing is an insane waste of money.'

Erin gazed calmly down the table at her husband, resting her chin on her woven-together fingers, never saying a word.

'I don't know,' Jenny said. She bobbed her head from side to side, making her hair bounce as she spoke. 'I'm kind of going off the idea. Maui is so far away from New York, it's going to make it really hard for a lot of people to come.'

'Yeah,' Mason replied with a mouthful of pumpkin pasta. 'I know, that's the point. Hopefully, my parents included.'

'But what about your brother and his kids?' she said, counting off excluded guests on her fingers. 'And I want to invite Angie's parents. They'd already be coming all the way from England, I can't ask them to fly to Hawaii.'

'Really, don't,' I insisted. 'We'll do just fine without them.'

'And I wanted Arianna to be a flower girl,' Jenny said, turning to Erin. 'You don't want to have to lug her and TJ all the way out to Maui, do you?'

Thomas leaned across the table to give Mason the full benefit of his manic eyes.

'Elope,' he hissed. 'Do it now.'

'So you don't want to go to Maui?' Mason asked.

'I don't know,' Jenny pinched her shoulders together, innocently spearing a lettuce leaf I had assumed was just on my plate for show. 'There are a lot of things I hadn't considered. Doing a beach wedding means doing a beach dress. Maybe I don't want to.'

'You could get married in a Hefty bag and I'd still love you,' Mason replied. 'Whatever you want, babe, we'll figure it out.'

I watched the muscles in her face tighten as he went back to his starter. I knew her well enough to know something was up.

'Has Sadie mentioned anything about her wedding?' Jenny asked, pushing her plate away.

And there it was.

'She emailed me yesterday to see if I knew anyone at Bravo,' Erin replied. I tried to kick her under the table but instead bashed my toe on a very hard table leg. 'Some producer approached them about doing a reality show or something.'

'How awful would that be?' I said loudly. 'Imagine someone following you around constantly, telling you what you can and can't do for your own wedding. You wouldn't want that; your wedding is going to be so classy and anything reality TV gets involved with ends up being tack central.'

'I guess you're right,' Jenny sniffed, her cheeks burning red. 'So tacky.'

'That's my idea of a nightmare,' Mason added. 'Some company pitched the idea of making a reality show at *Ghost* once, like a guy's version of *The Devil Wears Prada*? They killed it after two days. A bunch of dudes sat at laptops typing and scratching their asses didn't make for good TV.'

161

'And that's why all reality shows are scripted,' Erin replied. 'Reality isn't really very interesting.'

'Maybe we should have our wedding after theirs?' Mason said, nudging a still-silent Jenny in the ribs. 'Just so we know exactly what we don't want.'

'She sent me a photo of some custom Louboutins,' Jenny replied with forced lightness in her voice. 'I don't know if they're for the actual wedding or the rehearsal dinner, but they were kind of cute.'

'For two thousand dollars, shoes need to be more than kind of cute,' Erin said. 'Besides, Loubies are hell to stand around in all day. Don't sweat it, babe, you know we've got you. Your wedding is going to blow hers out of the water.'

Jenny's shoulders slipped back down and a small smile reappeared on her face.

'It'll bankrupt you, if you're not careful,' Thomas muttered as Erin rose to clear our plates. 'And if the wedding doesn't, kids will.'

Now it was my turn to colour up.

'And if the wedding and the kids don't do it, the divorce definitely will,' Erin said, kissing him on top of the head. 'Right, babe?'

That shut him right up.

Two hours and several courses later, Mason and Thomas were comatose in front of a football game in the TV room while Jenny and Erin were poring over bridal magazines. It was like I'd fallen asleep and woken up in the 1950s.

'Just going to pop to the loo,' I said, picking up my glass of wine and venturing off alone when neither of them looked up from the latest issue of *The Knot*.

Fully aware that Mason and Thomas had both

availed themselves of the ground-floor facilities in the last hour, I slipped off my ankle boots and tiptoed upstairs. The second floor was deadly quiet but I could hear music coming from the very top floor. And not just any music, Disney music.

'Hello,' I said, pushing open the door to the play-room. Arianna and TJ looked up from their child-sized sofa. Neither seemed especially impressed.

'Don't mind them, they're in turkey comas,' a voice called from the adjoining room. It was, of course, the nanny. 'Does Erin need something?'

'No, I just came to say hi.' I waved meekly, never quite sure how to talk to her. We'd met so many times but always in passing when she was either whisking the kids away or delivering them to say goodnight. 'What are we watching?'

'*Pocahontas*,' Mandy the nanny said with a healthy scoff. 'It is Thanksgiving, after all.'

'That is dark,' I replied, crouching down beside Arianna. 'And entirely admirable.'

The playroom was almost the same size as my entire apartment, I realized, and full of more toys than your average Toys R Us. I knew Erin tried not to spoil the kids, but it seemed Thomas had no such qualms. TJ, not quite three and Arianna, already four and a bit, were transfixed by the TV. Mouthing the words along with the characters and quietly holding hands, full of turkey and mashed potatoes and the joy of being a small, wealthy child.

'They have no idea how good they have it, do they?' I asked.

Mandy grinned from the little kitchen that peeked out onto Horatio Street.

'Not a clue,' she replied. 'And I hope they never

do. There are kids in Arianna's class at pre-school who already have their own iPhones.'

'No way,' I breathed. 'That's insane. Who are they calling?'

'They're mostly playing games and watching *Peppa Pig*,' she replied with a dishcloth over her shoulder. 'But there was one boy who ordered a series pass for *Game of Thrones* and believe me when I say that was an exciting day in show and tell.'

It seemed impossible that these teeny-tiny pink-cheeked angels could ever be any kind of trouble. They looked just like every other kid in the history of kidkind. They didn't know they were rich, they didn't know they lived in New York. They didn't even know it was weird that it was Thanksgiving and they were upstairs with a Swedish woman everyone called Mandy, even though that wasn't her actual name, instead of downstairs with the rest of their family. But that was for them – and their therapist – to work out in years to come.

'I know I'm going to sound like a knob however I ask this,' I asked, resting my wine on the little mid-century modern sidetable I was fairly sure TJ hadn't chosen from the Pottery Barn Kids website by himself, 'but is it weird? Looking after someone else's kids all day when they're right downstairs?'

Mandy laughed and poured herself a glass of water. Mandy laughed a lot, I noticed.

'No, because it's my job,' she replied, joining me on the floor. I watched as TJ's eyelids began to flicker, his little blond eyelashes fluttering against his cheek. 'People think of the nanny as someone to take the kids off the parents' hands, but it's not like that any more, at least not for me. My job is to give them peace of mind and hours back in their day. They're busy people, they have big jobs. If they didn't have a nanny, they would have to compromise part of their lives. It's kind of like having a cleaner, just on a bigger scale.'

I thought about the state of the apartment and Alex's any-day-now return from his trip. A cleaner would come in handy.

'I don't hide the kids away in the attic,' Mandy said, glancing around at our surroundings. 'Well, except for today. We're laying low today, huh, babies? TJ doesn't feel too good and Arianna is keeping him company.'

Ari nodded and stroked her brother's sleeping head before kissing him on the forehead and I shoved my entire fist in my mouth to stop myself from crying.

'They're good kids,' Mandy whispered. 'Erin is a great mom. Thomas is a New York dad.'

I gave her an understanding nod, fighting the urge to bawl my eyes out at the sight of Erin's angel babies, cuddling each other in front of my eighth favourite Disney movie.

'I know they both work ridiculous hours,' I said, imagining two other children, a brother and sister with Alex's black hair and my blue eyes. 'I know they need help.'

'It's hard being a parent here,' she agreed. 'Kids start school so early. How do you have them in class on the Upper East Side by seven forty-five and get yourself to work on time? How do you collect them at 2 p.m. without missing a meeting? Get them to soccer practice, or ballet class, or make sure they do their homework before it's time for bed?'

'School starts at seven forty-five?' I asked. She nodded. Surely she was mistaken. Maybe they read the time differently in Sweden. 'At least Erin doesn't have to worry about the homework bit just yet.'

'They have homework,' Mandy corrected. 'They're not doing quantum physics just yet, but they have a project or reading to do every day. Parents paying tens of thousands of dollars a year want their children to be challenged at school.'

'That much?' I whispered, very glad I was already sitting down. 'Arianna is four years old!'

'But if you don't get them in the right pre-school, they don't get in the right middle school, and some prep schools will only take from certain middle schools. And I don't need to tell you how important it is about which college you go to here in America.'

'No,' I said, shuffling forwards until I was resting on my knees. 'Please don't.'

I tried to remember exactly how much money we had in the bank at that exact moment. The fact I didn't know worried me almost as much as the fact that my baby would not be going to nursery with TJ and Arianna. Or middle school, or high school, or, apparently, university. My baby wasn't even born yet and it was already a failure.

'So, to me, it is not weird,' Mandy said, stretching to touch her toes. I was really starting to not like Mandy. 'Sometimes it is more strange when a parent comes to collect their child from school, you know? That's just how it is in New York.'

Puffing out my cheeks like a distressed blowfish, I looked out the windows at the cotton-wool clouds as they puffed past. We were in the roof of the house and each window had a little recessed seat with a padded cushion and a mini reading light, perfect for story time, or working on your trigonometry, or generally plotting to take over the world. Erin's kids might be the luckiest kids on earth, but it was all so much. Every second of their day was supervised and planned. How could someone already be strategizing for their child's university place when they were still walking around with a dummy in and watching Disney movies with their nanny?

'Oh, Arianna, no!'

I looked back to see Mandy wrestling my wine glass out of Arianna's tiny hands. She was already halfway through her second gulp, cheeks flushed and eyes bright, before she managed to snatch it away. On cue, Arianna opened her mouth wide and began to wail at the top of her tiny lungs.

'Like mother like daughter,' I said, hastily standing up as TJ followed his sister's lead and began to bawl. 'I'm sorry, is there anything I can do?'

'No,' she replied with a forced smile. Not laughing now, are you, Mands? 'We're all good. I wish I could tell you that was her first taste of wine.'

'I wish you could too.' I backed out of the room with my hand on my stomach. Maybe it would be for the best if our baby didn't spend too much time with their West Village buddies. 'I'll leave you alone, sorry again.'

'It's fine,' she promised. 'So nice to see you, Happy Thanksgiving!'

'Happy Thanksgiving,' I repeated, bolting down the stairs with my ankle boots in hand, wishing I'd never ventured up in the first place.

Even though we'd eaten an obscene amount of food at dinner, I was hungry again almost as soon as we walked out of Erin's house.

'The baby must be sugar deficient,' I explained, happily swinging my Duane Reade bag full of Ben & Jerry's through the air as Jenny and I walked home. When it was on offer at two for the price of one, it was rude not to get four. 'I would never eat this much if I wasn't pregnant.'

'Were you pregnant that first winter you lived here?' Jenny asked. 'When we got snowed in by that blizzard and you made a delivery guy come out and bring you Häagen-Dazs?'

I still felt bad about that and she knew it. By the time he got up to the apartment, the guy's fingers were blue. 'Remind me again why you aren't on your way upstate with your fiancé?' I asked.

'Because even though I would love to spend the remainder of the holiday in the bosom of my soon-to-be family, even though Mason's mom keeps suggesting I wear her 1980s Princess Diana-inspired wedding dress, I am so busy with my very important job, I have to work tomorrow,' she replied. 'Or it could be because I want to hit up the Black Friday sales at 6 a.m. tomorrow and he really doesn't. They're both super-feasible explanations.'

'You're such a martyr to your job,' I said, mustering up as much sympathy as I could. 'What a trouper.'

'This up-and-down weather is freaking me out.' Jenny rubbed her own pale hands together as we rounded the corner to her apartment. 'Make your mind up, New York. Is it autumn or is it winter? My hair can't cope with this.'

'Jennyyyy!'

A tall, shaggy-haired man was standing in front of our building, screaming my friend's name at the top of his voice. Before she could react, I grabbed hold of her jacket and yanked her into the stairwell of our neighbouring building.

'Shit, should we call the police?' I whispered, fumbling for my phone as he reached down to pick up a crumpled can from the floor and launch it at our window. Instead of smashing the glass, the light, aluminium projectile flew two feet up into the air and then came right back down and hit him in the face.

'Oh Lord,' Jenny sighed wearily and pushed her hair back behind her ears. 'It's Craig. So yeah, you should probably call them.'

'That's *Craig*?'

It had to have been months since I'd seen Alex's bandmate and those months had not been kind. Stills had been on hiatus for a while, even before Alex and Graham took off on their South East Asia adventure, so I hadn't spent any time with Craig in an absolute age, but whenever I did see him, he always asked after Jenny. I got the feeling he hadn't quite got over her ending things between them – she was the closest thing he'd had to a proper girlfriend in all the time I'd know him, which was in itself a sad statement. He'd hardly been in the running for boyfriend of the year when they were dating, or to be more accurate, when they were drunkenly hooking up, screaming at each other in the street, not talking for three weeks at a time, and then drunkenly hooking up again.

'He does this sometimes,' she said, starting back up the steps. 'I'm not usually here, but my neighbours have complained. He's totally going to get his ass thrown in jail if he doesn't cut it out.'

'He looks as though that's where he came from,' I said as I followed her into the street. 'This is not a man living his best life.'

'Craig!' Jenny barked as he bent back down to pick up his can and promptly fell over. He was wasted. 'What the hell are you doing?'

'You got engaged,' he said, pointing an accusing finger in her general direction from his comfy-looking spot on the filthy pavement. I looked down and saw a rat peeking out from behind a pile of abandoned cardboard boxes. Fantastic, we had an audience. 'You're engaged, and you didn't even tell me.'

'I was waiting to send you a wedding invitation,' she replied, equal parts annoyed and tired. I was equal parts concerned for Craig and concerned for my ice cream. 'We haven't been together in more than three years, Craig, what are you doing?'

'We're meant to end up together,' he said, slurring his words. He was so drunk for how early it was, I was almost impressed. 'We were the endgame, babe. We're Ross and Rachel, we're Carrie and Big.'

'Is he Carrie or are you?' I whispered over her shoulder. 'Because I know he's definitely not a Ross.'

'Oh, hey, Angela,' Craig muttered as he crawled around on the ground and tried to find his footing. The main problem with falling over drunk when you were over six feet tall was how incredibly hard it became to stand back up again. 'How's it going?'

'I really think you should go home,' Jenny said, hoisting him up to his feet and holding him in place until he looked somewhat steady. 'Do you want me to get you a taxi?'

'No,' he protested, pushing her away and pulling her closer at the same time. Craig had never been on the best of terms with a razor but his usual stubble had been replaced by a slightly rubbish ginger beard and his hair needed a good wash. As did his clothes and, I realized as I got closer, his entire body.

'I love you, Jen,' he insisted, slurring his way through his declaration of love. 'I know I'm drunk but that's because I'm mad, dude. You got engaged to some other guy and you weren't going to tell me? And I know why, I know why you didn't want me to know.'

'Enlighten us, please,' Jenny said, her forehead puckering slightly.

'Because you love me,' Craig said with a sloppy smile. 'You still love me and you knew if I knew that you knew that I knew you were engaged, you wouldn't be able to do it. You wouldn't be able to get married to this chump, this asshole, this – this—'

'Mason,' she finished his sentence for him. 'His name is Mason. And that's a super-fun theory, you asshat, but now it's time for you to go home. If you keep screaming in front of my apartment, the neighbours are going to have you arrested.'

'Your neighbours love me!' He shook her off and turned in a sharp pirouette, wobbling in place for just a second before he collapsed into a giggling heap on the ground, right next to the rat. 'Mrs Kleinmann used to give me cookies when you went to work. I think she wanted to bone me.'

'Goodnight, Craig,' Jenny called as I opened the front door, let her in, and quickly closed it behind us, leaving Jenny's former lover lying in the street. 'Get home safe.'

'Do you think he's all right?' I asked, following her up the stairs.

'I think he's fine,' she replied, searching for her own keys to open the apartment door. When she turned to look at me, her eyes were bright and her cheeks were pink. 'What a dick. What a douche. As if I'm in love with him! Like, I totally understand why he's still in love with me but wow, as *if* I'm in love with him.'

'As if,' I echoed as we walked inside and flipped on the lights. Pregnancy and parenting books were piled high on the coffee table, competing for space with bridal magazines and tear sheets from wedding dress catalogues.

'I was the best thing that ever happened to that man and he blew it,' Jenny went on, sailing past her little library. 'He doesn't get to show up now and announce we're meant to be. Who does he think he is?'

'He thinks he's Craig,' I replied. 'Remember? He's a massive wanker who loves himself and never thinks about anyone else. That's why you broke up with him.'

'Yeah, you're right.' She trotted right over to the window, pulled up the corner of the blinds, and looked out onto the street. I couldn't see Craig, but I could hear him. He was still there. 'Wanna watch a movie?'

'Why not?' I replied while I stashed my ice cream in the freezer. I looked back to see her still staring through the window. 'What were you thinking?'

'You choose,' she said in a faraway voice, biting her thumbnail while she watched her ex flail around in a pile of garbage. 'I'm easy.'

'Hopefully not that easy,' I said as I took myself off to the toilet.

Craig was a semi-unemployed drummer in his mid-thirties, who shared an apartment with four other dudes and had seemingly forgotten how to use a washing machine. Mason was a handsome, award-winning journalist who owned his own Manhattan apartment, believed cleanliness was next to sexiness and had put a chunk of ice on her finger, so big I had to keep checking it for polar bears. Even with her track record for self-sabotage, there was no way Jenny would do anything as stupid as even entertain Craig's nonsense.

Or at least, I didn't think she would. I came back into the living room bearing a bowl of ice cream to see her beaming at him through the window, a Puerto Rican Juliet to Craig's grubby, hipster Romeo.

'Oh, bugger,' I muttered to myself. 'We're going to need a bigger bowl.'

CHAPTER ELEVEN

'Good morning, roomie,' Jenny sang as she pushed my bedroom door open at 7 a.m. on Tuesday morning.

After Thanksgiving at Erin's, we'd spent the entire weekend planning her wedding. If Sadie was throwing the wedding of the century, Jenny would have the wedding of the millennium. I was more than a little bit relieved when she decided to stay over at Mason's on Sunday evening to discuss potential colourways and honeymoon destinations – I needed the night off. Monday had passed in a blur the way all Mondays did – press day was press day was press day – and finally it was Tuesday. Finally, it was time for my meeting with Joe.

'I've got herbal tea for you,' Jenny said, placing a loaded tray on the edge of my bed. 'I've got avocado on multigrain toast with a poached egg, and I've got your prenatal multi-vitamin.'

'And what have you got for you?' I asked, sitting myself upright while Jenny presented me with a breakfast tray complete with a single pink rose in a tiny vase.

'Leftover pizza.' She rammed half a slice of cardboard-looking pepperoni pizza into her mouth before I could protest. I didn't want to know how old it was. 'You need your wholegrains and your protein and your good fats. This is, like, a complete meal here.'

'Thanks, but I don't know if I can eat that much first thing in the morning,' I said. My stomach turned at the sight of the poached egg and I felt myself go green. Ever prepared, Jenny grabbed the little bin from beside my bed and shoved it in front of my face right before I hurled. I dabbed at my mouth with the cloth napkin on the tray and winced. 'Morning sickness, officially the least fun part of being preggers.'

'Shit. You're really, totally pregnant,' she marvelled in a muffled voice. I looked up to see her holding the bin in one hand, stroking my hair with the other, the remains of the pizza slice held between her teeth. It would take more than a vomiting pregnant woman to come between Jenny Lopez and her appetite.

'The ten pregnancy tests you made me wee on last week weren't enough proof for you?' I asked, lying back down. 'You actually need to see me puke?'

'That was mainly for the LOLs.' She looked into the bin, pulled a sour face, and then set it down on the floor at the side of the bed. 'I still can't believe I got you to pee on every single one of them.'

'I've never seen you look happy to see a pregnancy test before,' I said, pushing the tray away and forcing myself up in bed. 'Maybe my mum was right, there is a first time for everything.'

She grabbed the napkin from my tray and hurled it at my face. It was nice to be home.

'Don't take this the wrong way, but you're pretty good at being pregnant,' she said, pushing the bin away from the bed with her foot. 'Kind of assumed you might freak a little more.'

'Me too,' I admitted as she climbed under the covers beside me. 'Whenever I really stop and think about it, I sort of panic. Because the idea of having a child is mental. But when I'm not throwing up or fighting constant and complete exhaustion, it's not as bad as I thought it might be. Weird, but not bad.'

'Then it's the opposite of planning a wedding,' Jenny said. 'Thanks for all your help this weekend, by the way.'

'You didn't really give me much choice, did you?' I replied, shuddering at the memory of Pinterest boards flashing before my eyes.

In three short days, Jenny's wedding had gone from a small, private affair in Hawaii to the society event of the season. I'd talked her down from booking the Plaza, but we had still spent a good four hours debating whether or not they needed to host welcome cocktails, a rehearsal dinner, and a thank you brunch. A week ago, the only things she needed at her wedding were me, Erin, Mason, and a steady supply of champagne, now we were looking for a venue that could hold 200 people and would allow her to bring live doves in for the ceremony.

'Are you sure Mason is down for all this?' I asked. 'He did seem awfully keen on Maui.'

'Mason wants whatever I want,' she replied happily. 'Maui would be fine, but a wedding should be a celebration of love and I want to celebrate with as many people as possible and in a way that does our relationship justice. We're not barefoot on the beach people, Angie.'

'No,' I said as she waved her ring at me. Again. 'But

I'm not sure you're St Patrick's Cathedral ceremony, silver service dinner for two hundred, releasing live doves as you say "I do", people either.'

'I am,' she replied with complete conviction.

'But is Mason?' I asked again. 'It is his wedding too.'

'You're so funny,' she laughed. I wasn't sure why. 'Mason wants whatever I want.'

I raised an eyebrow.

'Mason wants to spend thousands of dollars on a flower wall?'

'The flower wall was so beautiful,' Jenny replied, climbing out of bed and picking bits of lint off her leggings. 'I've got to go, I have SpiritSprint in twenty minutes.'

'You're very brave,' I said, reluctantly following her out of bed. I had a big day ahead of me. 'I don't think I could show my face back there.'

Tying her hair up into a huge pineapple on top of her head, she rolled her eyes skywards.

'I'm going to a different location,' she admitted. 'We're kind of banned from the Union Square place.'

'We are?' I asked brightly. 'Oh, good.'

'I didn't think you'd be super sad about it.' She bent over and touched her toes, bouncing lightly up and down. I attempted to do the same and gave up when my back creaked as my fingertips struggled to reach the tops of my feet. 'Good luck with your meeting today. Let me know how it goes or if you need me to kill someone for you.'

'It's nice to know I can depend on you,' I said, throwing my napkin at her as she left. 'Love you.'

'Love you too,' she shouted from down the hallway. 'Now get your pukey butt in the shower. You stink and you have to wash your hair. Like, *have* to. Dry shampoo is not an option.'

You just couldn't put a price on a friendship like ours.

After setting hourly reminders on my phone, I arrived at the restaurant Joe had chosen for lunch fifteen minutes early. I couldn't decide if it was a good or bad sign that he'd suggested we meet outside the office. On the one hand, who didn't love a free meal? But on the other, what if they were removing all trace of me from the building the second I stepped outside?

'Ms Clark?'

A neat waitress in a white shirt and black tie appeared with a too big smile on her face as I approached her podium in my smart Sandro shift and Jenny's black-patent Louboutin Mary-Janes.

'Let me show you to your table, Mr Herman is already here,' she said, gesturing for me to follow her down the steps and into the brightly lit dining room of Union Square Café.

My pulse fluttered as I tiptoed through the tables. How was he already here? I was so early! Damn that man and his timely nature.

'Joe,' I said, accepting a socially acceptable cheek kiss then sitting down. He really was very tall. Too tall. No one needed to be that big unless they were a professional wrestler or part of the circus. I wondered if he had to buy his trousers somewhere special.

'Thanks for meeting me down here,' he said, nodding for the waitress to fill up my water glass. 'It's the only problem with Spencer: there are no good restaurants in Times Square.'

'You didn't fancy Red Lobster?' I quipped as I accepted a menu.

Joe looked back at me with a blank stare.

'I'm joking,' I assured him quickly. 'I never go there, obviously, it's terrible. Eurgh, chain restaurants. Who would eat at Red Lobster?'

He didn't need to know the staff at the one on 7th Avenue knew me by name and always rewarded me with extra biscuits for being such a regular customer.

'I know this place is a publishing cliché, but I love the chicken salad,' Joe said, smiling at the waitress.

What kind of a man ordered a salad when he was eating out on expenses?

'I'll have the chicken salad as well,' I said. I copied Joe's smile but the waitress couldn't quite manage the same cheery response. 'Sounds delish.'

He was right, Union Square was a publishing world cliché, a famous restaurant full of good old boys on three-martini lunches, wining and dining each other with everyone eyeing each other across the room. I'd been for dinner once before but never for lunch, and now I understood why. I was fifteen years and one penis out of place.

'A glass of wine?' Joe asked, scanning the wine list. 'The Chenin Blanc always pairs well.'

I looked around the restaurant. Every single person at every single table had a drink in front of them.

'I actually have to proofread some pages when I get back,' I told him tapping my temple as I spoke. 'Better keep a clear head.'

No one told you the first skill you needed to perfect as a new mother was lying through your back teeth, and fast.

'We'll stick with water then,' he replied, handing back the massive ring binder-cum-wine list back to the waitress. It was almost bigger than she was. 'Shall we get the difficult part of lunch out of the way so we can enjoy our food?'

'Difficult?'

I crossed my legs under the table and knocked my knee against the hard wood. Joe flinched but ignored the loud bang.

'Not difficult,' he replied, shaking out his napkin. 'I meant to say, let's get work out of the way before the food comes. I'm not as good with words as you.'

'Flattery will get you everywhere,' I laughed nervously before gulping down half my glass of water. I couldn't tell if it was hot in the restaurant or if it was just me. My deodorant was already working overtime.

'As you know, we've already made changes in the marketing team,' he said, pulling his iPad out of his leather briefcase and tapping away at the screen. Tablets and smartphones really had ruined the entire concept of lunch. I briefly considered spilling my water on it but the last thing I needed was to give him more reasons to sack me. 'And the new streamlined teams are already showing some real progress.'

I did know. When he said 'streamlined', he meant slashed to pieces. It was horrible, watching everyone stare at their phone as call after call came down from HR and person after person left but did not come back. No wonder the new team was doing so well: they were petrified they would be fired if they didn't.

'We're going to be implementing a similar strategy across the sales teams in the next two weeks,' Joe said, handing me a spreadsheet.

No good had ever come of a spreadsheet, it was one of life's absolutes. No one ever kept a spreadsheet that charted happy things like the number of kittens in the Tri-State area or the various talents of the Hemsworth brothers. *That* needed keeping track of. What if you wanted to know which one was the tallest, which one played guitar, important things like that? There wasn't always time for Google.

'What happens after you streamline the sales team?' I asked weakly.

'Two things.' He pushed up his sleeves, clearly ready to get down to business. 'Firstly, I want to bring a video content specialist in to grow the *Gloss* website.'

I blinked in surprise. He was giving me more staff? It was literally the last thing I'd expected him to say.

'Oh. Right, then.'

Underneath the table, my feet throbbed in my borrowed Louboutin pumps. How had they swollen to twice their original size already? And more importantly, why did my baby hate me? It was one thing to make me fat, it was another to make my shoes too small.

'There is tremendous potential for digital growth at Spencer,' Joe went on. I remembered what Erin had told me. He had run the digital publishing business at his last company, so this did make some kind of sense. 'And *Gloss* could be the right root for that growth. Delia very much believes you are the right person to nurture it.'

The man loved his gardening metaphors.

'I am quite the nurturer,' I agreed, silently shushing my unborn baby who had eaten nothing but sour sugary sweets for the first ten weeks of its in utero existence. Hmm. No wonder it was punishing me through foot-swelling torture techniques.

'The work you've done with *Gloss* has been fantastic,' Joe said, grabbing at the air as he spoke. 'It's a bold brand. It's fresh, it's young, it's in touch with what's happening in the world. It's social media, it's selfies, it's emojis and LOLs.'

'Right . . . ' I kicked Jenny's shoes off under the table. *Gloss* might be young and in touch but Joe had just made sure I knew he definitely wasn't. 'Thanks. Just to be clear, when we started *Gloss*, it wasn't as a brand, it was as a magazine. We created it, just me and Delia in the beginning, we created it for real reasons—'

'The magazine is great, but the brand has the potential to reach so much further,' Joe interrupted. 'A great mag can become an amazing brand, Angela. I want to see *Gloss* on the phones of every woman aged sixteen to thirty in the world.'

'That would be amazing,' I replied, thinking that he really shouldn't be looking at sixteen-year-olds' phones, no matter the reason. 'My team have some great ideas to grow the website going forward—'

Joe held up a finger to cut me off and it was all I could do not to slap it out of the air.

'Magazine, website, video content, skincare line, make-up line, slogan shirts, tote bags, designer collabs.'

'Right,' I said. 'What are you talking about?'

'The *Gloss* brand,' he said, punching the air and almost taking out the waitress at the same time. 'Brand extensions, brand growth. Maximizing our content, exploiting the product.'

'I usually try to stay away from terms like product and exploit,' I replied carefully. 'So far, the deal has been that we put out a really good magazine, make some money, and then corporate more or less leaves us alone.'

'Wasted potential,' Joe announced. 'You could be more.'

'Me?' I asked. 'Or *Gloss*?'

'Both,' he replied. 'Why aren't you giving your audience all that you could, Angela Clark?'

'We gave every reader a very nice lip gloss last week,' I pointed out. 'And there haven't been any complaints so far.'

Well, there had been one, but if someone was offended by the sight of a shirtless Ryan Gosling, the problem was with them, not us.

'To reach the audience, we've got to know that audience, we've got to *be* that audience,' he said, holding up his other hand to silence me. 'We have to know what women want.'

I pursed my lips and held my tongue, just for a second. Obviously, no one knew exactly what women wanted like he did.

'I want to bring in someone who knows those women because they *are* those women.' He was practically rabid. 'I want someone raw and fresh and hungry.'

'You already have those women, they already work at *Gloss*,' I reminded him. Where was my bloody salad? The sooner the food arrived, the sooner he could shove it in his gob and stop talking. 'And trust me, no one is hungrier than I am.'

At least that much was true. I hadn't eaten all day.

'Have you heard of evolution?' Joe asked.

It was a strange question, but I'd got used to those since I started working in the media.

'Yeah, they actually teach it in schools in the UK,' I replied. 'They do here as well, don't they?'

'No, I mean Eva-Lution, the YouTuber,' he said, his smile flickering.

'Actually, I have,' I said as he took the iPad back and pulled up Eva's YouTube channel. Her intro video popped up on autoplay and I automatically smiled back at her cheerful face. 'I think she's great. You want us to start doing her kind of thing?'

'Not quite,' Joe replied. 'I want you to do *exactly* her thing. I've had some preliminary conversations with Eva and she's prepared to put her channel on the backburner for a while and come work with me to develop our online presence.'

The video kept playing at our silent table.

'At *Gloss*?' I asked, eventually finding my voice.

'At Spencer,' Joe replied.

'And you've already spoken to her about this?'

'Clearly.'

'That's brilliant, obviously,' I said, choosing my words carefully. 'But I'm curious to how that fits in with the rest of the editorial team; we don't have any digital-specific staff at *Gloss*.'

I looked around. Surely there should be bread by now? I couldn't think this fast on an empty stomach and fancy places always had bread.

'And that's the second thing I want to talk to you about . . . ' Joe put away the iPad and leaned backwards in his chair with a very big, ever so slightly smug smile on his face. 'Angela, you know we think you have a bright future at Spencer Media.'

'That's always nice to hear,' I said, hoping he couldn't hear the loud rumblings of my disagreeing stomach. 'Thank you.'

'As I mentioned when we met before, it's my job to make sure the women's brands at Spencer flourish and that likely means some pruning.'

'You did mention that,' I agreed, very hot, very hungry, and very, very nervous. Why couldn't he have ended the conversation with the compliment?

'Condé Nast has *Vogue*, Spencer Media has *Belle*,'

he said, laying his hands on the table. 'Obviously, we're not going to close our flagship fashion magazine any time soon.'

'Well, that makes sense,' I replied, flapping my arms very, very slightly. Sweat stains were not going to help this situation. '*Belle*'s a great publication, they've got a great team.'

'Glad you agree. Keeping *Belle* leaves me with a clearer choice,' Joe said, looking me straight in the eye. 'In January, we'll be closing *Gloss* or *The Look*.'

I stared across the table and felt my entire body seize up.

'Spencer will have one weekly women's lifestyle magazine with a supporting website alongside *Belle*'s high-end fashion content,' he explained. 'The market does not currently support both. *Gloss*'s brand is young and has a great online presence, but *The Look* puts out three times as many copies as you do.'

My breath caught in my throat and I couldn't swallow. My nose began to tickle and I knew what was about to happen. Do not cry, I ordered myself. You will not cry in front of this man. You will wait and go back to the office to cry in the toilets like a normal Spencer employee.

'That's not to say we're definitely going forward with *The Look*. Their sales are in decline and your online presence is skyrocketing. We're conducting some market research before we make the decision,' Joe said. 'But you really are valued at Spencer, Angela, and I want you to know there is a position for you in the new structure.'

A position, he said. Not 'you won't lose your job'. Very big difference.

'Right now the plan is that Eva will be in control of the editorial voice on the website and we'll have an editor at the magazine.'

I breathed out slowly, paused for a second and took a slow, deep breath in. Someone's magazine was going to close. Dozens of people were going to be out of a job. However you looked at this, there was no genuinely good news, only news that made you feel like a terrible person because you keeping your job meant someone else losing theirs. Why hadn't I just stayed home with Jenny and spent the day researching photo booths and rentable doves?

'One editor,' I said, trying not to think about how much this felt like the first annual Spencer Media Hunger Games. 'At one magazine?'

'That's right,' he agreed as the waitress reappeared with two massive salads. Suddenly I wasn't very hungry any more. 'I understand this is a lot to take in. We really want to talk to everyone involved before we make any major decisions.'

'Other than the decision to close an entire magazine?' I replied as she placed them down on the table. 'That decision has been made, hasn't it?'

Dark stars began to sparkle around my field of vision and a red-hot flush rolled over my entire body. This wasn't good.

'Of course, I'm very excited to see the Generation *Gloss* event first-hand – something like that is really going to raise your profile and the brand's stock, so to speak. I'd also like you to pull together a presentation detailing your three-year strategy for *Gloss*,' he said, picking up his knife and fork and digging in to his lunch while I sat there stunned, 'taking into account Eva's involvement with the online component and the potential global expansion.'

He smiled at me as though we were both in on some sort of secret.

'Oh, OK then,' I said, secretly wanting to punch him in the throat. 'And when were you wanting that by?'

'Next Tuesday,' he replied. 'At 9 a.m.'

'Next Tuesday? Seven days from now?' I asked. What was happening on Tuesday? Oh shit, I realized, I had my twelve-week scan appointment with Dr Laura but of course, I couldn't tell him that.

'Next Tuesday doesn't give me a lot of time, Joe. We have Generation *Gloss* this weekend.'

'Yeah, I can't wait for the party,' he said, completely ignoring my concern. 'Delia says it's a lot of fun.'

'Delia says a lot, doesn't she?' I frowned.

If the presentation was at nine and my appointment with Dr Laura was at ten thirty, I could probably make it. Still, a 9 a.m. meeting was perfectly timed for me to puke all over him.

'This is a positive development, Angela,' Joe insisted, clearly not even slightly bothered by the fact he was about to make dozens of people unemployed. This was just business to him, we were numbers on a spreadsheet. 'I am very excited for us to work together.'

'Giddy as a kipper,' I said under my breath, staring at my food.

'Think of it as the beginning of a new season,' he said through a mouthful of salad. 'I am excited to see what we're going to bring in with the harvest.'

Sweating, shoeless, and starving, I picked up my fork and forced a piece of chicken into my mouth, leaving my knife on the table. Just in case my brain came up with a better use for it than cutting up lettuce.

'How was your meeting?' Cici asked as I sailed back through the office, doggy bag in one hand, Jenny's shoes in the other.

'Wasn't great,' I replied, looking at all the staff, beavering away in blissful ignorance. 'Any messages?'

'Alex called,' Cici said and my heart almost leapt out of my chest. 'He said he couldn't get through to your cell? I said he should call you back but blah blah no reception blah blah, he'll be home soon but he'll talk to you before then.'

'Soon? Did he say exactly when?' I pulled out my phone to see it was still in airplane mode. Damn me for being so professional during lunch. 'Did he say which day?'

'No,' she replied, pushing her glasses up her nose. Worryingly, I was starting to get used to them. 'What did you eat for lunch? You look weird, like, more than usual. Are you going to puke again?'

'I'm fine,' I insisted even though it was clearly not true. 'Can you cancel my stuff for this afternoon. I've got something I need to work on.'

'I need to talk to you about the Generation *Gloss* party,' she said, following me into my office. 'I can get both Gigi and Bella if we drop the costumes. They won't dress up.'

'Whatever you need to do.' I swiped around at the papers on my desk, looking for my mouse. Maybe Alex had emailed. 'Thanks.'

'My mom knows their mom,' she shrugged, dropping into a chair. The bottom of her cropped sweater rolled up to reveal an altogether too toned tummy. 'I'll figure it out and let you know. Everything went good with Joe?'

I looked up as I fumbled around for a hair tie, yanking my hair back in a ponytail. Could I tell her? Should I tell her?

'He wants me to pull together a presentation, that's

all,' I said. There was no point worrying her and I still wasn't entirely certain I could trust her. 'For next week.'

'Gross,' she replied.

'Yup,' I agreed.

'Did you talk about finding me a new role?' she asked.

'Didn't come up,' I said. 'Sorry, I'll sort it, but I really need to think about this presentation right now.'

'Famous last words,' she said, standing to leave as Jenny's name appeared on the screen of my mobile.

'Be careful,' I called as she walked away. 'That sounds like something I would say.'

'Super gross,' Cici muttered, looking disgusted with herself.

'What's up?' I asked, answering the phone.

'Do you have the number for Annie Leibovitz?' she asked.

'No?' I replied. 'But I could probably get Cici to find it? Actually, Cici might have it – she probably took her passport photo. You need it for a project?'

'Did you know she shot Kim and Kanye's wedding?' Jenny said. 'I know it sounds crazy, but I figured I'd call and see how much she charges. The photos are basically the biggest investment you can make in your wedding – they're the only part of it that lasts forever.'

'Other than your actual marriage,' I replied flatly.

'Oh, yeah, for sure,' she said. 'That too.'

'I can't talk right now,' I said, scanning my inbox for an email from Alex. Nothing. Maybe he'd just called for a random chat. Stupid bloody Joe and his stupid bloody lunch. Now I had another reason to dislike him. 'See you tonight?'

'I might be late,' she said, sounding distracted. 'I've got an appointment with a cake designer.'

'You haven't even got a wedding date yet,' I reminded her. 'Shouldn't you know when you're getting married before you start looking at cakes?'

'You have to book them a year in advance,' Jenny replied. 'People plan their weddings around these cakes, Angela. Ivanka Trump used them.'

'Even more reason for you not to bother,' I said. 'Let's talk about it tonight.'

'Yeah, sure.' I could tell she was already thinking about something else. 'If you could get Cici to shoot me Annie's details, that would be awesome. And maybe Patrick Demarchelier. So I have a backup.'

'Bye, Jenny,' I said, ending the call and sweeping my hands over my face. 'Blood pressure, Angela, blood pressure.'

It had been the shittiest day in recent memory and it was still only one forty-five in the afternoon. Joe wanted to close my magazine, Jenny wanted Annie Leibovitz to take photos at her wedding, and all I wanted was a quiet sit down and a chat with the man I had married. So why did it feel like I was the one with the most ridiculous request?

CHAPTER TWELVE

'Are you sure I don't look pregnant?' I asked, turning to review my costume from every angle. The flowing ice-blue dress skimmed over my changing curves, moving as I moved. 'I feel as though I look massive.'

'Look up,' Jenny instructed as I stood still so she could apply my mascara. 'Don't sweat it, doll face, no one is going to be looking at your stomach.'

'Fair point,' I replied, blinking.

My costume had been chosen with clear objectives. It had to be practical since I was technically working, it had to look good in photographs, it had to cover up my stomach and, most importantly, according to Jenny, it had to draw all attention elsewhere, just in case. Dr Laura had said I wouldn't really start to show until around eighteen weeks but the bump had missed that memo, as had my boobs.

'They're insane,' Jenny confirmed. She screwed the lid back on the mascara and threw it on her bed along with the rest of her entire make-up collection. 'And they're spectacular. After you push it out, you should totally consider a boob job.'

'Thanks.' I cupped myself and bounced up and down slightly, just to make sure I wouldn't fall out. The dress was gorgeous. Ice-blue silk with badass metal detailing around the waist and narrow shoulder straps, but despite its origins it really wasn't suitable for a skirmish of any kind. 'I couldn't have done this without you.'

'Of course not, babe,' she replied as though that was obvious, tugging lightly at the elaborately braided wig she had talked me into. 'Have you ever thought about going platinum blonde?'

I'd been concerned when Cici offered to oversee the Generation *Gloss* opening gala, but as far as I could tell, not a single person had died during the planning of the party. Having spent the entire week up to my eyeballs in PowerPoint slides, trying to edit the magazine, and save it at the same time, all while not letting on to the team that anything was wrong, the last thing I wanted to do was spend Saturday night pretending I wasn't pregnant. Who knew that was going to be more exhausting than actually being pregnant? It had been the most exhausting four days of my life and I badly wanted to spend my evening face first in a pizza and *Real Housewives* marathon. But the party was important, Joe had made that very clear. *The Look* didn't have an events side, they didn't have this kind of connection with their readers. I needed this party to go so well he had no choice but to choose us.

'I really need tonight to go smoothly,' I said, staring at the stranger in the mirror. Jenny could work wonders with an eyeshadow brush, so it barely even looked like me. Sometimes I forgot she was a fairy godmother disguised as an extra from *Sex and the City*. 'Jen, I'm just so tired all the time.'

'You're going to have a good time,' Jenny promised. 'Think about it. Dancing, hanging out with the only three genuinely cool people you work with, taking sneaky selfies of celebrities to post on Facebook which will make people you went to school with super-jealous. You've been working your balls off, Angie. Go enjoy yourself.'

'You're right,' I said, with a happy 'humpf'. 'I've forgotten what actual fun feels like. Maybe I need to blow off a bit of steam. Are you sure you won't come?'

'I wish I could but I can't.' A huge grin crept across her face as she admired her handiwork. 'Mason is taking me out for dinner. He's been crazed this week, I've barely even spoken to him and we have so much wedding stuff we need to lock down.'

'Like a date?' I suggested. 'And a destination? And a budget?'

'Quit worrying about my wedding and go kick some ass at your party,' she said, holding up her hand for a high five. 'Maybe you can smother Joe Herman with your epic cleavage.'

'I'd love to try to explain that to HR!' I gave her a kiss on the cheek, careful not to disturb my epic contouring and searched for my borrowed, diamanté-studded Judith Leiber clutch. 'Me and the bump might be late, so don't worry.'

'We'll probably stay at his,' she replied, patting my stomach goodbye. 'That's where we keep the sex swing.'

I paused as I bent down to slip on my shoes; her face was the picture of innocence.

'I don't even want to know if you're joking,' I muttered. 'Are you sure people will get my costume?'

'Oh yeah,' she said, stretching out her arms to bow down. 'This is the best costume ever.'

'You're right,' I said, checking myself over in the mirror by the door. 'It's good. Better than the *Ghostbusters* costume I wore last year.'

'Just because Bradley Cooper mistook you for a janitor doesn't mean it was a bad costume,' she argued. 'Maybe just not a good *Ghostbusters* costume.'

'I'll see you tomorrow,' I said, grabbing three stuffed dragons from the bed.

'Don't do anything I wouldn't do,' she cackled as I walked out the door, flipping up my middle finger as I went.

Whatever reservations I may have had about Cici managing the party were swept away the second my cab pulled up in front of Capitale. Outside the venue, huge pale pink banners sporting the *Gloss* logo billowed in the wind and there were just enough paps hanging around to make me feel confident she'd pulled in the right kind of famous types for me to impress Jenny later on. They all looked up as my driver opened the car door and I delivered a dazzling smile. En masse, they glanced at my face, gave my boobs a cursory once-over, then went back to fiddling with their cameras.

'Arseholes,' I muttered, jogging up the steps and adjusting my long, blonde wig.

Two extra-large security guards smiled at me as I walked up the staircase and rushed to open the doors for me.

'Thank you,' I said with a small curtsey. 'Nice to see there are still some gentlemen around.'

'Anything for the Mother of Dragons,' said the guy on the left.

'Thank god,' I laughed, relieved. 'I was worried no

one would get it. Last year everyone else had the most elaborate costumes and I looked like a right idiot.'

'I don't believe it,' said the guy on the right. 'This is definitely the best costume of the night.'

'I bet you say that to all the girls,' I said happily as I walked inside.

The huge smile on my face evaporated the second they opened the doors. The party was immense. Music was pumping so loudly I could feel it in my lungs and there were already so many people inside, laughing, smiling and dancing, a wave of body heat slapped me where I stood. He most certainly had not said that to all the girls.

Not a single person was wearing a costume. Except for me.

'Angela?'

Megan stood in front of me, gorgeous in a gold sequin mini dress, her hair framing her beautifully made up face in perfect beachy waves. Unless her costume was 'Stunning New York Beauty Editor', she had not even attempted to get dressed up. And neither had anyone else.

'No one's in costume,' I said, eyes flitting back and forth. 'No one is dressed up.''

'Cici sent a memo?' Megan replied, stepping back from me very slightly. 'You cancelled the costumes?'

'No one is dressed up . . . ' I breathed as people began to turn and stare. I was standing in the middle of one of the fanciest parties I had ever attended, a party hosted by *my* magazine, and I was dressed as stupid Khaleesi from stupid *Game of Thrones*, and if the obscene frock, ridiculous wig, and RuPaul's *Drag Race*-inspired make-up weren't drawing enough attention my way, the three stuffed dragons I was dragging behind certainly raised one or two questions.

There were two options. Run for the door, fly back to England, and pretend I'd never heard of New York City or, somehow, style it out.

'What would Jenny Lopez do?' I whispered to myself as people began to pull out their phones. I was seconds away from becoming a viral sensation. 'What would Jenny Lopez do?'

It was a long time since I'd had to invoke that little mantra. I rolled back my shoulders, raised my chin and took a deep breath. Platinum blonde hair was in. Super-slutty dresses designed for fantasy warrior queens not so much.

'If anyone asks,' I said, ignoring the burn of humiliation in the pit of my stomach, 'the dress is archive Versace.'

'Is it?' Megan asked, giving me a good once-over.

'Nope,' I replied. 'But the fact you asked instead of laughing in my face means I might get away with this.'

Leaving Megan behind, I pushed through the crowds and headed for the giant double doors that led to the dance floor and, most importantly, the VIP area. If I could make it onto the other side of the velvet rope, no one would look twice at me. Who cared about an overly contoured magazine editor when there was the very real possibility of a Kendall Jenner sighting?

Surreptitiously swiping at my overly bronzed cheeks, I pushed through the crowds, the pulsing music carrying me onwards until I found the promised land.

'Hi, I'm the editor of the magazine.' I smiled at a tiny black-haired girl holding a tablet and the enormous bald man beside her. Neither looked even slightly impressed. 'Angela Clark?'

'I'm going to need to see some ID,' the girl replied. The bouncer remained stoic and unmoving. Apparently, Targaryens strolling through New York parties were a regular thing.

'It's right here,' I said, pawing through my tiny borrowed clutch bag. I knew I'd put my driving licence in there; I remembered taking it out of my wallet with my credit card and – oh shit, leaving both of them on the kitchen top.

'Because I'm an idiot, I think I've left it at home,' I shouted over the music. 'But I can see some of my friends in there, if I could just pop in and get one of them, they'll confirm I'm me.'

'I'm sorry, but I can't let you in,' the girl replied as the bouncer stepped in front of her, legs spread, hands in front of his nuts, intimidating middle-distance stare.

'I'm the editor of *Gloss*,' I insisted, pointing up at the neon sign that buzzed above the stage. 'This is my magazine's event? Really, if you'd just go and ask those two people over there . . . ' I pointed towards Jason and Sophie who were laughing their heads off and edging as close as humanly possible to someone I thought I recognized as a Jonas Brother.

'If you could step aside, that would be great,' the girl said. 'Otherwise, we're going to have to ask you to leave.'

'By god, it's Angela Clark!'

A loud British voice boomed in my ear and I was suddenly hoisted into the air and thrown over someone's shoulder. I grabbed at the front of my dress and prayed that my knickers weren't showing. I'd already made a show of myself once, I didn't need a wardrobe malfunction to make matters worse.

'James?' I yelped, suddenly face to face with a very firm, tuxedo-clad arse.

'Expecting anyone else?' James Jacobs replied as the girl immediately unfastened the velvet rope and ushered us inside. 'Look at your tits!'

'I didn't know you were in town,' I yelped as he bounced me up and down on his shoulder. 'Why didn't you tell me you were coming? I haven't seen you in bloody months.'

'It's been more than a year, actually,' he sniffed, before slapping my arse. 'Which you'd know if you really loved me. Why are you dressed as Elsa from *Frozen*?'

'You know you broke my heart after you left *Les Mis*,' I ignored him as we sailed past the velvet rope, no questions asked. Such were the perks of being a legitimately famous actor. 'I wasn't sure I'd ever be able to speak to you again.'

'What if I told you I'd auditioned for *Doctor Who*?' he asked, setting me down in front of a red velvet corner booth, separated from the action by a sheer curtain.

'No way,' I gasped, hastily shoving my boobs back where they belonged.

He nodded as he slid into his seat. 'Yes, way. Didn't get it though, did I? Too scared of a good thing.'

'Well, that's their loss,' I assured him, trying not to look too disappointed and joining him in the booth. 'You would have been amazing.'

'I know.' He tipped his head to one side, his curly dark hair falling in front of his eyes and smirked. 'I did rub my balls on the TARDIS console, though, so good luck to the new Doctor.'

'Classy as always.'

Sonic screwdrivers were all well and good, but I hoped they had some Dettol wipes on board.

He yanked me into his lap and kissed me full on the lips. I was sure I saw a camera flash somewhere, but me and James Jacobs caught mid-snog was beyond old news. We could have had full sex in the middle of the dance floor and no one would have believed he was straight, his closeted ship had long since sailed.

'It's good to see you, Clark. Where's that devastatingly handsome husband of yours?' James asked. He glanced around the room to check out the quality of the other celebs and smirked to himself. He was easily the most A-list person here and I wasn't sure if that was a good or bad thing. Great for the ego but perhaps not so good for the profile.

'He's away,' I said, pulling the fabric of my dress neatly over my lap to avoid presenting my vagina to Justin Bieber. Hadn't Cici told me he wasn't coming? 'He's been travelling around South East Asia for a couple of months but he's due home any day.'

'South East Asia?' James wrinkled his perfect nose and nodded at the waiter who appeared with two glasses of water and two cocktails. 'Without you? Should I prepare his coming out party?'

'Maybe.' I took a sip of the water and then picked up the cocktail, preparing to nurse it for the rest of the evening. I was getting good at fake drinking. 'He did say he'd been spooning Graham.'

'Makes sense that he'd be a top,' he nodded confidently. 'While the cat's away, the mice must play. Let's get smashed.'

He raised his glass to mine before taking a deep glug.

'What's wrong?' he asked when I hesitated. 'Knocked up?'

I opened my mouth to give him one of my routine answers. I was on antibiotics, I'd drunk too much the night before, I needed to stay sober because it was a work thing. But before I could say a word, his eyes opened wide and he began to cough, spluttering his sticky cocktail all over the table.

'Jesus Christ on a bike.' He grabbed a napkin from a passing waiter with a tray full of canapés and wiped his mouth before the drink stained his white shirt. 'You *are* bloody well pregnant, aren't you?'

'Please be quiet!' I begged, edging around the booth until we were side by side. 'No one knows because I only just found out. I haven't even told Alex. You have to keep it a secret.'

'Everyone knows I can't keep a secret,' James whined, raking his hands through his hair and throwing his head back like the big drama queen he was. 'Unless it's about my sexuality for thirty-three years, then, yes, but in general, absolutely not.'

He had a point.

'Well, you're going to have to try,' I said, giving him my sternest mum look, complete with a mouth like a cat's arse. 'You massive bellend.'

'It's just unexpected, that's all.' He pulled me into another big hug, hiccupping as he kissed the top of my head. He smelled of cheap beer and cigarettes and I realized this was not James's first party of the night. 'I'm so happy for you. Is it Alex's?'

I replied with one arched eyebrow.

'Just making sure,' he said, slurping down the rest of his cocktail then eyeing mine. 'Does this mean you're not going to drink that?'

'So, this is like a terrible outfit, even for you.'

I gave James a gracious smile before turning to find Cici standing beside our table. She was wearing a floor-length white gown with two slits in the front running all the way up to her hip bones, barely skimming the underwear I hoped she was wearing. Her hair was piled up on top of her head and huge diamond solitaires sparkled in her earlobes. She looked like an actual goddess. Not someone dressed up as a goddess, of course, because I was still the only person at the entire event who was in fancy dress.

'Did we decide not to do costumes?' I asked while James busied himself by braiding the back section of my wig. 'Because I don't remember discussing that.'

'Yeah,' she replied, eyeing James over my shoulder. 'I told you, on Tuesday. And Wednesday. And Thursday, when I asked if you had something to wear tonight.'

I pursed my lips and tried to recall. She'd spent so much time in my office this week and all of it was a blur.

'Never mind,' I said, yanking my head away from James. 'Pack it in, I'm not a bloody Girl's World.'

'I always wanted one of those when I was little,' he sighed, holding out a hand to Cici. 'James Jacobs, charmed.'

'Yeah, sure,' Cici replied, entirely unimpressed. Her Upper East Side ice-queen personality was not an act. She genuinely did not care whether or not James was famous.

'The party is amazing,' I told her, still smiling at the look on James's face as he set about demolishing my cocktail. 'You've done such an amazing job.'

'I did pretty great,' she acknowledged, complimenting herself in the way that only millennials know how. 'Planning stuff is easy. You just tell people exactly how it is, what you need, when you need it, and how much they're getting paid. If they don't like it, there

201

are at least a million other people in New York who do what they do.'

'So, you threaten them?' James asked.

Cici shrugged and nodded.

'Oh, Angela,' he slurred into my ear. 'I like this one. Can I keep her?'

'No,' I replied without looking at him.

'Did you know she's pregnant?' he asked Cici.

'James!' I slapped his arm as he covered his mouth theatrically. 'What is *wrong* with you?'

'Oops,' he replied. 'She's not really, I made that up. She's just getting a bit fat and isn't drinking because she hates fun.'

'I need you on stage,' Cici said, ignoring James Jacobs for the second time in one night and probably only the fourth time in his entire life. 'You have to thank the sponsors.'

'Oh, shit.'

I looked down at my dress and my boobs looked back.

'Is it really obvious that I'm in costume?' I asked.

'No,' James replied.

'Yes,' Cici said at the exact same moment.

'Hello, hello!'

Joe sidled up beside Cici, resting an arm on her waist until she took a wide step sideways, moving out of his reach. Interesting.

'Great to meet you, I'm Joe Herman.' He reached out to shake James's hand. 'I'm a huge fan of your work. I see you're getting to know our editor, Ms Clark.'

'We're sharing secrets,' James replied, batting his lashes at my boss. I dug two fingers into his ribs until he squealed and remembered himself. 'No secrets! No secrets at all.'

'I'd love to stay and chat with you both,' I said, sliding out of the booth and taking Cici's arm, 'but I have to make a quick speech. Be right back.'

As I stood, Joe looked me up and down, eyes widening with confusion as he took in my ensemble.

'It's an inside joke,' I said hurriedly. 'I'll explain it later. James, behave.'

'Yes, Mum,' he replied before slapping his hand across his own face to silence himself. I flashed him one last warning look as we went. I was still trying to work out how to save my magazine and the last thing I needed was for Joe to find out I was knocked up. There was no in-office crèche on the spreadsheet he'd shown me.

'He is so gross,' Cici muttered as we crossed the VIP area and disappeared backstage.

She wouldn't get an argument from me.

'I heard you used to go out with him,' I said casually, keeping my chin high as every person we passed gave my outfit a double-take. 'Didn't end well?'

'That was years ago,' she replied, scoffing at the very thought. 'I can't believe Dee Dee hired him, he's an asshole. Actually, that's not fair, at least assholes are good for something.'

It was an interesting point.

'I'll tell the sound people to set up the mic,' she said, trotting off behind the stage and leaving me conspicuously alone.

Doing my best to ignore the whispering partygoers around me, I pulled out my phone to check my messages. Five missed calls from Jenny and two voice-mails. Tottering over into a quiet corner, I dialled in immediately. Something had to be wrong, Jenny hated to leave voicemails, why else wouldn't she text like a normal person?

'Angela?'

There were tears in her voice.

'Uh, so, Mason and I had a disagreement at dinner,' she choked. 'And he left and I don't know what to do and he won't answer the phone and yeah, can you call me?'

I closed my eyes and leaned back against the wall as the second message began to play. This was not good.

'Hey, it's me,' she shouted over loud guitar music. 'I don't want you to panic but the wedding is off.'

Why did people insist on telling you not to panic when the only rational response to what they're about to say is panic?

'Is that Angela?' Another familiar voice came on the line and my heart all but stopped. 'Hey, Angela!'

'Shut up,' Jenny hissed at her companion. 'It's OK, I'm OK. I just, it's off. The whole thing is off.'

Oh, sweet baby Jesus in the manger. The other voice on the line sounded far too familiar.

'I should have known I could never have anything that good,' she said, tears cutting through her words. 'Can you call me when you get this? I love you, Angie.'

A loud, Lopez sob was abruptly cut off as she ended the call, right as the music faded out around me. With my phone still pressed against my ear, I looked up to see Cici on the stage.

'Good evening, Generation *Gloss*,' she spoke into the microphone on stage with an easy grace, her expensive education carrying her words across the room. 'I'd like to welcome to the stage the editor of *Gloss* magazine, Angela Clark.'

She stepped back and began to clap, nodding for me to join her. Slowly, the whole room followed suit until the applause was deafening and somewhere in the back corner I was certain I could hear James whooping loudly and screaming my name, even as Jenny's words echoed in my ears. With my phone in my hand, I climbed up the steps and crossed the stage, wearing a waist-length white blonde braided wig and quite clearly dressed as Daenerys Targaryen. Unsurprisingly, the applause faded out quite quickly.

'Hi, everyone,' I said, my amplified voice not quite drowning out the mutter of comments that swept through the crowd. I blinked out into the venue as a spotlight repositioned itself to shine right in my eyes. 'I know we all want to get back to having a good time so I'll keep it quick.'

'Thank fuck!' James bellowed.

'When my friends and I created *Gloss*, we wanted to make a magazine that was for us and for you,' I said, trying to remember the speech I'd written days ago but my brain was a complete blank. All I could think about was Jenny, god knows where, doing god knows what with the worst person possible. 'We wanted a smart, savvy magazine that was fun to read, made us laugh and made us think. Basically, we wanted to know who was feuding with whom on Twitter but we didn't want to feel as though we needed to take a shower after we'd read it.'

A brief titter of laughter fluttered across the room.

'I'm proud of *Gloss*,' I said, inadvertently meeting Joe's eyes. He had taken my spot in the booth and James had his arm wrapped around his broad shoulders. 'And I'm proud to celebrate it with you all tonight.'

'Where are my dragons?' James screamed.

Joe winced.

I smiled.

Leaning in to the mic to finish my speech, I cleared my throat but before I could speak, the speakers squealed with echoing feedback as my phone began to ring. It was Jenny again. I looked at it for a moment before cancelling the call as everyone in the room pressed their fingers into their ears.

'I'm now going to hand back to the person who planned this entire evening, Cici Spencer,' I said, stepping out of the spotlight and waving her back onto the stage. 'Can we get a round of applause for Cici?'

To be filed under 'things I never thought I would say'.

Pushing her into the spotlight, I gave Cici a small hug.

'I've got to go, I'm sorry,' I whispered. 'This is amazing, thank you.'

'Are you all right?' she asked, her voice packed with seemingly genuine concern. 'Is there a problem with the baby?'

I shook my head as my phone began to vibrate again.

'There is a problem with *a* baby,' I replied, striding across the stage and yanking the wig off as I went. 'Just not mine.'

CHAPTER THIRTEEN

Walking into a ridiculously cool party dressed as a character from a television fantasy show had been embarrassing. The idea of walking into a super-hipster bar in Williamsburg was mortifying.

'ID?' A greasy-haired man sat on a bar stool flashed a tiny torch up into my face.

'I don't have it,' I replied, waiting for his sarcastic response. I just wanted to get this over with. 'But I'm definitely over twenty-one.'

'K,' he replied, turning his torch back onto his book, a tattered copy of a Bukowski novel, and kicking the door open. 'Cool outfit.'

Well, maybe this wasn't going to be as difficult as I'd expected.

The Drill was the diviest of dive bars on all of Driggs Avenue and Craig's favourite Brooklyn haunt. Nine on a Saturday evening was early for hipsters, but the cracked vinyl booths that lined the right side of the room were already full, and to the left, a tattooed bartender lined up shots along the old wooden bar. The Velvet Underground blared out of the speakers, making conversation all but impossible. In the back, the pool table was silently spoken for, stacks of quarters lining the bumper from one corner pocket to the other.

Not a single person looked up from their table as I shuffled through the bar. If a grown woman had walked into a Manhattan bar in full *Game of Thrones* cosplay, on her own, on a Saturday night, I would definitely have raised an eyebrow. At The Drill, no one so much as blinked. Being cool must be exhausting.

It took a minute for my eyes to adjust to the dim light and a minute longer to spot Jenny. I looked ridiculous, Jenny looked like she'd been transported in from another dimension. Everyone in the bar was wearing battered jeans and faded T-shirts or vintage floral dresses with black tights and ripped jumpers that looked like they'd been hand-knitted by their nanas. But Jenny sparkled in a silver sequin Alice + Olivia mini dress and sky-high over-the-knee boots I recognized from the latest Stuart Weitzman ad campaign. At the very back of the room, behind the pool table and tucked in beside a vintage Ms Pacman machine, she shone at a tiny table for two, covered in crumpled cans and empty shot glasses and, most worryingly of all, Craig.

'Right.' I marched up to the table and slammed my wig down on the sticky surface. So now I knew how it would look if Johnny Rotten had ever dated a Kardashian. 'You're coming with me.'

'Hey, Angie!' Craig leapt up out of his seat and threw his arms around me. He wasn't a bad man, just a stupid one. It wasn't his fault Jenny had dragged him into her spiral of self-sabotage but he certainly wasn't doing anything to get her out of it. 'Great outfit. What are you drinking?'

'A cup of tea, in my pyjamas, in my own home, in approximately fifteen minutes from now,' I replied, grabbing Jenny by the arm and hoisting her onto her feet. 'Lopez, up.'

'Get off me!' she squealed, pushing me away and falling backwards, back into her chair. 'I'm staying here. I don't want to go home.'

'I don't give two shits about what you want,' I replied. There was a time for hugs and tears and that would come later. This was the time for tough love and when it came to telling her how it was, I'd learned from the best. 'This is insane, and I'm not going to let you do it.'

'Me and Craig are having some drinks,' she said, over-enunciating every word, and I could tell she was already well on her way to being wasted. 'And then we're gonna go back to his place. Right, baby?'

'Sure?' he grinned like the cat that had got the canary. Or the cat who was on a promise with his really hot ex-girlfriend, who had recently got engaged to a much more suitable cat. 'Whenever you're ready, babe.'

'Craig,' I said, taking Jenny's arm once more and pulling her away from the table, 'don't be an arse.'

Jenny fought back, but not well, either because she knew I was right or because she was bladdered, I wasn't sure.

'I'm not going home,' she wailed as I dragged her into the disgusting unisex toilet stall and pushed her backwards onto the loo. Her eyes were glazed and her perfect make-up was smudged all over her face. 'I can't go home. Leave me here with Craig. I deserve to be here with Craig.'

'You know, I probably should,' I said, turning on

the cold tap and waiting for the slightly orange water to run clear. 'But this is going to be a lot easier to fix tomorrow if we stop the madness now. Look at me.'

She pouted as I grabbed her chin and pulled her head away, immediately head-butting the dark red painted wall. I grabbed a handful of toilet paper, grateful it was still so early in the night and there was even any left, and wet it before dabbing gently at the trails of mascara streaking her cheeks.

'Tell me what happened,' I ordered, kneeling down in front of her as her bottom lip began to tremble.

'He doesn't want to marry me,' she stuttered. 'He walked out of the restaurant.'

'And what happened before that?' I asked as I smoothed her hair behind her ears and away from her face.

Jenny covered her eyes with her hands and peeled away a pair of extravagant false eyelashes before chucking them in the overflowing bin.

'We were talking about the wedding,' she said. 'And I was suggesting some stuff, Angie, nothing crazy.'

'Uh-huh,' I replied, not quite sure I believed her.

'And he flipped out,' she sniffed, her voice wavering as the shots hit her system. 'Out of nowhere. Everyone was staring at us.'

Well, I knew all about that, I thought, looking down at my outfit.

'He started ranting about how much I was spending, how I was trying to bankrupt him, how I cared more about the wedding than I did about marrying him and that I was only trying to one up Sadie which, you know, is insane.'

'Completely mad,' I agreed. We'd do rational and honest once she sobered up.

'I love him, I love him so much,' she cried, a fresh course of tears pouring down her cheeks. 'I just want him to know how much I love him, I want *everyone* to know.'

'And did you tell him that?' I asked.

Jenny looked at me guiltily. 'More or less.'

'Jenny?'

There was that tone of voice again. Just like my mother.

'OK, so I kind of told him he was ruining everything,' she said. 'And that I hated him and wasn't even sure I wanted to marry him anyway.'

'And that's your version of more or less?' I asked.

She pressed her hands against her face and let out a fresh stream of tears.

'Admittedly, it probably wasn't the best thing you could have said,' I said as I rubbed my hand in circles up and down her back, ever the diplomat. 'But we all say things when we're upset.'

'And then I took off my ring and threw it in his face,' she wailed. 'Angie, what have I done? I told you he didn't want to marry me.'

Oh, bloody hell.

'He's been weird all week. He hasn't been texting, he won't talk to me about work, he's cancelling on wedding planning stuff,' Jenny continued to sob, hot tears carving a path through the rest of her make-up. 'I forced him into it, I know I did, and now he's having second thoughts. Now everything is "whatever" and I hate it. I never should have pushed him.'

'Jenny, I'm sitting on the floor of a dirty bar bathroom, dressed as a woman who considers three dragons to be her children,' I said, unable to listen to it for another second, 'and I'm just not having this. Genuinely, truly, tell me now, what is going on?'

'I told you,' she said, snorting back tears. 'It's not me, it's Mason. I want to give him this awesome wedding so I can show him how much I love him and he doesn't want to marry me at all. That's why he wants to hide away on some island, so he can pretend it isn't really happening. I should have stuck with Craig. I should have known better than to think someone like Mason would ever want to be with me. I don't deserve him and he knows it. All I deserve is too-drunk-to-stand, too-lame-to-live Craig *and* his herpes.'

'Did I know Craig had herpes?' I asked, thanking my lucky stars that Alex had been so careful when he was in his 'I'm with a band' shagger phase. 'Ignore me, that's not the point. You're wrong. No one deserves Craig, not even his herpes. Just because Mason has been busy and doesn't want to spend a hundred thousand dollars on a wedding does not mean he doesn't love you. Also, not to go off topic, but have you got any idea how much he's already spent on that ring?'

She splayed out her naked left hand and began to cry again.

'This is going to sound like a daft question, but have you tried calling him?' I asked, covering her hand with mine.

'I called and he hung up,' she hiccupped. 'He hates me. 'He told me not to call him again.'

'He doesn't hate you.' I grabbed her as she rolled forward off the lav and into my arms. 'I bet he's hiding out somewhere, just as upset as you are right now.'

'I don't think so,' she said, sobbing onto my silk dress until it was wet through, 'he told me to fuck off.'

'We'll maybe give him a bit of time to cool off, then,

212

shall we?' I suggested. 'But I think it's time we go home.'

Waiting for Jenny to cry herself out, I turned my attention to the graffiti carved into the dark red walls. Why were so many toilets in New York painted red? It couldn't be for the romance factor. Maybe it stimulated deep, theoretical debates. If I had to hazard a guess, I'd say at least 50 per cent of the most important conversations in human history must have taken place in the toilets.

'What about Craig?' Jenny said, as she calmed down. She smeared her make-up across the backs of her hands just in time to make way for new tears. 'I called him and asked him to meet me. I'm such a dick, Angie. Why did I do that?'

'Because you're human?' I suggested.

'Stop being nice to me,' she said into my boobs.

'Because you're an idiot who is determined to ruin her life?' I corrected.

Her shoulders shook with a half laugh, half wail.

'I know it's dumb but one of the things that really weirds me out about getting married,' she said, 'is the lack of drama. And not even real drama, but the potential for drama. I love Mason, I would never, ever cheat on him, but when Craig shows up on the doorstep or guys hit on me when I'm in the gym, it's still exciting . . . am I a terrible person?'

'People hit on you when you're in the gym?' I asked, marvelling at the concept. When I exercised, I turned into a human blueberry. No one had ever so much as asked me the time when I was in the gym. 'Sorry, distracted. No, I don't think you're a terrible person. You might be a slightly sketchy feminist, but I don't have the most up-to-date guidelines on that, so you could be in the clear.'

'I wouldn't ever do anything,' she insisted, pulling at her sheer, golden tights. 'But it's just that little buzz of knowing that you could. I guess maybe my brain hasn't caught up with my ring finger and it's still trying to keep my options open.'

'That's one theory,' I agreed. 'Another would be that you've been dating for so long, you don't know how to accept that this is it and move on to the next thing. Sound like a possibility?'

'So, you have read *Keeping the Love You Find*,' she said, momentarily delighted. 'Such a great book.'

I smiled and nodded, even though I'd only really read the first three chapters and then used it to prop up a bookcase that was standing on top of uneven floorboards.

'Mason is some sort of gorgeous, CrossFit-obsessed yeti,' I told her. 'By all laws of science and nature he should not exist. He is a prince among men and Jen, you kissed every frog in the Tri-State area before you found him.'

'And some from Canada,' she reminded me.

'And some from Canada,' I amended my statement. Oh, Jacques of Montreal, how I did not miss thee. 'Mason is not going to turn back into a frog so you don't need to keep one foot in the pond.'

'It's a pretty nasty pond,' she said, perking up all of a sudden. 'Want to go home and play a fun game called Delete the Numbers of All Jenny's Exes?'

'Yes,' I replied. I'd been waiting to play this game for years. 'Yes, I do.'

'OK.'

She looked up, mascara drawn all across her face like a Batman mask and her lip began to quiver.

'What's wrong?' I asked, looking around our location. 'Apart from the obvious.'

'I don't want to talk to Craig,' she whimpered.

'No one does,' I assured her. 'Is there a back exit?'

'There's a window?' she said, pointing at the small square of glass above us.

'I'm not climbing out of a window,' I said, helping her up to her feet. 'I am too tired and too pregnant for that. I'm going to open the door, we're going to walk out into the bar, you're going to apologize for calling him, explain it was a mistake and we're going to pray a taxi will agree to let us in and take us home. I am not getting on the subway like this.'

'Yeah,' Jenny replied as someone began to hammer on the outside of the door. 'I guess that would be the adult thing to do.'

'Yes, it would,' I confirmed, pleased she'd come around so quickly. 'Are you ready?'

She looked longingly at the window.

'No,' she replied. 'Sorry.'

'Fine,' I said, bending over and giving her a leg up onto the window ledge. 'I'll get your handbag.'

Opening the door, I legged it across the bar and nabbed Jenny's vintage Fendi baguette from the disgusting bar table.

'Hi, Craig,' I said as I stalked past. 'Bye, Craig.'

'Wait!' He looked at me then looked at the empty bathroom stall. 'What happened to Jenny?'

'Hopefully nothing,' I replied, picking up my pace until I was running out the front door. Making my way carefully down the alleyway at the side of the bar, I tied the skirt of my dress in a knot at my hip to climb over an abandoned crate blocking my path. My hand slipped against the cold brick wall as it started to rain.

'Perfect,' I muttered to myself. A downpour would

really cap off my most glamorous New York evening. 'Jenny?'

'In here.'

I could hear her but I couldn't see her. What I could see was a collection of Oscar the Grouch trashcans, big silver bins, all laid on their sides, spilling revolting bar rubbish out onto the wet floor. Very slowly, her face peered up from behind them.

'Angie, I think I'm gonna puke,' she said, holding out her arms for help. 'Help me.'

Standing in the smelly, dirty alleyway as the rain soaked through my dress and Jenny flailed around in stinky garbage, I smiled at my best friend.

'Why are you just standing there?' she wailed. 'I can feel something moving!'

'Because about six months from now,' I explained, holding my breath as I approached the disgusting bins, 'when I'm getting up at three in the morning to change a dirty nappy, I want to be able to remember the time when I had to rescue Aunt Jenny from the bins.'

'I hate you sometimes,' she said, clinging to my neck as I dragged her out from the trash wilderness, hopping on one shoeless foot. I didn't ask where the other had gone, it was lost to the night.

'And I love you too,' I replied, smiling as we limped back out onto the street and off to find a taxi.

CHAPTER FOURTEEN

'Special delivery for Angela Clark?'

Yawning, I rubbed my eyes to make sure I wasn't hallucinating. A gigantic teddy bear filled the door of my office, supported by a pair of human legs clad in the same navy blue work trousers our mailroom workers always wore.

'I don't want it,' I said reflexively. The bear gurned at me and I shuddered. 'Make it go away.'

'Funny,' the deliveryman said, dumping the six-foot bear on the tiny sofa in my office while not laughing. 'It came with this.'

He wiped the sweat from his forehead and tossed a regular-sized white envelope on my desk.

'Thanks,' I said, keeping one eye on the bear.

As he left, he patted the bear on the head and, very slowly, it sloped forwards before collapsing face down in the middle of my office. I opened the envelope at my desk and a multicolour glitter explosion blew out all over my grey cashmere sweater dress. Inside the envelope was a card that said, 'I'm Beary Sorry' and inside the card was a Polaroid picture of James, pulling his most apologetic face, both of his hands pressed against his cheeks.

'Perfect,' I whispered, trying to swipe the glitter off me but only succeeding in spreading it all over my dress, my palms and my face.

The rest of the weekend had been a disaster. No cabs were interested in picking up Jenny the Garbage Monster and Angela, Mother of Damp Dragons, and so we had suffered the indignity of the L train back to Manhattan. After I had physically put her in the bath, dressed her, carried her to the toilet, held back her hair while she threw up whatever shots she'd consumed with Craig and then put her right back in the bath again, Jenny had passed out in my bed, alternately sobbing and spooning me all night long. I'd planned to spend all day Sunday working on my presentation, but instead I was passed out on the settee while Jenny ate all the ice cream in our freezer and hate-watched *27 Dresses*. There were several aborted attempts at calling, texting, emailing and even Snapchatting Mason, but he was either ignoring us both or he'd done something that was completely beyond my comprehension – turned off his phone.

By Monday morning I was more tired than I had ever been and all the glitter in the world couldn't have distracted from the dark circles that had taken up permanent residence on my face. Cici had covered my desk in healthy snacks and herbal teas before disappearing for lunch, but none of it was making me feel any better. It was almost time to crack open the emergency Percy Pigs I kept in my bottom desk drawer.

'Is this a bad time?' Joe asked, replacing the bear in the doorway of my office.

'Yes,' I replied without thinking. 'Sorry.'

'I wanted to tell you what a fantastic night I had on Saturday,' he said, letting himself in regardless and staring at the bear. 'You did a great job with the event.'

'It was a team effort,' I said, putting my hair up in a ponytail. The smell of dry shampoo around my face was making me nauseous. Much like everything else. 'I'm glad you had fun.'

'It was a shame you had to rush off.'

He wasn't sitting, I realized. Maybe he wasn't staying?

'Cici said it was a family emergency, we were all very worried.'

'Everyone's fine,' I assured him, testing a smile on my face. Nope, didn't feel right. 'But you know how families can be.'

'Oh, family first, absolutely,' he said, still not moving. 'Glad to hear everything worked out.'

'I don't want to be rude, but it's actually press day today,' I told him, flapping a hand over the marked up pages on my desk. 'I really should be getting on with this.'

'I just need five minutes of your time,' Joe replied, sticking his head back out of the door and waving someone over. 'I wanted to introduce you to Eva Hanstock AKA Eva-Lution.'

Just what I needed. An overenthusiastic child running around my office with a video camera.

'Look, Joe—'

Before I could protest, a very petite young girl with huge brown eyes and cheekbones that could have sliced bread appeared under his left armpit. Her hair was puffed out in a gorgeous golden blonde afro and she was rocking a red glitter lip better than anyone had any right to on a damp Monday morning in December.

'Hi!' She practically ran across the room, her cropped, high-waisted pinstripe trousers swishing as she went. 'I am so excited to meet you. I can't believe I'm in the *Gloss* offices, this is so dope.'

'Yup,' I repeated. I had never felt so old in my life. 'Dope.'

'Angela is a huge fan of your videos,' Joe said as I rose to reach out my hand but was instead swallowed up into a massive hug. She was much stronger than she looked. 'Right, Angela?'

'Massive fan,' I agreed, quietly inhaling. She smelled amazing. I smelled like Alex's cheap coffee, Alex's deodorant, and the subway. The deodorant was on purpose, the coffee I'd spilled by accident – and the stink of the subway was just something that was going to get you eventually.

'I'm the biggest fan of *Gloss* ever,' Eva said, releasing me and hopping right into the clean seat in front of my desk. Joe took the coffee-stained one beside her. 'I've been reading it since it came out. I used to get the subway into the city every week, just to pick it up.'

'You weren't working in Manhattan?' I was smiling, in spite of myself. She was like human sunshine.

'I wasn't working anywhere,' she replied, pushing up the sleeves of her soft, white shirt. 'I was only seventeen.'

And there went my smile.

'So, you're how old now?' I asked.

'Ancient,' she replied, laughing at the look on my face. 'In vlogger terms, anyway. I'm going to be twenty-two at the end of the year.'

Ancient? She was practically younger than the foetus in my belly.

'I used to get the train from Queens after school just to sneak into this fancy boutique in Nolita and grab a couple of copies,' she explained. When she talked, her hands flew around her face, drawing pictures in the air. 'When I got home, I would read one copy and then cut out pictures from the other and write features around them. I used to make my own magazine because I never thought I would be able to write for a real one.'

'Me neither,' I said, ignoring the self-satisfied grin on Joe's face. 'I more or less had to start my own.'

'Like me with my channel,' she agreed readily. Eva grabbed a recent issue from the coffee table behind her and leafed lovingly through the pages. 'I always loved your features, you were so funny and honest. You don't really write any more though, do you?'

'I wish I did but I don't really have time,' I admitted, running my fingertips over the masthead of the page in front of me. Angela Clark, Editor. 'When you're the editor, you've got to manage the whole magazine, it's more like running a business to be honest.'

'See, I love having complete creative control over my videos,' she replied, frowning slightly. 'I can talk about whatever I want.'

'And you'd really want to give that up?' I asked as I marvelled silently at her perfect cat's eye liner, making a mental note to search her channel for a tutorial. 'If you come and work for a big corporate publisher, there's going to be much less freedom.'

Joe sat up sharply, like an electrocuted meerkat.

'You'll still have freedom,' he corrected. 'But with more structure and support to build.'

'Structured freedom,' I repeated. 'Sweet.'

'There's only so much I can do on my own,' she said to me, glancing back at her new boss. 'I didn't go to college, I don't have rich parents. Running a YouTube channel out of your apartment has limits and I'm not interested in limits. Yeah, I've got ten million subscribers on my channel, but what's next?'

Ten million? Sweet Jesus.

'A quiet sit down and a well-deserved drink?' I suggested.

'I want to be the best at what I do,' Eva went on, a fire in her eyes that I recognized from somewhere. 'I'm going to be Oprah, Ellen and Beyoncé, all rolled into one. I'm going to take over the world.'

Oh. Dear. God. I was looking into the eyes of a baby Jenny Lopez, only even more ambitious. I tried to imagine what Jenny would be like if she'd been a teenager during the YouTube revolution. It didn't bear thinking about.

'You remind me of my best friend,' I told her, glancing across at a framed photo of me and Jenny, doubled over laughing at Erin's wedding to Thomas. A much happier image than the one of her doubled over the toilet on Saturday night. And Sunday morning. And Sunday night. 'Which is almost entirely a compliment. I'm just not sure why you'd want to give up your own thing to come and work for someone else?'

'To learn,' Eva said earnestly, beating her hand against the issue of *Gloss* in her lap. 'I'm can't get any further in my career until I learn from other people. Did you know Delia Spencer is the youngest female president of a media company *ever*? I'm sure there's something she could teach me that I'm not getting from staring at a camera in my bedroom.'

I smiled as she smoothed out the wrinkles in the magazine with an awkward smile. I was impressed. Even though it was easy to be impressed when your own hashtag goals only stretched as far as making it through the day without throwing up on yourself.

'I love *Gloss*, I really do,' Eva said. 'When Joe reached out to me and asked for a meeting, I died. For real, I am obsessed with your magazine. I want to have *Gloss* babies and send them all around the world to tell everyone how great we are, like a reverse Angelina Jolie. I'm excited to join Spencer Media because of *Gloss*.'

'That's so cool,' I replied, touched and flattered and quietly scribbling down what she had said. It was a better global outreach strategy than I'd come up with. 'I really hope we get to work together.'

'You've got to keep growing, haven't you? Got to keep swimming, like a shark,' she said as Joe stood, signalling that it was time to leave. 'If you're not moving forward, what are you doing? Treading water? That's five minutes away from drowning.'

'Maybe you're floating?' I suggested, following them towards the door. 'Floating is fun.'

Especially if you were floating on an inflatable donut in Taylor Swift's Rhode Island pool, just like Eva had been, on Instagram, over the Fourth of July weekend.

'For a while,' she conceded. 'But before you know it, you've been swept out on the tide and there's no way back to the shore.'

The girl was deep. That would look great as an inspirational quote on Pinterest.

'It was really nice to meet you,' I said, taking a deep breath and bracing myself for another mega hug. She genuinely seemed like an intelligent, determined woman who was nice to boot and it took all my strength not to whisper, 'Run while still you can' into her ear.

'Can we get a selfie?' she asked, whipping an enormous mobile phone out of a tiny Chanel bag and tilting her chin downwards before I'd even had time to blink. 'Sorry, I'm so Gen Z *I* can't even stand it sometimes.'

'It's fine,' I assured her, choosing not to look at the photo on the screen. 'Just promise you'll filter the shit out of it before you post it?'

'Oh, I don't filter,' she said, shaking her head. 'I'm all about authenticity. But I can Facetune you, if you'd like?'

'I would like,' I said quickly. 'Thanks.'

'See you in the morning,' Joe said over the top of her amazing hair. 'Can't wait to see your presentation.'

'Me neither,' I replied. 'See you then.'

Heaving my giant teddy bear back onto the mini sofa, I sat down beside him and rested my head against his chest. Joe was right, Eva was great. She was bright, she was funny, she knew exactly what she wanted and she wasn't afraid to ask for help. So what if she was young? She had all the experience she needed and confidence by the bucket-load. Like Joe had said at lunch, Eva was the future.

Which only left one question. What did that make me?

'I'm going to have nightmares about that thing,' Cici said, side-eyeing the bear hours later. Most of the lights were out and everyone else had long since gone home. 'Are you planning on staying here all night?'

'I'm still working on my presentation,' I explained, turning the screen of my computer to face her. 'We were so late closing today I only just got to it.'

'I figured you'd have it done by now,' she replied, scanning the first slide and pulling a face. 'It's like a *Gloss* brand thing, right? You could do that in your sleep, what's so complicated?'

I looked across the desk at my assistant and saw someone who wasn't just a colleague, a rich bitch, and a face that stalked my nightmares. For the first time, I saw someone who was reliable, supportive, and hardworking – and also someone who could very nearly pass for a friend. Even if I knew she'd rather wear head-to-toe manmade fibres before she would admit it.

'Cici?' I said.

'Yeah?' she replied.

'Please can you take off those fake glasses?'

She tensed her jaw and pursed her lips.

'They're not fake,' she replied. 'I need them for driving at night.'

I looked around the empty office, saw her standing on her own two feet, twelve floors off street level, and burst out laughing.

'What's wrong with you?' she asked when I didn't stop. 'Are you having a psychotic break? Should I call an ambulance?''

'I don't know,' I said, wiping a welcome tear away from my dried-out eyes. 'Possibly, and no, I think I'm OK.'

'OK, yeah, because you're laughing like a psychopath,' Cici pointed out. 'Why do you want me to take off my glasses and why is it funny?'

'Because you don't need them,' I said, rubbing my eyes; I'd been staring at a screen for altogether too long today. 'You don't need to wear glasses to convince people you're clever – I know you're clever. I know you're good at your job. The Generation *Gloss* party was amazing and persuasive props are not necessary.'

Slowly, she reached up to her face and pulled off the glasses, turning the frames over in her hands for a moment before folding them up and placing them on my desk.

'Why, Miss Spencer, you're beautiful,' I said with a grin.

'You want me to call you a cab?' she asked, smiling back. She looked even more like her sister when she smiled, not that I could remember the last time I'd seen a truly joyous expression on either of their faces. 'It's too late for you to take the train.'

'I can't leave until I finish this,' I said, tapping the computer screen with a pencil. 'And I can't finish this because my brain is mush.'

'It's a presentation about *Gloss*,' Cici said again, flipping through the slides. 'You know everything about *Gloss*, you *are Gloss*. What are you having trouble with?'

'Finding a reason for Joe to choose us over *The Look* when he closes one of us in January,' I replied softly.

Cici whistled quietly. 'Whoa.'

'I didn't want to say anything to worry you,' I replied, scrolling back and forth over the same slides I'd been looking at for the last three hours. 'But the way it's going right now, he's not even going to wait until January.'

'You know, you could ask for help,' she said, pulling my keyboard towards her. 'You're editing a magazine, you're pregnant, and you're living with that lunatic of a friend of yours. This is a lot to take on, I would have helped you.'

'Thank you,' I replied as my screen lit up her carefully appointed features. Several generations of carefully selected breeding and another several thousand dollars of rhinoplasty, Botox and cosmetic dentistry stared at my presentation. 'What do you think?'

'Joe doesn't need to know why *Gloss* is already great,' she said, clicking on a group of slides and pressing delete. I closed my eyes and tried not to throw up in my mouth. I had not backed up. 'He wants to know where *Gloss* is going in the future. He wants to know why he should invest time, money and resource in us. What does *Gloss* have that *The Look* doesn't?'

'A lifesize cutout of Chris Pratt in *Jurassic World*?' I suggested.

'The fewer slides the better,' Cici said, ignoring my unhelpful suggestion. 'You want to go in, tell him how it's going to be and get out. Don't let the thought of closing *Gloss* even cross his mind.'

'I shouldn't be defending the magazine's existence,' I said, catching on to her point. 'I need to remind him how bloody lucky he is to have it in the first place.'

'Exactly,' she replied, opening a new slide, her long nails clacking across my keyboard. '"Why Spencer Media needs *Gloss*".'

'Cici Spencer, I don't know how I would manage without you,' I declared, stunned by my own words.

'Took you long enough,' she muttered in response. 'Now, can we get this done so I can get the hell out of here, please? Unlike you, I have a life.'

I nodded in agreement. Not because she was right, but because it just wouldn't do for us to be nice to each other for more than five minutes at a time.

*

It was so late by the time Cici and I spilled out of the office and into our cabs, Times Square was almost deserted. The neon madness had already slowed down, animated billboards stood static and the brightly lit marquees of the theatres had all gone dark. I texted Jenny to let her know I wasn't coming home. Working with Cici had given me new life and new life required a new outfit. The exact outfit that was hanging in my wardrobe back in Park Slope. My black leather pencil skirt, my black silk shirt and the little black Saint Laurent ankle boots that were covered in silver glitter stars. Jenny had 'acquired' them from a photoshoot the winter before, but they were too big for her. I was certain they would fit my swollen feet and wearing a grand's worth of designer goods on my feet would certainly help boost my confidence while I explained to Joe just how stupid he would have to be to close *Gloss*.

As my cab rattled down FDR Drive, hitting every pothole possible, I gazed out on the Brooklyn skyline that awaited me across the East River. Manhattan still towered above me, threatening to swallow me whole as we looped around on ourselves and rolled over the Brooklyn Bridge. I was tired but I was happy. The presentation was good and I knew it. Tomorrow was still going to be interesting, but at least I was going in with a better than fighting chance.

We rolled up outside the house a little after one and the street was silent. There were hardly any lights in any windows on our block. Someone had lied: New York was definitely sleeping. Inside, the apartment was the same, comforting mess I had left it – piles of clothes and notebooks everywhere I looked and an empty packet of Hobnobs on the coffee table. I took a quick look in the kitchen and saw the Hello Hole had been completely covered and my floor was spotless. The murderous builder's work was done.

Peeling off my ankle boots, I automatically turned on the TV just as an episode of *Law & Order: SVU* began. I closed my eyes happily and hummed along to the music, thanking the TV gods for rewarding my long and stressful day.

And then I heard the toilet flush.

'Oh. My. God,' I whispered, my hands creeping up to my own throat and covering my mouth.

There was someone in the house.

I heard the footsteps coming closer to the living room but I couldn't move a muscle. This was not a drill, this was not paranoia, there was someone in my house, and to add insult to injury, they'd just used my toilet. It had to be the homicidal builder.

'And they flushed,' I told Detective Benson on the television. 'Forensics won't be able to get DNA evidence from the lav if they flushed.'

The familiar creak of the floorboard in the hallway told me they were right outside the door. There was nowhere to go, nothing to do but hide or fight. I looked all around, assessing possible weapons. Biscuit wrappers, Cheez-Its, dirty tights, my old Jimmy Choos. I closed my eyes and swallowed, adrenaline surging through my veins. If I could distract the murdery builder, because it was obviously him, maybe I could run out the front door, lock him inside and scream bloody murder until someone called the police.

A shadowy figure appeared in the doorway before

I could make a run for it. I saw the outline of a beard and a startled look in his eyes as he noticed the TV and then me.

'Get out of my way!' I screamed, hurling shoes, tights and packets of Cheez-Its in his direction as I charged towards the door with a blood-curdling war cry. I was not going down quietly. The neighbours had given my keys to the psycho in the first place, the least they deserved was a poor night's sleep.

The intruder dodged the cheesy snacks but my Jimmy Choo hit him squarely between the eyes. His legs crumpled underneath him and I saw my chance as he dropped down to one knee and kicked him squarely between the nuts and ran for the door. Before I could get anywhere, he reached out and grabbed my ankle.

'Angela,' he gasped.

'Please don't hurt me!' I screamed, closing my eyes and wrapping my hands around my belly, hopping on one foot to stop myself from falling over, not stopping to wonder how he might know my name. 'I'm pregnant!'

'What?'

I opened one eye to see a hairy, confused version of a man who looked just like my husband staring up at me.

'Alex?' I whispered.

He nodded, shock all over his face.

'What did you just say?' he asked, still carefully guarding his balls with one hand and hanging on to my ankle with the other.

'So, I've got some news,' I said, my heartbeat thudding in my ears. 'We're having a baby.'

Alex let go of my leg and wiped a hand over his face, blinking at me in silence.

'Are you serious?'

'Almost twelve weeks serious,' I said, reaching out to touch his beard. Gross. It was really him.

'A baby?' He tentatively released his nads and looked at my stomach. 'You're pregnant?'

'Yes,' I replied. 'And please don't say it doesn't look any different, because it definitely does, and it wasn't funny when Jenny said it either.'

'Angela . . . ' Alex rolled forward onto his knees, covering my mini bump with both hands. 'We're having a baby?'

'I know, I've had more time to get used to it than you,' I said, laughing at the look of shock on his beardy face and kneeling down on the floor beside him. 'One hundred per cent real human baby, cooking up in this oven. Oh, and it's definitely yours, by the way. In case you were wondering.'

And there were the tears again. Alex pressed his mouth against mine, kissing me so hard. It felt new, strange in a good way, he'd been gone so long and I couldn't stop myself from joining in with a little sob. Even while he kissed me, even as his hands became caught up in my long hair, his beard scratching my hot face, I wanted to be closer to him, on him, with him. I needed him inside me. I clambered up into his lap, desperate to feel his entire body against mine.

'I missed you so much,' I said as I yanked his T-shirt over his head and ran my hands down the strong muscles in his lean back.

'I missed you too,' he replied, pushing my sweater dress up around my hips and tearing at my tights. 'Every goddamn day.'

We fell backwards, arms and legs moving without thinking until we were nestled between the settee and the coffee table, his jeans somewhere else, my dress acting as a very expensive pillow. Alex paused, framing my face in his hands as he hovered above me.

'We're having a baby,' he said, smiling.

And for the first time in a long time, it felt as though everything was going to be all right.

CHAPTER FIFTEEN

'You did such a great job taking care of the place while I was gone,' Alex said, stroking my hair as I nuzzled up underneath his chin. My alarm clock was going to buzz at any second but I really, really didn't want to get out of bed.

'Thanks, I tried,' I said into his armpit. He smelled disgusting and wonderful at the same time and I loved it.

'No, you didn't,' he replied. 'It looks like a shitstorm ran through here. Did you rent the apartment out to a homeless frat while I was gone?'

'I missed you so much I couldn't find the energy to clean,' I said. 'And the baby likes clutter. It feels more secure when there's mess everywhere.'

'Then it's definitely your kid,' he smiled.

His too-short hair had grown back and then some. It fell into his eyes, almost hitting his left cheekbone, and as a pale shaft of light sliced through the heavy bedroom drapes, it was almost like looking at him on our first date. I hadn't realized how much longer his hair had been when we met, he must have been trimming it up millimetre by millimetre every day.

'The baby wants what the baby wants,' I said. It was thrilling to say it out loud. So much of the last few weeks had been spent trying not to say the 'b' word, now I could shout it from the rooftops. 'The baby also likes ice cream, long hot baths, online shopping and monogrammed pyjamas from J. Crew.'

'Why do I feel like I'm going to be hearing that a lot from now on?' He pushed himself down the bed and rested his head on my stomach. 'Alex, the baby wanted it. Alex, I did it for the baby.'

'Funny you should mention that, because the baby saw a pair of Louboutins in Saks the other day and it was really, really keen.'

He rested a hand on the top of my thigh and held his breath. 'How long until it moves?' he asked. 'Have you felt it kick yet?'

'It most likely won't kick for another few weeks, maybe even months,' I told him as I rubbed his prickly beard. 'For now, it's just chilling out, making me hungry and emo and fat.'

'You're not fat,' Alex argued. 'You look amazing. And babe, don't make me say it.'

He pointed up at my boobs and gave me a double thumbs up.

'I have so much catching up to do.' He pulled up my T-shirt and kissed my belly before turning his attention back to my face, via my enormous rack. 'I can't believe you let me disappear to Thailand while you were going through all this alone.'

'Jenny was here,' I replied, combing his hair back from his face. 'I wasn't alone.'

'I can't believe you let me disappear in Thailand

while you were going through all this with Jenny,' he corrected himself. 'You should have told me, I would have been on the first plane.'

'To help with Jenny or the baby?' I asked, giving myself a quick sniff. He wasn't the only one who needed a shower. 'It wouldn't have made any difference and you wouldn't have seen all those amazing places. You're not mad, are you?'

He scooched back up the bed, ran his thumb over my bottom lip, and then curled his hand around the back of my neck.

'What did I do to deserve you?' he murmured, weaving his legs through mine.

'Something terrible,' I replied, right as my clock began to bleat on the bedside table. 'I don't want to alarm you but you may have been Attila the Hun in a past life.'

'Turn it off,' he ordered, hands in places hands hadn't been in such a long time. 'Call in sick.'

'I want to,' I said, reluctantly pushing him away and sliding a pillow between us. Physical barriers were necessary. I felt like a horny sixth former on the back of the bus on the way home from a day trip to Alton Towers. 'But I've got this big presentation this morning. There's a new boss and, well, I didn't want to worry you but they sort of might end up closing *Gloss*.'

'*What*?'

Now he was awake.

'How long has this been a thing?' he asked, the concern on his face juxtaposed somewhat with the boner in his boxers.

'I didn't want to worry you—'

'Angela Clark, if you say that one more time,' he

warned. 'How serious is this? What about Delia? Why are you not freaking out?'

'Because I've already freaked out,' I explained as I clambered out of bed, hunting for the knickers I'd tossed out of bed while declaring I would never ever need them again as long as I lived. A declaration that lasted all of six hours. 'Honestly, the whole thing is a bit creepy. The new guy keeps telling me how much they rate me and how I'm a superstar. It's like he's grooming me or something. I keep waiting for him to load the entire *Gloss* team into a van to see some puppies then drive us off into the Hudson River.'

'You really think they could?' he asked, wrapping his hand around my wrist.

'No, not really,' I said, yanking on my pants. 'I think he might sack us all, but I can't imagine drowning is actually a possibility.'

'You know what I meant,' Alex said, rubbing the sleep from his eyes. 'I hate that this has been happening without me here to help.'

'Apart from worrying about losing my job, the constant urge to puke and cry, my dodgy blood pressure, not being able to drink, Jenny's engagement followed by Jenny's break-up, the complete and utter exhaustion, things haven't been so bad,' I assured him.

'Same old, same old,' he agreed, shaking his head and pulling me into his chest. 'You know you're going to kill it at this presentation today?'

'Yes,' I said, forcing conviction into my voice. 'I am.'

'And you know you're going to be the best mom ever.'

'Mum,' I corrected. 'Not mom.'

'See?' he said, kissing my forehead. 'You're already such a stickler for the details.'

I rested my hands on his shoulders and rubbed my face against his beard. I didn't know how Jenny put up with this twenty-four seven from Mason, my skin was already itchy and red.

'I'm so glad you're home,' I told him, pressing my lips against his in a loving-but-entirely-chaste-because-I-really-did-have-to-get-into-the-shower-or-I-was-going-to-be-late kiss.

'Whatever happens today, it's going to work out OK,' he said. 'We will figure it out.'

It was all I needed to hear.

Joe had asked me to give my presentation in Delia's office, meaning, I assumed, that Delia would be there as well. At least it would be one friendly face to go with the irritatingly handsome and annoying one.

I sat in the waiting room, smiling politely at her assistant, bouncing my laptop on my knees while the clock ticked down towards nine. I hadn't been up here since Delia got promoted. Her old office was nice, lots of pictures, big window overlooking Times Square, and a comfy leather settee in case you needed an emergency lie-down. Which I did. My morning sickness seemed to be worse when I was anxious and, as unlikely as it seemed, the idea of having to stand up in front of a man I didn't like and explain why me and seventeen other people should keep their jobs made me feel antsy. I'd already puked twice and now there was nothing left.

'Thanks so much, Caroline.'

Double doors opened and Joe emerged, shaking hands with Caroline Galvani, editor of *The Look*. I'd been so worried about losing my own job, my own magazine, my own staff, I'd barely allowed myself to think about the reality of Caroline losing hers.

'Angela.'

She gave me a nod as she swept past, laptop under her arm, Manolos on her feet. We weren't friends, but I'd always liked Caroline. She made a difficult job look easy and no one had a bad word to say about her. Maybe I wasn't done puking just yet.

'Hi.'

I looked back to see Joe waving.

'Are you ready?'

'Yes,' I replied, gathering my bag, my laptop and my wits as the lift pinged to take Caroline back down to her floor. 'I'm ready.'

She glanced over her shoulder as she stepped inside, her face drawn and grey, and showed me a tight, tearful grimace. This was horrible.

'Then let's do this,' Joe said, holding the door open wide and inviting me inside. Caroline disappeared into the lift and I followed Joe into Delia's office without looking back.

'Wow.'

Joe tossed a pencil across the polished glass table and began to clap. Beside him, Delia smiled.

'Just, wow.'

'Just wow?' I asked, flipping down the screen on my laptop. 'That's it? Great, I'll go back down to my desk then.'

'She's so funny,' Joe said to Delia, who nodded along happily. 'It's a British thing, right? They're always funny.'

Delia had been almost entirely silent since the moment I walked into her ridiculously massive office. The new view stretched all the way up to Central Park and it was nice, but I really missed the little leather settee. This was not an office that lent itself to naps.

'Must be something in the water,' I replied, desperate to get out of there and back behind my own desk.

Even as I had delivered mine and Cici's presentation, talking them through each slide, explaining why *Gloss* was the voice of the future at Spencer, why we had the most potential, the best connections, the greatest opportunities, all I could think about was the defeated look on Caroline's face. By keeping my magazine open, I was talking someone else out of a job. Dozens of someone elses. The tiny crystal Christmas tree on the edge of Delia's desk didn't help. We were post-Thanksgiving and it was officially the most wonderful time of the year. Unless you were about to be made redundant.

'You really spoke to the essence of the *Gloss* brand,' Joe said, positively beaming. 'I had you all wrong, Angela. This is fantastic work.'

'All wrong?' I asked. 'How so?'

'Anyone can write listicles and five hundred word features on what to wear next season,' he said, tapping his blank notebook. He hadn't written down a single thing. 'You're more than that, you have vision.'

Joe Herman, the king of the backhanded compliment.

'What Joe is trying to say is you understand how to put together a good magazine *and* how to grow a brand,' Delia clarified quickly. The look on my face must have been a picture. 'It can be complicated, moving from editorial into corporate. You've delivered precisely what we wanted to see. That's very difficult for some people, Angela. Most people, in fact.'

And it had been difficult for me. Impossible, actually. I hadn't a clue what they wanted. But Cici knew.

'Well, this is what you asked me to do,' I said,

looking down at my laptop. 'You know how strongly I believe in *Gloss*.'

'It was just fantastic work,' Joe said, so enthused I was worried he might have an accident. 'We have some things to discuss but I think we'll be able to get back to you on this pretty soon, right boss?'

Eurgh, he called Delia boss?

'I would say so,' she agreed. 'Joe, if you want to go, I'm going to chat to Angela for a bit.'

A second of surprise crossed his face but he pushed it away quickly, like a pro. He clearly wasn't used to being dismissed.

'No worries,' he replied, grabbing his omnipresent iPad before he left. 'I'll catch up with you later.'

We both waited until he had left the room and closed the door firmly behind him.

'Really?' I sat myself in Joe's seat and rolled his pencil right off the desk and onto the plush, cream carpet. 'Anyone can write a listicle?'

'I know, I know,' Delia laughed, holding her head in her hands. 'I'm sorry, he didn't mean it like that.'

'Yes, he did,' I said, dropping my own face onto the glass table and admiring my Saint Laurent booties. My skirt was tight; this was the last time I'd be wearing it for a while. 'He doesn't have a lot of time for writers, does he?'

'He just doesn't understand but you know I do.'

She kicked off her stilettos and skipped over to a mirrored cabinet underneath her enormous flatscreen TV. It was like Willy Wonka's chocolate factory made miniature, there wasn't a single kind of snack I couldn't see. She held up a packet of Twizzlers for consideration and I held out my hands.

'Gimme,' I said, clapping my approval.

'Joe never worked on the editorial side of things. He studied business, went into marketing and ended up in publishing, not because he loves it but because it pays him the most,' Delia explained, as she tore into the packet of sweets. 'That's not to say he isn't incredibly good at his job, because he is. I wouldn't have hired him otherwise.'

I took a Twizzler from the packet and munched away.

'He's right, though, your presentation was impressive,' she said. 'If I didn't know better, I'd have thought he wrote it himself.'

'I had some help,' I replied. 'To put it mildly. And I'm really good at writing listicles. I miss writing listicles, I was the queen of listicles.'

'You just like saying listicles,' she said as I tried my best to swallow the strawberry-flavoured sweet and keep it down. 'Taking over the company from my grandfather is a huge honour, but between you and me, we're not in the best shape. I don't want to close magazines, I want to grow. Do you think it was my ambition to come in and fire people?'

'No,' I admitted.

'You're my friend, Angela, a really, really good one at that. But the business is my family.' Delia nibbled the very end of a Twizzler and gazed out of the window. 'And now I'm in charge, it's basically my baby. I truly thought I knew how hard this was going to be, but I had no idea. There have been so many times I've picked up the phone to call you for impromptu cocktails but when I look at the clock, it's already midnight. I know this job is what I always wanted, I know making it work is going to mean sacrifice.'

'Imagine that,' I said, hiding a smile. 'I do understand, you don't need to explain it to me.'

Cici and Delia might have had matching nose jobs when they turned sweet sixteen, but Cici had been far more dedicated when it came to her Botox regimen. Right in that moment, Delia looked much older than her sister now, but she also looked proud.

'You haven't sacrificed me,' I told her, loosening the zip on my pencil skirt just a touch. 'I'm still your friend, Delia. Regardless.'

'That's good to hear,' she said, looking relieved.

'Is *Gloss* going to be OK?' I asked, even though I didn't really want to.

'I don't know,' she replied. 'It's up to Joe. It has to be.'

I chewed thoughtfully on my Twizzler.

'I'm glad to hear we're still friends,' Delia said, changing the subject with aplomb. 'I thought maybe you'd replaced me with Cici.'

'Not replaced . . . ' I was still wrapping my head around the part where she might close my magazine. 'But we *are* getting along a lot better these days. It turns out she's not all bad after all.'

'I don't know how to feel about that,' Delia said with a forced laugh. 'I'm glad she isn't trying to blow up your luggage again but, well, you're *my* friend.'

She handed me a second Twizzler and rolled her eyes at herself.

'It's a twin thing,' she explained when I didn't reply. 'I'm just jealous. Cici always got first pick at everything growing up. Clothes, bedrooms, boys. This is the first thing I've had that's mine.'

'Me *and* a global media empire,' I said with a whistle. 'You've got basically everything a girl could want.'

'Ha ha,' Delia replied. 'Very funny.'

'I do try,' I replied. 'I really do try.'

I wasn't the first person to arrive at lunch. Right after my presentation, I'd legged it to a doctor's appointment where Dr Laura had confirmed to Alex that there was definitely a baby and not just an excessive amount of pizza in my belly. Leaving him in the waiting room to stare at the updated twelve-week sonogram, I ran down the street to Fig & Olive.

'You're late,' Cici said, already halfway down a glass of red wine. 'I was about to leave.'

'It's four minutes past twelve,' I replied, checking my watch. 'And you're drinking wine.'

She stared at me over the rim of the glass as she drank. I really should have made more effort to convince Delia she had nothing to worry about when it came to me and Cici being besties.

'How did it go?' she asked, signalling to the waitress for another glass of red.

'So great!' I threw my coat over the back of the chair and gulped down half a glass of water. 'It totally looks like a baby now, there's a head and a brain, a bladder, two arms, two legs, all the other bits that should be there.'

'I meant how did the meeting go,' she said, pushing her menu away. 'But thanks for the biology lesson. I guess I wasn't hungry anyway.'

As soon as she said it, I remembered. It was almost scary how quickly I'd forgotten about the presentation. Wow.

'The presentation was brilliant,' I told her as bread magically appeared at the table. There was a reason I'd chosen this restaurant. 'They loved everything, all your suggestions, all the parts about talking to new readers and engaging with the audience. Joe ate it up.'

'I bet he did,' she said, a tiny smile playing on her lips. 'So, how come we're out for lunch? We've never gone out for lunch before. Are you firing me?'

'No!' I exclaimed, my mouth already full of freshly baked bread. 'Why would I fire you? This is a celebratory lunch. It's a thank you.'

'Oh.' Cici looked as uncomfortable as I felt. 'Right. OK. Do I have to eat?'

'It is traditional,' I replied, pushing the menu towards her. 'They have nice salads here.'

'Yeah, I know,' she said, draping her napkin in her lap now she realized she was staying. 'But I'm on a daytime fast, right now. All I can eat is cruciferous vegetables and bone broth.'

'And red wine?' I asked.

She shrugged and drained the dregs.

'I wanted to tell you how much I appreciate all your help with the presentation,' I explained after ordering. 'And with the Generation *Gloss* party. Last year we paid an agency an absolute fortune and they didn't do half as good a job as you did. I almost can't believe you pulled it all together on your own.'

'Really?' she asked, her microbladed eyebrows strained against her Botox in surprise. 'It was kinda easy, if I'm honest. Like I said, all you have to do is tell people what to do and make sure they do it on time and in budget. If they don't, they get their ass delivered to them. How hard could that be?'

'For me, very hard,' I said, dipping another piece of bread in a tiny pool of olive oil.

Cici made a sour face, whether at my wussiness or at me consuming actual oil, I wasn't sure.

'Have you ever thought about moving into a more corporate position?'

She dropped her head backwards until the ends of her hair almost touched the floor and let out a loud, guttural groan. Across the table, I watched a middle-aged man reflexively press his hand over his crotch.

'You can't even have what she's having because she's not eating,' I joked to the horrified-looking old lady at the next table.

'So, that's a no on management, is it?' I asked, shoving more bread into my gob.

'I don't want to be my sister,' Cici said, visibly frustrated as well as audibly. 'It's bad enough that I have to work at that place, creeping around in her shadow, while she runs the world. I want to do my own thing – I thought you would understand that.'

'I would?' Obviously, I didn't.

'Yeah,' she replied as her second glass of wine appeared. 'You wanted something so you worked hard and you got it. I know everything is about to go to shit in the restructure, but you're pregnant now, so who cares, right?'

'There is so much to deal with in that sentence, I'm not sure where to start,' I said, holding my hands out to slow myself down. 'Why is everything going to go to shit?'

'Because everyone will hate you,' she replied as though I should already know. 'If *Gloss* closes and our team is fired, they'll know you knew about it and they'll blame you for not saving them. If *The Look* closes and everyone there gets fired, people will say it's because you're friends with Dee Dee and she stepped in to save your job.'

245

'But she isn't!' I argued. 'That's why Joe is in charge of the restructure, so she doesn't have to be involved.'

'Sure,' Cici replied. 'And would you believe that if it was the other way around and Caroline Galvani was BFFs with the president of the company?'

'Can I pleased have a very tiny sip of your wine?' I asked.

She obediently handed over the glass. I stared into the rich red liquid and sighed before handing it back untouched.

'It's not fair to say I don't care about my job because I'm pregnant,' I said. 'I care. I'm not going to leave when I have the baby. I love my job.'

Plus, I added in my own head, I really needed the money.

'You don't even know what your job is going to be,' Cici said, pulling the merest scrap from the edge of a piece of bread and guiltily popping it into her mouth. It wasn't even a crumb but I was so proud. 'And have you checked in with your old pal Dee Dee about the maternity benefits at Spencer? That could change your mind.'

'They're not good?'

'They're archaic,' Cici replied. 'Literally the legal bare minimum. Twelve weeks' unpaid leave, no guarantees after that.'

'I didn't want anyone to know until I was twelve weeks so I haven't asked yet,' I murmured. 'Which did your grandfather hate more, women or children?'

'He hated them both equally,' she replied. 'It's fairly well documented.'

It hadn't even occurred to me to check the maternity benefits at work. How could women in the UK get a whole year off work to bond with their baby while I only got twelve weeks of unpaid leave? How was I supposed to bond with my baby in twelve weeks? It was definitely going to grow up to be an axe murderer who went around chopping up women who looked like me. This explained Norman Bates perfectly.

'That's why we have approximately four mothers in the entire company,' Cici said. 'None of the women on *Gloss* have kids, do they?'

'No.' I ran through every woman on my magazine, every single childless one of them. 'No kids. But they're all so young.'

'Not that young,' Cici replied simply. 'It can't be done, Angela. You can't run a magazine and have a baby.'

'Anna Wintour does it,' I said, clutching at the fanciest straw I could think of.

'Please. She's not human and we all know it.'

'OK,' I said. Time to turn the tables. 'If you hate working at Spencer so much, why do you stay here? I'm sure you could get a job somewhere else.'

'Really?' she asked with an arched brow. 'You think? Who is going to hire me, exactly? My résumé isn't exactly overflowing with accomplishments. I know everyone loves working at *Gloss* but your name doesn't exactly open every door in town.'

It was harsh but fair. My name didn't even open the door to this restaurant: we'd only been able to get a reservation when Cici made it.

'I want to do something for myself,' she said, a fierce look on her face. 'I want my grandpa to look at me and tell me I'm just as good as *she* is, just for once. That's why I wanted to go into editorial. Dee Dee can't write, she can't edit. I really thought if I could excel at that, he'd be so proud. She was always the smart twin, the hardworking twin. But I'm smart too, Angela. I'm good at stuff. Just because I didn't want to leave college and immediately lock myself away in an office building like Rupert Murdoch meets Rapunzel doesn't mean I'm useless.'

Cici was jealous of Delia and Delia was jealous of Cici. It was all so *Sweet Valley High*.

'Of course it doesn't,' I said. 'I get it. I turned up here without any idea what I was doing. I didn't even know I could write for a magazine until someone gave me a chance. Everyone needs someone to point them in the right direction.

'So, what's my direction?' she asked in a soft, questioning voice, wrapping a long strand of hair around her index finger. 'Who's going to help me?'

I leaned across the table and she automatically leaned away.

'What are you doing?' she hissed.

'Helping,' I hissed back. 'Or at least trying to.'

'Really?' She didn't look convinced. 'OK.'

'You have a talent for managing people,' I told her, pushing on with my attempt to be the bigger person. 'The things you find easy, telling people what to do, knowing what people want before they do, that's a skill. I think you could be really successful if you could just work out where you want to be.'

'You do?' Cici let the piece of hair spiral away from her, a slight kink appearing where it had been wrapped around her finger.

'Really successful,' I said again. 'I think kicking ass might be in your genes.'

'Well, obvs,' she breathed out slowly, staring down at the floor. 'But if I took that route, if I did it here,

I'd always be under Dee Dee, wouldn't I? She's the total HBIC.'

'Probably,' I admitted. 'You really couldn't cope with that?'

She pushed her fingertips into her temples and shook her head.

'Then sod it,' I said, flinging my arm up into the air for effect, forgetting I was still holding a piece of bread. I watched as it sailed across the room and landed in an unsuspecting businessman's salad.

'Start your own company,' I suggested, turning quickly away as he inspected the carb missile. 'You're young, you're loaded. Work out what you want to do, be amazing at it and burn Spencer Media to the ground if you want.'

She made a pleased noise in the back of her throat as she considered the proposition.

'Only, don't actually burn it to the ground,' I added quickly. 'That was just a figure of speech. Arson has no place in this plan and I am not recommending it.'

'You really think I could run my own company?' she asked.

'I really think you could do anything,' I confirmed. 'As terrifying as that sounds.'

'Hmm.' She grabbed an actual, honest-to-goodness piece of bread and took a bite. 'Watch out world, here comes Cici Spencer.'

'Here she comes indeed,' I said, raising my glass of water to clink it against her wine. 'And may god help us all.'

CHAPTER SIXTEEN

That evening, I left work with a smile on my face for the first time in weeks. It was freezing in Manhattan and it was as though the entire island had just remembered Christmas was right around the corner. I pulled the collar of my parka up around my ears even though I wasn't really that cold. The baby had some kind of inferno magical powers that kept me nice and toasty, even when the temperatures dropped below zero. I was quietly hoping it meant my baby was a superhero, but Alex *and* the doctor had told me not to get my hopes up. They were such spoilsports.

The Times Square subway station wasn't even worth considering this close to the holidays – I had no interest in spending forty minutes with my nose stuck in someone's armpit, with another person's shopping bags poking me in the bum. Instead of taking the stairs deep, deep down under the city, I wandered along 42nd Street, smiling at people in Santa hats and reindeer antlers. On any given evening in December, you were guaranteed to run into someone's Christmas party. It had always been my favourite time of year; everyone looked happier, kinder, more forgiving, and I couldn't stop thinking, as I trotted along to Bryant Park, this time next year the baby would be here.

'Sorry! Happy holidays!'

A young couple in matching Santa outfits and enormous white beards buzzed by, turning me around as they went. I reached out for the wall to steady myself as they rushed by, grabbing hold of each other until they came to a dizzy stop in each other's arms and kissed, their red noses colliding in the crisp night air.

'Ahh,' I sighed, enjoying their romance while simultaneously checking they hadn't stolen my wallet. This was New York, after all.

The ice rink in Bryant Park was packed. Tuesday, Wednesday, Friday, Saturday, it didn't matter. New York had swollen to twice its size, taking in visitors from all over the world, looking to find their Christmas miracle. Or at least a fancy handbag that was slightly cheaper than it would be at home. Beyond the ice rink was a market, red-and-white-striped stalls selling knickknacks and tat − by far my favourite form of merchandise − and filling up empty stomachs with hot mulled wine and chestnuts roasted on an open fire. I stood still for a moment, trying to capture the moment. So many happy people in one place at once. It was not something to be taken for granted.

'Hey, babe.'

'Hi!'

Alex Reid, freshly shaven and armed with shopping bags of his own, leaned down to kiss my lips. His face was cold but his eyes were bright.

'Five days ago, I was on a deserted beach,' he said wistfully, looking over at the pulsating swarm of bodies in the Christmas market. Little puffs of warm air followed his words every time he spoke.

'You want to go back?' I asked, checking my phone and smiling. She was on her way.

'I'm good,' he replied, reaching into the Bloomingdale's bag in his hand. 'Hey, look, I couldn't help myself.'

'You went to Bloomingdale's without me?' I wailed, pressing my hands over my mouth as he held up a little white onesie with a guitar on the front. He turned it around and, on the back, it read 'I'm with the band'.

'I had to,' he said as I snatched it out of his hands. 'Really, what choice did I have?'

'This baby is going to be so well dressed,' I said, my heart stopping at the price on the tag. How could this possibly cost fifty dollars? 'Thick as a pig because we won't be able to afford to send it to school, but incredibly well dressed. Do you have any idea how much it costs just to make sure your child doesn't turn into a coked-out smack whore around these parts?'

'Why?' Alex asked. 'Is it cheaper in England?'

'It's funny, if you go to normal school in England, you'll probably just end up sniffing glue or doing poppers in GCSE science. You have to pay to go to private school to end up a cokehead,' I explained. 'But here, it seems fairly lose-lose. Send them to normal school and they've got no hope of getting into a good college. Send them to private school and they're going to end up working as a high-class escort to pay for their Molly habit and possibly drown in the basement swimming pool of their Upper East Side schoolmate.'

Alex met me with a stern look.

'Have you been rewatching *Gossip Girl*?'

'For research,' I nodded gravely.

'I know we're not rolling in money but we're not exactly living on the street either, we'll make it work,' he said, taking back the onesie and putting it safely inside the bag. 'My baby is going to have the best of everything, whatever it takes. Me and Graham have so many great ideas for the next record, it's going to kill.'

'And do you think there's a chance you can record it and tour it before the baby is born?' I asked. 'Because today I found out I only get three months' maternity leave and literally no pay while I'm off.'

'What did you tell me about keeping your blood pressure down,' he asked. 'You cannot get stressed about these things, we'll figure them out. We're not the first people in New York City to ever have a baby.'

'No, I know,' I agreed. He was right, I needed to calm down. And I needed some roasted nuts. 'At least I've got really good health insurance with work.'

'Good point, more things like that please,' Alex said, taking my hand and leading me into the market. 'I said I'd meet him by the mulled wine.'

'Might be a bit of a problem if I get the sack tomorrow,' I mused as we wove our way through the throngs of people. 'But heigh-ho.'

'Getting back to the positive stuff,' he urged gently. 'Have you thought about names?'

'What if they do sack me, though?' A warm flush of anxiety started at my toes and raced all the way up to my face. 'I can't be a stay-at-home mum forever, Alex. I'd lose my mind, I'd be the size of a house inside a week, you'd have to wash me with a rag on a stick. I need my life, I *love* my life.'

'I was thinking Patti for a girl and maybe Elliot for a boy,' Alex went on. 'Or even Elliot for a girl. That works too, what do you think?'

'Everything's changing so quickly,' I said, offering no response to his ridiculous names. 'Even Chocolate Oranges have changed. I bought one from the English shop while you were away and they've taken the middle bit out and the foil is basically plastic now; you can't rewrap them properly after you've had a bit.'

'Babe,' Alex took my manically waving hands in his and secured them against his chest. 'When was the last time you rewrapped a Chocolate Orange?'

'It took me three days to finish it,' I said fearfully. 'Maybe that was a sign. A terrible, terrible sign.'

'I might have some money coming in soon,' he said. 'I was catching up on my emails and there was something from the licensing team at the label. Someone wants to use "Night Song" in something. I'm not sure what yet, but they actually want to pay.'

Ooh, pay meant money.

'On a soundtrack or something?' I asked. 'Like, in a movie?'

'Night Song' was one of my favourite songs from Stills' last album, mostly because Alex said he'd written it for me. I really couldn't see the point in being married to a musician if you couldn't at least get a couple of good tunes out of it to brag about on Facebook.

'I guess, he didn't say.' He leaned in and kissed my cheek, gently patting my belly at the same time. 'I'm gonna talk to them tomorrow. I doubt we're talking retire-in-the-Bahamas cash but it's better than nothing.'

'I don't know,' I said. 'I bet you could retire in the Bahamas on next to nothing. Once you've bought our house, what else do you need? I'd probably do a lot less online shopping in the Bahamas and—'

'Hey,' he nodded across the ice rink, 'here she comes.'

254

'And he's over there,' I said, pointing to the mulled wine stand. 'Are you ready for Operation Jentervention?'

'Fuck no,' he replied, cheerful as you like. 'But let's go force our friends to get back together whether they like it or not.'

Breaking apart, I jumped into the crowd to intercept Jenny while Alex headed Mason off at the pass. Tricking them into meeting up had been my idea, but Alex was the genius who suggested the very public setting. They were far less likely to spill blood with lots of people watching.

'I know you're pregnant, but I need to get wasted,' Jenny said, leaning in for a double air kiss. 'I had the shittiest day in history.'

'Then this is going to be a wonderful surprise!' I said, standing to the side to reveal Alex and Mason. Even though I'd seen Jenny look better, Mason looked like he was in a world of pain. It was only three days since they'd called it quits but he looked like he'd been living out by the bins for a month.

'You start,' I said to Alex, patting the front of his leather jacket while our formerly affianced friends stared at each other, speechless. 'You're the song-writer.'

'You're the writer,' he replied, nervously flipping his attention between the two. 'Why aren't they saying anything?'

'Then I'll start,' I said, waving a hand in front of Mason's glassy eyes. 'Before I do, please don't hurt me, Mason, I'm pregnant.'

'I know,' he said, snapping to attention. 'Jenny told me.'

'You did?' I turned on my friend who shrugged.

'Sure,' she replied. 'He swore he wouldn't say anything.'

'How long have you known?' I asked, looking back up at Mason and trying not to get a crick in my neck.

'Uh, a couple of weeks?' he guessed, checking with Jenny. She nodded and made a more-or-less gesture with her hand. 'I don't know, when did you move into Jen's place?'

'You told him right away!' I wailed. 'Jenny!'

'I tell him everything,' she wailed back. 'You know I can't keep a secret!'

'Did you tell him what you told me on Saturday night?' I demanded, hands on my quickly expanding hips.

'Which part?' she asked quietly.

'The part where you said you just wanted to marry him and only wanted a big wedding to show people how much you love him,' I prompted. 'Not that part where I found you in an alleyway, covered in disgusting bin juice.'

'No, because he's an asshole who doesn't love me and never really wanted to get married in the first place,' she replied, folding her arms over her pea coat and refusing to look at Mason. 'And it's really hard to tell him anything when he won't return my calls.'

'You called me once!' Mason volleyed back. 'And when I tried to call you on Sunday, you'd blocked my number!'

'You did?' Alex winced. 'Cold, Lopez.'

'I did?' She pulled out her phone to check. He was right. 'Wow, old habits, huh?'

'I do love you,' Mason said, chopping one giant palm with his other giant hand. 'And I do want to marry you. But I don't want to spend the same amount of money on a wedding that we could use to put down a deposit on a house. The things you were talking about, Jen, we could put our kids through college with what you wanted to spend.'

'Our kids?' she asked, gnawing on her thumbnail.

'Yeah.' He pulled her hand out of her mouth. 'Don't bite your nail, you know how mad you'll be if it breaks.'

'I don't want to spend that much money,' she said, sticking her hands deep into her coat pockets. 'They were just ideas I was coming up with. You didn't have to be such an asshat about it.'

'I overreacted,' Mason admitted. 'I've been losing my mind about all the restructures at work and I didn't want to worry you. I guess I convinced myself if I couldn't give you the wedding you deserved, I didn't deserve you.'

'Look at them,' I whispered to Alex, resting my head on his arm. 'They're talking to each other!'

'All I want is to marry you,' Jenny said, biting her bottom lip and looking upwards. I recognized it as her I'm-not-going-to-cry face. 'I don't care where we do it, Mase.'

'Maybe we could do it at my brother's house upstate,' he suggested, reaching out to pull her into a hug.

'No,' she replied quickly, burying her face into his torso. 'I don't think so.'

'Hey, let's do this properly.' Mason released his re-fiancée and pulled his wallet out of his jacket pocket. 'I kept this with me, just in case.'

Lowering himself onto one knee, he held out Jenny's ring as people formed a circle all around us.

'Jenny Lopez, will you marry me possibly in Maui, possibly in New York but definitely not in my broth-er's house?' he asked.

'Yes!' Jenny said, tearing her leather gloves off with

257

her teeth and hurling them in my general direction. 'You know I will, dickface.'

'Young love,' Alex sighed, kissing the top of my head.

I, and approximately half the city, began to clap as Mason picked Jenny up off her feet and spun her around in a big circle. I gave her an enthusiastic thumbs up, holding her gloves in my teeth as she leaned towards me over his shoulder.

'You really didn't have to mention the alleyway part,' she hissed. 'Dick.'

'Those two crazy kids,' I said to Alex. 'Our work here is done.'

'Good, this jetlag is playing havoc with my appetite,' he said. 'Can we get something to eat? I'm starving.'

'How do you always know just what to say,' I said, embracing him happily. 'Pizza?'

'Pizza,' he confirmed.

Truly, there could not have been a better end to a worse day.

CHAPTER SEVENTEEN

My mum always loved to tell me a watched pot never boils. Utter nonsense, I would reply, of course it does. But I'd been watching the kettle in our little work kitchen for what felt like a lifetime and the bloody thing refused to boil. It was so long since I'd made myself a cup of tea at work, I assumed it had gone on strike. Enjoying a nice cup of Tetley's finest had become a home-exclusive activity. The office called for coffee – lattes, cappuccinos, Americanos, espressos if I was in a bad way, flat whites if I was feeling fancy. I wasn't sure when I'd switched from a lovely cup of tea to a bucket of rocket fuel, but I did know I missed it. Jenny had insisted I switch to decaffeinated beverages because caffeine was bad for the baby. So now I was both perpetually knackered and suffering caffeine withdrawals, a wonderful combination that definitely helped me get through the day with a smile on my face.

'Mine's with milk and two sugars.'

I turned around to see Joe gurning at me on the other side of the fridge.

'What?'

'Not really,' he said, straightening his tie. 'I don't do sugar or dairy.'

'Of course you don't,' I replied, heaping a teaspoon full of the good stuff into my decaf brew. They can take away my caffeine, but they'll never take my sugar, just like Braveheart said. Or something.

It was only a day since I'd given my presentation, I wasn't expecting any answers just yet. I was *hoping* for them but I'd long since learned that anticipation was the mother of all kicks to the tits. A watched pot never boiled and a constantly refreshed inbox never delivered. Maybe my mum was onto something after all.

'I'm very close to finalizing the new strategy,' Joe said, eyeing my sugar consumption with disdain. At least, I hoped it was just my sugar consumption. It could have been the massive pompoms on the front of my jumper, but since I'd had no coffee in three weeks and gave approximately zero fucks, I would never really know. 'I'm presenting to Delia and the board next week and we'll be able to share with the group before the holidays.'

'You're going to announce a restructure before Christmas?' I asked, stirring my milky tea. 'So, there aren't going to be any redundancies?'

'Obviously this is all hypothetical and confidential, but why would that mean there aren't going to be any redundancies?' He looked at me, confused.

I felt as though I was going to puke and unusually, it had nothing to do with the baby.

'You're going to put people out of a job, right before Christmas?'

'Better to get it done than drag it out into the New

Year,' he replied with his shark's smile. 'Wouldn't you agree?'

'Joe, can I ask,' I picked up my tea and took a small sip, 'who did you vote for in the last election?'

'I'll talk to you next week,' he said, rapping on the refrigerator before he left. 'I think you're going to be excited.'

'I can hardly contain myself,' I assured him, heading in the opposite direction and back to my empty office.

Only it wasn't empty.

Two very burly men and one officious-looking woman were removing the little settee that sat inside the door and bringing in a hot pink desk and matching chair.

'I think you might have the wrong office,' I said, holding my tea over my head to avoid spillage as I sidled around them to block their way. 'This is my office, I'm not expecting any new furniture.'

'Angela Clark?' the woman asked, consulting a clipboard as she spoke. 'Office 1223?'

I nodded.

'Then this is the correct office.'

Loading themselves up like a little human forklift, the two men picked up my settee and backed themselves out of the office. I followed as clipboard lady called the lift.

'The order was signed by Joe Herman,' she explained, flashing a scribble on a piece of paper at me. 'I'm sure he can explain.'

'I'm sure he can,' I replied. 'And I'm sure he won't.'

Half the office was out on lunch but those that remained were all ears. Constantly having to bite my tongue had aged me ten years in the last three weeks. I was going to start billing my sheet masks

261

back to the company and boy, did I love a sheet mask.

'What's happening?' Jason asked, clutching at his throat as I hovered by his desk. 'Are you leaving? Did you get fired? Are you supposed to be taking the furniture with you?'

'I didn't get fired, I'm not leaving,' I said, watching as it disappeared into the lift, 'but I'm not sure what's going on.'

'What's with Barbie's Dream Desk?' Megan popped up from her desk, three different shades of eyeshadow on each eye. 'Are you redecorating?'

'Do I really look like someone who would have a neon pink desk in her office?' I asked. They looked at each other and then nodded. 'Yeah, I totally would. Where do you think it's from? I wonder if Alex would let me have one at home.'

'Everything's all right, isn't it?' Megan asked, lowering her voice. 'Ever since they cleared out marketing I've been waiting for the other shoe to drop. One of the guys on *Ghost* told me he saw Caroline from *The Look* crying in the toilets yesterday.'

'One of my guys on *Ghost* told me they're firing their editor,' Jason confided. I tried not to look startled; if they fired Mason's editor, what would that mean for him?

'There's so much gossip going around at the moment, and I bet hardly any of it is true,' I said, trying to throw them off the scent. 'Do you really believe Caroline Galvani was crying in the toilets?'

Jason nodded. Megan looked doubtful.

'There's no way,' I insisted, even though I was quite sure she had been. The look on her face as she left Delia's office had kept me awake half the night. 'She's such a professional, it just wouldn't happen. Even *I* wouldn't cry in the toilets at work.'

'You cry all the time,' Megan replied. 'You cried in the morning meeting on Monday.'

'That was Sophie's fault for playing that video of the dog that hadn't seen his owner in five years,' I argued.

'And you were crying at your desk this morning,' Jason added. 'I didn't like to say, but basically we all saw.'

'I was watching the dog video again,' I replied. 'The point is, I would never cry in the toilets about work stuff and neither would Caroline Galvani.'

'Oh,' Megan snapped her fingers and pointed at Jason, 'what about that time Idris Elba came in and you missed him because you were buying cronuts? You cried in the toilets then.'

'As I was saying, I very much doubt anyone saw Caroline Galvani crying in the toilets yesterday and if she was, I'm sure she had a very good reason,' I replied. 'Maybe she was trying to get tickets to the Katy Perry concert and they'd all sold out.'

'Angela, I love you but you're a terrible liar,' Jason said. 'How long until we know whether or not we're all gonna get fired?'

I had two choices. I could tell them the truth or I could lie.

'I don't know what you're talking about,' I lied.

'Worst. Liar. Ever,' Megan replied.

'Fine, I should know what's going on by the end of next week,' I semi-admitted. 'I don't want you to panic. The best thing you can do right now is carry on as usual, don't give anyone any reason to doubt how great we are.'

'We are pretty great,' Jason acknowledged. 'And we know you've got our back.'

'Always,' I promised, relieved to see smiles on their faces. Smiles that promptly vanished as Cici appeared at my side.

'What are we talking about?' she asked, with a strained attempt at a smile.

'Angela was just telling us how we shouldn't worry about losing our jobs because she's got our backs,' Jason said, shooting me an OK sign. 'Right, chief?'

'Right,' I said, shooting one right back.

'Oh, sure,' Cici laughed, her hand fluttering over her chest. 'That's cute. Can I speak to you for a moment?'

'In my office,' I replied, drawing her away from my crestfallen staff and closing the door behind us.

'What's with this piece of crap?' Cici asked, prodding the desk with the toe of her Gucci loafer. 'Are you already ordering furniture for the nursery?'

'Why would I be ordering a hot pink desk for a nursery?' I asked.

'I don't know,' she replied, pulling a face. 'Looks like the kind of tat you'd be into.'

'Well, you're right, it is,' I said, leaning my bum on the edge of my desk. 'But I don't know why it's in here and I'd appreciate it if you could find out.'

'I guess I could,' she shrugged. 'But I probably won't. I'm gonna be leaving today.'

'Leaving early?' I asked.

'No, leaving,' she replied, dropping her head to one side. 'I quit.'

There had been days when I had sat at my desk and dreamed of this moment. For the first few years of our acquaintance, Cici Spencer had made my life

264

miserable. Even after she gave up trying to get me fired, destroy my relationship, and generally sabotage my life, the best we'd ever managed was an uneasy truce where I didn't fire her and she didn't spit in my coffee. To the best of my knowledge. But now things really had changed.

'I just talked to HR and I'm out,' she announced, her perfectly oval face entirely decided. 'My contract says I have to work a fourteen-day notice, but they didn't seem to care, said I could leave at the end of the day.'

I bet they did. I could only imagine how many champagne corks were popping in HR at that second. Cici had, for the most part, been a terrible assistant, but she'd been an actual terror of an employee. I'd had more emails from HR asking whether or not there was any truth in the reports people had filed against her than I'd had from Facebook asking whether or not I remembered taking a drunk selfie seven years ago.

'I was thinking about what you said yesterday and you're right,' Cici said. 'I don't want to be here any more. As long as I'm working at Spencer, I'm always going to be Bob's granddaughter or Delia's sister, and that sucks. I want to be taken seriously.'

'And you decided this overnight?' I asked, still slightly stunned.

'Yes?'

'And you're sure?'

'Totally,' she insisted and I could see that she was. Gone was the trademark smirk and the ever-present you're-boring-me-to-death-by-breathing expression and in its place, there was a smile. A simple, genuine smile.

'Wow.' I couldn't quite believe it but I was truly sad. Honestly, utterly, end-of-*The Notebook*-level gutted.

'I want to love what I do and I want it to be mine,' she explained. 'I don't want to live with something I had handed to me, I want to create something that is all me.'

'I get it, I really do,' I told her, so confused by how incredibly upset I was. It was the baby's fault, it had to be. My unborn child had imprinted on Cici Spencer and there was nothing I could do about it. 'You want to make something for yourself. What happens when you give a man a fish and all that.'

'If you give a man a fish, he has a fish.' She reached out to press her palm against my forehead. 'Have you eaten this afternoon? Do you have low blood sugar?'

'Don't worry about it.' I felt my eyes prickle and pinched the inside of my arm, determined not to scare Cici with outward emotion. 'So, is this you officially handing in your notice?'

'Yep,' she said, throwing up her arms and looking around the office. 'You're getting a temp tomorrow morning.'

'Obviously, I'm not going to cry,' I said, immediately bursting into tears. 'But I'll be really, really sad to see you go.'

'Quit it,' she snapped, snatching two tissues out of the box on my desk and pressing them into my hands. 'And I think you mean jealous, not sad.'

'What are you talking about?' I sniffed, dabbing at my cheeks.

'Please, Angela.' She rolled her enormous eyes and cackled. 'I'm like the least observant human on earth when it comes to feelings and even I can see how stressed you've been lately. This isn't the same place it used to be. Just because Delia is your buddy doesn't mean she's creating an Angela-friendly utopia for you

266

to work in. Things are only going to get worse for you and you know it.'

'You're just saying that because you're leaving,' I replied, unsure as to whether I was trying to convince her or myself. 'Things are going to be rough for a while but then it's going to go right back to how it was.'

'There's no such thing as how it was,' Cici argued. 'You know what? You're the worst editor ever.'

A gasp caught in the back of my throat and choked its way into the world like a baby seal with whooping cough.

'Not the worst *editor*,' she corrected herself as I fought to regain the power of speech. 'You're a good editor, but you suck at being in charge. It's like, you saw *The Devil Wears Prada* and said, "I guess I'll do the opposite of that." Anna Wintour would weep if she saw the way you break your back to have everyone like you. She would cry genuine human tears – and you know the rumour is she wears those sunglasses all the time because she had her tear ducts removed and it permanently damaged her eyesight and now she can only be exposed to sunlight for two hours a day.'

'That's ridiculous,' I sniffed, biting the inside of my cheek.

'No, it's totally true,' Cici said, examining her cuticles. 'I went to school with her kid and my nanny heard it from her nanny.'

'Not that part,' I argued, crossing my arms in a huff. 'The part about me only caring about people liking me. Although I also refuse to believe the Anna Wintour story until I have it verified by a doctor or see it on *E! News.*'

'I didn't mean to upset you,' she said for the first

time ever. 'I figured you already knew. I think you're going to be a great mom, Angela. You sacrifice everything for everyone else, all the time. You stay late so other people can go home early, you work on weekends so the team doesn't have to, and I know the reason this restructure is freaking you out is because you're worried about everyone else.'

'I'm worried about myself as well,' I said. 'It is possible to care about yourself and other people at the same time, you know.'

'Not in this job,' Cici replied. 'You've got to be ruthless to win at this.'

It was an eye-opening experience, getting life advice from Cici Spencer. I did not care for it.

'Joe is an asshole,' she declared. 'He was an asshole when we dated in college and he's an asshole now. It's not something I like to brag about, but he cheated on me and then told everyone I was the one who cheated and of course, everyone believed him.'

'That's what people do,' I replied with a pang of guilt. It hadn't even occurred to me to get Cici's side of the story before believing Joe's secondhand. What a massive shitbag I was, damn my internalized misogyny. What would Beyoncé think?

'But assholes are good at this job, that's why Dee Dee hired him and I'll let you in on a secret, she's kind of an asshole too.' Cici looked over her shoulder at the buzzing office outside my door. 'I know you love the magazine, but will you still love it when it's ten o'clock at night on a Monday, Sophie's pages still need proofreading, and you haven't seen your baby in fifteen hours?'

'Yes,' I said, sticking out my chin defiantly.

'And will Alex love that?' she asked.

'Might not love it,' I said quietly. 'But he'd understand.'

I looked down at my jumper and dried my eyes on a pink pompom. When did she get so insightful? Was it actually Delia doing an amazing Cici impression? Or was I tripping from caffeine withdrawals?

'To be honest, I'm kind of amazed he hasn't cheated on you already,' she said with what she thought was a supportive smile. 'You're always here and he's super hot. You got knocked up at just the right time, that was smart.'

'OK, so you're leaving.' I wiped my nose on the back of my hand and cleared my throat. 'Should we hug?'

'I quit, I'm not dying,' she replied, recoiling at the thought. 'Don't be mad at me, you made me think about stuff and now I'm returning the favour.'

Just what I needed, more things to think about.

'Much appreciated,' I said graciously. 'As insane as it sounds, I am going to miss you. Do you have any ideas about what you want to do?'

'I know exactly what I'm going to do,' she said. 'I never would have seen it if you hadn't given me the push. If there's something else out there for me, there's something else out there for you.'

She took an uncomfortable step towards me and closed her arms around my shoulders in a stiff, boxy hug.

'You'll figure it out,' she said, pulling away and patting me on the shoulder. 'Or you won't, whatever.'

With that, she walked through the door, slipped on her coat and grabbed her Givenchy handbag from underneath her desk.

'Office announcement,' she shouted as she strode

269

across the room to summon the lift. It dutifully appeared on command. 'I'm leaving. Peace out, bitches.'

'Is it true?' Jason panted as he sprinted through my door. 'Is she gone? You fired her?'

'I didn't fire her, but yes, she's gone,' I confirmed.

'She's gone!' Jason screamed around the door as the entire office burst into rapturous applause. 'Sophie, you go get the cupcakes and I'll grab the champagne.'

Lowering my blinds on the celebrations, I ran my hand over the cuckoo of a bright pink desk that had invaded my space. I hadn't really changed anything since I moved into the office, just added to my nest. My wedding photo sat on top of one of the filing cabinets, pictures of me and Jenny at Erin's wedding, dancing in Las Vegas, posing in front of the Thames with Louisa, and then another of me and Alex under the Eiffel Tower at sunset. The one thing I'd always had, the whole time I'd been in New York, was my job at Spencer Media. Even when Jenny disappeared to LA, even when me and Alex were working things out, I'd always had this. I'd just assumed I always would.

The giant teddy bear James had sent over sat in the corner next to my Alexander Skarsgård poster. How old was that now? How long had it been there? The edges curled and the white parts had turned yellow.

'Et tu, Alexander?' I whispered, taking a seat behind my desk before tapping the words 'Anna Wintour tear duct surgery' into a google search.

Enquiring minds had to know.

CHAPTER EIGHTEEN

'Of course, I'm incredibly happy that the wedding is back on,' I said, kicking my front door open to let Jenny and her endless bags into my apartment after me. 'And I'm always down for a crafternoon, but are you sure you've got enough time to organize an entire wedding in one week?'

Jenny dumped an armload of brown paper bags onto my sofa, revealing her grinning face.

'Have you met me?' she replied. 'Of course I have. And the sooner you quit talking and start stuffing, the sooner we'll be ready for the bachelorette.'

It really was my own fault. In the week and a half that had passed between Jenny and Mason patching up their differences, Jenny had decided she simply couldn't wait one more second to become Mrs Jennifer Lopez Cawston. Not that she was planning on taking his name, but she liked to say it for effect.

'It makes perfect sense,' Jenny said, licking the whipped cream off the top of her coffee cup. 'Break for the holidays on Friday, get married on Saturday and head off on honeymoon on Sunday. Ring in the New Year with mojitos in Maui. Boom.'

Somehow, I managed to stop myself from asking why she hadn't thought of this in the first place and saved everyone a lot of bother. I was truly growing as a person.

'Where's Alex?' she asked, making herself at home in my living room. 'Is he around? Is he going to help?'

'Alex is downstairs in the studio, recording demos with Graham,' I said, shaking my head at the panic in her eyes. 'It's fine, Craig isn't here.'

'Kind of sucks that I'll never be able to see a Stills show again,' she sighed, checking all her bags. Party City, Dylan's Candy Bar, Mood Fabrics, Blick Art Materials. We'd been everywhere. 'Do you think he'll get over it?'

'In time,' I promised. She didn't need to know Craig had stopped by the night before with his third new girlfriend of the month. If there was one thing New York was not running low on, it was hot girls who wanted to go out with cute musicians. Craig would survive, one way or another.

'I can't believe this time next week, I'll be getting married,' she said, fishing a handful of craft paper place cards out of one of the bags and throwing me a calligraphy pen. 'We're doing a walk-through at The Union tomorrow evening and confirming the menu Monday, and then that's it. Hey, how's your handwriting?'

'Terrible,' I replied, throwing it back. My living room was already covered in wedmin detritus, tear sheets from *The Knot*, printouts from Pinterest, rubber stamps, miniature mason jars, and every colour ribbon under the sun. 'You write, I'll stuff.'

'I don't know why I didn't think to do the wedding there in the first place.' Jenny plonked herself on the living room rug next to the coffee table, a huge Starbucks cup in front of her. 'What's more me than a super-luxe boutique hotel in the middle of Manhattan?'

'Especially when you used to work there and they let you use their events space for next to nothing,' I agreed, picking her coat up off the floor and hanging it on the coatrack. 'So, what's the deal then?'

'We have the penthouse suite with panoramic views of Manhattan for the ceremony,' she explained, capturing her curls in a topknot. 'Which they've refurbished since I left, it's so nice now. It'll be super intimate, just twenty people. Then it's dinner for fifty in the restaurant, and we've hired out the basement bar for the evening for everyone else. They tried to stiff me on that, but I offered to hold the next AJB after party there over fashion week and suddenly the price became much more affordable.'

'And you've got everything else sorted?' I asked. 'Flowers, photographer, hair, make-up?'

'Invitations have all been emailed, Erin is taking care of the flowers, Tess Brookes is going to do the photographs,' she replied, ticking each item off on her fingers, 'Gina is doing my hair, Razor is doing my make-up. All that's left is my dress.'

'Oh.' I pulled out an enormous sack of gummy bears and what seemed like hundreds of black, glittery favour bags. 'Just the dress.'

'I've called in every favour I was ever owed,' she said, the cap of her pen in between her teeth. 'And some I really didn't deserve. I'll have a dress by Monday for sure. You and Erin are figured out, right?'

'Right,' I confirmed.

'Mason took care of the photo booth, the cars, the cake and the rings, and he swears he's getting his suit and shoes today.' She took a deep swallow and smacked her lips together. When you didn't have time for a wedding diet, there was no wedding diet. 'I'm telling you, Angie, this is the way to do it. No muss, no fuss.'

'If I ever get married again, I'll bear that in mind,' I replied as I opened the sack of gummy bears. A rush of fake rosé scent escaped from the bag and hit me right in the face. 'Gross.'

'Are you gonna puke?' Jenny asked, suddenly alert. 'How are you still getting morning sickness? Aren't you past twelve weeks now?'

'Some lucky people get it all day, all the way through their pregnancy,' I said in between slow, calming breaths. 'It's getting difficult to hide it at work.'

'You still haven't told them?' She gave me a sympathetic frown. 'Because of the restructure?'

'I still have no idea what's happening,' I nodded. 'Every day I sit at my desk, waiting for the guillotine to fall, and nothing happens. I haven't laid eyes on Joe or Delia in days. Until I know what's going on, I'd rather keep my news to myself.'

'You won't be able to much longer,' she said, reaching out to pat my neat little bump. 'Sure, you can tell people you just got fat right now, but if he keeps growing the way he is, they're gonna know.'

'What makes you think it's a he?' I asked, considering my belly. 'I think it's a girl.'

'Definitely a boy,' Jenny said. 'A girl would have had more considerate timing.'

The instant I reached into the bag of rosé gummy bears to fill my first favour bag, the swell of sickness was back. I jumped to my feet, hand clapped over my mouth, and ran down to the basement toilet. It was roomier than the upstairs bathroom when it came to puking and, thanks to the bump, I'd had plenty of opportunity to try them both out. Clawfoot, roll-top bathtubs looked amazing, but they didn't half take up a lot of space.

When I first met Alex, he was an uber hipster, living the life in a cool Williamsburg loft that overlooked Manhattan. It was the most amazing place I had ever seen, huge open spaces and high ceilings with windows where the walls should be, and a neverending view of New York City. Now, here we were, married with a baby on the way, living in a two-bedroom apartment in a gorgeous townhouse in Park Slope. I missed the loft and its inherent cool factor but I loved our home. Rolling off the L train and traipsing through hipster-ville had been fun, even if I'd always felt more like I was visiting the zoo than moving in for good.

Our Park Slope place was still a fair bit different to all the other family homes on the block. Before Alex invested every penny we had, it had belonged to a music producer friend and our cavernous basement had been turned into a fully functioning studio. It was a muso boy's dream come true. Less awesome if you were the wife of said muso, and liked walking around in your pants of an evening. But thanks to the wonders of soundproofing, I never knew who was down there with him.

Post-yak, I washed my face and stuck my head around the studio door, just to say hello. Alex and Graham were locked in what looked like a very serious conversation behind the glass. Graham was still sporting his travelling beard, I noticed. It was a bold choice. Alex cradled his vintage Fender Stratocaster in his lap. I'd barely seen it out of his arms ever since he arrived home – I'd have been jealous if I wasn't carrying around my own actual human baby; he acted as though he had missed it more than he missed me.

I stared at the soundboard in front of me, dozens of dials and switches blinking with little red and green lights in the darkness.

'One of you turns the sound on,' I said, sighing as I tried to remember exactly what to press.

I was certain Alex only knew how to use half of these buttons, just like me with the dishwasher, but it made him feel like a very special boy to have such an important toy. Somewhere on there was a two-way mic, flick it one way and I'd be able to hear them, flick it the other and we'd both be able to hear each other.

'Ah-ha.' I spotted a dial covered in glittery nail polish and turned it all the way to the left. Alex and Graham's voices echoed over the speakers. Clearly my husband also remembered the night I'd spent five minutes screaming at him through the glass because our Chinese had arrived and I didn't have any cash on me to pay for it.

'I'm not against licensing out the music,' Graham was saying, smoothing down his moustache as he spoke. He looked like Charles Manson, it really had to go. 'But not to these guys. I don't want people to think about processed chicken every time they hear one of our songs.'

'But you do want my kid to get a shitty education?' Alex countered. 'I hear what you're saying, Gray, but I've got to think about these things now. I can't afford to make all my decisions based on your artistic integrity.'

I held my breath, hoping that they hadn't noticed me. I was definitely not meant to hear this conversation.

'If you want to whore yourself out, go ahead,' Graham replied. 'I heard Justin Timberlake bought an actual island with the money he got for a McDonald's commercial, but you're not selling our music to these people.'

'This isn't McDonald's,' Alex protested, holding the guitar in front of him like a shield. 'Craig's fine with it.'

'Then maybe you should record the next Stills record as a two-piece,' Graham said, hopping off his stool. 'I'm super psyched about you having a kid, Alex, but I'm not prepared to sell out so you can buy diapers. Why are you trying to destroy the band? You already cancelled all the summer festival shows without even consulting us. I always knew this would happen; I just figured Craig would be the one to accidentally knock up some chick, not you.'

'It's not like I planned this, it's not like I'm ready,' Alex shouted. I jumped back in the dark. Alex never raised his voice. 'There's a whole bunch of shit I'm gonna have to leave on the to-do list whether I like it or not. She's pregnant, Graham, and I have to deal with it.'

I reached out and flipped off the switch, burning with an entire selection box of emotions. Alex had been so happy about the baby. From the second I told him, he'd done nothing but smile like a loon. He was constantly plumping up my pillows, rubbing my feet, asking how I felt. Not once had he said anything about not being ready.

'Daddy didn't mean that,' I whispered to my

stomach, hoping it was true. Why couldn't I have been born super rich? Or at least super stupid. Stupid people didn't worry about anything.

Graham snatched the door of the recording booth open and made a small, shocked sound when he saw me lurking in the shadows.

'Oh, hey,' he said, not quite managing to look me in the eye. 'I guess congratulations are in order.'

'It is traditional,' I said, sliding a smile I didn't feel onto my face. I didn't want him or Alex to know I'd heard their conversation. 'Sweet beard.'

'You like it?' he asked, stroking the ends with a smile.

'No,' I replied. 'It's awful.'

'I'm headed out,' he said, looking back at Alex who was tuning his guitar in the booth. 'I have a ton of things to do today but it was great to see you.'

'Don't let me keep you,' I said, clapping him on the shoulder. 'Bye, Graham.'

Picking up the canvas messenger bag that sat on the knackered old sofa behind me, he nodded before jogging up the stairs and out the front door. Inside the booth, Alex looked up and smiled. I waved, pointing to my ears when he started talking to let him know I couldn't hear. And hopefully convince him I hadn't heard any of it.

'Hi, beautiful.' He emerged from the booth and slid his hands around my waist, bending down to kiss the bump. 'How's it going up there?'

It was as if the other Alex had vanished completely. There was nothing in his eyes or his voice but pure love. If he really was angry or upset, he was doing far too good a job of hiding it.

'I came down to throw up,' I said and he pulled

away from a kiss, sticking out his tongue instead. 'Graham went off in a bit of a rush. Everything OK?'

He bopped his head from side to side, his long hair skirting around his eyelashes.

'The company that wants to license "Night Song" is not to his liking,' he said. Pinching his shoulders together, he let out a light sigh. 'But they want to pay us a ton of money. Like, a really filthy amount of money.'

'Retire-to-the-Bahamas money?' I asked, raising an eyebrow.

'Retire to the Bahamas and set up our own drug-running business,' he nodded. 'But they're not the most morally sound group of individuals ever.'

I liked to think of myself as a morally sound person but he still hadn't really said exactly how much money we were talking about.

'Have I eaten there?'

'Babe,' Alex said. 'You've eaten everywhere.'

Good point.

'Well, have they ever killed anyone?' I asked.

'Not directly as far as I know,' Alex replied. 'But they've got some pretty shitty hiring policies when it comes to people who aren't straight white dudes and I totally understand why Graham isn't jumping for joy about selling them the song.'

'Then don't do it,' I said simply. 'You've been offered stuff like this before and you said no. The record label won't be massively shocked.'

'Yeah, but we weren't expecting a baby before,' he reminded me. 'I got to thinking about everything the baby is going to need, not just school. Did you know diapers alone cost more than a thousand dollars a year? And it's not like we can toilet-train that little sucker any earlier. A grand! Just so it can poop itself.'

'You could hold it over the lav for the first eighteen months,' I suggested. 'I can't imagine you'd be terribly productive but if we're saving the thick end of two grand . . . '

It was meant to be a joke but the crumpled look that had taken over his usually easy expression cut me off.

'You do what you need to do,' I told him, placing his hand on my little, round belly. I'd spent our entire relationship trying to keep his hands away from that area; I wanted to make the most of this while I could. 'It's not as though we're that hard up for money.'

Unless I lose my job. Unless your next album doesn't sell. Unless there's a recession and the economy crashes and people stop buying magazines and paying for music and, oh shit, both of those things are already happening.

'I'm not worried,' he said. Even as he spoke, I saw a flicker of uncertainty in his eyes and I didn't like it one little bit. 'Everything is OK.'

'Everything is going to be so beyond OK,' I told him, resting my hands on top of his. 'Everything's going to be fantastic, Alex Reid. And you're going to be the best dad in the world.'

'Angie!' Jenny yelled from the top of the stairs. 'There's someone at the door!'

'Answer it, then!' I bellowed back as Alex pulled away, shielding his ears. 'Probably just stuff for the wedding,' I reasoned. 'Or baby stuff.'

'More baby stuff?' he asked.

He looked pointedly at the pile of boxes I'd already stashed in the studio. Ever since we cleared twelve weeks, I hadn't been able to help myself. We'd agreed we wouldn't tell anyone other than the people we had to until I knew what was happening with work and we'd filled in our parents but that didn't mean I hadn't put some quality time in on BabiesRUs.com.

'I've been meaning to ask,' Alex bent over and picked up what looked like a bulletproof vest. 'What is this?'

'It's a breast pump bustier,' I explained, readily whipping it out of the box. I unzipped the front and slipped my arms through the sleeves. 'See? You wear it like a sports bra and then you clip two automatic breast pumps to these slots in the front and it literally milks you.'

I clipped in the pumps and held out my hands for him to inspect my latest purchase.

'It looks like a torture device from *Star Trek*,' Alex gasped in horror. 'Why are you smiling? This is horrifying.'

'It's amazing,' I said, parading up and down the studio with my hands on my hips. 'I can milk myself like a cow while still playing *Candy Crush* and you're taking care of the baby.'

'Angela!' Jenny yelled again. 'I think you ought to get up here!'

'I bet Jenny will like it,' I said, heading up the staircase, ready to show off my lactating leisurewear. 'Oi, Jenny, I think I've got my bridesmaid dress sorted.'

'Angela Clark, what the bloody hell are you wearing?'

Standing in the middle of the hallway, surrounded by suitcases and sporting almost offensive tans, were my mum and my dad.

'It's a breast pump bustier,' I said slowly, as Alex climbed the stairs behind me. 'What are you doing here?'

'Surprising you, obviously. We're here for the wedding,' Mum said. 'Why are you wearing a breast pump bustier?'

'Because I'm pregnant,' I replied.

'Who's surprising who, amirite?' Jenny asked, her face stretching into an enormous open-mouthed smile as she bumped my leather-faced father with her hip. 'Mr Clark? You OK?'

'You're what?' Mum dropped her handbag and four little Nespresso pods rolled out onto the hardwood floor.

'Angela is pregnant,' Alex said, bending over to recover Mum's treasures. 'We're having a baby.'

'You're pregnant?' Dad asked.

We both nodded.

'With a baby?'

'God, I hope so,' I said, pulling a worried face at Alex.

'And this isn't just one of your jokes?'

'Yes, Dad, it's a joke,' I replied, pulling up my T-shirt to show them my slightly swollen stomach. 'I thought it would be hilarious to put on a stone and walk around the house wearing a breast pump bustier just on the off chance that my parents, who don't even live in this country, might decide to pop round on a Saturday afternoon to surprise me.'

'Well, there's no need for that attitude,' Mum muttered. Her lips had disappeared into one bright fuchsia slash across her dark brown face and her hands were shaking. 'You're really having a baby?'

'I'm really having a baby,' I said. 'I've weed on fifteen tests, seen a doctor, and had a sonogram done from outside my belly and inside my vagina. I'm definitely having a baby.'

'You don't need to be crass about it,' she replied, bursting into tears. 'My baby is having a baby!'

'And I'm going to be a granddad!'

Roaring at the top of his lungs, my dad grabbed hold

of Jenny and began to waltz her around the living room, whooping at her, while my mum charged Alex with a hug that almost took him off his feet.

'Well, that's saved me a phone call,' I said, wiping away a tear of my own in the middle of the madness, hands resting on the bump, boobs squeezed into a breast pump bustier, heart absolutely bursting.

CHAPTER NINETEEN

'It wouldn't have been so bad if they'd had better food,' Dad said, huffing and puffing as he dragged his tiny carry-on into the spare bedroom. Behind him, Alex heaved two giant suitcases through the door. 'You wouldn't have liked it one little bit.'

'They had everything,' Mum shouted from the settee. 'Everything you could possibly want. Don't listen to it, Angela, you'd have loved every minute of it.'

Dad furrowed his brow, furiously trying to come up with something to prove her wrong.

'They didn't have sausages,' he replied, triumphant. 'Or cheese and onion crisps. Come on, Annette, how can you call yourself all-inclusive if you haven't got sausages or cheese and onion crisps?'

'You and your bloody crisps,' Mum muttered, raising her teacup to her lips and critically analysing the living room. 'What's different in here?'

'Nothing?' I replied, absently stroking Alex's back as he went by to get the rest of their luggage. 'Why?'

'This isn't a new settee?' she asked. I shook my

head. 'Hmm. It seems smaller in here than last time. I always forget how poky things are in New York.'

'Everything's the same as it was the last time you were here,' I said, yanking my cardigan over my skinny jeans. The baby was really starting to mess with my wardrobe. My fat jeans had already become my skinny jeans and I was certain it had nothing to do with the amount of ice cream I'd been inhaling on a daily basis. The baby loved ice cream. 'The apartment hasn't shrunk.'

'Probably life on the open seas,' Mum sighed as she flopped onto the settee. 'Nothing but sea and sky as far as the eye can see. I don't know how anyone can live like this, all piled on top of one another. You'll need more space for the baby.'

'Babies are very small, at least in the beginning,' I assured her. 'I reckon it'll cope with living in a two-bedroom apartment in New York until it's at least twenty-two. Do you need anything, Dad?'

'Earplugs?' he muttered, taking himself off into the kitchen. 'I can't find the Yorkshire Tea, where's it hiding?'

'We haven't got any,' I called while Mum repeatedly poked my stomach. 'They didn't have any in the English shop when I went so we've only got Tetley's.'

He stuck his head into the living room and both my parents gave me the same look as when I'd told them I got a C in GCSE Maths. I'd let them down, I'd let the school down, and most of all I'd let myself down.

'Jenny looks happy?' Mum said, a question rather than a statement.

Jenny could have answered for herself but the second my dad put her down from their dance, she grabbed her coat and scarpered, claiming she needed to get ready for her bachelorette. I suspected it was more to do with the fact that my parents turning up on my doorstep unannounced was entirely her fault. They had been included in the flurry of emailed invitations, but rather than RSVP, they decided the very modern thing to do would be to just show up, as though they'd just popped around the corner for a cup of tea rather than abandoned a cruise ship somewhere in Mexico and flown eleven hours without so much as a text message to warn me.

'Jenny is happy,' I replied. 'Mason is awesome.'

'Awesome? Hark at her,' Mum said, abandoning my bump and sniffing her tea. She carefully removed her shoes and placed them neatly at the side of the settee. 'There was a woman on the cruise, looked just like her. Mexican, I think she was.'

'Jenny is a Puerto Rican,' I said, reminding myself to breathe. 'Not Mexican.'

'Well, quite.' She waved away the distinction with a flip of her ever-so-slightly racist hand. 'She must be excited about the wedding. We were getting a bit worried, weren't we, David?'

'No?' Dad placed a fresh mug of tea on the side table next to me even though the one in my hand was still warm.

'Woman her age, not married, no kids?' Mum clucked. 'Very close to being left on the shelf. It doesn't matter how pretty you are, it gets to a point where people start to wonder what's wrong with a woman.'

'But not men?'

'There's something wrong with all of them,' she replied, 'but nobody gives a monkey's.'

It was a fair, if not especially reassuring, statement.

'And what's going on at work?' She moved down

the sofa as Dad dumped himself happily on the end. There was the smile of a man who was glad to see dry land. 'What have they said about the baby?'

'It's been a bit crazy, actually,' I said. 'Bob Spencer, who started the company, he retired and now his granddaughter Delia has taken over—'

'Delia? Isn't that the nice blonde girl we met at your wedding?'

'Yes, Mum,' I nodded.

'Very polite for an American,' she said approvingly. 'Lovely manners.'

'Well, she's president of the company now—'

'Neck like a swan.'

'And she's brought in all these new people to run all the divisions, so I've got a new boss. He's kind of—'

'I can't believe you're having a baby,' Mum said, biting her lip and looking at me with cow eyes. 'Thank goodness we abandoned ship, eh, David?'

'Thank goodness,' he agreed. 'I'd much rather be here on granddad duty.'

Alex stood behind me, massaging my shoulders. I looked up to see him smiling blankly at my parents and wondered if he'd been self-medicating while I wasn't looking.

'You're still on dad duty for a while,' I laughed. 'Unless you're planning to stay until June.'

No one said anything and Alex's grip suddenly became uncomfortably tight.

'You're not staying until June,' I said firmly.

'We were saying in the car, on the way from the airport,' Mum said, giving me a nudge, 'what if we stayed on for a little bit after the wedding?'

'What, for the holidays?' I asked, slapping Alex's hands away before he throttled me.

'Holidays,' Dad repeated, shaking his head in defeat. 'Christmas, love, it's Christmas.'

'That's only a couple of days.' I peered up at Alex to see the same blank smile. His mouth was turned up at the corners but when I looked into his eyes? Absolutely nothing. 'Of course, you can stay for Christmas.'

'And we'll fly back after New Year's,' Dad said. 'It's settled, then.'

'After?' I didn't want to sound too alarmed but I also didn't want my husband to leave me. 'But that's nearly three weeks away?'

Mum and Dad exchanged a look that could only be honed by forty years of marriage.

'Do you not want us here or something?' Mum asked.

'More than anything,' Alex said, clapping loudly and making me jump. 'This is so great, a family Christmas. I'm so happy right now, you guys. Hey, Angela, I need to run downstairs and finish up. OK? OK. Awesome.'

Both of my parents studied their teacups with the utmost care as Alex thundered downstairs and slammed the door to the studio.

'They were recording something this morning,' I explained feebly, pointing over my shoulder. 'He's probably got things plugged in and that.'

'And you can't be too careful with electrics in an old place like this,' Dad agreed. 'He's a clever lad, that Alex.'

'You haven't even got your decorations up yet,' Mum said, observing my naked living room with dismay. 'You've always had your decorations up on the first, I should have known something was wrong.'

'What's this, chopped liver?' I stood up and waved

my hands around in front of my nearly naked tree like a gameshow hostess gone wrong. *I'll take a vowel and a cyanide capsule, Bob.* 'Look, I've been really busy with work and I haven't had quite as much time as I might have liked to decorate, and I'm pregnant, so I'm tired all the time, and Alex was away and I'm trying to help Jenny plan her wedding and we're a bit worried about money and there's a chance I might lose my job next week but, fucking hell, Mum, I've put up a Christmas tree, what more do you want?'

'Looks like we got here just in time,' she replied, casting her eyes sideways at my dad. 'Don't worry, your dad's got a box full of Yorkshire Tea in his suitcase.'

'Oh good,' I said, swapping my first mug for my second. 'Everything'll be right as rain then.'

'You really didn't have to come tonight, Mum,' I said while applying liberal quantities of kohl to my very tired eyes in the back of the taxi. 'You can still go home if you want? Wouldn't you rather stay in with Dad than trek around the city after us?'

'I've been stuck on a bloody boat with the man for longer than I care to remember, so no thank you,' she replied. 'And besides, someone needs to look after you and the baby.'

'I'm not going to trek up Mount Kilimanjaro,' I said, watching as she checked the contents of her handbag for the fourteenth time since getting in the cab. 'I'm going on a hen do.'

'I haven't been on a hen in years.' Somewhere on her travels, she'd got hold of a very sparkly bronzer and her face glittered like a mirror ball in the back seat. 'Are we going to have those little deely boppers? With the willies on?'

'I couldn't say for sure,' I told her, not wanting to break her little heart. 'But I don't think so.'

She puffed out her bottom lip, fiddling with the sequins on her sparkly black top. Her favourite piece from the Annette Clark cruise collection.

'I'd have popped into Ann Summers before I left if I'd have known,' she replied.

I chose to ignore her as we rumbled over the Brooklyn Bridge into Manhattan for the #JennyFest17.

'Don't you look nice?' I leaned in to give my bestie a kiss, her sharp cheekbone colliding with my ever-softening face. 'Good frock.'

She spun around in a neat circle, no mean feat given the height of her stiletto heels. The long sleeves and high neck of her white dress were deceptively modest for La Lopez, but when I came in closer, I noticed the strategically placed sheer panels covered in iridescent sequins and bum-skimming split hem that left literally nothing to the imagination. Hopefully, she wouldn't need to bend over until we got her safely back home at the end of the night.

'It's Elie Saab,' she replied, sashaying her hips in time to music I didn't hear. 'Don't ask how much it should have cost.'

'How much should it have cost?' I asked immediately.

'Seven thousand dollars,' she mouthed. 'But Erin had a friend at *Belle* call it in for a shoot. That evil skank Carrie Ann Roitfeld does their PR.'

There was truly nothing sweeter than nabbing a free frock and putting one over on your work nemesis at the same time.

'I'll try not to spill anything on it,' I promised, flipping one errant curl over to the right side of her parting. 'Thanks for abandoning ship this afternoon, by the way, you cow.'

'I figured you wanted some family time,' she said, patting me on the shoulder and almost falling over. Maybe she wasn't quite as steady on those shoes as I thought. 'Can we go inside? I need to sit down.'

'Are you already wasted?' I whispered, wrapping my arm around her waist and propping her upright. 'Dude.'

'Don't tell anyone,' Jenny whispered, leaning as far away from my mother as humanly possible. 'But I got kind of stressed out while we were getting ready so Erin gave me a pot brownie and now I'm like . . . '

She held up her thumb and forefinger to make an 'OK' gesture but couldn't quite manage to make them meet.

'Fantastic,' I said, shepherding her in through the double doors of the Soho Grand. 'How could that possibly go wrong?'

'Since Jenny is joining the ranks of married women, I figured it was only right that we revisit some of Single Jenny's finest moments and give them the grand farewell they deserve,' Erin announced as we trotted inside. As well as me and my bloody mother, she'd rounded up what looked like half of Jenny's office, her friends Gina and Vanessa and, for better or worse, Sadie, who had of course insisted on wearing white. Only Delia was missing.

'So, it's champagne at the Soho Grand, cocktails at Pegu Club, dinner at Alta, and then, if everyone is still standing, we have a room booked at Planet Rose for some late night karaoke. Sound good?'

It sounded exhausting.

That said, Jenny's original bachelorette plans had swung between a vineyard escape in Tuscany and somehow hiring Richard Branson's private island for the weekend. Apparently, a friend of a friend of a friend had been with Kate Moss and she was certain she could get the hook-up. This was decidedly more low-key, but the bride-to-be didn't seem to mind.

'I'm so into this,' Jenny said, dragging herself up the industrial iron staircase that led us from the lobby into the hotel proper. 'It's got to be two years since I was last here. Good call, Erin.'

'For *my* bachelorette,' Sadie announced, pulling her minuscule Hervé Léger white bandage dress down over her arse, 'Teddy is going to hire us a jet and we're all going to fly to Cabo and take over a resort with the boys on one side and the girls on the other and—'

'Hey, Sadie,' Jenny said, the sweetest smile on her face.

'Yah?'

'Tonight is *my* bachelorette and I don't want to hear one more word about your goddamn wedding,' Jenny replied, still smiling. 'Got it?'

'Got it,' Sadie replied, sucking in her cheeks to keep in whatever it was she really wanted to say.

'Good.' Jenny grabbed Erin by the arm and led the way. 'Let's do this.'

'This sounds like a long night,' Mum muttered as we followed Jenny from a safe distance. I wanted to be able to catch her if she fell, and Mum wanted to stop anyone from seeing her very tiny knickers. 'Are you sure you're going to be all right?'

'I'm going to be fine,' I said, determined to make it through the evening. The baby had already taken away my ability to wear leather leggings, possibly forever, it was not taking Jenny's hen do as well. I would see this through to the end if I had to prop my eyes open with matchsticks, even if I was already knackered just from climbing the stairs.

All of West Broadway bustled by in high heels and sequins. There were far fewer big coats than you might expect for the middle of December, but then again, this was Soho and not the real world. I wasn't even sure rich people felt the cold – they were probably vaccinated against it. I'd have to ask Erin to make sure.

It wasn't quite seven but the bar was already busy. I couldn't remember why we'd stopped hanging out at the Soho Grand. When I'd first moved to Manhattan, we'd find ourselves propping up the bar at least once a week, knocking back Perfect Tens and hoping someone felt like expensing champagne. I looked around at the other guests for clues as to why we'd abandoned ship. Everyone looked the same, appropriately downtown, skinny jeans, leather leggings, smudgy eyeliner and a complete lack of interest. Exactly how I remembered it.

'I say we get this party started right,' Erin declared as we sat down. 'Shots all round?'

Jenny and my mum looked over at me as though I'd yanked both of their heads on a string.

'What?' Erin asked. 'What am I missing?'

'I might as well tell her,' I said, the secret smile I reserved especially for baby-related activity taking over my face. 'I'm bloody pregnant, aren't I?'

'Darling, that's the best news!' She threw open her arms and pulled me in. 'I'm so happy for you.'

'Thank you,' I sniffed, automatically pulling my

gorgeous midnight blue Rebecca Taylor frock tight around my belly to prove it. 'I've got approximately a thousand questions for you.'

'Get a caesarean, get a nanny, and buy shares in Touche Éclat,' she replied while Jenny and my mum cheered. 'You're going to be great at this, you've already been Jenny's mom for the last six years.'

'That was exactly what I wanted to hear,' I told her, dropping my head onto her shoulder and smiling. 'Thank you.'

'Any time, sweetie,' she said. 'We moms have to stick together.'

'But are the rest of us still doing shots?' I heard my mum ask. 'Because I'd take your arm off for a sweet sherry.'

It really was going to be a long night.

Several hours later, post-Pegu Club, after Alta, and only very slightly delayed by my needing to stop and use the toilet every three blocks, we arrived at the karaoke bar. Everything in New York moved fast, the cars, the people, the dating apps. One week you couldn't get a reservation at a restaurant because it was far too cool, and the next, it had gone out of business. But one part of the city was timeless. The East Village would always be the East Village. There might not have been so many punks loitering around St Mark's Place these days, but it was still the best place to go if you were looking for a cheap drink and a good time, and we were in search of both.

We piled into Planet Rose, filling the seedy-looking bar with twenty pairs of high heels, galloping down the narrow entryway with one sensible pair of Marks & Spencer's Footglove flats trotting close behind.

'Are you sure you don't want to go home?' I asked my mum.

Her eyes burned with the thrill of a girls' night out and three very large gin and tonics, plus someone, somehow, had found her a pair of penis deely boppers and, from the look on her face, this was the happiest she'd ever been.

'I'm fine,' she insisted. 'I wouldn't turn down a cup of tea, but if they haven't got any, I'll have a Scotch.'

She pushed past and grabbed the songbook out of Sadie's hands, scanning the pages like a pro.

'I'm going to sing a Taylor Swift song first,' Sadie babbled to anyone who would listen. 'She's the sweetest, her cats are the best, we hung out after the Victoria's Secret show and she baked a cake and no one ate the cake but you could tell it was a good cake. You know, I should call her, let me call her.'

'What has she taken?' I asked Jenny as Sadie began manically swiping at her phone. How she was planning to call Taylor Swift from inside the Amazon app, I wasn't quite sure. 'Is she going to die?'

'She is if she promises Tay-Tay and can't deliver,' Jenny bellowed before starting the girls in a chant. 'We want Tay-Tay! We want Tay-Tay!'

'Can I help you, ladies?' A short, stout man in a fetching white vest and too tight jeans leered at me from behind the bar. I smiled politely, ignoring the fact he was addressing my tits rather than my face. If you ever wanted to meet drunk, gorgeous women who wouldn't usually give you the time of day, open a karaoke bar in Manhattan.

'We've reserved a room,' I shouted over the bar as he openly perved on my friends. 'Under the name Erin White?'

'Room isn't big enough,' he replied, his gruff voice barely audible over the dulcet tones of someone murdering a Mariah Carey song in the background. 'New York City ordinances say no more than twelve to a room. How many of you are there?'

'Twelve,' I said confidently. It was clearly a lie. There were at least twenty of Jenny's best friends and well-wishers rammed into the shiny red walls and zebra printed sofas of Planet Rose's main room. 'Definitely no more than twelve.'

He looked each and every one of us up and down. Sadie got the once-over twice.

'OK.'

Either he couldn't count or he didn't care, but I was grateful either way.

'I'll need a credit card,' the bartender barked, and I handed mine over reluctantly. I wasn't sure our baby budget covered drunk girl karaoke, and not one of these women was in a fit state to Venmo anyone anything. But it was Jenny's hen do, a night for the ages. I would rally.

'It's tough, I know,' Erin said as the girls piled into the room, Sadie still hammering away at her phone, even though it was almost 2 a.m. Taylor would be ecstatic. 'Wanna get some fresh air?'

I nodded and followed her back through the bar. I hated being sober sister, especially on a hen do, and especially at karaoke. It was not fun, watching your friends peel off their shoes and run through the streets barefoot without so much as a sniff of booze in you. All I could think about was whether or not they would cut themselves, and what exactly they were stepping in, and enduring endless flashbacks of all the times I'd done exactly the same thing.

'How are you doing?' Erin asked, leaning against a sad tree a couple of doors down from Planet Rose. An all-night bodega hummed with fluorescent lights, tepid hot dogs and fridges full of foul-looking energy drinks. 'Really?'

'I'm good,' I replied, stifling a heroic yawn. 'I've been the full seven dwarves – hungry, sleepy, dopey – but I'm mostly all right. Apart from how I keep crying all the time, though. What's that all about?'

'That's to prepare you for the next eighteen years,' she said. 'I heard it gets slowly better over time; you have one huge relapse when they leave for college and then it clears up, just like that. How's Alex doing?'

'Honestly, I'm not sure.' I flashed back to his argument with Graham. Thanks to my parents' unexpected arrival, there had been no time to discuss it. 'He's really happy about the baby, but he's definitely more stressed than he's letting on.'

'Even Thomas worried about money and he has all of it. Seriously, I'm sometimes amazed that anyone else in the world has any money,' she said, shaking her head at her own good fortune. 'I think it's a throwback Neanderthal thing. They can't kill a woolly mammoth and bring it home to you so they worry about their 401k and college funds instead.'

'Makes sense,' I replied, wishing it was that simple. Maybe if we got really stuck, I could nick one of her rings and pay the mortgage with that. I could always replace it with a fake from Claire's Accessories, no one would ever know the difference.

'So, how come Delia isn't here tonight?'

The question caught me off guard.

'She's probably working,' I said, twisting my own

297

engagement ring around my finger. 'No rest for the wicked.'

'She's certainly getting a reputation for that,' Erin replied. 'She's making more cuts than Bob ever did. Who knew she was secretly the evil twin?'

'I know that's a joke but I'm not sure you're that far off.' I rubbed my hands up and down my arms. We'd had a mild winter so far, but it was the middle of the night and even with my internal super-furnace, I was feeling the chill without my coat. 'We had a really fun conversation about whether or not my job is safe.'

Erin sucked the air in through her teeth. 'And is it?'

'It is not,' I replied. 'And how am I supposed to find another one when I'm pregnant? New York isn't exactly known for its kind-hearted attitude towards women with children.'

'I'd give you a job, but you would suck at PR,' she said, tucking her hair back behind her ears. 'You're one of the worst liars I've ever known.'

'I will take that as the compliment it was not intended to be,' I said, annoyed even though I knew she was right. 'Things are changing far too fast. I feel like it's something else every day at the moment. I've had to stop reading the news altogether – between work and home and the Lopez-Cawston nuptials, I've got more than enough to worry about.'

'Angela, things are going to change, like it or not.' Erin sifted through her tiny Prada evening bag and produced a pack of chewing gum. She held it out and I shook my head as she unwrapped a piece and started chomping. Cinnamon flavour, the devil's work. 'But things are always changing. Do you feel the same way you did before you moved to New York? Shit, do you feel the same way you did last week? We change, constantly, we just don't always think about it as much as we usually do when something as big as a baby comes along.'

'I have been a very different person since *The Vampire Diaries* finished,' I replied thoughtfully. 'And I prefer it when things come about one at a time. This feels like a lot at once.'

'Yeah?' she agreed. 'Kind of like finding out your boyfriend is cheating on you and your best friend knew all about it and is moving to another country without consulting a single soul?'

'What kind of a fool would do something like that?' I asked through gritted teeth.

'Everything is going to be different,' Erin said. 'And not all of it is going to be great. There will be days when you don't shower, when you hate your baby and its constant pooping, and you detest your womb-less husband – but you know what? By the time you've changed that shitty baby and googled how much it costs to get a divorce, you'll feel better. And the next day won't be quite so bad.'

'You paint such a beautiful picture of motherhood,' I said, catching sight of some split ends lit up by the neon sign in the window of the bodega. I needed a trim badly. 'Thanks for the pep talk.'

Across the avenue, the door of a bar swung open and a bubble of music and laughter popped out onto the street. A group of friends, two men and three women, grabbed on to each other's necks, heads thrown back with laughter. Two of the women sang a song I didn't recognize and one of the men gave the other a piggyback ride down to the end of the block.

'Don't they look happy?' I bounced my weight from one foot to the other, my feet were really starting to sting. 'And possibly underage.'

'They look drunk,' Erin replied. 'You don't remember that because it's been a while, right? You're going to be a great mom, Angela, but yeah, things are going to change.'

'I fear change,' I said, pulling the sleeves of my dress over my fingertips. I was officially cold. 'Change is bad.'

'No such thing as good and bad change,' she corrected. 'Only easy change and difficult change. You know who said that?'

'Oprah?' I guessed.

'No, I was really asking – I can't remember.' She scrunched up her face and shrugged. 'It does sound like Oprah. Maybe it was Jenny. Or I might have heard it on *The Real Housewives.*'

'Shall we go back inside and find the bride-to-be?' I suggested, rubbing my arms. 'You must be freezing in that.'

'Me?' She looked at the goose bumps on her bare skin and blinked. 'I'm great, babe, I'm so drunk right now, I can't feel anything.'

I sighed as I followed her back into the karaoke bar. It was hard to take solace in advice from a woman so wasted she kept trying to pull the door open when there was a great big 'PUSH' sticker right in front of her face.

'*In vino veritas,*' I told myself as we worked our way back through the crowded bar. 'So much vino.'

'The minute you walked in the joint—'

Through the window of our room, I saw my mother, standing on a coffee table, microphone in one hand, bottle of exceptionally cheap champagne in the other, belting out Shirley Bassey's greatest hits like she was in the middle of the sing-off on *The X Factor.*

'I could see you were a man of distinction, a real big spender.'

At the end of the line, she gave a kick much higher than I would have suspected she was capable of. I watched as her shoe flew through the air, arcing gracefully across the room before landing square in Sadie's face.

'My nose!' she screamed. 'You've broken my nose.'

'Oh pish.' Mum's eyes followed the words on the screen above her. 'I bet it's not even bruised. They're a very light shoe, you know. It's a Marks and Spencer Footglove.'

'You've ruined my life,' Sadie wailed. 'It's definitely broken.'

'Pinch your nose and tip your head forward,' Mum ordered, sadly climbing down from the table. The backing track to 'Big Spender' continued to blare out of the speakers as everyone descended on Sadie and her million-dollar face. 'Or is it back? I don't know . . . Can you taste pennies?'

'Might be time to head,' Erin said, pointing over at Jenny. Our bachelorette was curled up in a corner, covered in coats and smiling to herself, fast asleep. She looked like an incredibly glamorous dormouse. 'I'll call a cab.'

'Good idea,' I said, patting the bump and congratulating it on a relatively successful evening. 'Good idea, indeed.'

CHAPTER TWENTY

'Oh. My. God.'

'What?' I stuck an earbud in my ear, proofreading the final fashion pages as I answered Jenny's call. 'What's wrong?'

'Nothing's wrong. Everything is right. I think I'm dreaming,' I could practically hear her bouncing off the walls. 'You won't believe this, but I called Amy, that British girl who runs AJB, to see if they had anything I could wear for the wedding and it turns out Bertie Bennett is launching a bridal collection next season and he's gonna let me wear one of the sample dresses. Bertie Bennett is making me a wedding dress and I have to go meet with him tonight.'

'Does he definitely know it's you and not the other Jennifer Lopez?' I asked, a little dazed. This was *huge*.

'I don't know and I don't care,' she sang. 'You have to come.'

'Jenny, I can't.' I stared at the clock to try and turn it backwards. AJB dresses were so beautiful and Bertie Bennett was a fashion legend, if it had been any other day, I would have happily murdered almost anyone

302

for the opportunity to hang out with him. Jenny had been handling their PR for the last couple of years, but this was an incredible coup, even for La Lopez. 'It's press day and I've still got more than half the magazine to approve. There's no way I'll be done here before ten.'

'You can't sneak out early, maid of honour?' she tried her best, most wheedling tone of voice. 'For your best friend? Your old pal, Jenny?'

'You know there is nothing I would love more,' I said, circling a typo in the second paragraph. 'But I really can't. Is there any way you could move it to tomorrow?'

'When Bertie Bennett offers to *give* you a wedding dress, you don't ask questions, you just go,' she replied. 'I just cancelled a new business meeting I've had in the diary for months. Wait, no, I haven't. Don't tell Erin.'

'Send me photos,' I said, holding the marked-up pages out to Sophie who was waving from the doorway. 'And if some sort of miracle happens, I'll let you know.'

'What if I call in a bomb threat?' she suggested. 'I know that's not funny, but Angie, this is Bertie-fricking-Bennett.'

'There's a nuclear bunker underneath the building with WiFi, Censhare, and an FTP server,' I answered. 'If you do that, I'll never get away.'

'Wild,' she whistled in response. 'Fine, I'll take photos. Maybe Sadie can come with.'

'Is she still wearing the protective face mask?' I asked. 'I saw it on Instagram last night, Mum was well tickled.'

'Yeah, maybe I'll go on my own,' Jenny replied in a sulk. 'Go finish your magazine. Love you.'

'Love you,' I said, popping out the earbud and opening up the news pages.

'Is there really a nuclear bunker underneath the building?'

I looked up to see a confused look on Eva's face. Of course, the neon pink desk had been for her. Of course, Joe had decided the best way for her to integrate into the company was to share an office with me. Of course, I was ready to chuck myself out of the window after dealing with it for three-quarters of a day.

'I don't know,' I replied, offering her my best attempt at a smile. 'It was a joke.'

'Was that your friend?' she asked. 'The one who's getting married?'

'Yep,' I said, studying my computer screen very closely.

'That's exciting. I've never been a bridesmaid,' Eva said, picking up a tablet and tapping out a note. 'You should vlog it. For the website.'

'Probably won't,' I said, catching sight of her deflated face in the corner of my eye. 'Good idea, though.'

Why would anyone think it was a good idea to move someone into my office on press day? Because that person is a wanker, the voice in my head whispered. The voice in my head spoke so much sense.

It was already dark outside. Even though it was only three in the afternoon, we'd had an entire day of terrible weather, rain, rain and more rain and the sun hadn't even made an attempt at putting in an appearance. The weather forecast was better for the weekend but I was still keeping everything crossed for sunshine at the wedding.

In the bottom of my computer screen, I noticed a new message notification. It was my mum.

CAN YOU SEE HAMILTON 2NITE?

Hamilton? They had *Hamilton* tickets?

You got tix? I replied, fingers like lightning.

UR DAD MET NICE MAN IN THE PARK. HE'S IN IT. IS IT
GOOD?

I had been trying to get tickets to *Hamilton* for two
years. They were like unicorn poop rolled in diamond
dust, completely unobtainable unless you were
insanely lucky or obscenely rich. Alex had pulled
every string in his musical book to snag two for my
birthday the year before, but I decided it was a good
idea to eat three-day-old Mexican leftovers for lunch,
and when I should have been enjoying the vocal styl-
ings of Lin-Manuel Miranda, I had a front seat to the
inside of my toilet bowl. Jenny and Mason went instead
and she called me during the intermission, in tears
because it was so good. I still hadn't forgiven them
for not lying.

It's v good, I told Mum. Get tix and go!!!

U AND ALEX 2?

She doesn't mean to shout, she just likes the bigger
letters, I told myself, letting out a cleansing breath.

I have to work, I replied. Take Dad, he'll like it. It's
historical.

MAN SAID ITS FUNNY. WILL SEE MIGHT GO XXX

I turned my attention back to my computer screen, groaning as all the letters swirled together.

'Hey, chief,' Jason knocked on my door and grinned. 'Hi, Eva.'

'Hi, Jason!' she replied, practically leaping out of her chair with emoji hearts in her eyes when he walked in. I wasn't sure who was going to tell her just how very gay he was but it certainly wasn't going to be me.

'You look so great today, chief,' he said, holding out a Snickers bar. 'Is that a new highlighter?'

'Yes,' I replied, angry at myself for being pleased. 'What do you want?'

'Would it be OK if I run out for an hour?' he asked, holding his hands together in prayer. 'My roommate's boyfriend is dancing with Justin Timberlake at this thing they're recording for *Extra*. It's only at Radio City, I will be gone for mere moments. You'll barely even believe I left my desk.'

'It's press day,' I said, holding up a handful of white pages in case he, the managing editor, wasn't sure what that meant. 'I need you here.'

'Yeah, I know, but I'll make it up,' he bargained, carefully placing the Snickers on my desk. 'I'll stay as late as you need me, I swear it.'

'What if I don't want to stay late?' I asked, tearing into the Snickers before he could take it back.

Jason began to laugh, slapping his thigh to illustrate just how amused he was.

'Good one,' he said, clicking his fingers as he left. 'You almost had me there. I'll be back ASAP, call me if you need me. I won't be more than an hour, two at most. We'll get this baby to bed by ten!'

What an arsehole. I couldn't make my best friend's

first wedding dress fitting, my parents had scored free tickets to *Hamilton*, and my staff were taking the piss.

'Cici was right,' I realized. 'I *am* a bad boss. Anna Wintour probably has snipers at the ready to take out staff who bunk off on press day.'

I looked out the window and waited for the flying pigs. Cici Spencer was right.

Grabbing my phone, I started a text to Alex. I wasn't entirely sure what I wanted him to say but I was certain he could come up with something helpful.

The baby wanted a Snickers, I typed, adding a photo of the half-eaten chocolate bar. What are you doing?

Working, he replied. No kisses, no emojis. Super harsh.

On new music? I asked.

Yep, he texted back. Talk later.

'Fine,' I muttered, shoving the rest of the Snickers into my mouth and undoing the top button of my jeans. 'We will talk later, arse.'

'You want to talk later?' Eva asked.

'Don't mind me,' I said, fake laughing. 'Sometimes I talk to myself.'

'That might be kind of distracting,' she frowned, scratching her head behind the neon pink desk Joe had shoved directly in front of mine. 'I guess I'll have to get used to it.'

'I guess,' I replied with a manic grin.

Outside my window, the sky blackened, thunder rumbled across the city – and I really hoped Jason had forgotten to take an umbrella.

The rain still hadn't let up when I eventually approved the last pages, dead on the dot of seven. Leaving Jason to send everything to print, I practically ran across the lobby, desperate to leave the building. I hadn't set foot outside all day and I needed fresh air, I needed to get home, and I needed to talk to Alex.

'I thought you were never going to leave.'

Cici stepped out of the shadows of the neighbouring building as I fought with my umbrella.

'Are you trying to give me a heart attack?' I asked, chucking my umbrella up in the air. Rain hammered the top of my head, soaking my hair through as I bent over to retrieve it. 'What on earth are you doing?'

'Waiting for you?' she replied, as though it was obvious. She held out her own massive golf umbrella, her blonde blowout untouched by something as vulgar as weather. 'I need to talk to you about a thing.'

'And you couldn't do that, say, in the warm, dry confines of the massive office building behind me?' I asked.

'Uh, no,' she replied. 'Grandpa had all the offices bugged years ago – you didn't know that?'

'I bloody well absolutely did know it,' I said, punching the air and almost two passersby at the same time. 'Regardless, this is bad timing, I'm knackered. Can we catch up another time?'

'Look, Angela, we both know you're going to give in eventually,' she said impatiently. 'So, let's just get it over with. I made a reservation at the Four Seasons.'

Just in case I'd forgotten how obscenely rich she was.

'Cici, the Four Seasons is ten blocks away, it's hammering it down, and I haven't been to the toilet in seventeen minutes,' I said. 'There's no way we're walking all that way. If you've got something to say, you can say it here or you can get on the subway and come back to my house.'

'Brooklyn?' she recoiled. 'Eww.'

'As much as I'd love to stand here getting piss wet through, I've got to go,' I said, popping my own umbrella and showering myself in the face in the process. 'So nice to see you, we must do this again some time.'

'No!' She stamped her shiny black Hunter rain boot and her umbrella shook itself off like a wet dog. 'This is really important. I stood out here in the rain to wait for you, and you know I hate admitting this, but I really need your help. Will you please come to the Four Seasons with me?'

'If you want someone to check out your Tinder date before you go into the bar again, I am not your girl,' I warned. 'Don't think I didn't hear about that.'

'I only did that maybe five or six times,' she replied sulkily.

So many interns had suffered under her reign of terror.

'This is important,' Cici said with a straight face and something that looked like earnestness in her eyes. 'I wouldn't ask if it wasn't.'

I pressed my mouth into a hard line, raindrops dripping down the back of my neck and a baby pressing on my bladder. The internet said it was still only the size of a lime but never in my life had a lime made me need to pee this much. At least, not unless it came on the side of a shot of tequila.

'Angela,' she said, reaching out to take my hand in hers. 'Please.'

Whoa. This was an unprecedented moment. I wasn't entirely sure what to do and I wasn't entirely sure she hadn't been taken over by body snatchers.

'OK,' I said slowly, gesturing for her to lead the way. 'Four Seasons it is.'

'Thank you,' she muttered, waving to a black town car that pulled a sharp U-turn across 42nd Street and came to a stop right in front of us. 'Please don't pee in the car.'

Of course, she had a town car waiting for her, I thought, whipping out my phone to send Jenny a notification in Find My Friends, just in case.

'You're doing what?' I asked, pinching myself under the table while Cici calmly sipped a Scotch on the rocks.

'I've set up my own media company,' she replied. 'Why do you look so shocked? It makes perfect sense when you think about it.'

'But your grandfather already owns one of the biggest media companies in the world,' I reminded her. 'And your sister, your identical twin sister, is the president of that company.'

'Yeah, I had not forgotten about that, but thanks for the heads-up,' she said. Along the bar, two handsome men in suits threw her smiles, only to be shut down with nothing more than a roll of her crystal-clear blue eyes. 'After we had lunch, I was thinking about what I'm good at, what I know, and that's when it hit me. I'm good at managing people and I know media. I don't know how to write, but I know what good writing looks like, and I have the most important skill already, I know how to make people do what I want.'

'I don't know if that's the most important,' I said, still struggling to grasp what she was telling me. 'But yay?'

'I know how to manage people who know what they're doing,' she said, spinning her bar stool around so that her long, slender legs were pointed directly at me. 'Which is why you're here.'

'You want me to come and work for you?' I asked, unable to hold in a little gasp of surprise.

'Oh, my god no.' A little flutter of laughter escaped her mouth and echoed over the quiet piano music. 'I know you would never leave Spencer, you're too much of a martyr. But some people will, right?'

'So, let me check I've got this straight. You're not trying to headhunt me but you expect me to point you in the direction of the people you should headhunt from the company I work for, including my own employees?' I drew out a mental map of her ridiculous request on the bar with the tip of my finger, just so I could be sure.

'Yes,' she replied, placing her drink back down on its plush napkin. 'What?'

'You can't see why that's weird?' I questioned. She shook her head. 'You don't think there's a conflict of interests here?'

'No, not really,' Cici said, offering the bartender a polite smile as he refilled our water glasses and placed a bowl of bar mix in between us. Without a word, she pushed it towards me. 'Besson Media is going to be web-based. I know Spencer has websites, but only websites based on magazines. We're going to be quick and modern and instant, everything you aren't. Spencer is like the fat old housecat, we're the panther that smashes down the front door and tears that housecat apart with our teeth.'

'Beautiful visual,' I said, choking on a dry roast peanut. 'I'm still not going to give you a list of who you should nick. They'd sack me and they'd be right to. Also, not to be funny, but you didn't get on with people that well. What makes you think people are going to come and work for you in the first place?'

'Because I have tons of cash,' she said, tilting her head to one side. 'My business manager has already had so many people approach us. I thought it would be harder than this, to be honest.'

'You have a business manager?' I asked.

'Yep,' she nodded. 'I have a COO, a CBO, a CMO and of course, I'm CEO.'

'Wouldn't have expected anything else,' I said, feeling oddly proud. 'This sounds so great, Cici.'

'I know,' she shrugged. 'It's going to be the perfect company. Flexible working hours, great healthcare, the offices are in Brooklyn, but, you know, sometimes you have to make sacrifices.'

'Commuting to Brooklyn isn't a sacrifice,' I told her. She pulled a sour face and shivered dramatically. 'You really did all this in two weeks?'

'What can I say?' Cici took another tiny sip of her drink. 'I'm motivated.'

'That I can see,' I said, tapping my bitten-down nails against my water glass. 'And it's slightly terrifying.'

And I'd thought an unexpected pregnancy was a lot to process. Cici was starting her own rival media company? It was a Ryan Murphy miniseries in the making.

'Well, it's been lovely to see you,' I said, hopping down off my stool, scooping up a handful of bar mix and shoving it in my pocket. I needed train snacks. 'And this all sounds fantastic, but I need to go home.'

'For sure,' she said, without blinking. 'So, you'll call me.'

A statement, not a question.

'Probably not, if I'm honest,' I said, walking backwards out of the bar and into the ridiculous marble lobby, longing to be back out in the rain. I needed to clear my head. 'Bye, Cici.'

'Bye, Angela.' She raised her hand in a wave. 'And I know you said I shouldn't try to headhunt you, but just so you know—'

'Don't say it,' I warned, wrapping my glittery scarf around my neck.

'Whatever,' she said with a glittering smile on her face. No longer an underfed hyena but a housecat-eating panther. 'Just think about it.'

I had a horrible feeling I wouldn't be able to do much else.

'I know you weren't raised Catholic, but can you remember exactly how it went when the devil tempted Jesus in the desert that time?' I asked Alex, hurling my parka in the general direction of the coatrack and missing completely. 'Because I'm pretty sure I am having my faith in something tested.'

'Don't know,' he said, not looking up from his laptop. 'Bad day?'

'Bizarre day,' I replied. I kicked off my ankle boots and collapsed on the sofa, pointing my feet in his general direction. It was definitely foot-rub time. 'Where are Mum and Dad?'

'Your dad said he met a man called Miranda in the park and tonight they were going to see him sing.' Alex continued to stare at the computer, his pale skin glowing with the light from the incandescent screen. 'So no, I have no idea.'

'Oh yeah,' I remembered. They were at *Hamilton*. The bastards. 'So, long story short, Cici is setting up her own media company and wants me to be the editor of the first website.'

Alex didn't move.

'Or at least I think she does,' I said, trying to recall exactly what she'd said. 'It was very confusing, but then, it was Cici.'

'Yeah, that's funny,' he said, looking up at me with tired, dry eyes. 'Did you eat?'

'I'm not sure funny's the right word.' I shuffled down the sofa until I was properly laid down and my feet were closer to foot-rub distance. He was not taking the hint this evening. 'I know it sounds ridiculous, but if you took the Cici part out of the equation, the whole thing sounds kind of like a dream. Seriously, if it was anyone but her—'

'You'd still be ignoring it because you're almost four months pregnant and need health insurance and a steady job and you don't throw away a career to go dick around at an internet startup,' Alex replied, closing up his laptop with a loud clap. 'What is this, 1999? Are you trying to get in on the dotcom boom?'

'Why are you so angry?' I asked, tearing up the second I opened my mouth. 'I'm only telling you what happened. Of course I'm not going to take a job working with Cici, I know I have to stay at Spencer.'

'Thanks, I feel so much better knowing you're passing up an amazing opportunity because you have to,' he said. He anchored one hand on the back of his neck and swung the other around in the air, chucking an invisible tennis ball into the kitchen. 'Did she offer you a pony as well?'

'You know full well if she'd offered me a pony I'd have taken it,' I said, sitting upright. 'Alex, what's wrong?'

'Nothing's wrong,' he said, picking up the tiny Baby-gro he'd bought in Bloomingdale's. 'I sat down

314

and looked at our budget today. It's going to be tighter than I realized if we want to do this properly.'

'People have babies on far less than what we have, every day,' I said, refusing to let myself cry. This was the problem with hormones, I told myself, the first sign of a disagreement and the waterworks started. It wasn't my fault. 'What's got you so freaked out?'

'People who don't live in New York City,' he said, standing before beginning to stride up and down the room. 'People who don't have huge New York City mortgages to pay and New York City childcare to worry about.'

'Non-New York City mortgages and non-New York City childcare aren't cheap either,' I reminded him. 'Louisa and Tim had to tighten their belts when they had Grace.'

'So tight they can't breathe?' he muttered. 'Because that's what's going to happen to us.'

'Yeah, so we'll have to make a few sacrifices,' I told him, trying to sound as soothing as possible, but it was hard when he wouldn't bloody well stand still. 'It won't be that bad.'

He turned and looked right at me.

'Like what?'

'I don't know,' I said, looking at my shocking nails. 'I'll stop getting manicures and I won't buy coffee on the way into work any more.'

He took a deep breath and pushed all his hair back from his face with both hands.

'And I suppose I'll take myself off the waiting list for a Chanel Jumbo Flap Bag,' I muttered into my chest.

'We are not ready for this.' Alex swiped at a cushion and knocked it across the room. 'We are not ready at all.'

You will not cry, I told myself, you will not cry. Did Hillary Clinton cry when she didn't win the election? No, she didn't, and so I wasn't going to cry just because my husband was being a massive dick.

'Chanel bags are bit obvious, anyway,' I said quietly, puffing out my cheeks to stop my eyes from prickling. 'Not really me.'

'I'm going downstairs,' he said, grabbing his laptop as he crossed the room.

'Do you want anything to eat?' I called as he went, holding my breath as he slammed the door.

'No,' he answered abruptly from the other side. 'I'm fine.'

'Well,' I said, breathing out and patting the bump gently, just in case it had heard. 'At least that makes one of us.'

CHAPTER TWENTY-ONE

By the time Friday morning rolled around, I felt as though I'd been alive for a thousand years. Alex woke up the morning after his hissy fit, acting as though nothing had happened, Cici had stayed silent, my parents were relatively well behaved, and the rest of the week passed in a whirl of last-minute wedding preparations and work.

Delia knew I was leaving at lunchtime. Jenny's rehearsal dinner was taking place at Prune at seven and we were both going. I only knew Delia had RSVP'd yes because Jenny had told me. I hadn't seen her once since our chat in her office over two weeks ago but finally, I had been summoned. Not to Delia's office but to Joe's. It didn't seem like a great sign, but it still felt better than being ordered in to HR, like half the sales team had been the week before. Erin had not been wrong, Delia was slashing staff left, right and centre. I'd even heard some of the girls at *Belle* refer to her as The Butcher in the Starbucks on 7th Avenue on my way in.

The almost unbelievably shiny young man who sat

outside Joe's office smiled his animatronic smile as I paced up and down in front of his desk. I couldn't stop moving for fear of actually falling over. I'd worn heels, which I now realized was a mistake, but since I couldn't button up any of my clothes that morning, I needed something to dress up my Topshop maternity jeans. And to think Jenny had said it was early for maternity wear. Now I'd tried these on, I doubted I would ever take them off.

'He had a meeting in HR at eight thirty,' the assistant blustered when I pointedly looked at the clock again. 'He said he'd be back here by nine.'

'Brillbags,' I said, clicking my tongue at him and walking the length of the room once again.

'Angela, there you are.' Joe marched towards me with an all-business look on his face. 'Shall we get started?'

'Here I am,' I agreed, wondering where else I might have been given that our meeting was supposed to start ten minutes ago. My baby-related emotional melt-downs had given way to the world's shortest temper and I couldn't say I was too upset about it.

'How are things going with Eva?' he asked, closing his office door behind us and automatically handing me a tiny bottle of water from his mini fridge. Joe's office was the opposite of mine: sleek and neat and devoid of personality. No sign of his British girlfriend, I noticed. Or evidence that he wasn't actually an android. I'd watched *Westworld*, I knew these things were possible. I hadn't entirely understood the show, but I got the general gist.

'If I'm being brutally honest, I wouldn't choose to share an office,' I said, a sentiment he was already aware of thanks to a somewhat emotional email I'd sent upon finding out about his plan. 'I think she'd do better in with everyone else, not stuck in my office, listening to me all day.'

'But that's exactly what we want,' Joe corrected. 'It's the best method of immersion. You and Eva are something of a pilot programme for us, Angela, you're her mentor. It's really a huge honour when you think about it – we could have done this anywhere in the company but we did it with you.'

'I'm sorry, I must have bumped my head and missed about seventeen meetings where all this would have been discussed,' I replied with a painfully pleasant laugh. 'But she's there now, isn't she?'

'She is,' he agreed.

'And she's not going anywhere?'

'She isn't.'

'Right.' I sat down on the black and chrome chair opposite his desk and crossed my legs. Why did I already need a wee?

'I've got a lot of these meetings to get through today, so let's get to it,' Joe said. 'There's a reason I wanted to see you first thing.'

'Did my name come out the hat first?' I asked.

He leaned forward across his desk, pointing at me with both fingers.

'You, Angela Clark, have potential.'

'No, I definitely tested negative for that on my last smear,' I replied. Joe looked confused. 'Sorry, I make jokes when I'm anxious. I get it from my dad.'

'No need to be anxious,' he insisted, tapping the desk with both index fingers.

'Really?' I asked. 'Because I'm fairly sure you're about to tell me whether or not you're closing my magazine and sacking twenty people I'm responsible for.'

'You're looking at this all wrong,' Joe replied. 'This is the day, this is *your* day. We're pulling you out and lifting you up.'

'Pulling me out of where?' I looked around as though there would be actual people with actual forklift trucks. 'Where am I going?'

'We're closing *Gloss*,' Joe said with a shrug, cutting me off when I opened my mouth to scream. 'It's done, it's agreed. We're shutting the print edition next week.'

'I'm going to be sick,' I said very quietly. I could see my feet. I couldn't feel my feet. I couldn't feel anything.

'We're also shutting *The Look*,' he added. 'And in January, we will be launching a new hybrid print-and-media-content platform, *The Gloss*.'

He clapped his hands together and held them out, waiting for a reaction.

Without a word, I grabbed the brushed chrome wastepaper basket under his desk and threw up. Giving Joe a quiet thumbs up, I reached out and took a tissue from the box on his desk and wiped my mouth.

'Don't worry about that,' I said. 'Please continue.'

'You just vomited,' he said, staring at me in abject horror. 'In my trash can.'

'I did,' I agreed. 'But I'm quite all right. Let's say it's lactose intolerance. You're closing both magazines and opening one new one?'

'Yes,' he said, visibly disturbed. 'In January.'

'What will happen to the staff?' I asked, clutching my tissue.

'The editor-in-chief will select which staff move to *The Gloss* and which staff are surplus,' he replied. 'It won't be down to me.'

'And who is going to be the editor?'

My heart was racing so fast, I could see little sparkles appearing at the edge of my vision. There was only one answer, one reason I was brought in first and staring at this gurning goon. But did I want this? Could I even deal with this right now?

'Caroline,' Joe said, resting backwards in his chair. 'Caroline is going to be the editor.'

'I think I'm going to throw up again,' I said, lurching forwards and grabbing the bin.

'Should I call someone?' he asked, not making any effort to move. 'Do you need a doctor?'

'No, it's just all that pesky lactose,' I said, blinking into the bottom. How could one man eat so many protein bars? 'Carry on.'

'I'm going to offer Caroline the editor-in-chief position,' Joe said as I slowly sat up, keeping the bin in my lap. 'And I'd like to offer you the position of Junior Global Brand Director for Women's Lifestyle Brands.'

I gripped the sides of the bin very, very tightly.

'You'd like to what?'

'I'd like to offer you the position of Junior Global Brand Director for Women's Lifestyle Brands,' he repeated, pushing a piece of paper across the desk. It was a job description. 'It's a new role, working with me to oversee the expansion of *The Gloss* into all our territories. All the editors would be reporting in to you on a global scale. It's a very exciting role for someone with your passion, Angela.'

Someone so passionate she'd just thrown up twice.

'Say the title again?' I whispered.

'Junior Global Brand Director for Women's Lifestyle Brands.'

'It's got the word brand in it twice,' I said. 'Can a title have the word brand in it twice?'

'We can work on the title if you don't like it,' Joe offered. 'But this is such an opportunity. You know how hard it is for someone to come out of the editorial melee and move into a bigger role. This puts you on the fast track to VP.'

'VP of what, though?' I asked, lightly resting two fingers against the inside of my wrist and attempting to take my pulse. Oh good, it was going so fast I couldn't even count.

'That's a hypothetical point, much further in the future,' he said, furrowing his manly brow. 'Right now, I need you to think about this role. Moulding *The Gloss* brand, hiring the global teams, managing the brand expansions. It's travel, it's people management, it's making the most of your creativity and your passion for this brand that you created.'

'Is it, though?' I was asking myself more than him. 'There would be no editorial at all, right? I wouldn't have anything to do with the actual magazines themselves?'

'You'd have *everything* to do with the magazines!' he cheered. Pointed to various framed titles behind him, *Belle*, *Gloss*, *The Look*, *HQ*, *The Spencer Report*. All safely behind glass where he couldn't possibly be expected to read a single word. 'I know it's going to be a strange shift, but this is such an exciting challenge.'

'And if Caroline takes over the magazine and the website, she could just sack everyone from *Gloss* and keep everyone from *The Look*?' I said. 'My entire team could be out on their arses?'

'I get that perhaps this looks a little like a, uh,' Joe flapped a hand around in the air, looking to pull the right word from the ether, 'forgive my terminology, a shit sandwich right now, but we're elevating you, Angela, we're making you a focal point in the company. If this works out, you could be in my job two years from now.'

It was the most horrifying thing he could have said.

'It's not a shit sandwich, Joe, it's a shit buffet,' I said loudly. 'There's no bread, there's no butter, there's just shit. Loads of different kinds of shit. One kind of shit held together by two other kinds of shit and forced down someone's throat and that someone is me.'

He blanched at the metaphor as I fell back against my chair and carefully covered my stomach with my arms. Wasn't it my passion he said he was interested in? It probably wasn't a good idea to expose my unborn baby to so many expletives at once, but if it was going to live with me for the next eighteen or so years, it was better that it became desensitized as early as possible.

'I don't want your job,' I told him, pushing my hair back from my hot face. 'I know that might not make sense to you, but it was never in my plans. It's not what I'm good at.'

'I think you're underestimating yourself,' Joe replied, straightening his tie. 'You have a skill for nurturing talent, you're good at it. And you're the heart and soul behind *Gloss*, I know that. You're the person who made this brand a success.'

'I didn't make the brand a success, I made the magazine a success,' I insisted, standing up on the other side of his desk. I paused for a moment to steady myself in my badass high heels and wished I'd listened to my gut instead of my Pinterest board. '*Gloss* is my magazine, not my brand. I care about every word that goes into it, and every person that writes every word, every person who reads every word. Delia made it a real magazine, Spencer made it a brand, what I did was show up every day and do something I loved.'

He looked up at me, considering his response without a flicker of emotion in his eyes.

'I hear what you're saying.'

When he finally spoke, his words were perfectly measured and managed, all his years of executive training shining brightly, and I really, really wanted to punch him right in the mouth.

'And I understand your concerns.' He stood up too and was suddenly towering over me. 'You don't have to give me an answer right away, of course you should take the weekend to think about this, it's a big move, but we would like an answer on Monday.'

'Monday,' I said, nodding to myself. 'OK. And what happens if I don't take the job?'

Joe shrugged, the easy smile completely vanishing from his face.

'Then we no longer have a role for you at Spencer Media,' he said, returning to his seat. 'And I'll be very sorry to see you go.'

Nodding to myself, I turned to leave with the job description in my hand.

'Could you take the trash can with you?' Joe asked just as I reached the door. 'And you should look into some of those lactose pills. You can buy them over the counter now.'

'Awesome, yeah, thanks,' I said, coming back for the bin and tucking it under my arm as I let myself out of his office. 'I'll definitely do that.'

A shit buffet and a bin full of vom.

What a way to start the weekend.

CHAPTER TWENTY-TWO

'What would you do?' I asked Jenny in the car on the way from The Union to Prune. 'I mean, really, what can I do? I've got to take the job, haven't I?'

'It's not like they're moving you down to the mail-room,' she replied, scanning the job description as we bumped over another pothole. 'This is huge, Angie. You'd be a director, you'd be in charge of an entire global brand, the travel alone . . . it would be really exciting for the right person.'

'For the right person,' I agreed. 'But I don't know if that's me. How can I nick off to Sydney to check on the Australian edition of the magazine if I'm breast-feeding?'

'Are you sure they won't hire you a wet nurse?' she asked, handing me back the piece of paper. 'If not, it's the only thing they aren't going to give you.'

'I get that it's an amazing offer,' I said, gazing out the window as we slowed down in front of Webster Hall to let someone cross the street. We'd seen Alex play there so many times. 'And I am in no position to be turning down that kind of money right now. Joe made it very clear that it's this job or no job. So why do I feel sick?'

'You always feel sick,' she reminded me. 'You have for months now, you're pregnant, remember?'

'It's not baby sick,' I said, punching her in the arm. I exhaled as we pulled away and turned down 3rd Avenue. 'It feels wrong.'

'What would you do if there was no baby? No mortgage, no Alex? What would you do if it was just you?'

'Get on a plane in my bridesmaid dress and move to another country without consulting anyone?' I suggested, hopefully.

'Only an idiot would do something like that,' she replied, resting her head on my shoulder. 'Did you talk to Delia?'

I shook my head. It was a sensible question, but every time I'd picked up the phone to dial her extension, I hadn't been able to do it.

'Did I tell you she cancelled on dinner?' Jenny asked. 'She swears she's still coming to the wedding, but something came up tonight or so she says.'

'I hope she didn't cancel because she didn't want to see me,' I muttered. I didn't mean it in the slightest. I very much hoped that was the reason she'd cancelled. 'Plus, there's the Cici thing to think about. That could be amazing if it's done right.'

'But that really would be a crazy risk,' she said. 'Alex is right, startups are hard, even if they have all the money in the world and all the best people. Plus, it's Cici, and she's kind of the devil.'

'She has sort of grown on me,' I admitted. 'A bit like a very attractive form of mould. Or Justin Bieber.'

'And what did Alex say?' Jenny pulled out a Chanel mirror and tapped at her cherry red lip gloss. 'He's smart about this stuff, right? That's why you married him.'

I opened my bag and checked my phone for the thousandth time that day.

'He hasn't said anything,' I told her, trying to control my wavering bottom lip. 'I haven't been able to get hold of him all day. He was gone when I woke up – I assumed he'd gone for a run. Now, nothing.'

'What do you mean he was gone?' Jenny looked puzzled. 'He's coming tonight? To dinner?'

'I hope so,' I nodded. 'He's supposed to be bringing Mum and Dad, and if they had to find their own way on the subway, we'll all be in trouble.'

'I'm thinking about getting Mason tagged,' she said with a disgruntled sigh. 'A little microchip in the back of his neck, like they do with shelter dogs? It's really the only way to be sure you know where they are all the time.'

'Twenty-four hours ago I would have told you not to be ridiculous,' I said, putting my phone away and placing the folded job description beside it. 'But if you find someone who will do it, can you let me know?'

'Your mum said I had to dress up,' Dad said, meeting me and Jenny at the door of the restaurant, umbrellas in hand.

'You look nice,' I replied. 'It's nice, but it's not fancy.'

'I knew it wasn't dressy,' he said, loosening his tie and throwing evils at my mum who innocently busied herself with her handbag.

'On the cruise, we dressed for dinner every night,' Mum said. 'We were asked to sit on the captain's table five times. That was more than anyone else, you know. Until your dad started reading books about serial killers . . . '

'Impressive,' I said, looking over her shoulder for my husband. 'Did he have any fish fingers?'

'Not a one,' Dad replied, indignant. 'That's another thing to add to the list, thank you, Angela.'

'Any time,' I told him. 'Where's Alex?'

'He sent your dad a text message to say he might be late,' Mum said. 'We thought he was with you.'

Alex had sent Dad a text message? He'd ignored me all day but he'd sent my dad a text message?

'Can I see?' I asked, as nonchalant as humanly possible.

Dad handed me his phone. There was a smiley face emoji. This wasn't from Alex, he didn't speak emoji, he'd definitely been kidnapped. Someone had kidnapped my husband and I'd been so preoccupied with some corporate twonk, I hadn't even noticed. I handed the phone back.

'Are you coming inside or are you going to stand out there in the rain?' Dad said, holding the door open. 'I'm sneezing just looking at you.'

'I'm coming,' I said, joining everyone inside, shaking off my umbrella and placing it carefully in the rack by the door.

'What time do you think Alex might get here?' Dad asked, sticking to my side as Mum ran across the room to hug every single woman who had been on Jenny's hen. I stifled a smile as Sadie reared backwards, shielding her nose with both hands.

'Not sure,' I replied, texting said errant husband as we spoke. 'I think his phone must have died, I haven't heard from him.'

'Hope he didn't lose it,' Dad chuntered, eyeing the entire room with great suspicion. 'Expensive things, phones. Pricey bit of kit.'

'I'm sure it's fine, Dad,' I said. 'He was probably working on something with Graham and forgot to charge it. Wouldn't be the first time.'

'Not cheap,' he added, just to make sure I understood.

Ignoring him as best I could, I checked my own phone to see if Alex had replied but there was nothing. His backpacking extravaganza had really taken the shine off the boy's texting skills. Before he'd been sans WiFi for two months, he'd been very good at letting me know where he was and when he'd be home. I didn't need him on a digital leash, but when I'd sent several poop-face emojis and one 'I really need to talk to you' message, a quick unicorn in return and maybe a 'how's the mother of my unborn child doing?' wouldn't have gone amiss.

'Dad,' I said. 'How did you feel when Mum told you she was pregnant?'

'Chuffed to monkeys,' he replied, looking at his watch. We hadn't even sat down to dinner yet and I could tell he was counting down the hours until he could leave. 'Couldn't have been happier.'

'You didn't freak out or anything? I asked. 'You didn't panic? You were loads younger than me and Alex, surely you must have had a bit of a wobble.'

'Maybe a bit,' he said. 'But things were different back then, sugarplum. You didn't worry about things, you put your head down and you got on with it. We were married, we wanted kids. I knew it would happen sooner or later and well, here you are.'

Clearly I was the most wanted baby in the history of the world.

'So, you weren't worried about anything?' I knew I was pushing my luck. My dad was a wonderful man

329

but unless he'd had a couple of sherries after Christmas dinner, the likelihood of getting an emotional break-through was slim to none.

'I worried you'd have two arms, two legs and one head,' he said, crossing his arms as my mother tittered like a schoolgirl at something Mason's brother said across the room. 'Other than that, I was just happy to have you.'

'Great,' I said, an eye still on my silent phone. 'Thanks.'

'Of course, there was that one day right before you were born when I went a bit loopy and took myself off to Skegness for fish and chips and your mother thought I wasn't coming back,' he added. 'But other than that, no, it was all right as rain.'

'Wait, what?'

'What about what?' he asked.

'You nicked off to Skeggy without telling Mum, right before I was born?' I prompted. 'How long were you gone for?'

'Only overnight,' he said, as though a man going missing for twenty-four hours in the mid-Eighties was no cause for concern. 'I just fancied a day at the seaside, that was all, and it occurred to me that I wouldn't be able to pop off for the day once you arrived. Your mother wasn't best pleased and your grandmother was even less impressed, but I had a lovely time. Even had a Mr Whippy on the seafront.'

'You drove hundreds of miles to spend the day in Skegness right before I was born and you didn't tell Mum you were going?' I just wanted to make sure I had my facts straight before I had my breakdown. 'What were you thinking? Mum must have been so worried. They didn't even have mobile phones back then.'

'Your mother is always worried,' he said with an

added 'pfft' just to make sure I knew he thought I was overreacting. 'I went for a drive to clear my head. It's different for dads, Angela. You've got that baby with you all the time. Even before it's moving around and kicking, you know it's there, don't you? It can take a bit longer for a dad to come to terms with how much his life is going to change.'

'How much *his* life is going to change?' My voice picked up an octave and I noticed Erin and Thomas looking over. 'I'm going to push a human being *out of me*. The only thing that's been removed from my person until now is that piece of Lego I got stuck up my nose when I was six and I can't say that was a treat.'

'Why don't I get us a drink?' Dad suggested. 'Get me a drink, I mean. Do you want some pop?'

'Maybe I would like to run off to the seaside for the day and eat ice cream and ponder the meaning of life. Not a Mr Whippy, though, because I can't have soft serve, because I can't have anything, because I'm bloody pregnant.'

I was shouting. I was shouting at the top of my voice.

'What time did you say you thought Alex might get here?' he asked, looking for an assist from his wife. 'You seem a bit tense.'

'Because I *am* a bit tense,' I snapped. 'And I don't know when he's bloody well going to get here because I don't bloody well know where he is, do I?'

'Hey, Angie?' Jenny tapped me on the shoulder with a pointed look on her face. 'Could you come to the bathroom with me for a moment?'

'Yes,' I said, still staring daggers at my dad. My poor, clueless dad. 'I'm coming.'

'What the fuck is going on?' Jenny hissed, locking the door to the single stall behind us. 'Where is Alex?'

'I don't know,' I replied, laughing hysterically. 'He's gone. Won't answer my texts, told Mum and Dad he'd be late. Your guess is as good as mine. Thailand maybe? Cambodia? Who knows.'

'No, he's not ruining my wedding.' She pulled her iPhone out of her bespoke Edie Parker 'Mrs' clutch and dialled Alex's number while I panted at myself in the mirror. Hysterics were not my best look.

'Hey Alex, it's Jenny,' she said. I knew she was leaving a voicemail and I knew he wouldn't listen to it, but there was no point in trying to stop her. 'I'm not sure where you're at right now but I would love it if you could get your sorry ass into a goddamn cab and show up to my goddamn rehearsal dinner because if you don't, so help me god, Alex Reid, your baby is going to grow up with a single mother and that is not fair. I'm serious, if you don't get here inside sixty minutes, I'm going to hunt you down and murder you, you motherfucker. OK! See you soon!'

She hung up the phone, inhaled, smiled and exhaled happily.

'And that's how we deal with that,' she said, scrunching up her nose and kissing me on the cheek before letting herself out of the lav. I turned on the tap and ran the water until it was icy cold, dipping my hands under the flow. As if by magic, my phone buzzed into life with a message. A message from Alex.

'Shit shit shit,' I gasped, fighting with the paper towel dispenser as the screen went black. Rubbing my hands dry on the arse of my borrowed Marchesa mini dress, I prayed I hadn't pulled off any sequins and opened Alex's message.

Hey, can't make dinner, tell Jenny I'm sorry. I'll be back in tomorrow.

What. The actual. Fuck.

Before I could type exactly what I was thinking, another message came through.

I love you xo.

I stared at the screen, trying to make sense of it all. This wasn't like him. He knew you don't bail on someone's rehearsal dinner, let alone Jenny Lopez's rehearsal dinner. He didn't even know what sorry meant, she was going to kill him. And most importantly, where on god's green earth had he gone?

'Are you still in there, love?' I heard Dad ask on the other side of the door.

'Yes,' I replied in a quiet, dangerous voice. 'Sorry. I lost my temper.'

'That's all right,' he said. 'No worse than when you were sixteen. There's about to be dinner, if you're coming out.'

'I'll be out in a second,' I promised. 'Don't eat my mash.'

It was still raining outside, I could hear it from inside the bathroom. It had to be pouring it down. I sat down on the toilet and attempted to calm down, still wondering where Alex might be.

'You're overreacting,' I said out loud. 'He's probably recording with Graham, lost track of time, and realized it was too late to make dinner. That's all this is.'

Not showing up just wasn't like him. Ignoring my messages just wasn't like him. Shouting at me and throwing cushions around the living room just wasn't like him.

Oh fuckityfuckfuckfuck. Fuckadoodledo.

He'd gone to Skegness for fish and chips and he was never coming back.

'It's nothing,' I told myself. 'Dad came back and Alex will too. At least you know he's OK.'

My blood pressure aside, everything was fine. I wasn't going to ruin Jenny and Mason's evening by having a meltdown in the toilets. We'd already had one of those while planning this wedding, and I was fairly sure that was the limit. Alex hadn't left me, he hadn't gone back to Thailand, he hadn't got on a plane to England then driven himself to Skegness for fish and chips, and he wasn't dead.

At least, he wasn't yet.

CHAPTER TWENTY-THREE

'So,' Jenny held out her hands. 'Whaddya think?'

I opened my eyes, already holding a tissue underneath each one. I was nothing if not prepared. I'd expected her to look good, I'd anticipated a very pretty dress, but even if I'd been able to magic up a dress from my own imagination, I'd never have been able to create something this wonderful. Her hair was pulled back, braided into a perfect crown and threaded through with the most delicate strings of Swarovski crystals, making it look as though fairies had kissed her on the head as she'd walked by. Delicate curls hung around her face, grazing her cheekbone perfectly and framing Razor's stellar make-up job. Rose-pink lips, soft smoky eyes, flawless skin. Maybe there was something to this giving up sugar malarkey.

And then there was the dress.

Yards and yards and yards of ivory tulle flowed from her waist, falling in dozens of different layers that floated with her as she moved while the bodice sparkled subtly with the same crystals she wore in her hair. High neck, long sleeves and then dipping low in the back, almost all the way down to her waist. It was so obviously a Bertie Bennett design, and so perfectly Jenny at the same time. A timeless, vintage shape, made with modern touches and just the right amount of sparkle. It was almost impossible to imagine it hadn't been designed especially for her.

'You look awful,' Erin said, throwing back an entire flute of champagne. 'We should cancel the wedding.'

'Just the worst,' I agreed as tears began to pour down my face. 'I've never seen anyone look so bad. I'm embarrassed for you.'

'It is a real piece of shit,' she said, staring at herself in the mirror. 'And the best part is, when they actually make this dress, it won't have all the beading and shit. This is, literally, the only dress in existence that is exactly like it. I'm getting married in a Bertie Bennett original, bitches.'

'And she's such a lady,' Erin said, holding a hand against her heart and a tissue to her nose. 'What a beautiful moment.'

'Do not fucking cry,' Razor instructed from the bathroom. 'I am not reapplying anyone's false eyelashes, I already put away the glue.'

'We won't cry,' Erin and I chorused together, sobbing into tissues not ten feet away.

'You two look OK,' Jenny said, cocking her head to the side to consider our matching Jenny Packham dresses.

I should have known, when Erin gave me my frock, that Jenny's dress was going to be such a stunner. What kind of woman put her bridesmaids in impossibly beautiful dresses like ours unless she was so very certain about her own? I swished my hips around in a shimmy, thankful the bump had played nicely and just about managed to squeeze in without my having to torture it with Spanx.

'I suppose you're going to have to get married now,' Erin said, handing her a glass of champagne. It was almost three forty-five, the wedding was scheduled to take place at four, just in time for sunset. 'Poor Mason.'

'Any word from Alex?' Jenny asked. I could tell she was trying not to sound concerned, but I knew that she was. So was Erin. So was I. My dad, on the other hand, was on the warpath. Part of me hoped that Alex stayed well away, he was not safe anywhere in New York City.

'It's fine,' I said. It was the opposite of fine. I'd been up all night and panicking all day. He'd said he'd be home and he wasn't. 'I'm sure he'll be here.'

'Could you wish for me to win the lottery real quick?' Jenny said, nodding towards the door of our hotel room. Peering inside, opening it only as much as he had to, was Alex Reid.

'Hi?'

'Erin, Razor, I need you in the other room,' Jenny ordered, picking up her skirts and swishing all the way into the bathroom. 'Now, please.'

'But the other room is the bathroom,' Razor whined. 'We won't all fit in there with you in that dress.'

'We'll fit in there if you stand on the toilet,' Jenny barked. 'Go!'

'Can I come in?' Alex asked, silhouetted in the doorway with head hanging low.

'Depends,' I said, reaching for fresh tissues. 'Are you planning on staying?'

He came into the hotel room and I saw that he was wearing his suit, albeit with his battered old Converse.

'I'm sorry,' he said without making any attempt to come closer. 'It's a long story.'

'We don't have time for a long story,' I said, looking down at my bridesmaid's dress. 'But I'd love to hear the short version.'

'I sold my vintage Strat.' He held out his arms and let them clap loudly against his sides. 'I sold my vintage Strat and I had to drive upstate to deliver it.'

'Alex, you didn't,' I breathed. 'You *love* that guitar.'

'And I love our baby more,' he replied, rubbing the heel of his hand against a tired eye. 'I got fifty grand for the guitar. Now we don't have to sell "Night Song" to the fast-food place.'

'Fifty thousand dollars for a guitar?' Razor gasped on the other side of the bathroom door.

'You didn't have to do that anyway,' I said, ignoring Razor's squeal and silently thanking whoever had made him be quiet. 'We would have made it work, you shouldn't have to give up something you love.'

'I sold it to a friend upstate, he says I can still borrow it to record if I want to. It's cool.'

He very much wanted me to think this wasn't a big deal but I knew it was and I hated it.

'I thought I could drive up there and back down in a day, turns out I was wrong.'

I felt terrible about him selling his guitar, but he was going to have to do better than that, if only to stop Jenny from breaking the door down and killing him dead.

'Really? That's it?' I asked, concentrating on breathing. 'You couldn't have called and told me that?'

'I could but I didn't,' he replied. His eyes found the floor and his long black hair covered his face. 'I don't know why. After I dropped off the guitar, I started thinking and driving and suddenly it was the middle of the night. My phone died, I lost track of time. I stopped to buy a charger at a gas station and I was gonna call, but then I got that message from Jenny and shit, Angela, I was scared. Mason is a brave man.'

'Lucky man,' I corrected as the threat of violence rumbled behind the bathroom door. 'Mason is a *lucky* man.'

He looked up at me from his safe space across the room and even though I was angry and sad and confused, my heart shattered. He looked so afraid.

'Please come here,' I said, holding my voice together for as long as I could. Faster than I could blink, he was right in front of me, holding my face in his hands. Neither of us said anything at first. I took his hand in mine and led him over to the loveseat in front of the window. He sat first, pulling me into his lap and I laid my head against his chest, listening for his heartbeat. He stroked my hair and held me close, as though he would never let me go.

'I'm so sorry . . . ' Alex's long, calloused fingers combed through my gently curled hair. 'I know I fucked up, I don't know what I was thinking. I don't want to let anyone down. You, the band, or the baby, and somehow that's exactly what I did.'

It was perfectly sound baby-brain logic. Apparently, you didn't need to be physically carrying the baby for it to affect you.

'You didn't,' I told him. 'I promise, you haven't let anyone down.'

'It's so dumb,' Alex said, moving his hand to massage the nape of my neck and I leaned my head back, pushing harder against his fingers 'Clearly, I was not of sound mind. Also, I didn't really eat anything other than a ton of Sour Skittles and a Seven-Eleven hot dog all day – they should do a study into what that does to a person's brain.'

'They could just check mine,' I suggested helpfully. 'Although maybe they shouldn't.'

He kissed the top of my head and nodded in agreement.

'I swear I'll never do it again,' he said. 'I'm so fucking sorry, it was such a weird, cowardly thing to do. My brain got stuck thinking about all the times I've been away touring and all the time you spend away at work. We barely have enough hours in the day for each other – what if a kid is too much? I don't want to screw this up, I really don't.'

'There's a difference between being physically in the room with a person and being there for somebody,' I said, shuffling upright so I could look him in the eye. 'Trust me, I've done that before. I spent years under the same roof as someone but we were never really in the same place. We are not those people.'

Alex took in a deep breath and blew it out hard, pressing the heels of his hands against his eyebrows.

'I'm just going to say it,' he said, releasing his hands, the skin around his eyebrows rushing red. 'I'm scared.'

He laughed at the words as they came out of his mouth and I offered up a lopsided smile.

'God, it actually feels good to say it. I'm chicken-shit scared. Of losing you, of you hating me. I'm so scared I'm gonna mess up, Angela. Like, what if the band is really successful but it means missing out on my child growing up? Or if I pass up band opportunities and end up resenting my kid? I don't want to wake up one day, ten years from now, and realize I screwed everything up.'

'I'm going to suggest something incredibly controversial,' I said, placing Alex's hand on my mini bump. 'Rather than panicking and driving around the countryside and eating sour sweets and manky hot dogs, how about we actually talk to each other about stuff like this?'

He looked at me in surprise. 'That is a wild idea.'

'I know,' I nodded. 'Having another brain inside me has made me a super genius.'

'Huh,' Alex gave a low whistle. 'No wonder they want to put you in charge of the world at work.'

'You read my email?' I asked. He nodded and leaned in to kiss me gently.

'Whatever you want to do, we'll do it,' he said. 'But I know you would hate that job, Angela, it would make you miserable. There has to be another option.'

'There might be,' I said, tightening up his skinny black tie. 'We'll talk about it after. I do still have two questions, though.'

'Shoot.'

'How come it took you a whole day to get home and,' I looked down at his Converse, 'how come you're in your suit but you don't have your shoes?'

'You said we didn't have time for a long story,' he replied. 'But I'll tell you later because it's a really good one. There's a broken down rental car, a very angry gas station attendant, three pairs of socks *and* a raccoon.'

'I wanna know what happened with the raccoon,' Jenny wailed, bursting out of the bathroom in a cloud of ivory tulle. 'Don't make me kick your ass, Reid.'

'Whoa!' Alex's eyes opened wide at the sight of the world's angriest bride. 'Lopez, you look incredible.'

'More than I can say for you,' she said, fluffing out

the layers of her skirts. 'Now, for real, there was a raccoon?'

'It is actually almost four,' I said, reluctantly drawing her attention to the clock on the wall. 'Everyone will be waiting, we should get up there.'

'I'll tell you on the way upstairs,' Alex said, holding out his arm. 'It's more of an elevator story anyway.'

'Oh, my god,' Jenny whispered, holding a hand over her mouth. 'I'm getting married.'

'Yeah,' I replied. 'That's a thing that's happening.'

'And you're having a baby,' she whispered, pointing at my belly.

'And I'm halfway to being wasted,' Erin said, grabbing her around the waist and pushing her towards the door. 'So, can we get this show on the road before I lose my buzz?'

'It's a solid plan,' Alex agreed. 'Lopez, are you gonna do this or not?'

'I guess,' she replied, turning to me with tears in her eyes. 'I can't believe it's happening.'

'I can,' I said, folding her into a very careful hug. 'You're incredible, Mason is the luckiest man alive. Are you ready?'

'As I'll ever be,' she said, taking a deep breath.

I followed Jenny out of the suite, my hand in hers, with Alex close behind while the bump bubbled happily in my belly. Everything I wanted, everything I needed, was right there with me at last.

CHAPTER TWENTY-FOUR

'You're not serious?'

Delia and Joe stared at me from the other side of the boardroom table.

'Pretty serious,' I said. 'It would be a really rubbish joke if I wasn't.'

'You're not taking the job?' Delia asked. She looked upwards as she spoke, as though she was trying to translate the words from another language. 'You're going to leave?'

'That is the gist of it,' I confirmed. 'Yes. I don't want to be Junior Global Brand Director for Women's Lifestyle Brands.'

It had taken me all weekend to learn how to say that without looking at it written down.

'You haven't thought this through,' Joe said, shaking his blond head. 'Weren't you at a wedding this weekend? Take a couple more days, there's no rush.'

'There is, actually,' I replied. 'I've still got all my holidays to take this year, and if I hand my notice in today, I can leave at the end of the day and that ties up nicely with the Christmas break, so yeah, it's all very neat and tidy.'

'You're going to walk out on your magazine?' Joe did not look impressed. 'I thought you loved that magazine.'

'I do,' I said, wanting this part of the day to be over. 'But the team will manage without me for a couple of weeks. They're really good – you should keep that in mind before you go and fire half of them.'

'Is this because you're pregnant?' Delia asked, lowering her gaze to my carefully disguised stomach.

'You know?' I asked, protectively covering my belly.

'Everyone knows,' she replied, looking slightly hurt. 'I figured it out when I ran into you at the doctor's office, and everyone knows you've been throwing up and skipping out on drinks. Plus, you have a huge bump, it wasn't hard to guess. I thought maybe you would tell me at the wedding, but you were too busy avoiding me all night.'

It was fair, I had been avoiding her, but I'd also been trying to keep my dad off the Sambuca shots and Mum away from Sadie's surgically reconstructed nose, so I'd had my hands full for most of the night.

'She's pregnant?' Joe yelped. 'Now?'

Well, at least I'd managed to keep it a surprise from someone.

'Weren't you the one who told me she was sick in your trash can?' Delia asked.

'Yes, but I assumed that was from the excitement,' he said, throwing his hands up in the air. 'And she said something about lactose intolerance. How was I supposed to know she was pregnant?'

'You picked a real winner to be running women's brands,' I told Delia. 'Good work.'

'You don't have to leave,' she said, moving right past my snarky comment. 'If you don't want to take the director role, we'll figure something else out.'

It was hard. Harder than I thought it would be. Gritting my teeth and closing my eyes, I shook my head.

'It's time for a change,' I told her. 'Spencer Media has been the most amazing place for me, and now it's going to be an amazing place for someone else. It's not that I don't want to be here any more, it's just that there's something else I want more.'

'And what's that?' Joe asked, his gaze turning steely next to Delia's arch disappointment.

'I don't know yet,' I said, standing up to leave. 'But I'll figure it out.'

'Happy Christmas Eve,' Alex said. 'How did it go?'

He was waiting for me outside the office, all bundled up in his Brooklyn Industries padded coat, skinny black jeans, and a red and white Santa hat on his head. I bit my lip to stop myself from crying as he stooped down to kiss me.

'Joe was confused, Delia was pretty upset, and everyone else cried,' I said, tucking my Alexander Skarsgård poster into my tote bag. 'Me included. Actually, mostly me. Alex, it was so weird. I can't believe I quit *Gloss*.'

'I'm proud of you,' he said, taking a second Santa hat out of his pocket and resting it on top of my head. 'Want to go for a walk?'

'Why not?' I said, following him up Broadway. 'I've got nothing else to do, have I?'

Times Square was manic. There were always at least three times as many people as could comfortably fit inside one city block, especially when that city block also had moving traffic flowing through but Christmas was the exception. New York emptied out for the holidays: it was like Jenny always said, not many people were from New York, they came here to become someone new. At Christmas, they all went back to wherever they came from, either to play at being their old selves for a few days or to show everyone at home how much they'd changed, because that was a certainty. Everyone who came to New York changed, one way or another.

For the first time in months, there was room to breathe in the streets. I held Alex's hand but walked in my own space, not huddled into him, trying not to be knocked over or pushed out of someone's way. The city was mine again, if only for a couple of days.

'Have you talked to Cici?' Alex asked, flipping the white fluffy pompom on the end of his hat over to a more rakish angle.

'I have.' I tightened my glittery Marc Jacobs scarf around my neck. It was getting really cold. 'We're going to meet in January. She can't really try to hire anyone away until Joe and Caroline have done their cull, but there are definitely a few people who are way too talented to be unemployed who are going to be looking for jobs. I would imagine the promise of a bigger pay cheque and health insurance will help them overlook the fact they'd be working for Cici Spencer.'

'Technically,' he corrected me as we crossed 59th Street into Central Park, 'they'll be working for you.'

'Maybe,' I reminded him, walking towards the ice rink. I could barely stay upright in regular shoes when I was on solid ground, but I still loved to watch other people skate. Everyone was happy when they were skating. 'I still haven't accepted her offer.'

'And there's no rush,' he insisted, pausing at the top of one of the little stone bridges, looking down on the frozen pond. 'I know you made the right choice.'

Alex moved behind me to cuddle me and the bump as we watched all the little kids skate by. Bundled up in hats and scarves and mittens, they whirled around the ice with grins on their faces and their arms flapping at their sides. One little girl with long blonde hair stuttered back and forth, stomping rather than skating as she chased a bigger boy in a blue hat. They were both laughing, not a care in the world between them.

'I know I did,' I agreed, leaning in for a kiss, revelling in our warm lips and cold noses. 'And everything else will work itself out.'

It didn't seem quite possible. If I could have popped back in time to give Past Angela a heads up, she would never have believed me. Sitting on the sofa with Mark, probably staring sadly out the window and daydreaming about a life so far away from her every day. But here I was, standing side by side with a man so wonderful you couldn't make him up, walking out on one adventure, right into another and to top it all off, I was completely full of baby. It only seemed like two minutes since I'd arrived in New York with nothing more than a weekend bag, a broken heart and the four Toblerones I'd bought at the airport. And now . . . it really didn't seem possible.

'It'll all be great,' Alex promised, interrupting my thoughts with a squeeze of my hand. 'Everything is going to be perfect.'

I took a deep breath and felt my waistband strain against my stomach.

'Everything already is,' I replied, meeting his eyes as I breathed out and smiled. 'Everything already is.'

EPILOGUE

'Alex?'

I let myself in and breathed in deeply. Whatever he was cooking smelled amazing.

'I'm in here,' he called. 'Come see.'

Throwing my parka onto the coatrack, I leaned on the back of the settee as I prised my feet out of my trainers before tiptoeing barefoot into the bedroom.

'Don't come in until you get changed,' Alex warned. He was poised on the top of a stepladder, paint roller in one hand, black plastic tray in the other. 'Everything's still wet. I'm almost done, give me two minutes and I'll shower before we eat.'

'It looks amazing,' I said, marvelling from the doorway. 'I can't believe you did all this in one day.'

'And cooked the world's best pasta Bolognese,' he added. 'I know, I know, I'm kind of amazing.'

'Completely amazing,' I corrected as he climbed down the stepladder to meet me with a kiss. 'And I'm not just saying that because I'm starving and desperate for a wee.'

'How are you feeling?' he called as I waddled to the bathroom. 'Any movement?'

'Nothing,' I replied through the door, holding my breath and giving a little push. Nope, nothing. 'I don't think I'm having this baby, ever. I think it wants to stay right where it is.'

'I'm afraid that's not going to be possible,' Alex called through the door, running a paint-covered hand through his paint-speckled hair. 'I just painted a bedroom and I don't do manual labour for the good of my health.'

I finished up and washed my hands before peeling off my leggings and swapping them for my favourite pair of extra-large Victoria's Secret pyjama bottoms.

'Do you like it?' Alex asked when I reappeared. The broken streetlight outside the undressed window fizzled in and out and we stood side by side on dust-sheets, admiring his handiwork.

'I do,' I nodded. 'But Jenny's going to hate it. She says we shouldn't reinforce assigned gender stereo-types from birth.'

'Jenny can suck it,' Alex replied, swiping my nose with the roller. 'If the baby hates it, we'll change it. I'm not picking up a roller again until it's old enough to help.'

I wiped my face with the back of my hand, a smear of baby pink paint stuck to my skin, then, startled, I grabbed hold of Alex's arm.

'What?' He dropped the roller on the floor, splashing pink paint all up the leg of his jeans. 'What's wrong?'

'I think she does like the colour,' I said, looking down at my pyjama bottoms. 'My waters just broke.'

'Are you OK, should I call Jenny? Should I call your mom?' he looked around the room wildly. 'I knew we

350

should have done this last week. You shouldn't be around all these paint fumes, we've got to get you out of here.'

'Alex, relax,' I said, pressing my hands down on his shoulders. 'It's not going to fall out right here. Is it? WAIT, IS IT?'

He pulled up my jumper and placed his palms on my enormous stomach. Inside, the baby kicked.

'We're having a baby,' he whispered. 'Shit, Angela, we're having a baby.'

'Please don't be an arsehole and hurt Mummy,' I said, rubbing my hands up and down my stomach. 'I love you very much and we've been very nice to you so far.'

'I'll get the hospital bag, you go sit down,' Alex ordered, running out of the nursery. 'In the living room! Away from the paint!'

'Think I might change my pants first,' I muttered, gazing around the formerly spare room, the gorgeous cot Alex had made by hand, the vintage mobile my mum had sent over from when I was a baby, the monogrammed cashmere blankets from Jenny. And finally, I rested my narrowed eyes on the bustier breast pump.

'I so can't wait to meet you,' I told the bump as my baby kicked impatiently. She was an anxious traveller, just like her mum. 'Please don't be a dick.'

'Angela!' Alex called from the other room. 'Are you OK?'

'Yes,' I replied, turning out the light and closing the nursery door, wondering what came next. 'I really am.'

The only thing I knew for certain was that everything was exactly how it was supposed to be.

And that was enough.

ACKNOWLEDGEMENTS

As always, major thanks to the entire team at HarperCollins. Lynne, Martha, HAHAHHHAA, it's a book, madness. Special shout out to Lucy Vanderbilt for assorted cat photos sent in times of need, thank you, thank you, thank you. And to everyone else at HCUK, US, Australia and Canada, you're the bestest.

I owe thanks to more people than I could hope to list here but there's a big old gang of writers who have given me more support than I think they know, so hey Mhairi McFarlane, Kevin Dickson, Rowan Coleman, Rosie Walsh, Gi Fletcher, Paige Toon, Will Hill and Gillian McAllister, YOU'RE ALL RIGHT.

Can't say enough nice things to all the people on Twitter, Insta and Facebook who are always there to chat when things get rough (or I just need to laugh), especially those of you who humour my constant tweets about the WWE and my lovely pal, Nicki Yates. I really hope you like this one!

To Terri White, Della Bolat, Ryan Child, Louise Doyle, Harriet Hadfield and Kevin Dickson (again. You poor fool, you), thank you so much for dealing with me IRL while I wrote this book. And all the others. You're either gluttons for punishment or I did something right in a previous life.

And to Jeff Israel, thanks for dealing with the litter box for three straight months while I hid in a cupboard and wrote a book. You're so lucky. I mean, I'm so lucky. Wait, did I? Yes, yes I did.

I HEART YOUR QUESTIONS!

What inspires you when you're writing your books? Although your books are fiction, do some of your scenes resemble to your own life or people you know? For instance, relocating to America from London, this is what you have done isn't it? *Emily Mallinson*

I did move from London to New York but that actually happened after *I Heart New York* had been published. The book was inspired by a holiday in New York with my brother. I just fell in love with the city and I was feeling so miserable and uninspired in my real life back at home, I couldn't stop wondering what my life might look like if I was ever able to move to New York.

A lot of things that happen in the books are inspired by things I've done or life experiences I've been through but they're usually very different by the time they make it to print. A lot of people think they recognize people they know in my characters but they're usually a combination of lots of different people – it's almost impossible to take a real person and drop them into a work of fiction and make it work, they always seem to stick out in the worst way. I'm constantly inspired by conversations I have with my friends, I figure if we're talking about the same thing again and again, it must be something other people are experiencing too and then my brain starts ticking!

What's the one thing you miss about New York? *Morgan Tarr*

Other than my friends, I genuinely miss the city itself. Walking the streets of New York is like charging a battery, you never know what you're going to see, who you're going to meet. When you're out and about, it feels like literally anything could happen, every second is the beginning of a new adventure and I don't think there's anywhere in the world that has that kind of energy.

What was the last photograph you took on your phone?
Kerry Woolford

Right this second, it's a photograph of my cat, Anderson Cooper, passed out on the living room rug with his legs in the air. What a little tart.

If you could be one of your characters for a day, who would it be and what would you do? *Nicola Aldgate*

That's so difficult! I think I'd actually be Tess because she's a photographer and I've always wanted to learn how to be a proper photographer and maybe I'd acquire her snapper skills. Also, she gets to travel to lots of exciting locations, her best friend Amy is hilarious and I'd definitely be up for a date night with Nick . . .

If you had a unicorn, what would you name it? *Katja Kane*

Roy. Roy the unicorn. He'd be awesome.

What's the best thing about being an author and what made you start writing in the first instance? *Sarah Haddock*

There are so many great things about being a writer. I get to indulge my creative nonsense for a living, experience all the different lives of my characters, I can make my own schedule, travel around the world while still getting my work done and best of all, I don't have to commute in a morning! It's hard to say what made me start because I've been writing for as long as I can remember. Ever since I was a little girl, I wrote stories for myself but I truly never expected them to be published.

What kind of a writer are you? Do you plot it all out meticulously first and then go from there? *Natalie Sorrell*

Someone once told me there are plotters and panters – authors who plot out every moment of their books and authors who fly by the seat of their pants. I'm a panter, which sounds really sketchy! When I'm writing the first draft, I have some character notes, a rough outline of where I want the plot to go and then, once that's done, I write more notes and work through all the changes I need to make. When I was writing *I Heart Forever*, I made a story-board to keep track of all my scenes after the first draft and it was really useful so maybe I need to be more of a plotter! I honestly don't believe there's a wrong or right way to be a writer, just do what feels natural to you. Don't be afraid to experiment, as long as you're doing it, you're doing it right!

If you write another *I Heart* book, which city would you choose and why? *Carine Durie*

I don't know if it would definitely be an *I Heart* book but I'd love to visit and write about Tokyo. I've always been fascinated by Japan but for whatever reason, I've still never made it over there. I just love Japanese culture and I'd love to see it firsthand.

Who, what or where is your biggest source of inspiration? *Natalie Sorrell*

My friends and New York City, without shadow of a doubt. My friends all live such interesting lives, they're always giving me ideas for characters and I could write about New York forever, even though I don't live there anymore. You could sit on one street corner for half an hour and get enough material to write twenty books. It's my forever love.

If you had to give up either Percy Pigs or wrestling for the rest of your life, which would it be? *Ellie Mould*

That's just cruel! I guess I would give up Percy Pigs and find another snack. I couldn't give up wrestling, I know, I've tried.

The *I Heart* books have taken me to a different place and time when I've needed it, what do you do to escape the reality of everyday life? *Kim Hopkins*

I love to read as well but it's not always a relaxing hobby for me! When I'm deep into writing a book, it's hard to get out of my head and difficult to concentrate on someone else's writing. For my birthday last year, my boyfriend bought me a membership to the LA Zoo and I love to go and visit the otters. There's a little alcove built into the outside of their tank with a ledge big enough for me and my buddy, Kevin Dickson (who's a writer as well), and we'll sit down, talk about our books and right all the wrongs with the world. What bad could happen while you're hanging out with otters? It's kind of like *Breakfast at Tiffany's* only, you know, not.

What is your go-to karaoke song? *Annalee Slark*

I have quite a few but my faves are *I Touch Myself* by The Divinyls and *Torn* by Natalie Imbruglia. I love karaoke so much.

Which one of your books is your 'favourite child'? *Samra Dzumhur*

I Heart New York will always be really special because it was my first book and I'm still shocked it ever made it out into the world! Other than that, I really love *We Were on a Break* because it was so much fun to do something a little bit different. Also, I'm obsessed with Daniel Craig, the three-legged cat.

How are you and Angela alike and how are you different? *Annaleigh Putze*

When I started writing the *I Heart* series, Angela was very much based on me, basically living my dream life. I was confused and uncertain of what to do with myself and the idea of having a Jenny Lopez-fairy godmother appear to help me was really appealing! I can be socially and physically awkward, two characteristics I unfortunately passed on to Angela, and we definitely share the same issues with communication! I've always struggled to ask for what I want if I'm worried it'll rock the boat and Angela and I both prefer to avoid conflict but we're also hardworking, romantic and loyal to our friends. I think they're great qualities. I'd say I'm more cynical than Angela – she seems to have her anxiety under better control than I do – but overall, I'd say we're still quite similar.

If you weren't an author what would like to be? *Sarah Harris*

Either a makeup artist or an events planner. I'm obsessed with makeup (and co-host Full Coverage, a podcast about everything beauty) but I've always loved planning parties and events. Last year I threw a western-themed baby shower for a friend and it was the best thing ever. I had real wagon wheels, bandanas, cowboy hats for everyone and we played lasso the rocking horse. I'd honestly love it so much.

DISCOVER LINDSEY'S

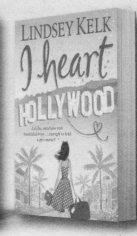

I heart SERIES

There are lots of ways to keep up-to-date with Lindsey's news and views:

lindseykelk.com

facebook.com/LindseyKelk

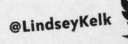

@LindseyKelk

@LindseyKelk